EON

Greg Bear

A Legend book

Published by Arrow Books Limited
62–65 Chandos Place, London WC2N 4NW

An imprint of Century Hutchinson Limited

London Melbourne Sydney Auckland
Johannesburg and agencies throughout
the world

First published by Victor Gollancz Ltd 1985
Legend edition 1987

© Greg Bear 1985

This book is sold subject to the condition that it shall
not, by way of trade or otherwise, be lent, resold,
hired out, or otherwise circulated without the pub-
lisher's prior consent in any form of binding or cover
other than that in which it is published and without a
similar condition including this condition being
imposed on the subsequent purchaser

Printed and bound in Great Britain by
The Guernsey Press Co. Ltd, Guernsey, C.I.

ISBN 0 09 953470 3

EON

Farley brought the vehicle to a halt and Patricia descended from the cab to stand on the roadway. Then she clambered up a ladder to a platform on top of the cab and looked down the straight line of the road. The road went to its own vanishing point— no cap, no barrier. Above, the rest of the landscape did much the same.

"It's bigger," she said. Farley and Lanier stood by the truck, looking up at her. Wu and Chang joined them. "It's bigger than the asteroid. It goes beyond the end. Is that what you're trying to tell me?"

"We don't tell," Lanier said. "We show. It's the only way."

"You're trying to tell me it doesn't stop, it goes right on out the other end?" She heard the touch of panic and high-pitched fascination in her own voice.

The Stanford professor, six years before, had been wrong. Someone beside extra-terrestrials and gods could appreciate her work. She now knew why she had been brought up from Vandenberg, carried to the Stone by shuttle and OTV.

The asteroid was longer on the inside than it was on the outside.

The seventh chamber went on forever.

For Poul and Karen
with much appreciation
and love

EON

Prolog: Four Beginnings

One/ Christmas Eve 2000
New York City

"It's going into a wide elliptical Earth orbit," Judith Hoffman said. "Perigee about ten thousand kilometers, apogee about five hundred thousand. It'll make a loop around the moon every third orbit." She pulled back from the video screen to let Garry Lanier have a look from where he sat on the edge of her desk. For the time being, the Stone still resembled a baked potato, with no meaningful detail.

Outside the door to her office, the noise of the party was a distant reminder of ignored social obligations. She had brought him into the office just a few minutes before.

"That must be an incredible fluke."

"It's not a fluke," Hoffman said.

Tall, with close-cut dense black hair, Lanier resembled a pale-skinned Amerindian, though he had no Indian blood. Hoffman found his eyes particularly reassuring—gently scrutinizing, the eyes of a man used to seeing across great distances. She did not put her trust in people on the basis of looks, however.

Hoffman had taken to Lanier because he had taught her something. Some had called him bloodless, but Hoffman knew better. The man was simply competent, calm and observant.

He had a kind of blindness to people's foibles that made him peculiarly effective as a manager. He seldom seemed to recognize petty insults, bitchiness or backbiting. He saw people only in terms of their effectiveness or lack of it, at least as far as his public reactions showed; he cut through their surface dross to find the true coin beneath. She had learned some interesting things about several people by observing

1

their reactions to Lanier. And she had adapted her own style, picking up on his finesse.

Lanier had never been in Hoffman's at-home work area before, and now, in the video's cool light, he inspected the shelves of memory blocks, the broad, empty desk with its basic secretary's chair, the compact word processor beneath the video.

Like most of the party-goers, he was a little in awe of Hoffman. On the Hill, she was called the Advisor. She had acted in official and unofficial capacities as a science expert for three presidents. Her video programs reviving and re-exploring science had been popular in the late 1990s, in a world just recovering from the shock of the Little Death. She had served on the board of directors of both the Jet Propulsion Laboratory and now ISCCOM—the International Space Cooperation Committee. Though she could not disguise her solid build, her taste in clothes was immaculate. There was a conscious limit to her style, however; her fingernails were short and unpainted, well-manicured but not elegant, and she wore little makeup. She allowed her brunette hair to find its own shape with a minimum of interference; it tended to make a nimbus of fine curls around her head.

"You must be on the Drake Hookup," Lanier said.

"I am, but this is a Deep Space Tracking picture. The Drake is still locked on the Perseus Gemstar."

"They won't turn it on the Stone?"

She shook her head, grinning wolfishly. "Feisty old bastards are on a tight schedule—won't turn it around even for a look at the biggest event of the twenty-first century."

Lanier raised an eyebrow. The Stone, as far as he knew, was just an asteroid. The oblong chunk wasn't going to hit the earth, but if it was going to orbit, it would be in perfect position for scientific probes. That was interesting, but hardly worthy of so much enthusiasm.

"Twenty-One isn't until next month," he reminded her.

"And that's when we'll be getting busy." She turned toward him and folded her arms. "Garry, we've been working

2

together for some time now. I trust you a lot."

He felt a tightening at the base of his spine. She had seemed tense all evening. He had dismissed the fidgeting as none of his business. Now she was making it his business.

"What do you know about the Stone?" she asked.

He thought a moment before answering. "DST located it eight months ago. It's about three hundred kilometers long, a hundred kilometers across at midsection. Medium albedo, probably a silicate body with a nickel-iron core. It had a kind of halo around it when first spotted, but that's dissipated. That made a few scientists speculate it was an exceptionally large old comet nucleus. Some conflicting reports on low density revived the old Shklovskii Mars—moon speculation."

"Where did you hear the density reports?"

"I don't remember."

"That reassures me a little bit. If you haven't heard much more than that, probably no one else has, either. DST had a leak, but we've plugged it now."

Lanier had entered her circle while working as a public relations manager for AT&T Orbicom Services. Before being employed by Orbicom, he had spent six years in the Navy, first as a fighter pilot, then flying high-altitude tankers. He had flown the famous Charlie Baker Delta route over Florida, Cuba and Bermuda during the Little Death, refueling the planes of the Atlantic Watch whose vigilance had played such a crucial role in limiting the war.

After the armistice, he had received an OK from the Navy to take his expertise in aerospace engineering over to Orbicom, which was tuning up its world-wide civilian Mononet.

There had been a few calls at first to Orbicom headquarters in Menlo Park, California, then requests for help on position papers, then an abrupt and unexpected transfer to the Orbicom building in Washington, which he later learned had been engineered by Hoffman. There was no question of romance —how often had he quelled *that* rumor?—but their ability to work together was remarkable in a Washington atmosphere of perpetual partisan bickering and funding squabbles.

3

"Why the secrecy?" he asked.

"DST has been ordered to mask all data given to the community." By which she meant the scientific community.

"Why in hell should they do that? Government's relation with the community has been awful the last few years. This certainly won't help."

"Yes, but I concur this time."

Another chill. Hoffman was very dedicated to the community.

"If there's a blanket over everything, how do *you* know?" Lanier asked.

"Connections through ISCCOM. I've been put on oversight by the President."

"Jesus."

"So while our friends are partying out there, I need to know if I can rely on you."

"Judith, I'm just a second-rank PR type."

"Bullshit. Orbicom thinks you're the best personnel coordinator they have. I had to wrestle Parker for three months to get you transferred to Washington. You were lined up for a promotion, know that?"

Truthfully, he had hoped to avoid another promotion. He felt he was getting away from the real work, higher and higher up the tower of power. "And you got me transferred, instead?"

"Pulled enough strings to look like the puppet master I'm supposed to be. I may need you. You know I don't pick candidates unless I'm sure they'll yank my ass out of the fire later."

He nodded. To be part of Hoffman's circle was to be groomed for importance. Until now, he had tried to overlook that as a truism.

"Do you remember the supernova sighted about the same time as the Stone?"

Lanier nodded; it had made a brief splash in the journals, and he had been too busy to find that low-profile coverage odd.

"It wasn't a supernova. Just as bright, but it didn't match any of the requirements. In the first place, it was first recorded

4

by DST as an infrared object just outside the solar system. Within two days, the flare became visible, and DST detected radiation of frequencies associated with every atomic transition. The flare temperature started at a million degrees Kelvin and peaked at just over one billion degrees. By that time nuclear explosion detectors on satellites—the new GPS super-Vela—were picking up thermally excited gamma rays from nuclear transitions. It was clearly visible in the night sky, so DST had to make up a cover story, and that was the discovery of a supernova by space defense installations. But they didn't know what they had."

"And?"

"The display went out, everything got quiet and then a visual sighting was made in the same portion of the sky. It was the Stone. By that time, everybody knew they weren't dealing with a simple asteroid." The video pictures flickered and a chime sounded.

"Well, here it is. Joint Space Command has taken over the Drake and rotated it."

The Drake was the most powerful orbiting optical telescope. There were bigger instruments being built on lunar farside, but none yet in operation matched the Drake. It had no Defense Department connection. Joint Space Command legally had no jurisdiction—except in time of national security crisis.

The Stone appeared on the screen greatly enlarged and cradled in numbers and science data graphs. Much more detail was evident—a big crater at one end of the oblong, smaller craters all over, a peculiar band running latitudinally.

"It still looks like an asteroid," Lanier said, his voice lacking conviction.

"Indeed," Hoffman said. "We know the type. A very large mesosiderite. We know the composition. But it's missing about forty percent of its mass. DST confirmed that this morning. That chunk's profile through the center resembles a geode. Geodes don't occur in space, Garry. The President has already accepted my recommendation that we organize an investigation. That was before the elections, but I think we can

5

push it with the new administration—cracker-barrel mentality or not. Just as a precaution, we're scheduling six orbital transfer vehicle flights before the end of February. And I'm laying my bets down early. I think we're going to need a science team, and I'd like you to coordinate for me. I'm sure we can arrange something with Orbicom."

"But why the secrecy?"

"Why, Garry, I'm surprised." She smiled warmly at him. "When the aliens arrive, the government *always* goes in for secrecy."

Two/ August, 2001 Podlipki Airfield, near Moscow

"Major Mirsky, you are not concentrating on your task."

"My suit is leaking, Colonel Mayakovsky."

"That is irrelevant. You can stay in the tank for another fifteen or twenty minutes."

"Yes, Colonel."

"Now pay attention. You must complete this maneuver."

Mirsky blinked sweat from his eyes and strained to see the American-style docking hatch clearly. The water was already up to his knees in the pressure suit; he could feel the stream entering through the seam at his hip. There was no way of telling how copious the flow was; he hoped Mayakovsky knew.

He had been instructed to wedge the bent metal bar into the two sensor ports. To get the necessary traction to jam it home, he hooked his ankle and right wrist to the circular lip of the hatch, using the L-shaped attachments on his boots and glove. Then with his left hand

—(how they had tried to discourage him in school in Kiev, now gone, all of his teachers and their nineteenth-century ideas; how they had tried to get him to use his right hand exclusively, until finally, in his late teens, an edict had come down officially pardoning *gauche* children)—

Mirsky slammed the bar. He unhooked his wrist and ankles and pushed back.

The water was up to his waist.

"Colonel—"

"The hatch will pause before opening. Three minutes."

Mirsky bit his lip. He twisted his neck around within the helmet to see how his teammates were doing. The five lined-up hatches were manned—two men and Yefremova. Where was Orlov?

There—pushing his helmet back, Mirsky saw Orlov being hauled to the surface of the tank, three wet-suited, scuba-equipped divers assisting him to shadowy obscurity. The surface, the lovely surface, sweet air and no water streaming in. He couldn't feel it now. The level was above his hip.

The hatch began to move. He could hear the mechanism whining. Then it stopped, only one-third open.

"It's stuck," he said, stunned. He was reasonably sure the exercise was supposed to be over as soon as he could enter the hatch, and the hatch was supposed to be foolproof, it was supposed to open when properly *jimmied*—American word, American technology, reliable, no?

"Loosen it. Your bar is obviously not positioned properly."

"It is!" Mirsky insisted.

"Major—"

"Yes, yes!" He jammed the heel of his heavily gloved hand against the bar again. He hadn't hooked his ankles and right wrist; he floated away from the hatch and had to waste precious seconds reeling in his line and dragging himself back. Hook. Pound. Unhook. No result.

Water up to his chest, cold, slopping past his neck seal into his helmet when his angle shifted. He swallowed some accidentally and choked. *There. Colonel will think I'm drowning and show mercy!*

"Jiggle it," the colonel suggested.

His gloves were almost too thick to reach into the groove where the bar now resided, held in place by the partly open

7

hatch. He pressed, his sleeves filled with cold and his fingers numbing. He pressed again.

His suit was no longer neutrally buoyant. He was starting to sink. The bottom of the tank was thirty meters below, and all three of the divers had accompanied Orlov. There was nobody between him and drowning if he could not make it to the simulated Soviet hatch on his own power. And if he did not leave now—

But he didn't dare. He had wanted the stars since adolescence, and panicking now would put them out of his reach forever. He screamed in his helmet and slammed his glove tip into the groove, causing a sharp freezing jolt of pain to go up his arm as his fingers crammed into the inner fabric and casing.

The hatch began to move again.

"Just jammed," the colonel said.

"I'm drowning, goddammit!" Mirsky shouted. He hooked his wrists onto the lip of the ring and sputtered water from his mouth. The suit's air entered and exited just above the neck ring of his helmet, and he could already hear the suck and gurgle.

Floodlights came on around the tank. The hatches were suspended in watery noon brightness. He felt hands under his arms and around his legs and saw the three other cosmonaut trainees vaguely from the corners of his foggy faceplate. They kicked away from the hatch complex and hauled him higher, higher, to his grandmother's archaic and welcome heaven.

They sat at their special table away from the two hundred other recruits and were served fine thick sausages with their kasha. The beer was cold and plentiful, if sour and watery, and there were oranges and carrots and cabbage cores. And for dessert, a big steel bowl of fresh-made, rich vanilla ice cream, unavailable for months while they trained, was set before them by a smiling mess officer.

When dinner was over, Yefremova and Mirsky strolled

across the grounds of the Cosmonaut Instructional Center with its hideous black steel water tank half-buried in the ground.

Yefremova came from Moscow and had a fine eastern slant to her eyes; Mirsky, from Kiev, could as easily have been German as Russian. Still, coming from Kiev had its advantages. A man without a city: this was something Russians could sympathize with, feel sad about.

They spoke very little. They thought they were in love but that was irrelevant. Yefremova was one of fourteen women in the Space Shock Troops program. Her femaleness kept her even busier than the men. She had trained as a pilot in the Air Defense Forces before that, flying Tu 22M training bombers and old Sukhoi fighters. He had come into the military after graduating from an aerospace engineering school. His deferment had been most fortunate; instead of being inducted into the army at eighteen, he had qualified for a New Reindustrialization scholarship.

In the engineering school, he had gained excellent marks in political science and leadership, and they had earmarked him immediately for the difficult position of *Zampolit* in a fighter squadron in East Germany, but then had transferred him to Space Defense Forces, which had only been in existence for four years. He had never heard of it before the transfer, but such a stroke of luck . . . He had always wanted to be a cosmonaut.

Yefremova's father was a high-ranking Moscow bureaucrat. He had put her into what he thought would be a safe military training program rather than let her run wild with Moscow's infamous Young Hooligans. She had turned out to be very capable and very bright; her future was promising, though not what her father had expected.

Their backgrounds were worlds apart, and chances were they would never even have a chance to date, much less conduct an affair or get married.

"Look," Yefremova said. "You can see it clearly tonight."

"Yes?" He knew immediately what she meant.

"There." She leaned her head close to his and pointed

above the summer's long blue twilight to a tiny spot of light just beside the full moon.

"They will get there before we do," Yefremova said sadly. "They always do, now."

"So pessimistic," Mirsky said.

"I wonder what they call it," she said. "What they will name it when they land."

"Not 'the Potato,' surely!" Mirsky chuckled.

"No," Yefremova agreed.

"Someday," Mirsky said, squinting to make the spot out more clearly.

"Someday what?"

"Perhaps the time will come when we will take it away from them."

"Dreamer," Yefremova said.

The next week, a two-man vacuum chamber imploded on the outskirts of the airfield. Yefremova was testing a new suit design in one half of the chamber. She was killed instantly. There was great concern about the political repercussions of the accident, but as it turned out, her father was not unreasonable. Better to have a martyr in the family than a hooligan.

Mirsky took an unscheduled day's absence with a bottle of brandy smuggled in from Yugoslavia. He spent the day alone in a Moscow park and did not even open the bottle.

After a year, he finished his training and was promoted. He left Podlipki and spent two weeks in Starry Town, where he visited Yuri Gagarin's room, now a kind of shrine for spacefarers. From there, he was flown to a secret facility in Mongolia, and then . . . to the Moon.

And always he kept his eye on the Potato. Someday, he knew, he would go there, and not as an ISCCOM exchange Russian.

A nation could only stand so much.

Three/ Christmas Eve 2004, Santa Barbara, California

Patricia Luisa Vasquez opened the car door to release her seat harness. She was anxious to get into the house and start the festivities. The psychological testing at Vandenberg the past few days had been exhausting.

"Wait," Paul Lopez said. He put a hand on her arm, then stared at the dashboard. Vivaldi's *Four Seasons* played on the car stereo. "Your folks aren't going to want to know—"

"Don't worry about it," she said, pulling back a strand of very dark brown, almost black, hair. The lower half of her round face was illuminated by an orange streetlight, light olive skin pink in the sodium glow. She regarded Paul solicitously, tying her hair into two braids parted in the middle. Her square, intense eyes reminded him of a cat's gaze just before pouncing.

"They'll love it," she said, laying hand on his shoulder and stroking his cheek. "You're the first non-Anglo boyfriend I've ever introduced them to."

"I mean, about us rooming together."

"What they don't know won't hurt them."

"I feel a little awkward. You keep talking about your parents being old-fashioned."

"I just wanted you to meet them, and to show you my home."

"I want that, too."

"Listen, with the news I have tonight, nobody's going to worry about my maidenhood. If Mom asks how serious we are, I'll let you answer."

Paul grimaced. "Great."

Patricia pulled his hand toward her and made a rude sound against the palm with her lips, then opened the door.

"Wait."

"What now?"

"I'm not . . . I mean, you know that I love you."

11

"Paul . . ."

"It's just . . . ."

"Come on inside and meet my family. You'll calm down. And *don't worry.*"

They locked the car door and opened the trunk, pulling groceries out of the back. She huffed up the front walk with a box, her breath clouding in the cold night air. She wiped her feet on the front step mat, swung the screen door wide, caught it with her elbow and shouted, "Mama! It's me. And I brought Paul, too."

Rita Vasquez took the box from her daughter's arms and laid it down on the kitchen table. At forty-five, Rita was only slightly plump, but the clothes she wore invariably conflicted with even Patricia's rudimentary sense of fashion.

"What is this, a care package?" Rita asked. She held her arms out and folded Patricia in them.

"Mama, where did you get that polyester suit? I haven't seen one of those in years."

"I found it in the garage, packed away. Your father bought it for me before you were born. So where's Paul?"

"He's carrying in two more boxes." She removed her coat and savored the smells of tamales steaming in corn husks, baking ham and sweet potato pie. "Smells like home," she said, and Rita beamed.

In the living room, the aluminum tree was still bare— decorating the tree on Christmas Eve was a family tradition— and a gas log burned brightly in the fireplace. She reacquainted herself with the old plaster bas-reliefs of grapes and vines and leaves beneath the cornice, and the heavy wooden beams across the ceiling. She smiled. She had been born in this house. Wherever she went, however far, this would be home to her. "Where are Julia and Robert?"

"Robert's been stationed in Omaha," Rita answered from the kitchen. "They can't make it this year. Be out in March, maybe."

"Oh," Patricia said, disappointed. She returned to the kitchen. "Where's Papa?"

12

"Watching TV."

Paul came in the kitchen door heavily loaded. Patricia took one of the boxes from him and laid it on the floor next to the refrigerator for unloading. "We were expecting an army, so we brought lots of stuff," she said.

Rita pushed through layers of food and shook her head. "It'll get eaten. We're having Mr. and Mrs. Ortiz from next door, and cousin Enrique and his new wife. So this is Paul?"

"Yup."

Rita hugged him, her arms barely meeting around his back. She took hold of both his hands and stood away, surveying. He smiled. Tall, thin Paul, with his brown hair and light skin, looking more Anglo than the others. Still, Rita smiled as they talked. Paul could hold his own.

She walked down the hall to the den where her father would be sitting in front of the television. They had never been well-off, and the TV was a twenty-five-year-old model that made a rainbow ghost whenever it received 3-D transmissions.

"Papa?" Patricia said quietly, sneaking up behind him in the half-dark.

"Patty!" Ramon Vasquez looked around the rear cushion of his chair, a big grin lifting his pepper-gray mustache. He had been partly paralyzed by a stroke three years before and even with surgery hadn't fully recovered. Patricia sat on the divan beside him.

"I've brought Paul home with me," she said. "I'm sorry Julia can't be here this time."

"Me, too. But that's air force." Ramon had been in the air force for twenty years before retiring in 1996. Except for Patricia, the family was enmeshed in the air force. Julia had met Robert at a party on March Air Force Base six years ago.

"I've got something to tell everybody, Papa."

"Oh? What's that?" Had his speech improved since they last talked face to face? It seemed so. She hoped so.

Rita called out from the kitchen. "Daughter! Come help me and Paul put away this stuff."

"What're you watching?" Patricia asked, reluctant to leave.

13

"News."

A commentator—and his scarcely less formidable ghost—was leading into a story about the Stone. Patricia lingered despite her mother's second call.

"As more and more personnel are sent to the Stone, citizen and scientific groups are asking for an open forum. Today, in the fourth year of a joint NATO–Eurospace investigation, the cloak wrapped around the Stone is as impenetrable as ever, and—"

So it was no news after all.

"—Russian participants are particularly unhappy with the requirements for secrecy. Meanwhile, protestors from the Planetary Society, the L-5 Society, the Friends for Interstellar Relations and other groups have gathered around the White House and around the so-called Blue Cube in Sunnyvale, California, protesting military involvement and alleging a cover-up of major discoveries within the Stone."

An earnest, clean-cut and conservatively dressed young man appeared on the screen. He stood in front of the White House and spoke with exaggerated gestures. "We know it's an alien artifact, and we know there are seven chambers inside—huge chambers. We didn't put them there. There are cities in every chamber—deserted cities—all but the seventh. And there's something incredible there, something unimaginable."

"What do you think it is?" the interviewer asked.

The protestor flung his hands up. "We think they should tell everybody. Whatever's there, we as taxpayers have the right to know!"

The commentator added that NASA and Joint Space Command spokespersons had no comment.

Patricia sighed and placed her hands on Ramon's shoulders, automatically rubbing his muscles.

Paul watched her closely at dinner, waiting for her to find the right opportunity, but she didn't. She felt uncomfortable with the friends and neighbors present. This was something only her immediate family should know, and she couldn't tell even them as much as she wanted.

Rita and Ramon seemed to accept Paul. That was a plus. Eventually, they would have to know about the living arrangements—if they hadn't figured it out already: that Patricia and Paul were more than just dating acquaintances, that they were living together in that haphazard way reserved for coed dormitories.

So many secrets and discretions. Perhaps they wouldn't be as shocked as she expected—wanted?—them to be. It was a little disturbing to think that her parents might regard her as a grown-up, sexual being. She was not nearly as open about it as most of her friends and acquaintances.

Eventually, she and Paul would be married, she was sure. But they were both young, and Paul was not going to ask until he felt he could support them both. Or until she convinced him that *she* could—and even with her doctorate, that wasn't likely for several more years.

Not counting, of course, the pay she would receive from Judith Hoffman's group. That money would go into a separate security account until her return.

When the dishes were cleared and everyone had gathered around the tree, family and friends helping to decorate, she signaled her mother that they had to talk in the kitchen. "And bring Papa." Rita helped Ramon into the kitchen on his aluminum crutches and they sat around the battered wooden table that had been in the family for at least sixty years.

"I have something to tell you," Patricia began.

"Oh, *madre de Dios,*" Rita said, clasping her hands and smiling rapturously.

"No, Mama, it's not about Paul and me," she said. Her mother's face stiffened, then relaxed.

"So what, then?"

"Last week, I received a phone call at school," Patricia said. "I can't tell you all about it, but I'm going to be gone for a couple of months, even longer. Paul knows about it, but I can't tell him any more than I've just told you." Paul entered the kitchen through the swinging doors.

"Who was it called you?" Ramon asked.

15

"Judith Hoffman."

"Who's that?" Rita asked.

"The woman on television?" Ramon asked.

Patricia nodded. "She's an advisor to the President. They want me to work on something with them, and that's as much as I can tell you."

"Why should they want you?" Rita asked.

"I think they want her to build a time machine," Paul said. Whenever he had said that before, Patricia had become angry, but now she shrugged it off.

She couldn't expect Paul to understand her work. Very few people did—certainly not her parents and friends. "Paul has some other crazy theories, too," she said. "But my lips are sealed."

"Like a clam," Paul said. "She's been hard to live with the past few days."

"If you wouldn't keep trying to get me to talk!" She sighed dramatically—she was doing a lot of that lately—and looked at the cream-colored ceiling, then turned to her father. "It's going to be very interesting. Nobody will be able to reach me directly. You can send mail for me to this address." She drew the phone pad across the table and wrote down an APO address.

"Is this important to you?" Rita asked.

"Of course it is," Ramon answered.

But Patricia didn't know. It sounded crazy, even now.

After the guests had left, she took Paul on a nighttime tour of the neighborhood. For a half hour, they walked in silence, passing from one streetlight glow to the next. "I'm coming back, you know," she said finally.

"I know."

"I had to show you my home, because it's very important to me. Rita, Ramon, the house."

"Yes," Paul said.

"I think I'd be lost without it. I spend so much time in my head, and what I do there is so different . . . so bizarre to

16

most people. If I didn't have a center, a place to return to, I'd get lost."

"I understand," Paul said. "It's a very nice home. I like your folks."

She stopped him and they faced each other, holding hands at arm's length. "I'm glad," she said.

"I want to make a home with you, too," he said. "Another center, for both of us to come back to."

Her expression was so intense she seemed about to leap on him. "Cat's eyes," Paul said, grinning.

They circled back and kissed on the front porch before going in to join her parents for coffee and cinnamon cocoa.

"One last pit stop," she said as they prepared to drive back to Caltech.

She walked down the hall to the bathroom, past the graduation pictures and the framed contents page of the issue of *The Physical Review* her first paper had appeared in. She stopped in front of the cover and stared intently at it. Suddenly, her heart seemed to miss a beat, leaving a peculiar hollow in her chest, a brief, almost pleasant sensation of falling, fading, then returning to normal.

She'd felt it before. It was nothing serious, just a cold wind down the middle of her chest, every time she truly accepted the idea of where she was going.

Four/ 1174, Journey Year 5 Nader, Axis City

The Presiding Minister of the Axis City, Ilyin Taur Ingle, stood in the broad observation blister, staring out across the Way through the city's blue glow at lanes bright with the continuous flow of traffic between the gates. Behind him stood two assigned ghosts and a corporeal representative of the Hexamon Nexus.

"Do you know Olmy well, Ser Franco?" the Presiding Minister picted, using graphicspeak.

17

"No, Ser Ingle, I do not," the corporeal representative replied, "though by reputation he is famous in the Nexus."

"Three incarnations, one more than law allows because of his extraordinary service. Olmy is one of our oldest citizens still corporeal," the minister said. "An enigmatic personality. He would have long since forfeited his majority rights and retired to City Memory if it wasn't for his usefulness to the Nexus." The P.M. instructed a sprayer to release his special variety of Talsit. The mist filled a cubic area surrounded by faintly glowing purple traction fields. Ingle entered the field and took a deep breath.

The ghosts hadn't moved, their images fixed until called upon, visible only to indicate their City Memory personalities were tuned in to the chamber, listening and watching.

"He is of Naderite background himself, I believe," the corporeal assistant said.

"Yes, he is," the minister said, nodding. "But he serves the Hexamon regardless of who is in power, and I have no doubt where his loyalties lie. A most unusual man. Tough, in the old sense of the word—a man who has lived through great changes, great pain. I've had him recalled from one point three ex nine. He's been supervising our preparations for the Jart offensive. But he can be of more use to us here. He is the one to send now. Axis Nader can't disagree with him or accuse us of partisan assignment; his reports to them are always detailed and accurate. Inform the President that we are accepting the task and sending Olmy."

"Yes, Ser Ingle."

"I believe the ghosts have their questions answered, now?"

"We listen," said one ghost. The other did not move.

"Fine. Now I will meet with Ser Olmy."

The ghosts faded and Corprep Franco left, fingering his neck torque to pict a flag of official business over his left shoulder.

The P.M. turned off the traction fields and the chamber became smoky with more Talsit. The smell was disconcerting, sharp like old wine, as Olmy entered.

18

He approached the minister quietly, not wishing to interrupt his reverie.

"Forward, Ser Olmy," the minister said. He turned as Olmy walked up the steps to the blister platform. "You're looking fit today."

"And you, ser."

"Mm. My wife made me a wonderful forgetting last turn. Removed much unpleasantness from my twentieth year. That was not a good year, and the loss was a relief."

"Excellent, ser."

"When will you marry, Olmy?"

"When I find the woman who can purge my twenty-first year, first incarnation."

The minister laughed heartily. "I hear you keep a fine advocate company in Axis Nader. . . . What's her name?"

"Suli Ram Kikura."

"Yes, of course . . . She's been active smoothing things between the Nexus and the Korzenowski hot heads, has she not?"

"Yes. We seldom discuss it."

The minister sucked in his breath, looked concerned and stared down at the platform. "Well, just so, then. I have a difficult mission for you."

"My joy to serve the Hexamon."

"Perhaps not this time. No mere investigation of illegal gate commerce. Every few decades, we send someone back to the Thistledown to check stability. But we are doubly motivated this time. The Thistledown has been reoccupied."

"Someone crossing the Forbidden Territories?"

"No. More puzzling. Nothing has disturbed our sentries at the first barrier. Apparently the occupants have entered the Thistledown from outside; perhaps more startling, they are human. Not in great force, but they're organized. There's no use speculating where they come from; the information is too equivocated. You'll have authority, of course, and the necessary transportation. Ser Algoli will inform you about the other requirements. Understand?"

Olmy nodded. "Ser."

"Good." The minister leaned over the railing and peered at the surface twenty kilometers below. A maelstrom of lights swirled around several of the lanes. "There appears to be a jam-up at that gate. Ah, it's the season for worries. The month of the Good Man." He turned to Olmy. "Good luck. Or, as the Eld put it: Star, Fate and Pneuma be kind."

"Thank you, ser."

He stepped back from the platform and left the chamber, taking the lift up the long, slender pylon to the Central City, where he arranged his affairs for a protracted absence.

The assignment was a privilege. Return to the Thistledown was forbidden for any purpose not essential to the Nexus. Olmy hadn't been there for well over four hundred years.

On the other hand, of course, it could be a very dangerous mission—especially with information so equivocated. He could help ensure his mission's success by bringing along a Frant.

If there were humans in the Thistledown, and they weren't city renegades—the most likely explanation—then where did they come from?

Far too narrow and equivocated for his ease.

Chapter One: April 2005

On the first leg of the trip, in the passenger cabin of the long-bed shuttle, Patricia Vasquez had watched the Earth's cloud-smeared limb on a video monitor. Before her own transfer, cameras mounted in the shuttle bay had shown her the long waldos maneuvering the huge cargo out of the bay into the waiting arms of the OTV—orbital transfer vehicle—as if two spiders were trading a cocoon-wrapped fly. The operation had taken an hour, and with its slow fascination had distracted her from thoughts about her present circumstances.

When her own turn came and she donned the passenger bubble to be guided across the ten meters to the OTV's lock, she worked hard to appear calm. The bubble was made of transparent plastic, so she did not suffer from claustrophobia—almost the opposite, in fact. She could feel the immensity of the blackness beyond the spacecraft, though she could not make out stars. They were outdone by the glow of the Earth and the close, brightly lighted surfaces of the OTV, a train of clustered tanks, balls and prisms wrapped in aluminum beams.

The three-man, two-woman crew of the OTV greeted her warmly in the narrow tunnel as she "hatched," then guided her to a seat just behind theirs. From that vantage, she had a clear, direct view, and now she could see the steady pinpoints of stars.

So confronted, with none of the comfortable separation of a video monitor frame, space seemed to extend into a mating of infinite, star-cluttered halls. She felt as if she could walk down any one of the halls and become lost in altered perspective.

She still wore the black jumpsuit she had been handed in Florida just six hours before. She felt dirty. Her hair, even though tied up in a bun, let loose irritating wisps. She could smell her own nervousness.

The crew floated around her, making last-minute checks,

punching readings into slates and processors. Patricia examined their colored suits—the women in red and blue, the men in green and black and gray—and idly wondered how they were ranked and who commanded. Everything seemed casually efficient with no deference in voice or manner, as if they were civilians. But they were not.

The OTV was a registered unarmed military vehicle, subject to the restrictions imposed after the Little Death. It was one of dozens of new vehicles that had been constructed in Earth orbit since the appearance of the Stone, and it differed substantially from the vehicles that had serviced the Joint Space Force's Orbital Defense Platforms. It was larger and capable of traveling much greater distances; by treaty, it could not carry cargoes to the ODPs.

"We're leaving in three minutes," said the shuttle's co-pilot, a blond woman whose name Patricia had already forgotten. She touched Patricia on the shoulder and smiled. "Everything will be hectic for a half hour or so. If you need a drink or have to use the lavatory, now's the time."

Patrica shook her head and returned the smile. "I'm fine."

"Good. Virgin?"

Patricia stared.

"First flight, she means," the other woman clarified. Patrica remembered her name—Rita, just like her mother.

"Of course," Patricia said. "Would I be sitting here acting like a cow in a slaughterhouse, otherwise?"

The blond laughed. The pilot—James or Jack, with beautiful green eyes—looked over his shoulder at her, his head framed by the belt and sword of Orion. "Relax, Patricia," he said. So calm. She was almost intimidated by their professional assurance. They were spacefarers, originally assigned to the near-Earth orbit platforms and now working the distances between Earth, Moon and Stone. She was just a young woman fresh out of graduate school, and she had never in her life even left the state of California until traveling to Florida for the shuttle flight from Kennedy Space Center.

She wondered what her father and mother were doing now,

sitting at home in Santa Barbara. Where did they imagine their daughter to be? She had said good-bye just a week ago. Her stomach still churned at the memory of her last few moments with Paul. His letters would get to her, that was guaranteed—forwarded through the APO address. But what could she tell him in her return messages? Very likely, nothing. And her time in space had been estimated at two months, minimum.

She listened to the rumble and purr of the OTV machinery. She heard fuel pumps, mystery noises, gurgles like large water bubbles popping behind the passenger cabin, then the sharp *ting*s of the attitude motors driving the craft away from the shuttle.

They began rotating, their axis somewhere near the middle of the cocoon cargo, clamped where a spare hexagonal fuel tank would have otherwise been. The OTV lurched forward with the impulse of its first engine burn. The blond, still not in her seat, landed on her feet against the rear bulkhead, flexed her knees with the impact and finished her sequence on the processor.

Then everyone buckled in.

The second burn took place fifteen minutes later. Patricia closed her eyes, nestled into the couch and resumed work on a problem she had put aside more than two weeks before. She had never required paper during the initial stages of her work. Now, the Fraktur symbols paraded before her, separated by her own brand of sign notation, invented when she was ten years old. There was no music—she usually listened to Vivaldi or Mozart while working—but nevertheless, she became immersed in a sea of abstraction. Her hand went to the pack of music coins and the slate stereo attachment in her small effects bag.

A few minutes later, she opened her eyes. Everyone was in their seats, staring intently at instrument panels. She tried to nap. Briefly, before dozing off, she ran through her Big Question again:

Why had *she*, in particular, been chosen from a list of mathematicians that must have been meters long? That she had

23

won a Fields Award didn't seem reason enough; there were other mathematicians of far greater experience and stature . . .

Hoffman hadn't really offered an explanation. All she had said was, "You're going to the Stone. All that you'll need to know is up there, and it's classified, so I'm not allowed to give you documents while you're here on Earth. You'll have a hell of a lot of studying to do. And I'm sure it will be glorious fun for a mind like yours."

As far as Patricia knew, her expertise had no practical use whatsoever, and she preferred it that way.

She didn't doubt her talents. But the very fact that they were calling on *her*—that they might need to know about (as she had expressed it in her doctoral dissertation, *Non-gravity Bent Geodesics of* n-*Spatial Reference Frames: An Approach to Superspace Visualization and Probability Clustering*)—made her even more apprehensive.

Six years ago, a Stanford math professor had told her that the only beings who would ever fully appreciate her work would be gods or extraterrestrials.

In the dark, sleepily drifting away from the OTV noises and the sensation of her stomach pressing always upward, she thought of the Stone. The governments involved did not discourage speculation but provided no fuel to feed the fires. The Russians, allowed on the Stone only the last year, hinted darkly at what their researchers had seen.

Amateur astronomers—and a few civilian professionals who hadn't been visited by government agents—had pointed out the three regular latitudinal bands and the odd dimples at each pole, as if it had been turned on a lathe.

The upshot was, everyone knew it was big news, perhaps the biggest news of all time.

And so it wasn't incredible that Paul, putting a few odd facts together, had told her he thought she was going to the Stone. "You're just too far-out a mind to be going anywhere else," he had said.

Gods and extraterrestrials. Still, she managed to nap.

When she awoke, she saw the Stone briefly as the OTV swung around for its docking maneuver. It looked much like the pictures she had seen many times before published in newspapers and magazines—bean-shaped, about a third as wide in the middle as it was long, heavily cratered between the smoothly artificial excavated bands. Ninety-one kilometers in diameter at its widest, two hundred ninety-two kilometers long. Rock and nickel and iron and not nearly as simple as that.

"Approaching south polar axis," the blond said, leaning around in her chair to look back at Vasquez. "A little briefing, in case they haven't told you already. Blind leading the blind, honey." She glanced meaningfully at her shipmates. "First, some facts and figures important to mere navigators. Note that the Stone is rotating on its long axis. That's nothing surprising—everyone knows that. But it's rotating once every seven minutes or so—"

"Every six point eight two four minutes," James or Jack corrected.

"That means," the blond continued, unfazed, "that anything loose on the outer surface will fly away at a pretty good clip, so we can't dock there. We have to go through the pole."

"There's stuff inside?" Patricia asked.

"Quite a lot of stuff, if they're keeping everything—and everyone—we've been bringing up in the past few years," James or Jack said.

"The Stone's albedo matches any of a number of siliceous asteroids'. Apparently, that's what it was at one time. Here's the south pole now," Rita said.

In the middle of the large polar crater was an indentation—judging from the scale of the Stone itself, quite tiny, no more than a kilometer deep and three or four kilometers wide.

The Stone's rotation was easily discernible. As the OTV matched course with the Stone, then began its approach along the axis, the crater enlarged and showed even more detail. With hardly any surprise at all, Patricia realized the floor was marked by shallow hexagons, like a beehive.

25

At the center of the indentation was a circular black spot about a hundred meters across. A hole. An entrance. It loomed larger and larger but lost none of its intense blackness.

The OTV slid into the hole.

"We have to maintain our position about five minutes, until they bring the rotating dock up to speed," James or Jack said.

"We did all this?" Patricia asked, her voice unsteady. "In just five years?"

"No, honey," the blond said. "It was here already, I'm sure you've heard the Stone is hollow inside with seven chambers. We have a fair number of personnel and thousands of tons of equipment in there, doing God knows what and finding things we'd give our eyeteeth to see, believe me. But this is where our knowledge stops, and we've been instructed not to pass along rumor. You won't be needing it."

"We've been riding a docking signal for the last seven minutes," James or Jack said. "Voice contact any second."

The radio chimed. "OTV three-seven," a calm tenor male voice said. "We have prime dock rotating. Advance at point one meters per second."

Rita flipped a switch and the OTV's floods came on, partially illuminating the inside of a gray cylinder that dwarfed the craft. Four rows of lights appeared ahead of them, wobbling back and forth slightly as the rotating dock adjusted its speed. "Here we go." The OTV advanced slowly.

Patricia nodded and held her hands tightly in her lap. The bump was hardly discernible as the OTV motors went *ting* all around and brought them to a stop inside the tunnel. A hatch opened ahead of the ship and three men in space suits floated into view, carrying cables. They used suit thrusters to fly around the OTV and tie it down.

"You're hooked, OTV three-seven," the radio voice said a few minutes later. "Welcome to the Stone."

"Thanks," James or Jack said. "We have a big load in the hopper and precious cargo up front. Treat them gently."

"Foreign or domestic?"

"Domestic. Best California vintage."

26

Patricia didn't know whether they were talking about a cargo of wine or her. She was too nervous to ask.

"Got you clear."

"Any more mysteries to leak to us, guide?" the blond asked.

"My people want the hopper cargo released in five minutes."

"Timing on."

"More mysteries. Let's see. Why is a raven like a writing desk?"

"Bastard. I'll think on it," James or Jack said. He switched off the mike and floated up from his couch to help Patricia with her belts. "Closemouthed, all of them," he said, guiding her to the lock access corridor. "I leave you to their tender mercies. And promise us, someday—pretty please?—" he patted her shoulder paternally "—when all this is settled and we're reminiscing in a bar in Sausalito . . ." He grinned at her, knowing how ridiculous the image was. "Tell us what the hell happened up here, step by step? We'll savor it the rest of our lives."

"Why do you think they'll tell me?" Patricia asked.

"Why, don't you know?" Rita joined them in the lock. "You've been given top billing. You're going to save their collective hide."

Patricia climbed in to the transfer bubble and they closed the lock behind her. Watching through the lock port, she could see the curious hunger in their faces. The lock hatch swung open and two men in spacesuits reached in to pull the bubble from the OTV. She was passed along hand-to-hand through a circular opening in the dock's dark gray surface.

Chapter Two

Twenty-five kilometers below the axis, the Stone's spin produced a force of six-tenths of a g. Garry Lanier took daily advantage of that to perform gymnastic feats difficult or impossible for him on Earth. He swung back and forth, blowing out his breath forcefully and grunting, holding his legs straight together and propelling himself high over the parallel bars and the pit of fine white sand. It was easy to twist and reverse his position. Almost as easy was swinging his legs into the air, spinning and doing a reverse that way.

The exercise cleared his mind of everything else—for a few minutes, at least—and took him back to his days as a college gymnast.

The Stone's first chamber, viewed in cross section, resembled a squat cylinder, fifty kilometers in diameter and thirty across the floor. Since each of the Stone's first six chambers were wider in diameter than in length, they resembled deep valleys, and that's what they were sometimes called.

Lanier paused for a second with toes pointed together and stared up at the plasma tube. Rings of light passed through ionized gas only slightly denser than the near-vacuum around them, sweeping along the axis from the bore hole to the opposite side of the chamber with such speed that the eye interpreted their passage as a continuous hollow shaft or tube. The plasma tube—and extensions in the other chambers—provided all the light for the Stone's interior and had been doing so for some twelve centuries.

He dropped to the sandy bed and rubbed his hands on his sweatpants. He worked out for an hour—no more—whenever his schedule allowed, which wasn't often. His muscles were feeling the lack of Earth gravity. At least he was acclimated to the thin air.

He ran his hand through his short black hair, face expressionless, pumping his legs slowly to cool them down.

Soon, back to the small office in the administration bungalow, back to signing slates allocating materiel to the various experiments, looking over the science team shifts in the five cramped labs, scheduling equipment and central processor time . . . back to the memory blocks and the

28

information coming out of the second and third chambers . . .

And to the security squabbles, the Russian team's constant complaints about limited access.

He closed his eyes. Those things he could handle. Hoffman had once called him a born administrator, and he didn't deny it—handling people, especially brilliant, capable people, was his meat and drink.

But he would also go back to the tiny figurine in the top drawer of his desk. For him, the figurine symbolized everything peculiar about the Stone.

It was a lifelike three-dimensional image of a man, encased in a block of crystal. On the base of the block, which stood just under twelve centimeters high, a name had been engraved in neat round letters: KONRAD KORZENOWSKI.

Korzenowski had been the main engineer on the Stone, six hundred years ago.

That was where it began—the Library Beast, he thought of it, threatening to consume him—the knowledge that had every day taken a bit of his humanity and rubbed it thin, pushing him closer to some sort of personal crisis. There was no way— yet—to deal with what he knew—he and only ten other people. Soon, an eleventh would arrive.

He felt sorry for her.

The gymnastics pit was half a kilometer from the science team compound, midway between the compound and the barbed wire fence that marked the boundary beyond which no one could go, unescorted, without a green badge.

The valley floor was covered with a soft, sandy layer of soil, not dusty though dry. A few scrubby patches of grass grew out of the soil, but for the most part the first chamber was arid.

The compound itself, one of two in the first chamber, resembled an old Roman encampment, with an earthworks rampart and a shallow, dry moat surrounding the buildings. The rampart was topped with electronic sensors mounted on stakes every five meters. All these precautions dated back to the days when it was reasonable to suspect there might still be

Stoners in the chambers and that they might present some danger. Out of force of habit—and because the possibility had never been completely ruled out—the precautions were maintained.

Lanier crossed the sturdy wooden bridge spanning the moat and climbed a set of steps on the rampart, waving his card at a reader mounted on one of the stakes.

He passed the men's and women's barracks and entered the administration bungalow, tapping his finger on Ann Blakely's desk and waving as he walked past. Ann had served him as secretary and general assistant for over a year. She swiveled on her chair and reached for the memo slate.

"Garry—"

He shook his head without looking at her and continued on up the stairs. "Five more minutes," he said.

On the second floor, he slipped his card into the verification lock on his office door, pressed his thumbs onto the small plate and entered. The door swung shut automatically behind him. He removed his sweatpants and shirt, substituting the blue science team jumpsuit.

The office was neatly organized but still looked cluttered. A small desk manufactured from OTV tank baffles was flanked by chromium bins filled with rolls of paper. A narrow shelf of real books hung next to racks of memory blocks sealed behind tough, alarm-equipped plastic panels. Maps and diagrams were taped to the walls.

A broad window looked out over the compound buildings. North across the valley's barren floor of dirt, sand and scrub loomed the massive gray presence of the far chamber cap.

He sat on a lightweight director's chair and propped his feet on the window frame. His dark eyes, underscored by fatigue lines, focused on a distant point at one o'clock high where the plasma tube butted up against the cap. Through the tube's diffuse glow, it was difficult to make out the hundred-meter-wide bore hole that pushed through the cap into the second chamber. The bore hole opened five kilometers above the atmosphere in the chamber.

In two minutes, his private time would be over. He organized his slates and processors, looking over the day's schedule, preparing himself mentally to be a mover-and-shaker.

There was dirt beneath one fingernail. He removed it with another fingernail.

If he could only explain the simple things—the figurine, the barbed wire used to string up the fence, the crate wood used to make the bridge over the moat—it would all fall into place.

The Stone would explain itself.

The only explanations he had now were much too incredible to be sane.

His comline hummed.

"Yes, Ann."

"Are you on duty now, Garry?"

"That I am."

"Transmission down the hole. OTV approach."

"Our savior?"

"I presume."

Hoffman had said this young woman was important, and the Advisor's word was one of the few things Lanier felt he could count on. In the four years since that night at the party, he had learned a great deal about politics in and out of world capitals, and how nations handled crises. He had come to realize how truly extraordinary Hoffman was. Capable, and with uncanny intuition.

But at that party, she had been dead wrong about one thing. The Stone's appearance did not signal the arrival of aliens, not in the strict sense of the word.

He picked up two slates and a processor. "Anything else?" he asked, standing by Blakely's desk.

"In and out," she said and handed him a cube of messages.

There was always a mild, cool breeze flowing down the almost vertical slope of the cap. Sometimes snow fell, piling up in drifts against the nickel-iron wall. The elevator entrance, a perfect semicircular arch, had been blasted out of asteroid material, as had all the tunnels, serviceways and bore holes of

31

the Stone, by a fusion torch of extremely high power and efficiency. The sides of the short hall had been polished smooth and etched with acid by the Stoners to reveal the beautiful triangular Widmanstätten patterns, veined with rocky troilite intrusions.

The elevator was cylindrical, ten meters in diameter and five meters high, and was used for both personnnel and freight. There were handgrips along the perimeter and tie-downs dimpled the floor. It followed a sloping tunnel to the staging areas surrounding the external bore hole. As the elevator climbed, its angular velocity declined, weakening the centrifugal force of the Stone's rotation. By the time it reached the vicinity of the bore hole, the spin produced only one-tenth of one percent g.

The trip took ten minutes. The elevator decelerated smoothly and stopped, its opposite hatch flush with a pressurized tunnel leading to the staging areas.

Taking an electric miner's cart, one of the two dozen or so brought up from Earth, Lanier rose most of the remaining distance along a magnetic rail.

The cart whined to a stop and Lanier drifted the rest of the way, pulling himself along guide ropes.

The first landings in the bore hole had been tricky. There had been no power to the rotating docks at that time, and very little illumination. The OTV pilots had proved their skill again and again. The first spacesuited explorers had shown great courage in leaving their craft and approaching the bore-hole walls, which rotated at about three-quarters of a meter per second. Now that the dock and staging area equipment had been refurbished and brought back into operation, the transfer process was much easier.

The three docks were simple, massive and efficient. Cylinders within the hole rotated to compensate for the Stone's spin, each accelerated like the rotor in a giant electric motor. One engineer in a booth below the prime dock controlled all of the docks, opening and closing hatches, coordinating cargo and passenger unloading.

The staging areas themselves had been thoroughly customized by the engineering team, outfitted with near-freefall workshops and machine shops. Here was where bulky cargoes were checked out, repackaged and either shipped down the elevators to the valley floor or flown along the axis to the next hole and chamber down the line.

The director of the engineering team, Lawrence Heineman, was talking to a slight, dark-haired young woman in the prime dock staging area as Lanier pulled himself in. They stood in a broad oval of light, hands on guide ropes, watching as large vacuum doors slid across to reveal the OTV's cocoon cargo resting on joists. The cargo dwarfed them.

Heineman, a short, crew-cut, muscular aerospace technician from Florida, smiled broadly and waved his hands, explaining something to the young woman. As Lanier approached, Heineman turned, held out the palm of one hand and bowed slightly in his direction. "Patricia, this is Garry Lanier, the closest thing to a civilian boss we have. Garry, Miss Patricia Luisa Vasquez." He shook his head and blew his breath out with an enthusiastic "Whoo!"

Lanier shook Vasquez's hand. She was small and pretty in a fragile way. Round face, silky dark brown hair, thin wrists, narrow legs, broad hips for her size: an altogether unpractical-looking woman, he thought. Beneath wide square eyes as black as his own, and a small, sharp nose, she had drawn her mouth into a tight line. She looked scared.

"My pleasure," Lanier said. "Larry, what have you told her so far?"

Heineman parried the question with a sidelong glance. "Patricia, I'm only a blue-badge for now—and I hear you're going to get a green. Garry is worried I might pass along some of the ignorant suppositions of an axis-hugger. I've only been telling her about this level of operations, I swear." He held up his right hand and clapped his left to his chest. "Garry, I've read some of this lady's papers in a half-dozen math and physics journals. She's fantastic."

33

There was a question on his face, however, which Lanier had no trouble interpreting. *What in hell is* she *doing here?*

"So I've heard." He pointed at the cocoon. "What's that?"

"My ticket to a green badge, finally," Heineman said. "Packing slips say it's the tuberider. And the V/STOL is coming in on the next OTV, a few hours from now."

"Then let's get it unwrapped and see what sort of modifications we'll have to make."

"Right. Pleased to meet you, Patricia." Heineman started to leave, then stopped and turned back slowly with a puzzled expression. "What you write about, it's really more a hobby for me, way beyond my expertise." He raised his eyebrows hopefully. "Maybe we can talk more later, though, when I get my green badge?"

Patricia smiled and nodded. Teams of men and women in gray jumpsuits were already gathering around the cocoon like ants tending a queen. Heineman joined them, calling out orders.

"Miss Vasquez—" Lanier began.

"Patricia's fine, really. I'm not very formal."

"Neither am I, if I can help it. I'm the science team coordinator."

"So Mr. Heineman told me. I have so many questions . . . Mr. Lanier, Garry, is this really a spaceship, a starship, the whole thing?" She swung her arm wide, her feet lifting from the deck momentarily.

"It is," he said, feeling the familiar, peculiar pleasure. Even though the Stone had nearly driven him crazy in the past few years, with its endless layers of surprise and shock, he was still more than a little in love with it.

"Where did it come from?"

Lanier held up his hands and shook his head. Vasquez suddenly noticed how exhausted he appeared, and that subdued her excitement some.

"First, I'm sure you'll want to rest and get cleaned up. Our facilities in the valley—the chamber floor—are quite nice.

34

Then you can visit our cafeteria, meet a few of the team scientists, take it from there. One step at a time."

Vasquez examined him intently. Her eyes made the inspection seem less than sympathetic, even aggressive. "Is something wrong?"

Lanier raised his brows and glanced to one side. "We have a name for what this place does to you. We call it getting Stoned. I'm just a little Stoned, is all."

She looked around the staging area and experimented with the centrifugal force, pushing herself up a few centimeters with a nudge of her toe. "It looks so familiar," she said. "I expected an alien artifact to be mysterious, but I can identify almost everything, like it was built on Earth, by us."

"Well," said Lanier, "Heineman and his people have been busy up here. But keep an open mind. If you'll follow me, we'll descend to the floor of the first chamber. Use the ropes. And if Larry hasn't already said it, allow me to welcome you to the Stone."

Chapter Three

Patricia lay on the air mattress, keeping still so the synthetic fiber sheets wouldn't squeak against the vinyl. Surrounded by darkness, she was clean, warm, well fed—the cafeteria food had been more than palatable—and now that she wasn't walking around, not nearly so breathless. Tired but unable to sleep. Her memory kept tossing up visions:

The thirty-kilometer-wide chamber floor, a mottled gray-and-brown valley landscape, capped at each end by impassive rock and natural metal walls, run through by the glowing plasma tube.

The peculiar perspective as she stood outside the valley level zero elevator entrance, facing the immensity, the landscape for kilometers around looking flat and normal, a desert on a bright cloudy day. Off to either side, however—spinwise and counter-spinwise—the curve became more pronounced. She seemed to stand under a vast arching bridge with the plasma tube a bright milky river flowing overhead. Directly north, the land rose to curve in snug conformity with the circular cap. Looking up, everything distorted as if seen through a fish-eye lens, the cap accepted the embrace of the opposite side of the chamber, completing the circle behind the plasma tube.

The Stone was still active, even though these chambers had been deserted centuries before.

Lanier hadn't answered many questions, telling her it was "the process" to let her see and experience the Stone, step by step. "Otherwise," he had said, "why should you believe what we tell you?" That made sense, but she was still frustrated. What was so mysterious? The Stone was magnificent and startling, but not—so far as she could tell—anything to arouse her professional interest. Straightforward physics, however advanced.

It was simple, really. Take one large asteroid, rock with a core of nickel-iron—your average billennia-old chunk of primordial planet-stuff—and push it into an orbit around your planet. Hollow out seven chambers, each connected by an axial bore hole, then worm-hole some of the remaining volume with tunnels, accessways, storage depots and elevators. Bring up supplementary carbonaceous and ice-volatiles asteroids and begin transferring their material into the chambers. Send it on a journey into deepest space, and *voila*!

The Stone.

She had learned a few key facts so far. Each chamber floor was connected by tunnels dug through the intervening asteroid material. Many of the tunnels were part of an extensive train transport system. There were no trains in the first chamber because it had served as a reserve and storage area and had been infrequently visited in the time when the Stone was populated. The seventh chamber had apparently served a similar purpose, which made sense—the outermost chambers doing double duty as buffers against damage to the compara-

36

tively thin ends of the asteroid. The wall between the first chamber cap and space was only a few kilometers thick in places.

But there was something peculiar about the seventh chamber. She had felt it in Lanier's voice and seen it in the expressions of those she had met in the cafeteria. And there had been the rumors on Earth . . .

Somehow, the seventh chamber was different, important.

She had met five team scientists so far, three in the cafeteria: Robert Smith, tall and bird-boned with red hair and down-angled eyes that made him seem sad, an expert on asteroid formation; Hua Ling, the slender and intense senior member of the Chinese team and a plasma physicist who spent most of his time at the south polar bore hole; and Lenore Carrolson, a round-faced woman of fifty with gray-blond hair and a permanently friendly, sensual expression, heavy-lidded eyes surrounded by smile lines.

Carrolson had greeted Patricia with motherly solicitude. It had taken Patricia several minutes to realize that this was *the* Lenore Carrolson, Nobel laureate, the astrophysicist who had discovered and partly explained gemstars eight years before.

Carrolson had taken Lanier's hint that it was her duty to show Patricia the women's quarters in the compound. They were in a long, fiberwall barracks on the north end of the quadrangle. The rooms were small and spare but comfortable in their own ingenious ways, everything lightweight and compact. In the building's lounge, Carrolson had introduced her to two other astronomers, Janice Polk and Beryl Wallace, both from the Abell Array in Nevada. They sprawled on couches that looked as if they had been assembled out of scrap metal in a high school shop class. Polk resembled a fashion model more than Patricia's image of an astronomer. Even in a jumpsuit, her dark beauty was elegant and distant, her expression not so much disapproving as skeptical. Wallace was attractive enough, but about twenty pounds overweight. She seemed perturbed about something.

Carrolson had pointed out the social roster located near the

37

main door. "There are thirty women here on the science team, and sixty men. Two married couples, four committeds—"

"Five," Patricia had added.

"And six married but spouses back on Earth. I'm one of those. That means slim pickings for the single men. But committed or not, you're fair game if you put your name on the roster. There's an old saying that has to be bent a bit here: 'Don't dip your pen in the office ink.' Since office ink is all there is, some pen dipping is inevitable. But nobody has to take abuse." Carrolson glanced at Polk and Wallace. "Right, girls?"

"Paradise," Polk said flatly, looking up from her slate and widening her eyes. "Better than university."

"Any trouble," Carrolson said, "and you just tell me. I'm senior female here, in age at least."

"I'll do fine," Patricia had replied.

She had never been a social butterfly, tending to fall hard and fast—and usually without reciprocation. Still, with Paul to think of, that was the least of her concerns here. Although— and she smiled in the darkness—Lanier was a pretty fellow. So worried, though.

Patricia wondered if she would look just as worried when she had the whole picture.

Without knowing she had slept, she heard the chiming alarm on her comline. Beside her bed, a pleasant amber light switched on with the signal. She blinked at the bare, off-white walls and had no trouble remembering where she was. She felt right at home, in fact, and a little excited. She swung her feet over the edge of the bed.

Patricia had never been adventurous. Hiking and camping had not been missing from her life, but she had never felt inclined toward outdoor activities other than bicycling. Every six to eight months, she became an avid bicyclist, spending two hours each day riding around the campus. The urge would pass after several weeks and her sedentary habits would return.

There had always been too much to do in her mind or on paper. The mindwork could be done almost anywhere, but not while climbing precarious trails or being dead tired after a long march.

But here . . .

Sometime in the night, she had made the Stone her meat and drink. She was familiar with the feeling, having approached math problems with similar zeal. She was exhilarated, her pulse was up and she colored like a young girl.

When Lanier knocked, she had dressed and combed her hair. She opened the door with eyes wide.

Carrolson stood behind him. "Breakfast?" Lanier asked. Wearing the standard zipper-and-button blue jumpsuit of the science team, she looked more practical, he thought.

The clear pale light of the plasma tube never varied and cast only the vaguest of shadows beneath their feet as they walked. The cafeteria, adjacent to an experimental agricultural station, was feeding breakfast to the 1500–2400 shift. "Night" for Patricia had been from six in the "morning" to two in the "afternoon." Lanier said he slept irregularly; Carrolson was just finishing her shift.

About twenty of the science team clustered around a video screen at one end of the cafeteria. Lanier joined them briefly, then came back while Carrolson and Patricia sat down with dinner and breakfast. An automatic chef produced trays of food, each segment at the proper temperature, each dish surprisingly tasty. A tap near the unit carried a sign announcing, "Genuine STONE water—an experience not to be missed. H_2O from the stars!" The water was flat but not unpleasant.

Lanier gestured at the group around the screen. "Football," he explained. "Hunt and Thanh have patched into the bore-hole microwave and the outside array. Some commercial outfit is relaying a scrambled game to subscribers and we happen to be in the same section of the sky as the satellite. They've unscrambled the signal."

"Isn't that illegal?" Patricia asked casually, sorting out the bites on her tray.

"Height hath its privileges," Carrolson said. "Nobody will ever prosecute."

Fresh orange juice was available. Citrus trees prospered under the tubelight. The maple syrup on her pancakes was also genuine, but not homegrown. Lanier noticed her expression of surprise.

"What we can't grow in the Stone, we might as well ask for the best from Earthside. It's so expensive to ship up anyway, quality only hikes it a fraction of a percentage point—and we have them convinced we should be fed at least as well as submariners and lunar settlers. Eat hearty—that's a two-hundred-dollar breakfast."

Carrolson chatted amiably through the meal, talking about her husband's work on Earth—he was a mathematician employed by the U.S. Office of Science and Technology. Lanier said little. Patricia was also quiet, taking her cues from him, watching him from the corner of her eye whenever she thought no one would notice. His Indian features attracted her, but the dark circles under his eyes made him look as if he hadn't slept in weeks.

"—really good for you," Carrolson was saying.

Patricia regarded her blankly.

"The tubelight, you know," Carrolson reiterated. "Has everything we need, and nothing harmful. You could lie out under it for days and not be burned, but you'd get your share of vitamin D."

"Oh," Patricia said.

Carrolson sighed. "Garry, you're having that effect again."

Lanier seemed puzzled. "What effect?"

"Look at the girl." Carrolson drummed her fingers on the lightweight metal table, rigged out of OTV tank baffles, as was so much furniture in the compound. "Watch out for him, Patricia. He's a heartbreaker."

Patricia glanced between them, mouth open. "What?"

"I'm going off shift now," Carrolson said, picking up her tray. "Just keep it in mind. Every woman on the team has had their letch for Garry. But he's responsible to someone back

40

home—someone very important." She smiled mysteriously and walked toward the dishwasher unit.

Lanier sipped his cup of coffee. "I'm not sure she's reading you correctly."

"She most certainly is *not*."

"She means I'm responsible to the Advisor—to Judith Hoffman."

"I met her," Patricia said.

"And I'm not on the social roster because there's too much work to do here and not nearly enough time. Besides, there's rank to consider." He finished the cup and set it down.

"You'd think with so many intelligent people around, rank wouldn't be that much of a factor," Patricia said. She felt naive the instant the last word was out of her mouth.

Lanier folded his hands on the table and looked at her directly until she glanced away.

"Patricia, you're young, and this might seem very romantic to you, but it's deadly serious. We're working under agreements which took years to iron out—if they're ironed out even yet. We're an international team of scientists, engineers and security forces, and whatever information we find is not necessarily going to be available to every person on the globe, not for some time yet. Since you'll have access to almost everything, you must be particularly responsible—as responsible as I am. Please don't waste your time concerning yourself with . . . Well, I suggest you stay off the social roster. Another time, another place, sure, romance and adventure. But not on the Stone."

She sat stiffly, hands knotted in her lap. "I have no intention of going on the roster," she said. She hadn't been called on the carpet, exactly, but she was still upset.

"Good. Let's get your green badge and take a ride across the valley." They deposited their trays in the scrubber and left the cafeteria. Lanier walked a few steps ahead of her, eyes on the ground as they approached a small building near the northern side of the ramparts. A stocky broad-shouldered woman in a black jumpsuit, with a green belt and red sergeant's stripes on

41

her sleeve, opened the door for them, then sat behind a desk made of more baffle metal to fill out forms. When they were done, she opened a locked box and pulled out a green badge with an outline of the Stone printed in one corner, surrounded by a silver circle.

"Our security is tight here, Miss Vasquez," she said. "Make sure you know the rules. A green badge is a great responsibility."

Patricia took the indelible pen and signed the badge, then pressed her fingers onto an ID scan plate for storage in the security system computers. The woman clipped the badge to her breast pocket. "Pleased to have you with us. I'm Doreen Cunningham, head of security for First Chamber Science Compound One. Any questions or problems, feel free to visit."

"Thank you," Patricia said. Lanier led the way out of the guardhouse and up the rampart steps.

"If you like to exercise, we have a running path around the inner perimeter of the compound, with an extension that takes you to the second compound. There's a gym pit not far from here. I recommend pretty strenuous exercise whenever possible. The low-g is a bit easy on us. I tend to get flabby if I don't maintain. And exercise will acclimate you more quickly to the air pressure."

"I think the low-g is pleasant," she said as they walked to the front of a wide plastic-sheet quonset hut. "Buoyant."

Inside the hut were two vehicles resembling large snow-cats, mounted on six rubber-tired band-steel-spoke wheels instead of treads. Patricia bent down to look beneath, then straightened. "Very rugged," she said.

"Our trucks. Easy to drive—you'll learn soon. But today, you're just going along for the ride. Keep your eyes peeled."

He unlocked a door and helped her up the high step into the shotgun seat. He paused before closing the door. "I'm sorry I came down on you so hard. I'm sure you understand how important you could be here, and—"

42

"I *don't* understand," Patricia said. "I haven't the faintest idea what use I'll be."

Lanier nodded and smiled.

"But you were right, anyway. If I'm so important, then I need to keep my nose to the grindstone."

"Looks like the Stoned work ethic will come natural to you," Lanier said. He climbed into the driver's seat and reached into his pocket, pulling out a slate. He offered it to her. "Slipped my mind. You'll probably want to make notes at some point or other. Government issue."

He switched on the electric motor and drove the truck out of the shed. "We're going into the second chamber now, into the first city. We'll spend a few hours there, then take you on the Thirtieth Century Limited."

"One of the trains?"

He nodded. "We'll skip the third chamber today—too much, too soon. It could overload you. We'll stop at the fourth chamber security compound for a break and lunch, and then go right through to the sixth chamber."

The truck approached a chain link fence stretching for several kilometers east and west.

"Would it be premature to ask questions now?"

"We have to start somewhere," Lanier said.

"That's real dirt outside. You could grow things in it."

"It's moderately fertile," Lanier said. "We have several farming projects under way, mostly in the fourth chamber. Most of the dirt is straight carbonaceous asteroid material, with supplements."

"Mm." She turned to survey the scrub and the low plume of dust behind them. "Is the Stone still powered-up—I mean, can it leave?"

"It's still powered-up," Lanier said. "We don't know whether it can leave or not."

"I was wondering . . . if we could be trapped inside, if it decided to leave. Then we would need to farm, wouldn't we?"

"That's not why we're farming," Lanier said. She waited

43

for him to elaborate, but he stared straight ahead, slowing the truck as they approached the gate in the wire fence.

"The motors are very old. Some of the engineers think they're worn out," he said, as if he had half listened to her and half followed his own chain of thought. He removed an electronic key from his pocket, dialed a number and opened the gate with a radio signal. "We don't understand the drive yet. The motors' last effective act was to slow the Stone down for insertion into the present orbit. They used chunks of mass removed by robots from the outside of the Stone—mostly in the deep bands. Mass-drivers lobbed the chunks towards a point just above the northern crater. That end is sealed off— you'll soon discover a second reason why. What happened to the chunks at that point, we don't know; the documentation is difficult."

"I should imagine."

The truck hummed through the gate and across a track marked by tire ruts and an absence of scrub.

"All that chain link," Patricia said. "Once you prescreened everyone coming up here, you'd think that would be enough security. Must have cost a lot to have all that stuff shipped up here. Could have shipped up science, instead."

"The chain link wasn't shipped here. We found it."

"Chain link fence?"

"And figurines," Lanier said.

"What are you talking about?"

"Humans built the Stone, Patricia. People from Earth."

She stared at him, then tried to grin.

"Built it twelve hundred years ago. At least, it's about twelve hundred years old."

"Oh," she said. "Pull the other one."

"No, I'm serious."

"I don't expect to be made fun of," she said quietly, straightening in her seat.

"I'm not making fun. Do you think we'd ship eight or nine kilometers of chain link?"

44

"I'll believe that before I believe Charlemagne or whoever had the Stone made to order."

"I didn't say it came from *our* past. Before this goes any farther—please, Patricia, be patient. Wait and see."

She nodded, but inside she was furious. This was some sort of initiation. Take the young woman out on a ride, terrorize her, stick her hand into a spaghetti-worm mystery, bring her back and have a good laugh. She's now a true Stoner. Great.

She had never stood for that sort of treatment, even as a thirteen-year-old whiz-kid at UCLA.

"Look at the scrub," Lanier said. "It's grass. We didn't bring it with us."

"It looks like grass," she acknowledged.

The ride across the valley took thirty minutes. They approached the slate-gray cap. A silvery metal arch stood before the entrance to the tunnel, which was about twenty meters wide. A ramp rose from the dirt to the entrance. Lanier accelerated up the ramp.

"How is the air maintained?" she asked. The silence made her uncomfortable. Lanier switched the truck lights on.

"The middle three chambers have large ponds buried beneath them. The ponds are shallow and filled with several varieties of duckweed, water hyacinth and algae. Plus some other plants we're still identifying. The biggest pond is shaped like a doughnut and circles the fourth chamber. There are ventilation ducts in the caps at about three kilometers—you can see them with binoculars, or if you have sharp enough eyes—and the Stone is honeycombed with other shafts and ducts."

Patricia nodded, avoiding his eyes. *She's going to be Stoned soon,* Lanier thought. Resentment was the first sign. Resentment and disbelief were much easier than acceptance. And the most careful introductions to the Stone didn't prevent the cycle. Here, everyone came from Missouri. Everyone had to be shown first. All other learning and refinement came later.

Six minutes after entering the tunnel, they came to a heavy chain link hurricane fence completely covering the tunnel mouth. Lanier opened another gate with his key, and they emerged in the second chamber.

The ramp leading down from the tunnel had been fortified on each side with masonry walls. More fence had been strung between the walls, and a guardhouse stood to one side of the next gate. Three marines in black jumpsuits came to attention by the guardhouse as the truck rolled toward them, its tires grumbling on the ramp paving. Lanier braked the vehicle and shut it off, then swung down from his seat. Patricia remained where she was, staring at the vista before her.

Beyond the ramp was a two-kilometer-deep shelf of park-land, irregularly spotted by copses of trees and numerous broad, flat white concrete structures, resembling thick building foundations. Beyond the parkland, a narrow lake or river about a kilometer across ran east and west completely around the chamber. A suspension bridge with tall, slender, curved towers crossed the water, set between massive concrete anchors.

The bridge pointed toward a city.

It could have been Los Angeles on a very clear day, or any other modern terrestrial city, except for the surreal exaggeration. It was bigger, more ambitious and ordered, more architecturally *mature*. And scattered throughout the city, like bumpers on a pinball board, were the biggest structures she had ever seen in her life. Easily four kilometers tall, they resembled upright chandeliers made of concrete, glass and shining steel. Each facet of the nearest chandelier-structure was as large as entire buildings in between. The chandelier resemblance increased as she looked up and saw them suspended from the chamber floor overhead. Across the two layers of atmosphere, fifty kilometers away, the city became beautifully unreal, like a model behind dusty glass in a museum.

Her eyes swept to either side, head swinging as if she were watching a slow tennis match between progressively taller players.

46

"Good morning, Mr. Lanier," said the senior officer, approaching to inspect his badge. "She's new?"

Lanier nodded. "Patricia Vasquez. Unlimited access."

"Yes, sir. General Gerhardt passed the word yesterday to expect you."

"Any activity?" Lanier asked.

"Mitchell's survey squad is going through the K mega now, at thirty degrees and six klicks."

Lanier leaned back into the cab. "The 'megas' are the big buildings," he explained. She shielded her eyes against the plasma tube, trying to see the opposite side of the chamber more clearly. She could make out parks and small lakes, systems of streets—laid out in alternating concentric circles and square blocks.

She was as far from the opposite wall as Long Beach was from Los Angeles. Despite its scale, the city was definitely human-built.

Lanier stepped up on the running board and asked if she would like to stretch her legs before they continued.

"What do you call it?" Patricia asked.

"Its name is Alexandria."

"You named it?"

Lanier shook his head. "No."

"We're going all the way to the seventh chamber today?" she asked.

"If you're up to it."

"How long do we stay here?"

"A few hours at most. I want you to get a look at the library before we continue."

"A library?"

"Indeed," Lanier replied. "One of the highlights."

She settled back in her seat, eyes wide. "Is the city deserted?"

"Most of us think it is. We've had scattered reports, but I put it up to nerves. Boojums, the security team calls them. Ghosts. We've never found a live Stoner."

"You've found dead ones?"

"Quite a number. There are mausoleums in this chamber, and in the fourth chamber. The main cemetery in Alexandria is at two-six degrees and ten kilometers. Do you understand the coordinate system?"

"I think so," Patricia said. "Measure from the axis for angle, then distance from the cap. But what's zero, and which cap?"

"This is the zero bridge, and we measure from the south cap."

"This isn't an initiation, then—you weren't telling me a story. Humans built the Stone."

"They did," Lanier said.

"Where did they go?"

Lanier smiled and waggled a finger.

"I know," Patricia said, sighing. "Wait and see for myself." She stepped down from the truck and stretched, then rubbed her eyes. "I'm impressed."

"The first time I saw Alexandria, I felt kind of at home," Lanier said. "I was raised in New York, moved to LA when I was fifteen—lived in big cities all my life, practically. But this really impressed me, even so. We could move twenty million people into just this chamber and still not be crowded."

"Is that why the Stone is important—as real estate?"

"No," Lanier said. "We don't plan on selling condos. We have fifteen archaeologists on the team, and they'd kill anyone who even suggested it. They hold briefings every few days— I'm sure you'll attend several soon. They're working around the clock, and have been since we brought them up here three years ago. They haven't let us touch anything since that time, except when one of the security team commanders or myself has overruled them. And even then, we needed damned good excuses."

Patricia nodded to the three guards, who returned the greeting cordially, one tipping the visor on his cap. A radio in the guard house beeped and crackled. The senior officer answered. Patricia couldn't catch the guttural message, but the guard replied in what sounded like Russian.

"I could have sworn they were all clean-cut American soldiers," Patricia said.

"They are. There are Russians working with Hua Ling in the southern cap bore hole."

"The marines speak Russian?"

"This one does, obviously. And three or four other languages. Cream of the crop."

"Is there anybody up here who isn't brilliant?"

"No common grunts, if that's what you mean. We can't afford them. Everyone has to do double and triple duty." He sat in the driver's seat again. "When you're ready, we'll cross the bridge and drive to the library."

"Anytime," Patricia said, resuming her seat.

Lanier advanced the tractor and the gates swung wide for them, then closed after.

They crossed the four-lane bridge, tires chattering and whanging on the asphalt. Patricia reached into her pants pocket to pull out the slate. Using its ten-key shorthand board, she typed:

Weather—or rather, the absence of it. Sky is quite clear. Perspective—really startling. Land appears flat nearby, then just above the horizon (looking north) seems to curve, the curve getting more radical up the side of the valley. The chamber overhead has lots of detail, visible through slight haze.

She played back what she had keyed in, hunting for errors. She had learned to type on a slate in high school, but that had been many years ago, and she preferred writing by hand. Paper, however, was obviously an expensive commodity on the Stone, to be used sparingly.

She continued to type as they passed down a broad thoroughfare. *Street about fifty meters wide, divided down the middle by what might have been grass at one time, and trees. Two lanes each side. None of the plants look healthy. Gardening systems deteriorating—not working at all? Shop windows on street level, nearly all broken. Lobbies of*

49

businesses, agencies, open to the air. One window—humanoid mannequin. Long-necked. Poised, but nude.

She spotted a sign above what might have once been a jewelry store. "Kesar's," she read. Latin alphabet—and on the other side of the sign, as they moved on, she saw that the same name had been spelled out in Cyrillic. Some shops had Oriental ideograms—Chinese and Japanese. Others were in Laotian and the modified Vietnamese–Roman alphabet.

"Lord," she breathed. "I could be back in LA."

There was something peculiar about the shops, the designs, even a few window displays. She squinted, trying to resolve the discrepancies. "Wait a minute," she said. Lanier slowed the truck. "This is all supposed to be quaint, isn't it? I mean, like back home, where we have shopping malls built to make us think we're in Old England. This is supposed to be old-fashioned."

"As good an observation as any I've heard," Lanier said, shrugging. "I've never really paid this area much attention."

"Garry, I'm very confused. If the Stone was built a thousand years ago, how does all this fit in?"

Lanier swung around a gentle curve and brought the truck to a stop in the middle of the street. He pointed to a large, umber-toned building on the northern edge of the greenspace. "That's one of the libraries—one of two we're investigating now. All the others are closed off."

Patricia clutched her lower lip between her teeth. "Should I be nervous?" she asked.

"Probably. I would be."

"I mean, it's as if—" She shook her head. "Why should I go in there? I'm a mathematician. I'm not an engineer or a historian."

"Believe me, nobody enters the libraries on whim. You're uniquely qualified. You've been working in an area with no practical value—until now."

"I'm going to stop asking questions," Patricia said, sighing. "I don't even know the right questions to ask."

Electronic sensors had been placed around the building.

Chain link fences topped by wicked-looking razor-wire curls enforced the gentle suggestions of sensors and cameras. Four guards stood before the entrance, carrying Apples—antipersonnel lasers—and looking very serious. As Lanier and Vasquez approached, an amplified voice boomed out, "Mr. Lanier. Stop and allow scan. Who's that with you?"

"Patricia Vasquez," he said. "Index under science team, reference memo from General Gerhardt."

"Yessir. Advance and present ID."

They left the truck and walked to the gate. "We brought the razor wire and sensors up from Earth two years ago," Lanier told her. "When we began to realize what we had, in there."

They presented their IDs and laid their hands on a plate carried by a woman in black and gray. After being cleared, they entered the enclosure.

The ground-floor windows had been broken here, as well. No signs or maps were evident within, but it had the definite feel of a library—though once again, it seemed artifically quaint. The interior was dark and deserted.

"The outside guards can't enter the library, only special security—black-and-gray uniforms. There's one person on duty inside at all times, with a video monitor—the voice we heard."

"Very fancy," Patricia said.

"Necessary."

A strip of fluorescent lighting hanging from the ceiling on a bolted track flashed on. More strips glowed in sequence, making a path of light across the ground floor and up a flight of steps near the center of the building.

"We have portable generators at four locations in Alexandria," Lanier said as they walked down the path. The floor was bare and dusty, with a few well-cleared tracks in the dust. "Most of the city's power nets aren't functioning. We haven't tracked down the power supplies yet, but they're probably not discrete plants. The Stone itself seems to carry a reserve of power, with concentrations in supercooled batteries."

Patricia's brow wrinkled. "Batteries?"

51

"Like the hundred-meter cells in Arizona and the Greater African Conservatory."

"Oh." She wasn't much on practical physics, but she didn't want Lanier to know that.

"The electrical system is pretty conventional, otherwise. Control and information channels are optical, more so than back on Earth. The buildings are dark because most of the circuit breakers—or whatever served that function—have been tripped, and nobody's going to reset them until we know more about fire hazards."

"Why are the windows broken?" Patricia asked as they continued climbing.

"Glass gets brittle with age, slumps. Pressure surges in the atmosphere crack the windows."

"Weather?"

"Of a sort. There are high- and low-pressure systems in the chambers, updrafts and coriolis, downdrafts near the caps. Even storms. Snow in some of the chambers, infrequently. Most of it seems controlled, but we don't know whether the controls are built-in, static, or whether machines are still hard at work someplace."

In the shadowy halls beyond the light strips on the second floor, she saw man-sized metallic cylinders arranged in rows, marching off into obscurity.

"We've been pulling data out of these storage banks for a year," Lanier said. "The programming languages weren't familiar to us, so we've only had success producing readable copy and useful images for about six months. As it turns out, the library in the next chamber is even larger, so we're concentrating on it, now. But . . . I still prefer this. There's an extensive hard-copy center on the fourth floor. That's where I did my early research, and where you'll be doing some of yours."

"I feel like I'm on the *Mary Celeste*."

"The comparison's been made," Lanier said. "At any rate, here or anywhere else, the rule is, Don't disturb anything you can't put back exactly the way it was. The archaeologists are

52

just finishing their gross surveys and they're still touchy. We have to break the rule now and then—repairing necessary equipment, tinkering with the computers—but no excess meddling is allowed. If the Stone is a *Mary Celeste*, we can't afford not to know why."

On the fourth floor, they entered a large room filled with reading cubicles, each with a viewer and a flat gray panel mounted in a small desk. One of the desks had been equipped with a recently imported Tensor lamp connected to the new power supply. Lanier pulled out a chair for her. She sat.

"I'll be back in a moment," he said. He walked to the opposite side of the room, passed through a door and left her alone. She fingered the viewer on the desk—was it for video, microfilm? She couldn't tell. The screen was flat and black as ebony, no more than a quarter of an inch thick.

There was something unusual about the chair. A small cylinder was mounted horizontally in the middle of the seat, fitting with some discomfort between her buttocks. There might have been cushions at one time, covering the cylinder— or perhaps the chair created its own cushion when powered up.

Patricia glanced nervously at the rows of empty cubicles, trying to imagine those who had last used them. When Lanier returned, she was very glad to see him. Her hands were trembling.

"Spooky," she said, smiling weakly.

He held out a small book bound in milky plastic. She thumbed through the pages. The paper was thin and tough. The language was English, though the typeface was unusual— too many serifs. She opened to the title page.

"Tom Sawyer," she read, "by Samuel Langhorne Clemens, Mark Twain." The publication date was 2110. She closed the book and put it down, swallowing hard.

"Well?" Lanier asked softly.

She looked up at him, frowning. Then a kind of understanding passed between them. She opened her mouth to speak and shut it again.

"You've wondered why I'm so tired looking," Lanier said.

"Yes."

"Do you understand, now?"

"Because of this . . . library."

"Partly," he said.

"It's from the future. The Stone is from our future."

"We're not certain of that," he said.

"But that's why I'm here . . . to help you figure out how."

"There are other puzzles, equally mystifying, and perhaps they all tie together."

She opened the book again. "Published by Greater Georgia General, in cooperation with Harpers of the Pacific."

He reached down and took the book from her hands. "That's enough for now. We'll go outside. You can rest for a bit, or we can spend a couple of hours at the security base."

"No," she said. "I want to go on." She closed her eyes for a few seconds. He left to reshelve the book, then returned and walked ahead of her to the ground floor.

"The subway entrance is a two blocks from here," he said. "We can walk it. Exercise clears the head."

She followed him across one corner of the park, looking at without really seeing the buildings and their signs in the various languages of Earth, knowing she was past the point of assimilation.

They passed beneath a half-moon arch and walked down a double-back incline into the subway station.

"You said the Stone wasn't from the future," Patricia commented.

"From *our* future," Lanier corrected. "It may not be from our universe."

Her skin felt warm. She blinked rapidly, not sure whether she was going to cry or laugh. "Damn."

"My sentiments exactly."

They stood on a broad platform, near a wall ornamented with large, flat, rose-colored crystals arranged in irregular tesselations. Direction signs hung from the ceiling, letters scabbed and peeling: "Nexus Central, Line 5" "This side for

Alexandria" "San Juan Ortega, Line 6, 20 minutes." More of the ebony-black flat display screens hung near the signs, all blank.

Patricia felt a small tremor of dizziness. Was she really where she was, or suffering through a work-induced dream?

"You're getting Stoned," Lanier said. "Watch yourself."

"I am. Yeah. Watching myself getting Stoned."

"Depression is usually the next step. Disorientation, fantasies, depression. That's what I went through."

"Oh?" She looked down at the white tiles beneath her feet.

"Should be a train coming in the next five, ten minutes," Lanier said. He put his hands in his pockets and joined her in regarding the floor.

"I'm doing fine," Patricia said. She didn't believe herself, but on the other hand, she had felt worse before exams than she did now. She'd hold up. She had to. "I'm just wondering if there are better ways to indoctrinate newcomers. This seems pretty haphazard."

"We tried other ways."

"Didn't work?"

"No better, some worse."

A puff of air advanced out of the train tunnel. Patricia thought to peer over the edge of the platform to see what kind of mechanism the subway cars rode on. The floor of the channel was featureless, no rails or guides of any sort.

Out of the tunnel hissed a giant aluminum millipede, its nose windowless and crossed by a radiance of green lines. It stopped with neck-jarring suddenness and hummed softly as its doors slid open. A marine guard stood in the lead car, holstered pistol and laser rifle prominent.

"Mr. Lanier," he greeted, saluting smartly.

"Charlie, this is Patricia Vasquez. Another green badge. Patricia, this is Corporal Charles Wurtz. You'll probably be seeing a lot of each other. Charlie is our main man on the zero train line."

"Keep all the boojums from bumming a lift," Charlie said, grinning and shaking Patricia's hand.

55

Lanier beckoned for her to enter first. The interior. examined for basics, was like any reasonably new rapid transit system vehicle. The plastic seats and metal fixtures were in good repair. The cars had obviously not been designed for crowding—no handstraps or rails for standing passengers—and the arrangements were spacious, with lots of leg room. And no advertising. Indeed, within the car there were no signs at all.

"Like an old BART in San Francisco," Patricia said. She hadn't ridden on the BART or the LA Metro in years.

They settled back in their seats. There was no sensation of motion until she looked out the large round windows spaced at irregular intervals along the sides of the car. The station was a passing blur. Then there was only darkness relieved by flashing white vertical bars.

"It just doesn't look that much like the future," she said. "It's recognizable. I always thought the future would be so different, it wouldn't be recognizable. Particularly a thousand years in the future. But there are buildings, subways—I mean, why not matter transmitters?"

"Alexandria and this rail system are a lot older than other parts of the Stone. When you get around and see things in more detail, you'll notice big differences between our technology and this. Besides . . ." He paused. "There's history to consider. Delays. Handicaps. And holdovers."

"Which I'll know about soon enough."

"Right," Lanier said. "Did you feel any motion just now? Acceleration?"

She frowned. "No. But maybe we started out slowly—"

"The trains accelerate at four g's."

"Wait." She turned to a window and looked at the passing bars of white, then frowned. "Alexandria . . . I mean, it wasn't designed right."

Lanier regarded her patiently. She was supposed to be brilliant, but in many ways she was so *young*. Struggling to maintain her decorum as if she were a schoolgirl.

"The Stone has to accelerate and decelerate, right? Just like this train. But I don't feel any motion now, and . . . the chambers should have angled floors, to compensate for the thrust, for the wash of water in the lakes and ponds—higher walls on one side. Acceleration slosh. Angled walkways to compensate."

"There aren't any provisions for acceleration in the chambers," Lanier said.

"So they accelerated slowly?"

He shook his head.

"They had some way to compensate?"

"The sixth chamber," Lanier said. "But that's part of the big picture, too."

"You're making me sort everything out for myself."

"Whenever possible."

"As a test."

"No," Lanier said emphatically. "The Advisor said you can help us. I don't doubt that. But if this were a test, you'd be doing just fine." Though he had reservations.

The tunnel walls passed behind them and the train rushed into light. They passed over water, doing at least two or three hundred kilometers an hour. "In the elevated stretches, there are three rails under the cars, magnetic induction," Lanier said.

"Oh." She turned her attention to the sea, a uniform expanse of rippling blue-gray, stretching north to a bank of fog against the cap. Above the gray expanse she could see the chamber's arch, and to the northwest and northeast the distant edges of the fog bank, and a shoreline at three o'clock high.

About seven kilometers from the train, its lower extremity hidden in white mist, was the hexagonal top of an upright tower, perhaps fifty meters tall and half as broad. Another tower appeared only a kilometer or so distant, fully visible and mounted on a slender round pylon.

The fog rushed up to meet them, and suddenly, they were over land. Rich pine forest blurred beneath, appearing healthy—if slightly blue—in the tubelight.

"Fourth chamber was a recreation center, as near as we can

tell," Lanier said. "And of course, a reservoir and air-purification system. There are four distinct islands here, each with a different habitat. There were underwater habitats, too—coral gardens, freshwater ponds and river systems. Resort, wildlife preserve, fish farm—it's all returned to an untended state, a bit wild but prospering."

The train slowed and slid with a faint humming noise over an elevated platform. Two men in black jumpsuits ran next to the cars as they came to a stop. Lanier stood and she followed him to the door. It opened as silently as before.

Forest, water, dirt—all in one glorious sniff.

"Later, Charlie," Lanier said. Charlie saluted smartly and took a stance in the doorway behind them.

A platform guard stepped up to examine Patricia's badge. "Welcome to summer camp, Miss Vasquez," he said. She looked down from the platform railing. They were six meters above the ground. The platform was surrounded by a compound much like the one in the first chamber, with fiberboard buildings and earthen ramparts, but a much larger greenhouse-agriculture laboratory.

Everyone in the compound wore black, in combinations of black and khaki, black and green, and one black and gray. "Security forces?" she asked. Lanier nodded as they descended the platform stairs.

"We keep a small science group here, and we let people take their vacations or liberty here, when there's time for such things, which isn't often. This chamber is strategic. It divides the relatively livable parts of the Stone from the business end."

"The propulsion system?"

"That, and the seventh chamber. Anyway, you'll have a chance to stretch your legs, assimilate what you've seen so far."

"I doubt it," Patricia said.

Lanier guided her to the compound cafeteria.

In most respects, the cafeteria was little different from the one in the first chamber. They sat at a table with British and

West German soldiers. Lanier introduced her to the German commanding officer, Colonel Heinrich Berenson. "He'll assume command of the seventh chamber security forces a week from now. You'll be working together quite a bit."

Berenson was a colonel in the West German Space Force, sandy-haired and freckle-faced, as tall as Lanier but more obviously muscular. He appeared more Irish than German; with his non-German name and sophisticated manner, he seemed truly international to Patricia. His manner was friendly but slightly distant.

She ordered a salad—fresh greens from the agrilab—and looked at the faces of the men and women around her. Not all of them had green badges.

"How does the badge system work?" she asked Lanier. Berenson smiled and shook his head, as if this was a sore point.

"Red badges are confined to the bore hole in the first chamber," Lanier said. "Mostly engineering support. Blue can go anywhere in the Stone except the sixth and seventh chambers, but in all chambers but the first, must be escorted and must be performing specific duties. Green badges can go to any of the chambers but are always subject to security checks."

"I am here more than three years," Berenson said, "and I only get a green three months ago." He glanced down at her badge and nodded meaningfully. "Fortunately, I found a loophole. I can be considered to have escorted myself."

Lanier grinned. "Let's just be thankful things are going as smoothly as they have been."

"Amen," Berenson said. "I would hate to see true confusion."

"For green badges, there are three levels of clearance. Level one is lowest—no access to designated secret areas. Level two is limited access for duty purposes—the special security guards have level two green badges. Level three is the clearance we share."

"I will be level two," Berenson said.

As they returned to the train, Patricia asked, "Being level two means he won't know exactly what the Stone is?"

"When you get to the seventh chamber, you have to know a lot."

"But not about what's in the libraries."

"No," Lanier said.

That sobered her. Berenson was morose, and he didn't even know about the libraries.

The four spacesuited soldiers ran in long, graceful leaps across the lunar surface with only the stars and a quarter-Earth to light their way. Mirsky watched them from the top of a boulder, only his white helmet showing. In his right hand, he held an electric torch, pointed back toward his team comrades waiting in a gully carved by a rolling rock millions of years before. When the four were in the proper position, he flashed the light on and off three times.

The objective—a mock-up of a lunar settlement bunker— lay a hundred meters beyond the boulder. The four defenders were now by the airlock. Mirsky raised his AKV-297— automatic vacuum-adapted Kalashnikov projectile rifle—and pointed it at the airlock hatch.

The hatch opened and Mirsky raised the rifle slightly, centering it on a cross-barred target near the hatchway signal lights. With one gloved finger, he depressed the side-mounted trigger and felt the rifle kick three times. A thin line of burning gunpowder discharge from the barrel glowed briefly in the darkness. The target blew out in tatters of plastic as the door opened.

Mirsky heard the exercise supervisor read off the numbers of the four space-suited defenders and order them to assume a reclining posture. "Your airlock is also incapacitated," the supervisor added laconically. "Fine work, Lieutenant Colonel . . . You may proceed."

Mirsky and his three comrades advanced toward the mock-up. The defenders lay on the lunar soil outside the open hatchway, motionless except for the advancing numbers of their backpack life support displays. Mirsky leaned over and winked at one of them through his visor. The defender glared back at him, not in the least amused.

"Look over your shoulder at two o'clock, Comrade Lieutenant Colonel," one of his men advised. Mirsky turned around and followed the line of the corporal's thickly protected arm and gloved finger.

The Potato, a sharp point of light with a clearly discernible oblong shape, had just risen above the Moon's horizon.

It seemed that all his life, people had been pointing it out to him—Yefremova three years before, the first among them.

"Yes, I see," Mirsky acknowledged.

"That is why we train, is it not, Comrade Lieutenant Colonel?"

Mirsky didn't answer. The supervisor cut in and demanded they stop the useless chatter.

"The stars have ears, Corporal," Mirsky advised the soldier. "Let's take our objective and get home in time for more political lessons." The corporal met Mirsky's glance and grimaced but said nothing more.

In their own bunker, four hours later, the exercise supervisor walked down the aisle between the sleeping slings of the victorious team, shaking hands and congratulating them warmly, and then handing out letters from home. All the men received letters, if only from party cell coordinators in some outlying village. The supervisor stopped by Mirsky's sling last.

"Only one letter for you, Comrade . . . Colonel," he said, handing Mirsky a thick and carefully sealed and taped envelope. Mirsky took the envelope and stared at it, then at the supervisor.

"Open it."

He carefully tore off the end and took out five folded sheets of paper. "A promotion," he said, unwilling to be very emotional about the whole thing.

"And your orders, Comrade," the supervisor said. "Gent-

lemen, are we interested in discovering where our new
Colonel Pavel Mirsky is going?''

"Where?'' several asked.

"Back to Earth,'' Mirsky said.

"Back to Earth!'' the supervisor echoed. "This is, what—
your fourth training tour on the Moon in two years? And now
back to Earth.''

The men watched him carefully, grinning.

"To the Indian Ocean,'' Mirsky said. "For final training as
battalion commander.''

"To the Indian Ocean!'' the supervisor shouted, pointing
one finger at the floor—symbolically indicating the Earth—
and then raising both his hands, looking upward and nodding
at the ceiling.

The men cheered and broke into applause.

"Now, you will have the stars you have always wanted,
Colonel,'' the supervisor said, shaking his hand firmly.

Chapter Four

The rest of the fourth chamber slipped by the train windows
quickly, a blur of hilly terrain, small lakes and outcroppings of
what looked like granite.

"The line ends at the sixth chamber. We'll be met by Joseph
Rimskaya and some of the Chinese team at the terminal
annex.''

"Rimskaya? I had a teacher with that name at UCLA.''

"Rimskaya is why you're here. He recommended you.''

"But he left the university to join the Bureau of Math and
Statistics.''

"And he met the Advisor while working in Washington,''
Lanier added.

Rimskaya had been her professor in a special math seminar.
She hadn't liked him much; he was a tall, blocky man with a
wiry red beard, loud and assertive, a political science

professor and expert in statistics and information theory. A rigorous mathematician but not, in her opinion, in possession of the insight necessary for truly valuable research, Rimskaya had always seemed the perfect academician to her: rigid, demanding, an unimaginative taskmaster.

"Why is he here?"

"Because the Advisor finds him useful."

"His specialty was statistical theories of population behavior. He belongs in sociology."

"That's right," Lanier said.

"How—"

Lanier appeared irritated. "Think, Patricia. Where did the Stoners go? Why did they go there, how did they get there?"

"I don't know," she answered quietly.

"We don't know, either. Not yet. Rimskaya is head of the sociology group. They might be able to tell us."

"This is such an ass-backwards way of teaching."

"I'll be patient if you will," Lanier said.

Patricia was silent for a moment. "No guarantees," she said. "I wish you'd stop seeming so peeved at me when I just ask straightforward questions."

Lanier raised his eyebrows and nodded. "Please don't take it personally."

So he's under strain, she thought. *Well, so am I. Only he's had time to get used to it. If you can ever get used to something like the library . . . or the Stone itself. Then again, there's almost certainly more. . . .*

She had the sudden vision of a maze of chalkboards waiting for her in the seventh chamber, filled with wandering mathematicians working on some grand, unified problem. Over them all, on a huge video screen, the Advisor watched patiently, like God. Lanier was her avatar.

"Rimskaya's half Russian," Lanier continued. "His grandmother was a widower and an immigrant and her name was applied on the U.S. entry papers to her son, as well. He speaks Russian like a native. Sometimes he acts as interpreter between the Russians and us."

The train's hum increased in pitch and they plunged into the fourth chamber's northern cap.

The fifth chamber was darker than the previous sections she had visited. A canopy of flat gray clouds painted the cylinder's upper atmosphere, cutting out half the tube light. Beneath the clouds was a Wagnerian landscape of barren mountains, resembling ragged lumps of anthracite mixed with dark-rainbowed hematite. Between the mountains were rusty abyssal valleys, cut by waterfalls feeding into quicksilver rivers. The mountains toward the middle of the chamber floor were startling in their contortions—arches, giant rugged cubes, broken-tipped pyramids and causeways of irregular slab steps.

"What in hell was *this*?" she asked.

"A kind of open pit mine, we think. Our two geologists— you met Robert Smith, he's one—speculate that when the chambers were hollowed out, the fifth wasn't finished off. They left it for raw material. And the Stoners used it. These are the scars."

"Perfect for fans of old horror movies," Patricia said. "Can't you just see Castle Dracula here?"

They said nothing throughout the short trip down the next tunnel into the sixth chamber. As the train's hum decreased in pitch and the tunnel dark brightened, Lanier stood and said, "End of the line."

The lower terminal was a cavernous construct of unpainted slabs of reddish concrete and mottled gray-and-black asteroid rock. The platform was marked with faint lines, as though long winding queues had once formed there.

"This was a worker's station once," Lanier said. "When they modified the sixth chamber, this served as a debarkation point. Six hundred years ago, perhaps."

"How long has the Stone been deserted?"

"Five centuries."

They walked up a ramp into a building constructed mostly of thick transparent panels, giving an excellent view of the sixth chamber.

The valley floor was layered with gigantic inert mechanical forms, cylinders and cubes and stacks of circular plates laid on edge, resembling a monstrous circuit board. Just outside the terminal building, a row of spherical tanks marched off to a distant wall. The wall was at least a hundred meters high, and the tanks half that in diameter. Below this level of the terminal, between the spheres and a parallel row of cylinders resting on their sides, was an immense gully filled with glistening water. The channel was lined with pipe ends and cyclopian pumping apparatus. Over it all, thick black clouds floated in clumps, dropping curtains of rain and flurries of snow. Somewhere was a constant pulsing, less heard then felt, like the infra-sound beats of moving mountains or the grinding of distant sea bottoms.

Looking up at an angle, between decks of clouds, she could dimly see the opposite floor of the chamber, bumped and ridged with a carpet of mysterious mechanism.

"No moving parts in the whole chamber except for large pumps, and not many of those," Lanier said. "The builders relied upon a built-in weather cycle. Rain falls, picks up heat, flows down channels into shallow ponds, evaporates, carries heat up, and the atmospheric maintenance systems drain it off, we're still not sure how."

"What does it all do?"

"When the Stone was first designed, the sixth chamber was going to be another city. But the builders had specified that the Stone could only accelerate at three percent g. Just before the Stone was outfitted—and before the completion of the major excavation—they found a way to allow the Stone to accelerate to the limit of its power. The method was complex and expensive, but it gave the Stone a versatility the builders couldn't pass up. So the sixth chamber was equipped with selective inertial damping machinery, which makes up a small fraction of what is here now." He nodded at the vista through the glass. "That's why none of the chamber floors are inclined, and none of the ponds or rivers are equipped with slop barriers. They don't need them. The sixth chamber can selectively damp the effects of inertia on any object in the Stone. On a large scale, it overcomes acceleration and deceleration of the entire ship. On a small scale, it prevents inertial effects in the trains. It's self-regulating, though we haven't found any 'brain' yet.''

The rain hit the transparent roof and ran down the forty-five degree slope over the stairwell. Lanier paused to look at the beads and rivulets of water.

"Since that time, the machinery has been modified and expanded. It once covered about three square kilometers, and the rest of the sixth chamber was used for industry and research, things that couldn't be done in the cities. Now, it maintains the seventh chamber as well.''

Four people, all clad in yellow rain gear, marched along the edge of the channel beyond the terminal. They had parked their truck a few meters away, on a raised roadbed.

"Our reception committee," Lanier said. They walked to the head of the staircase. Cold air pooled in the stairwell, and Patricia shivered as an outside gust blew some of it over them. Rain sang softly overhead. Between the rivulets on the glass, through a trench-like break in the clouds, Patricia saw the opposite northern cap. All the other caps had been virtually blank, featureless. This one was furrowed by a row of rectangular boxes, spaced at equal intervals like a steep flight of stairs. On the face of each box was an elliptical design. The boxes, she estimated, were at least a kilometer wide, and the ellipses half that along their major axis.

The first of the four to reach the top of the stairs doffed his rain cap. Patricia looked down to see her former professor, his face ruddy and bearded, eyes small and suspicious as if from some long-harbored hurt. Rimskaya was just as she remembered him. He returned her stare defensively, then nodded to Lanier. Behind him, a tall, even-featured blond woman and two Chinese, a man and a woman wearing green caps, removed their gear and shook water off onto the floor.

Rimskaya approached Patricia, his every gesture conveying aloofness, if not disgust. "Miss Vasquez," he said. "I hope you are up to this. I hope you do not make me seem like a fool for choosing you."

She opened and shut her mouth like a carp, then laughed too loudly. "Professor, I hope so, too!"

"Don't mind him," said the blond woman, her voice pleasant and deep, with a faint British accent. "He's said nothing but good about you for four months now." She clutched her own cap under her arm and held out her hand. Patricia shook it. Her grip was firm and warm. "I'm Karen Farley, this is Wu Gi Me, and Chang i Hsing." Chang smiled broadly at Patricia, her straight black bangs hanging down over her eyebrows, the latest Chinese fashion. "We're from Beijing Technological University."

Rimskaya still studied Patricia. His gray eyes narrowed. "You are healthy, no space sickness, no emotional distress?"

"I'm fine, Professor," she said.

"Good. Then you—" he indicated Farley, Wu and Chang "—you take care of her. I'm going to the first chamber to rest. I'll be gone a week, perhaps longer." He held his hand out to Lanier and they shook once, firmly. "I am tired," Rimskaya said, "not least because I have no idea what this all signifies. I have never been an imaginative man, and this place . . ." He shuddered. "Perhaps it will suit you better, Miss Vasquez." He bowed stiffly to his colleagues, then picked up his gear and walked toward the ramp leading to the train platform.

Patricia looked after him, nonplussed.

"I envy him . . . a bit," said Wu in perfect California English. He was about her height, just on the edge of plumpness, with a stiff crew cut and a childlike face. "I have read some of your papers recently, Miss Vasquez."

"Patricia, please."

"They are quite beyond me, I'm afraid. Chang and I are electrical engineers. Karen is a physicist."

"Theoretical physics. I've been very impay-tient to meet you," Farley said.

" 'Impay-shent,' " Lanier corrected.

"Yes." Farley grinned at Patricia's puzzlement. "I'm

a Chinese citizen also. I can fool most people most of the time. Correct me, please, when I blunder.''

Patricia looked between them owlishly. She felt a bit strungout, not yet ready to meet new people and stretch her sociability.

"We're escorting Patricia to the seventh chamber,'' Lanier said. "But she may want to rest here awhile.''

"No." Patricia shook her head firmly. "I'm going for the big picture today.''

"That's a woman,'' Farley said. "Suicidal doggedness. Something I admire. Chang has it. Gi Me—we call him Lucky—Gi Me's a lazy fellow, though.''

"Both she and Professor Rimskaya are slave drivers,'' Chang said. Her English accent was markedly less proficient than Wu's and Farley's. She produced two packets of rain gear from a pouch in her own coat and gave them to Lanier and Patricia. They suited up quickly and left the shelter of the annex.

The air smelled of clean rain, ozone and metal. The rain had slowed to a drizzle and the snow had stopped. Water slid in sheets from sloping metal walls below the elevated road, collecting in gutters and washing to a catch basin meters below. Patricia peered into the basin and saw the smooth funnel of water descending into darkness.

The truck on the roadbed was a replica of the vehicle which had taken them across the first chamber. Farley offered Patricia the shotgun seat again, and the others climbed into the back, pushing aside boxes of fabric-wrapped scientific gear. Farley edged the truck forward, then brought it up to speed.

The roadbed expanded into a broad flat ribbon, winding through complexes of tanks and gray shapes hidden behind a rapidly spreading fog. Wu leaned between the two seats. "This stuff that looks like asphalt—it isn't. It's asteroid rock, all the metals removed, ground up and mixed with a plant-based oil. Very tough, no cracks. We wonder who's going to patent it.''

Somehow, Patricia found the dreariness invigorating. There

68

was a bluish quality about the fog that made her feel as if she were within a sapphire. The rain resumed, and the drum of water on the truck's roof—combined with a gentle surge of warm air from the heater—made everything seem secure, no more strenuous than watching an entertainment on a video.

She snapped herself out of that feeling quickly. Lanier was watching her. She angled her face toward him and then looked away. How *could* they consider her so important? In the face of this monumental mystery, what could she possibly do?

The size alone was enough to paralyze thought. Looking up through gaps in the cloud cover to the opposite side, she could just as well have been looking from the window of a shuttle reentering the atmosphere.

The truck followed the gently curving highway and crossed the sixth chamber in twenty minutes. The familiar arch and tunnel entrance loomed ahead. Farley switched on the lights as the tunnel enveloped them.

After the stormy sixth chamber, the clarity and brightness of the unhindered plasma tube light was welcome.

"You can almost hear the birds singing," Patricia commented.

"I wish," Farley said. They descended the ramp. Ahead stretched an arrow-straight road, about half as broad as the sixth chamber highway and made of the same material. To each side of the road, sandy hummocks topped with stiff yellow grass dotted the floor for several kilometers. A short hike away were stands of low, scrawny trees. To the west, up the curve of the chamber floor, Patricia saw small lakes and what looked like a river emerging from one of the cap tunnels. A few fleecy clouds clung to the cap. The landscape was equally homogenous and bland right up to the limits of the tube light both east and west. The plasma tube itself emerged from the center of the cap in a straight, unobscured beacon.

Patricia could feel the anticipation building in the cabin, centering on her. They were waiting for her reaction.

Reaction to what? If anything, this chamber was less

impressive than the first. Her shoulders tensed. So what was she supposed to say?

Lanier reached between the seats to touch her arm. "What do you see?" he asked.

"Sand, grass, lakes, trees. A river. Some clouds."

"Look straight ahead."

She looked. The air was clear. Visibility was at least thirty kilometers. The northern cap seemed to be obscured, not nearly as obvious as the looming gray presence in the other chambers. She looked up and squinted, trying to make out the end of the plasma tube.

It didn't end. It went on, certainly more than thirty kilometers, getting dimmer and thinner until it almost merged with the horizon.

Of course, on a non-curved surface—as the cylinders were, viewed parallel to the axis—the horizon was much higher. Given unlimited distance, the horizon would begin at a true vanishing point in the perspective. . . .

"This chamber's longer," she said.

"Yes," Wu agreed cautiously. Chang nodded, grinning as if at some joke, her hands folded demurely in her lap.

"Now, let me get this straight. We've traveled about two hundred and twenty kilometers into the Stone, which is about two hundred and ninety kilometers long. So this chamber could be, maybe, fifty kilometers across." Her hands were trembling. "But it isn't."

"Look closely," Lanier said.

"It's an optical illusion. I can't see the northern cap."

"No," Farley said, all too sympathetic.

"So?" Patricia looked around the cab. The others kept their faces impassive, except for Chang's secretive smile. "What the hell am I supposed to see?"

"You tell us," Lanier said.

She figured furiously in her head, looking up at the opposite side of the chamber, trying to calculate distances in the strange perspective of the huge cylinders. "Stop the truck."

Farley brought the vehicle to a halt and Patricia descended

70

from the cab to stand on the roadway. Then she clambered up a ladder to a platform on top of the cab and looked down the straight line of the road. The road went to its own vanishing point—no cap, no barrier. Above, the rest of the landscape did much the same.

"It's bigger," she said. Farley and Lanier stood by the truck, looking up at her. Wu and Chang joined them. "It's bigger than the asteroid. It goes beyond the end. Is that what you're trying to tell me?"

"We don't tell," Lanier said. "We show. It's the only way."

"You're trying to tell me it doesn't stop, it goes right on out the other end?" She heard the touch of panic and high-pitched fascination in her own voice.

The Stanford professor, six years before, had been wrong. Someone besides extraterrestrials and gods could appreciate her work. She now knew why she had been brought up from Vandenberg, carried to the Stone by shuttle and OTV.

The asteroid was longer on the inside than it was on the outside.

The seventh chamber went on forever.

Chapter Five

Patricia had slept—she checked her watch—nine hours. She lay on the cot, listening to the gentle sound of tent canvas clapping in the breeze.

In at least this region of the seventh chamber, there was little need for solid-walled buildings. The weather was dry and mild, the air temperature warm. She stared up at the awning stretched between aluminum poles, at the smoky outline of the plasma tube through the cloth.

I am here. This is real.

"You bet your life," she whispered. Inside the tent, a complex of partitions and tarp floors covering about a hundred

71

square meters, Farley and Chang were speaking Chinese in muted tones.

The first few hours in the chamber, while they had arranged a cubicle in the tent for her and prepared for a cookout, Patricia had been hyperactive, darting about like a moth, asking questions that sometimes made little sense. Lanier had watched her glumly for a while; she had felt she was somehow disappointing him. But later he had joined the others in laughing at her—with her—and had produced a surprise bottle of champagne. "To christen your new self," he had said.

On the first round, they had tried to find something more fitting in the way of names for what everyone had, heretofore, referred to simply as the "seventh chamber," or "the corridor."

"Spaghetti world," Farley had suggested. No, Wu countered—more like macaroni world, hollow in the middle. Chang tossed in pipe world. "Tube" and "tunnel" had already been appropriated for other parts of the Stone; the words and shapes seemed to echo against each other, a sexually charged confusion of fittings-within-fittings.

A couple of glasses of champagne and Patricia had become desperately drowsy. They had barely set up a cot under the awning before she was sound asleep.

She stretched and propped her head on her elbow, looking across the scrub and sand, and up at the enormous cylinder of land stretching into the haze. Farley came out of the tent and sat beside the cot.

"Dreaming?"

"No," Patricia said. "Musing."

"When Garry gave us the grand tour, a year and a half ago, I thought I'd go crazy. What's your opinion of the indoctrination? I mean, it's really just beginning for you, but . . ." She trailed off, regarding Patricia with very blue eyes. Farley was perhaps ten years older than she, and there was humor evident in the lines around her lips and eyes. She had a demanding directness in her manner—almost a female version of Lanier, Patricia thought.

"Seeing is not quite believing," she answered. "So just hearing about it certainly wouldn't be enough."

"After a while, we tend to become complacent," Farley said, staring down the gray-green road. "It worries me sometimes. When new people arrive and see what we see every day, we're shaken back into realizing how strange it really is. Sometimes I feel like a beetle crawling through a fusion power plant. I can feel a certain amount, see a certain amount, but I sure as hell don't understand everything." She sighed. "I'm not sure Garry approves, but I think you should be warned about the boojums."

"He mentioned them. What are they?"

"Some of us have seen boojums. Spooks. I haven't, and none of our group have. The consensus is they're psychological, a sign of the strain. There haven't been any really clear sightings, photographs or anything. So be wary of what you see. And be doubly wary—no one has proven that the Stone or the corridor is completely deserted. We're just too few to adequately explore and police all the chambers. So if you see anything, report it, but don't believe it." She smiled. "Does that make sense?"

"No," Patricia said, swinging her legs over the side of the cot. "Do I have a work schedule, some idea of what I'm supposed to be doing, when?"

"Garry will tell you all about that in a half hour or so. He's sleeping now. Exhaled. I mean, exhausted. We're all a bit worried about him, you know."

"You and the others—you have green badges, but do you have third level clearance?"

"Heavens, no." Farley laughed, tossing her long blond hair back over her shoulders. "We're Chinese. We're lucky to have gotten this far. We're here by courtesy and because our governments happen to be friendly this decade. All the same, we're much better off than the poor Russians. They get to study the bore holes and the plasma tubes, and very little else. Everyone perceives plasma physics to be their specialty, so they're stuck on the axis. Americans have no conception what

73

fine archaeologists they have. Now, as for their sociology . . ." She shook her head ruefully. "I'm a born and bred Marxist, but I'm not sure the Stoners would fit strict Leninist dogma."

"Garry hasn't given me any details on the agreements. I read about them at home. . . . But I know we weren't told everything."

"NATO–Eurospace vessels were the first to reach the Stone and begin exploration. By the ISCCOM agreements, NATO has the right to control exploitation, and NATO is dominated by the United States, of course. The Russians have protested this is a special case, but they haven't gotten anywhere so far. The Chinese have never been tebbly—terribly—interested in deep space, so we've accepted what little we've been allowed. By being quiet and subservient, we've come much further than the Russians. No Russians in the seventh chamber, you'll notice."

"You don't sound Chinese."

Farley laughed. "Thank you. Everyone says my accent is good, but sometimes my words . . . Well. What you're really saying, I think, is I don't *look* Chinese. I'm a second-generation Caucasian immigrant. My parents were British expatriates in Czechoslovakia. They were agricultural specialists, and China welcomed them with open arms when they emigrated in 1978. I was born there."

"I've spent all of my life in California," Patricia said. "I feel so protected compared to you. Out of touch with the real world."

"The world of intrigue and international politics? Me too. I spent most of my life on a farm in Hopeh. Rather cut off. And now . . . we're *both* here." She looked down at the ground, shaking her head. "For various reasons, there are a lot of things we shouldn't talk about. Garry trusts me, and I respect his trust. We've all done our best to be courteous and trustworthy. That's why we've come this far. So. Technical matters directly relating to our work, that's okay. But anything having to do with subjects off limits to Wu, Chang and me—no discussion. None at all."

"Okay," Patricia said.

Farley looked north, directly down the throat of the corridor. "The Stoners made this. They were humans, just like you and me. Beyond that, we're encaved—in the dark. But sometime, we will run into them—or something even stranger." She smiled thinly. "Is that a prediction strong enough for you?"

Patricia nodded. "Anything more specific, I'll get the shakes."

Farley patted her on the shoulder. "Must get back. Garry will be with you shortly."

She entered the tent.

Patricia stood and smoothed down her jumper, then walked a few dozen meters across the sand. She bent down and ran her hands through the blades of a clump of grass.

The length of the corridor was so startling, compelling, that her breath slowed. It was spare, economical, incredibly beautiful. The even lighting, the gradually receding but nevertheless clear details; the sand, the bushes, the lakes and rivers flowing from southern cap condensation . . .

Despite what Farley had said, Patricia felt safe walking another dozen or so meters west. And having gone that far, still within a few minutes' run of the tent, it seemed no big deal to go an equal distance beyond. She reached the edge of the dwarf forest in ten minutes, then glanced back to orient herself to the tent and the ramp emerging from the cap tunnel.

The trees resembled scrubby pines, none more than two meters tall, their gnarled branches intertwined into an impenetrable thicket. She had never seen anything precisely like them on Earth, but their needles were similar to those on the Douglas fir Christmas trees her family used to buy before settling on an aluminum substitute.

She bent down to peer under the low canopy but saw no sign of life.

How strange, that the Stoners should take every living,

75

moving thing with them. Stripping the Stone. Where did they all go?

That much was obvious, now. She could feel the compulsion each time she looked down the corridor. They headed into the infinite north, if the corridor truly was infinite.

"Patricia!" Lanier called from the tent. She jumped, slightly guilty, but there was no urgency or rebuke in his voice.

"Yes?"

"Work to do."

"On my way." She returned to the tent.

They sat by a folding table arranged under the awning. Lanier took a slate and plugged in a memory block, then set the apparatus between them. "You should have some idea now why we need you here. We have a couple of mysteries to figure out, and that"—he pointed down the corridor—"may not be the greater."

"I wouldn't think so," she said.

"I've already programmed a first-draft schedule for you. You'll get a tour of the third chamber city—concentrating on a library there. That city was called Thistledown, just like the Stone itself. It's a couple of centuries newer than Alexandria. And you'll make several return visits to the library in the second chamber. That'll take a week or two, just getting you started." He pointed to the slate and tapped a RUN button. Instructions scrolled down the screen. "Here's how to use the subways, schedules, and precautions. Obviously, I won't be able to guide you all the time, or even very often. Work piling up all over. And I'll probably be returning to Earth for a short while. During that time, you'll report to Carrolson. Most of the facts you need to know, regarding security, are in that block. Who to talk to, who not, protocol, that sort of thing. Farley, Wu and Chang are fine people, but be circumspect. Be circumspect around anyone who doesn't have the same privileges you do."

"Who else can I talk to, besides you?"

"Carrolson. You can talk to her about everything but what you read in the libraries. I'm working to get her clearance

76

for that, too. But not yet. You'll meet others in a couple of days. Some will have library clearance, and you'll be working with them, coordinating, cross-checking. Clear enough? For the next couple of weeks, it's going to be study, study, study."

"How far from the camp can I go?"

"As far as you can walk, but take along a radio. We have a security base about fifty kilometers down the corridor, with sensors set to pick up any activity in the corridor for several hundred kilometers. If they call a retreat, get back to the tunnel as soon as possible."

"What's the likelihood of that happening?"

"Small." Lanier shrugged. "Maybe nonexistent. Hasn't happened yet. I hope you don't resent kid-glove treatment. If anything happened to you, the Advisor would have new hairless rugs all over her floor."

Patricia grinned. "So who's my *duenna*?"

"Until Carrolson gets here, Farley. Questions?"

"Let me get started, then I'll ask questions."

"Fair enough." Lanier left her at the table. She picked up the slate and began the first memory block.

Chapter Six

Lanier left on the next shift, saying he would be back in two days to begin the next part of her education. Carrolson arrived a few hours later, carrying a box of memory blocks and a more powerful processor recently shipped from Earth. "At least I can take part of my work with me wherever I go," she said. Farley, Wu and Chang immediately began submitting some of their problems to the new processor.

Patricia studied the cubes that contained information on the corridor. The length of the corridor was unknown, but radar signals sent from the bore hole had not yet returned after the passage of four months. It was assumed that either the corridor had no end or that the signals had been absorbed in some as-yet-unexplained way.

Exploration teams had made several forays into the corridor, but until recently, none had proceeded farther. than five hundred kilometers. To that point, the corridor was indistinguishable from the seventh chamber it adjoined: a thick layer of dirt, atmosphere at Stone-normal pressure—650 millibars—and the normal intensity of flux tube lighting.

The corridor differed from the seventh chamber in one respect: 436 kilometers down the line, it was surrounded by a circuit of artificial structures, four motionless cupolas floating without support above wide dimples in the soil. Each of the four cupolas stood alone, spaced at equal distances from the others around the circumference. What they were made of was unknown, but the substance didn't match any of the characteristics of matter except for solidity. Eight hundred seventy-two kilometers down the line was another circuit, and a new expedition was exploring in that area now.

Patricia tapped the slate's burnisher against her tooth, then reached into her personal effects bag and brought out the stereo attachment and a coin of Mozart. The attachment fitted easily in the standardized socket and played *The Magic Flute* as she read on, undisturbed.

She cut the music and took a break after an hour and a half.

Despite Carrolson's protestations that she wasn't Vasquez's nursemaid, to Patricia that described her role exactly. She had no immediate duties in the seventh chamber, and her expertise wasn't complementary to Patricia's. Still, there was a certain comfort in having the older woman around. She was relaxed, self-confident and easy to get along with. A good person to ask questions of, if only to bounce thoughts around.

The intricacies of Stone protocol and organization were not easy to master. A chart in the memory block Lanier had left with her showed it all clearly. Under the supervision of the ISCCOM regulatory committee, NATO–Eurospace—more directly, NASA and the European Space Agency—were in charge of the Stone's exploration.

The Joint Space Command had a very large say in how the studies were conducted. Despite the civilian overgarments, this was largely a military operation. Judith Hoffman, nominally coordinating the civilian and military agencies from her offices in Sunnyvale and Pasadena, tempered this reality a little.

The Stone security team consisted of some 300 Americans (about half), 150 British and 100 Germans; the remaining 50 were from Canada, Australia and Japan. France was not a member of NATO–Eurospace and had declined an invitation to send its nationals to the Stone, no doubt partly in protest of NATO pressure to join in the major rearmament of the first two years of the twenty-first century.

Through their respective commanders, the Stone security team took orders from U.S. Navy Captain Bertram D. Kirchner—commander of external security—and Army Brigadier General Oliver Gerhardt, in charge of internal security.

The six hundred team members worked throughout the Stone to defend the civilians in case of attack. Who might attack was unspecified, but in the beginning, obviously, attack was expected from the seventh chamber, or from hidden elements in the unexplored second and third chamber cities.

Lanier acted as Hoffman's direct voice on the Stone. He coordinated science, engineering and communication. Carrolson was the senior science supervisor; Heineman was in charge of civilian engineering; and a woman named Roberta Pickney, civilian communication.

The structural breakdown of the science team was informative. There were mathematicians, archaeologists, physicists, social scientists (including historians), computer and information specialists, and medical/biology experts. There were also four lawyers.

Engineering consisted of support—with a military adjunct—and mechanics. Communication also had a military adjunct, in charge of coded transmission. Pickney, assisted by Sylvia Link, was responsible for internal Stone communications and Earth-space-station-lunar settlement networks.

Patricia thought she would never be able to remember even the most important names. Names had never been her strong suit—faces and personalities she did better with.

Besides the United States and Eurospace civilian personnel, representatives from Russia, India, China, Brazil, Japan and Mexico had been invited to serve on the science team. Some Australians and one Laotian were to arrive soon. Carrolson intimated there had been trouble with the Russians. They had only been on the Stone for a year, after finally agreeing to certain restrictions. Despite their agreement, they had been demanding (reasonably enough, Patricia thought) access to all information on the Stone, including the libraries. The libraries, Carrolson explained, were a purely American preserve, by direct order of Hoffman and the President.

"They'd save us all a hell of a lot of trouble if they just opened everything up to everybody," Carrolson said. "I despise secrecy." But she enforced her orders.

"So who's handling the science team while you're here with me?" Patricia asked.

Carrolson smiled. "I put Rimskaya on it. He's snarly, but efficient. And people will certainly think twice before coming to him with complaints. Me, I'm just a pussycat. I *need* this kind of vacation."

Lanier's memory block specified precisely whom she could talk to, and whom not, about her studies. If she wished to discuss the library, she could only speak with Rimskaya, Lanier and one science team member she hadn't met yet— Rupert Takahashi. He was on the current corridor expedition.

Patricia ate lunch with Carrolson and the three Chinese, napped for half an hour, then took her slate and a camp stool across the flat to the dwarf forest, where she sat and began to make her own notes. Carrolson joined her an hour later, carrying a thermos of iced tea and a couple of bananas.

"I'll need some tools," Patricia said. "A compass, a ruler, some pencils, or . . . I've been thinking. Is it possible that one of the engineers or electronics people could make a tool for me?"

"Name it."

"I'd like to know what the value of *pi* is in the corridor."
Carrolson pursed her lips. "Why?"

"Well, so far as I've read, the corridor is definitely not made of matter. It's something else entirely. Last night—I mean, last sleep, Farley and I talked and she explained what she knew. This morning I peeked at some of the papers Rimskaya and Takahashi put together before my arrival."

"Back in the amateur days of superspace mathematics," Carrolson said wryly. "Rimskaya probably should have stuck to his expertise."

"Perhaps, but he made some interesting suggestions. Tomorrow, Karen is going to take me to the bore hole." She pointed up at the plasma tube and the southern cap axis. "If I can have a *pi*-meter by that time, maybe I can learn some things."

"Done," Carrolson said. "Anything else?"

"I don't know if it's even possible, but as long as we're measuring *pi*, I'd like to measure slash aitch and the gravitational constant, whatever else they can think of pertaining to the qualities of the universe. A kind of multi-meter."

"You think the constants will vary here?"

"Some of them, at least."

"Slash aitch, the quantum of momentum? We wouldn't even exist."

"There could be a difference in ratio. I'd just like to know."

Carrolson stood, picked up the empty thermos and the banana skins and returned to the tent. Minutes later, she and Wu left in the truck, taking the tunnel back to the sixth chamber.

Patricia stared down the corridor, frowning slightly.

She had very real, if limited, power. She had just made a Nobel laureate jump to do her bidding.

For much of her life, Patricia had spent her most important moments in her head, lost in a world that would have been completely incomprehensible to the vast majority of people on Earth. Now, sitting by the dwarf forest, listening to the Mozart

Jupiter Symphony and staring down the length of the corridor, she felt at first nervous, then irritated that the state wasn't coming fast enough.

She knew where to begin. If the corridor wasn't made of matter, there were only a few alternatives. Either it was a tube of restraining forces, passing beyond the end of the asteroid through some superspace trickery, or it was not. If not, then it was likely to be constructed itself of superspace trickery. (She considered, and dismissed as philosophically useless—for the moment—the notion that the corridor was an illusion.)

Superspace trickery was the more difficult concept to work with. If the Stoners had used the machinery in the sixth chamber to distort space-time, there would be consequences. When the multi-meter arrived—if it did what she had requested—she could begin laying down parameters. Curved space on the scale of the corridor would probably produce fluctuations in the value of *pi*, since the diameter of a circle, in any seriously distorted manifold, would vary in relation to its circumference. Other constants would vary depending on distortions in higher geometries.

She gave up trying to force the state after a while. The facts weren't sufficient to warrant straining herself.

There was nothing she could do, for the moment, but relax and read. She plugged another memory block into the slate.

"How long did it take you to get used to living without night?" Patricia asked. Farley tapped her fingers impatiently against the wall of the arch, waiting for the axis elevator. They stood fifty meters east of the tunnel ramp, on a smooth-polished square of nickel-iron.

"I'm not sure I *am* used to it," Farley said. "I live with it, but I miss starry nights."

"With all their technology, you'd think the Stoners would have come up with some way to have darkness."

"Shutting off the plasma tube would be a huge waste of energy," Farley mused. "Especially for the seventh chamber. I mean it does seem to go on forever—and how could you shut off something like that?"

Patricia pulled out her slate and typed, *Seventh chamber plasma tube—power supply? Maintenance? Same as other chamber tubes?*

The elevator door opened and they entered the large circular cabin. The door closed as Farley pressed a button. They both grasped bars mounted in the walls. At first, the acceleration of the elevator increased their total weight, but as they rose—approaching the axis—the effects canceled out. The elevator reached a steady velocity after traveling about a third of the way up the shaft. Their weight had decreased considerably by then. Shortly after, they began to decelerate, slipping smoothly into near-weightlessness. The door opened and a guard in black and gray greeted them.

The axis compartments surrounding the seventh chamber bore hole had been pressurized and heated, but otherwise they remained much as the Stoners had left them, centuries before. Ribbons of newly wired lighting crisscrossed the cavernous staging area.

"We're going to the singularity monitor," Farley said. The soldier gestured for them to board a cart. They followed the ropes and took their seats, buckling themselves in.

"I have a feeling you're going to show me something else astonishing," Patricia said accusingly. "I'm not even used to the other wonders yet."

"Ancillary wonder," Farley said mysteriously. "A result of the other wonders, if you follow Rimskaya and Takahashi's theories. But you're the space-time expert here."

"I'm not so sure," Patricia said distantly.

"If the corridor is a matrix of bent geodesics, a warped tube of space, what would you expect to find at its center?"

"I wondered about that yesterday afternoon." She paused as the cart neared the end of the staging area. "It's not going to work down the center. There's going to be a region where all the rules fail."

"Precisely."

"A singularity?"

"That's where we're going," Farley said.

The guard pulled the cart alongside an airlock mounted in the rock wall. Farley gripped a guide bar and helped Patricia out of her belt. The guard saluted and said he would wait for them.

They entered the airlock. Farley switched on a light and pulled down two rumply, one-size-fits-all pressure suits from a rack. "You can snug the arm and leg lengths a bit with these straps. Mobility and finesse aren't really needed here, just pressure and temperature and air. This isn't the most visited spot on the Stone."

The rear wall of the airlock was equipped with a broad-runged ladder, ascending to a wheel-opened hatch in the ceiling. Bits and pieces of equipment—some obviously long-abandoned—lay stacked in the corners and under the ladder.

"Just watch your step. Take everything slowly. There's no danger if you're careful. If anything happens to your suit—very unlikely—we can be back in the lock in less than two minutes."

Farley checked Patricia's suit seals and pressed a red button on a panel mounted near the ladder. The air was quietly pumped out of the chamber until Patricia could hear only her own breathing. Farley switched on their suit radios.

"Up the ladder," she said.

"I've never been in a spacesuit before," Patricia said, climbing the rungs after Farley.

"You didn't get spacesick, according to the OTV crew."

"Being weightless is fun."

"Hmm. Took me three days to get used to it."

Farley spun the wheel on the hatch and pushed it open. It glided slowly upward, then stopped until she ascended another rung and gave it a push. It swung out of the way. Compact floodlights had been installed in the bore hole, though the opening to the seventh chamber was only a dozen meters away, and the milky glow of the inner plasma tube spread faintly throughout.

Patricia turned to look south. The walls of the bore hole—rough and grooved with irregular lines—faded into inky blackness. At the end of the blackness was a circle of light the size of a BB held at arm's length. She looked up as best she could and saw a wide intrusion of dark rock in the asteroidal metal.

"Plasma tube begins anew in each chamber," Farley said. "It butts against the caps, sustained by a very weak bottle. The bottle also acts to keep the atmosphere in—otherwise, it would all have licked out through the bore holes. Leaked, I mean. Leak?"

"Leaked is fine," Patricia said. "Wouldn't air be kept down in the chambers because of the rotation?"

"Scale height is the key. Without the bottle, the atmospheric pressure at the bore holes would still be about a hundred and eighty millimeters of mercury."

"Um," Patricia said.

"We think there are charged plates inset in the cap material around the circumference of the tube, but we haven't investigated yet. And the corridor tube is quite a different thing from the other tubes. We have even *less* idea how it works."

They moved along the bore-hole wall using the ubiquitous ropes and stanchions. Near the rim of the hole stood a scaffold about fifty meters high. Running from the bottom to the top of the scaffold was a ladder in a long cylindrical cage.

"You first," Farley said. Patricia entered the cage and pulled herself up hand-over-hand, letting her legs swing unused behind, as she had seen Farley do in the airlock. "When you're above the cage, link your suit ring to a cable. If you somehow manage to float free, I'll come after you with a tether."

At the top of the scaffold, now aligned directly on the Stone's axis, Patricia took hold of the safety cable and pulled herself out of Farley's way. Another cylindrical cage poked five or six meters beyond the rim. Farley gestured, and they climbed out over the sloping walls of the cap.

"The plasma's pretty clear from this angle, as you can see,"

Farley said. They had an incredible view of the corridor. Without the obvious clues of distorted perspective, the landscape could have been painted on a huge bowl. The details were rendered faintly milky by the plasma tube, which concentrated into a bright circle at the center of the far cap.

"The Russians aren't allowed this far. They're working in the other bore holes, however."

At the end of the second cage was something that gave Patricia's eyes a twinge. Farley motioned for her to approach.

"This is it," she said. "Where everything goes haywire in the corridor."

It resembled a half-meter-wide pipe made of quicksilver, stretching off to its own vanishing point, not in a straight line and not in a curve, not moving and not standing still. If it could be said to reflect at all, it did not behave like a mirror, imaging instead barely recognizable imitations of its surroundings.

Patricia approached the singularity, trying not to look at it directly. Here, the laws of the corridor were twisted into a neat, elongated knot, a kind of spacial umbilicus.

It distorted her face as if with a gleeful malevolence.

"It doesn't look straight, but it is. It resists penetration, of course," Farley said, reaching out with a gloved hand to touch the blunt end. Her hand slid gently to one side. "It seems to produce the force that acts like gravitation in the corridor. The net effect is an inverse-square force which is ineffective within the length of the seventh chamber but goes to work right outside the connection with the corridor. The transition is very smooth. Out in the corridor, the farther from the singularity you are, the greater the force, until you reach the corridor walls. Makes it seem like the walls are *pulling* you. *Voila!*— weight."

"Is there any difference between walls pulling and singularity pushing?"

Farley didn't answer for a moment. "Damned if I know. The singularity stretches down the middle of the corridor within the tube. There's speculation it has something to do with maintaining this plasma but . . . honest, we're all ignorant here. You have a wide-open field to explore."

Patricia reached out with her hand. The twisted-mirror surface reached back to her with an out-of-focus something, not a hand. The hand and its opposite met. She felt a tingling resistance and pressed harder.

Her hand was gently pushed down the length until she lifted it away. Patricia—somewhat to her surprise—understood the principle immediately.

"Of course," she said. "It's like touching the square root of space-time. Try to enter the singularity, and you translate yourself through a distance along some spacial coordinate."

"You slide along," Farley said.

"Right."

Patricia maneuvered herself to the rounded beginning—or was it the end?—of the singularity, then reached around the zone with both arms as if to hug it. Her fingers squeezed the twisted surface and she was pulled against the base, then bounced back.

"Touch it," Patricia said, "and it repels the pressure with a force parallel to the axis." She touched it twice in succession. The ring and cable stopped her reacting twist. "I pinch it at this angle, I'm propelled by the singularity, going north. The opposite angle, south. No torque—unidirectional. Either I'm pushed straight outward, or I'm shunted along the line."

Farley smiled enviously through her faceplate. "You catch on fast."

"Glad you think so," Patricia said. She sighed and backed away. "Okay. Let's go back. I'm going to have to think this over."

Farley took hold of her shoulder and directed her back along the cage, down the scaffold and into the airlock. Patricia was already glassy-eyed, musing.

She hardly noticed the elevator ride. At the tent camp, she sat down with the slate and Carrolson's processor. Farley wandered off for a few minutes to eat. When she returned, the linked processor and slate were flashing requests for the next sequence of instructions. Vasquez appeared to be napping. Farley glanced at the slate display.

From the—a future(?) Singularity. Longer—passing through the asteroid wall. Inverse-square repulsion increasing. Where did the Stoners go? Why, down the corridor, of course.

No set curvature near the twisted mirror. Must have the multi-meter to check that out—certainly seems likely, however. If I regard the setup as predesigned technology, technology manipulating geometry, use of spaces and altered geodesics as a tool. A singularity, perhaps infinitely long, beginning here, just before the boundary where chamber and corridor meet.

Energy to maintain the plasma tube in the corridor. Could that be made a function of the separate universe the corridor obviously is? Where did the matter come from—all that dirt, and the atmosphere? Not from the Stone, not all of it; that's obvious.

The warm air coming down the corridor lapped at the tent, brushed the grass near the camp and mingled with the cold air pouring down from the cap, forming dust-devils.

Chang and Wu played chess under the awning.

After a time, Farley took a nap, too.

Chapter Seven

Heineman murmured to himself testily. Walking slowly along the Velcro pad surrounding the assembly area, he scrolled through the cargo manifest on the slate. The cargo—removed from its cocoon and assembled—fit all the specifications the engineering team had made up six months before. That had been a crazy time—trying to design a device which had ridiculous properties to do a job that none of the engineering team understood. But back then, green badges had been very rare items.

There was no way now for anyone to deny him a green

badge. He was the only one who could test the device and teach others how to use it.

It was a beautiful piece of work: a hollow cylinder twenty meters long and six wide, resembling a giant jet engine with all its guts removed. He peered down the middle of the assembly at the sickle-shaped metal pieces that would clamp down on the mysterious *something* the cylinder would surround. The clamps now rested on plastic inserts, which would be removed when the device was in place.

It was called a tuberider. Sitting next to it—brought up in three cocoons by a subsequent OTV—was a highly modified Boeing–Bell prop-driven vertical/short takeoff and landing aircraft, V/STOL for short, model number NHV-24B.

It was the most peculiar aircraft he had ever seen. Developed initially for the U.S. Air Force, designed for search and rescue missions, it could rotate its two wingtip-mounted engines through 120 degrees. The five broad blades of each prop could be folded back into the engine nacelles. And in the tail, aimed slightly above the centerline, was a kerosene-oxygen rocket engine, no doubt to provide extra thrust—but under what conditions?

Its wings were rakishly forward-swept and were mounted three-quarters back on the fuselage, almost touching the V–tail. It could carry eighteen people and a crew of two, fully loaded, or fewer passengers and a lot of equipment. It was at once airplane and helicopter and rocket.

He loved it just from reading the specs. He had always had a weakness for Rube Goldberg gadgets.

The V/STOL could be fitted to the tuberider in three positions: like an arrow sticking from the side of a log, nose and refueling nozzle inserted mid-cylinder; in the configuration of its first mission, inserted "up the cylinder's ass" as Heineman thought of it, as its rocket propelled the tuberider down the middle of the plasma tubes and bore holes to the seventh chamber; or clamped to the cylinder along its belly.

He didn't have the slightest idea what it would do once it

was in place. From an aeronautical or astronautical perspective it was pure craziness. How would the cylinder be stabilized on its track—whatever that was—while the V/STOL docked? The cylinder had no maneuvering engines. The whole contraption would be just barely stable enough to ride down the axis with the rocket pushing—

'Tis not mine to reason why, he thought, marking the final check on the slate. Despite his initial enthusiasm, no aircraft, Heineman felt, was truly beautiful until he had flown it—and survived.

The cocoon had also contained contraband. Not on the manifest—not the official one, at any rate—were two metal boxes the size and shape of coffins. Heineman had a good idea what they contained—high-speed radar-controlled Gatling guns.

He could also guess where they would be installed, and for what reason. They were Joint Space Command items, and the only man who needed to know about their arrival was Captain Kirchner. They were in direct violation of ISCCOM guidelines for the Stone.

Heineman was used to serving two masters. He knew Kirchner and JSC had their reasons for breaking the rules. He knew Lanier and Hoffman would appreciate those reasons when the time came.

Heineman made sure the crates were delivered to the external security staging areas and then forgot about them.

He floated past the assembly and looked at his watch. Garry was late.

Lanier pulled himself along the ropes to the third dock staging area. The tuberider and V/STOL occupied center stage like grand ladies of the theater awaiting costumers' attentions.

Heineman eyed him unenthusiastically as he approached. "You look exhausted," he commented, handing the slate over for inspection. Lanier handed it back without a glance or comment. "You'll spook people, coming out of the chambers like that."

90

"Can't be helped," Lanier said.

Heineman shook his head and let out his breath in a dubious low whistle. "What in hell have you got down there?"

"Are they ready?" Lanier asked. Heineman nodded and pulled the box of memory cubes out of his beltsack.

"For now. I'm pushing them down the tube next week. If I get my badge . . ."

Lanier reached into his inside jacket pocket and produced a green badge, flipping it around to show Heineman. "Yours. Second level. Go and find out for yourself. You're so eager."

"That's my nature," Heineman said. He clamped the badge to his lapel. "How's the girl doing? She any help?"

"I don't know," Lanier said. "She's resilient." He raised his eyebrows and took a deep breath. "Seems to be a survivor." He seemed anxious to change the subject. "I'll have provisional greens for your flight crew."

"I'm going to fly it into position alone," Heineman said. He was surprised when Lanier simply nodded; he had expected some argument. "Who'll take the first sortie with me?"

"I will, if I have time," Lanier said.

"You haven't flown in years."

Lanier laughed. "Neither of us has ever done this kind of flying. Besides, it's not a skill you forget. You should know that."

A guard drifted across the staging area toward them. Lanier glanced in her direction, held out his hand and received a sealed envelope. She left without a word being exchanged.

"You expected that," Heineman said.

"I did." He opened the envelope, read the enclosed note, then stuck it in the pocket where Heineman's badge had resided. "My orders Earthside. I'm going to spend another couple of days here, then take the next OTV. Larry, get the tuberider in position, prepare for a flight test, but hold everything until I return."

"Advisor wants you?"

Lanier patted his coat pocket. "Priority. But I have to make

91

sure Vasquez is going to work out." He turned toward the hatchway.

"I'll be waiting," Heineman called after. He looked at the tuberider and V/STOL, eyes bright.

Chapter Eight

Lanier escorted Carrolson in a truck to the seventh chamber. In the tunnel, Carrolson turned on the cab light and removed a pouch from the box in her lap. "Give electronics high marks this week," she said. "Patricia asked for something and they got it to me in twenty-four hours."

"What is it?"

"You really want to know? It might upset you."

He smiled. "It's my job to be upset."

"She asked for a meter to check out local values of *pi*, Planck's constant—slash aitch, rather—and the gravitational constant. Electronics threw in speed of light, ratio of proton mass to electron mass, and neutron decay time. I don't know whether she'll use them all, but she's got them."

"Sounds pretty high-tech to me."

"I asked how they managed to squeeze some of the tests into a package this size. They smiled and said they've been building defense satellites for CSOC for years, and the multimeter was easy in comparison. They scavenged circuits from some surplus security devices. I don't know how it works, but it does. At least, it seems to. Look." She pushed a button marked with the Greek letter *pi*. The luminous display read "3.141592645 *stable*."

"My calculator will do that."

"It won't tell you if *pi* changes."

"So who's this billed to?"

"Science, of course. Is there no poetry in your soul—does everything reduce to billing?"

"It's in my blood. Anyway, remove it from science and

92

charge it to a new, special category. Mark that category 'Vasquez' and keep the expenditures confidential.''

"Yes, sir." Carrolson put the multi-meter back in its felt bag as they came down the ramp into the tubelight. "Will she be expensive?"

"I don't know. I want to separate science in the first six chambers from anything done here. I'll be back on Earth in a couple of days, and part of my time may be spent arguing money with senators and congressmen. It's a complicated subject."

"My curiosity is checked," Carrolson said. "You think she'll work out?"

Lanier cast a peeved glance at her. "Don't you start. Give her whatever she wants, treat her kindly, keep her on the straight and narrow after I'm gone. She'll do fine."

"Because the Advisor says?"

Lanier halted the truck near the tent. "She seems to get along well with Farley. If something important drags you away, what say we have Farley chaperone her? Even if she is Chinese."

"I don't foresee any problems there."

"Nor I. You'll take Vasquez back and forth to the libraries, with a military escort, not Farley. That's my only stipulation."

"Fine. Now for some real sore points," Carrolson said. "What?"

"The Russians are grumbling about pulling out their members. If the Russians go, my sources tell me the Chinese might pull out as well. A knee-jerk response. They've been complaining, too, and they don't want anyone to think they're more gullible than the Russians."

"Hell, Farley's been feeding them stuff about the seventh chamber for months now. That doesn't keep them happy?"

"No. The Russians know the basics, too."

"The hell with all of them," Lanier grumbled. "That sums it up."

"Admirably." Carrolson grinned.

"Just make sure Patricia doesn't talk to anyone she shouldn't."

"Got you."

"Including you."

Carrolson bit her lower lip, crossed herself and shook her head fervently. "Hope to die. Seriously, aren't I just about due for my upgrade?"

"I hope to bring it back with me. I'll be talking with Hoffman. Patience."

"Patience is," Carrolson said.

Lanier stared at her sternly, eyes flickering back and forth across her face. Then he cracked a broad smile and reached up to touch her shoulder. "Our watchword. Thank you."

"*De nada,* boss."

Wu approached the truck as Carrolson and Lanier stepped down. "Expedition to the second circuit is back," he said. "They're about sixty kilometers away. Security has them on track, and messages have been relayed."

"Good," Lanier said. "Let's get ready for the home-coming."

The second expedition consisted of four trucks and twenty-six people. Sitting near the dwarf forest, Patricia watched the column of dust as the vehicles approached. She picked up her slate and the processor and strolled back to the camp.

Two more trucks entered from the sixth chamber tunnel, rumbling and whanging down the ramp. They parked by the tent and Berenson—commander of the German security forces, and now in charge of security in the seventh chamber—stepped down from one, Rimskaya and Robert Smith from the other. Rimskaya nodded cordially at Patricia as he passed by. *His mood's improved,* she thought.

Lanier and Carrolson emerged from the shadow of the tent overhang.

"How far did they go?" Patricia asked Lanier.

"Nine hundred and fifty-three kilometers—half battery range." He held the felt-bagged instrument out to her. "Your multi-meter. We've logged it into the equipment list, and now

94

it's yours. Treat it carefully. Electronics won't be able to duplicate it quite as quickly."

"Thank you," Patricia said. She removed the instrument and the instructions on a folded slip of paper. Carrolson looked over Patricia's shoulder.

"It has a range of about ten centimeters," she commented. "Strictly local."

Rimskaya came up behind them and cleared his throat. "Miss Vasquez," he said.

"Yes, sir?" *Old habits die hard.*

"How do you like the problem?"

"It's marvelous," she said, her tone level. "It will take time to solve—if it *can* be solved."

"Certainly," Rimskaya said. "I trust you have become aware of our hypotheses?"

"Yes. They've been helpful." They had been, too. She didn't want to overstress the point, however.

"Good. You've been to the singularity?"

She nodded. "I wish I'd had the multi-meter." She passed it to him and he examined the device, shaking his head.

"A fine idea. I see you are making progress. Much better than I. That is as it should be. There is a gentleman on the expedition who might be able to help you more. His name is Takahashi, the expedition's second-in-command. A very experienced theorist. I trust you've read some of our joint papers."

"Yes. Very interesting."

Rimskaya fixed his stern gaze on her for an uncomfortably long five or ten seconds, then nodded. "I must speak with Farley now," he said, walking away.

The expedition trucks parked twenty meters from the camp. Lanier walked out to meet them. Carrolson stayed with Patricia. "That's as far as we've gone down the corridor," she said. "From what they radioed back, we still haven't found much."

The arrival was something of an anticlimax. Nobody left the vehicles; and one by one, at Lanier's instructions, they moved past the camp and up the ramp into the tunnel, vanishing into the sixth chamber.

Lanier returned with three memory blocks. He gave one to Carrolson and one to Patricia, pocketing the third. "Expedition report, unedited," he said. "Nothing spectacular, according to Takahashi, except . . ."

He glanced behind him, down the corridor.

"Yes?" Carrolson urged.

"The second circuit is more than just floating cupolas. There are openings beneath the cupolas. They appear to be wells of some sort. They didn't find out where the wells lead, but they're definitely open."

"Then the corridor has holes," Carrolson said. "All right, Patricia, it's time we made plans for a trip to the first circuit. When are you going to be free?"

Patricia took a small breath and shook her head. "Any time. I can work wherever I am."

"Make it day after tomorrow," Lanier said. "Patricia and I have to spend some time in the library." He discreetly gestured to Carrolson: time to leave. She made her excuses and glanced back at them as she entered the tent.

"Part two of the indoctrination will begin next shift," he said. "The most difficult part of all. Are you ready for it?"

"I don't know," she said, feeling her chest contract. "I must be. I've survived so far."

"Good. Meet me at the ramp in twelve hours."

Chapter Nine

The Axis City had moved a million kilometers down the corridor since its construction five centuries ago. Olmy and the Frant had covered that distance in less than a week, flying their craft in a smooth stretched spiral around the plasma tube.

In the history of the Thistledown and the Way, no one had ever entered the asteroid from the *outside*.

96

Olmy and the Frant had surveyed the Thistledown's new occupants for two weeks and had learned a great deal. They were indeed human, and not even Korzenowski himself could have expected what Olmy now knew.

The Thistledown had come full circle. Geshels had warned there might be displacement, but no one had suspected what kind of displacement, or what the results might be.

Having completed his principal duties for the Nexus, Olmy then turned off his data and mission recorders and returned to his old home in the third chamber. The cylindrical apartment building where his triad family had lived, where he had spent two years of his childhood, stood right at the edge of Thistledown City, not quite a kilometer from the northern cap. Once, the building had held twenty thousand people, chiefly Geshels, technicians and researchers employed on the Sixth Chamber Project. It had then served as temporary home for hundreds of orthodox Naderites expelled by the Nexus from Alexandria. Now, of course, it was empty; there was no evidence it had even been visited by the asteroid's new occupants.

Olmy walked across the lobby and stood near the credit counter, one eyebrow lowered as if in puzzlement. He turned to the broad illusart window and spotted the Frant in the courtyard, sitting patiently on an empty light-sculpture pedestal. The window made it appear that the Frant was in a luxurious Earth garden, complete with glowing sunset. The Frant would appreciate that, Olmy thought.

He picted graphicspeak at the credit counter and received a confidential response: the apartment was blocked, as were all apartments in the building. None could be occupied or even viewed until the present interdict was revoked.

Those orders had been issued after the last of the Naderite families had been transferred from the cities. Only public buildings had been left open for the use of the last scholars, finishing their exodus studies. The Earth people had already put some of those facilities to use, the Thistledown City Library chief among them.

He picted a Nexus coded icon into the credit counter and

said aloud, "I have authorization to temporarily revoke interdict."

"Authorization recognized," the counter replied.

"Open and decorate unit three seven nine seven five."

"What decor do you wish?"

"As it was when occupied by the Olmy-Secor-Lear Triad family."

"You are of that family?" the counter asked politely.

"I am."

"Searching. Decoration completed. You may ascend."

Olmy took the lift. In the round cloud-gray hallway, walking a few inches above the floor, he felt a most unfamiliar and unpleasant emotional tug—the long-past pain of dreams forgotten or lost, of youthful hopes destroyed by political necessity.

He had lived so long his memories seemed to contain the thoughts and emotions of many different people. But one set of emotions still transcended the others, and one ambition remained foremost. He had worked for centuries on behalf of the ruling Geshels and Naderites, never playing favorites, that someday he might be allowed this opportunity.

His apartment number glowed red at the base of the circular door, the only glowing number in the hallway. He entered and stood for a moment in the surroundings of his childhood, engaged in a brief moment of nostalgia. The furnishings and decor were all here, reflecting his natural father's attempt to duplicate the apartment they had been driven from in Alexandria. They had spent two years here, awaiting decisions on their case before their triad family could be moved to the newly finished Axis City.

They had been the last family to live in these buildings, and Olmy had had considerable opportunity to explore the co-op memory and experiment with programming. Even in his childhood, he had shown a proclivity for things technical that dismayed his orthodox Naderite parents. And what he had discovered in the building's memory five centuries ago, quite by accident, had changed the direction of his life. . . .

He sat in his father's sky-blue chair before the apartment

data pillar. Such pillars were now obsolete in the Axis City, used only as charming antiques, but he had spent hundreds of hours as a child in front of this very device and found it familiar and comfortable to work with. Picting his own coded icons, he activated the pillar and opened a custom channel to the building's memory. Once, the memory had served the needs of thousands of tenants, keeping their records and acting as a depository for millions of possible decor variations. Now it was virtually blank; Olmy had the impression of swimming in a vast dark hollowness.

He picted a stack and register number and waited for coded questions to be picted. As each appeared before him, he answered precisely and correctly.

In the hollowness, there appeared a presence, fragmented, grievously incomplete, but powerful and recognizable even so.

"Ser Engineer," Olmy said aloud.

My friend. The nonvocal communication was level and strong, if toneless. Even incomplete, Konrad Korzenowski's personality and presence were commanding.

"We've come home."

Yes? How long since you last spoke to me?

"Five hundred years."

I am still dead. . . .

"Yes," Olmy said softly. "Now listen. There is much you must know. We've come home, but we are not alone. The Thistledown has been reoccupied. It is time for you to come with me now. . . .*

Chapter Ten

Patricia and Lanier passed through the fence and security checks, entered the second chamber library and followed the strips of lights across the empty floor and up the stairs. On the fourth floor, they entered the reading area with its dark cubicles. Lanier sat her down in the lighted cubicle and went off into the stacks, leaving her alone to again feel the chill, the spookiness that seemed—even amid all the strangeness—reserved for the library alone. When he returned, he held four thick books in his arms.

"These are among the last books printed for mass distribution, before all information services became solid state. Not on the Stone, but on Earth. Their Earth. I suppose you've already guessed what sort of library this is."

"A quaint one. A museum," she said.

"Right. An antique library, better suited to those with antique habits, no? When you get to the third chamber library, you'll become acquainted with the Stoners' state-of-the-art systems."

He held out the first volume. It was printed in a style similar to that of the Mark Twain book, but with heavier boards and thick, even tougher plastic paper. She read the spine. "*Brief History of the Death*, by Abraham Damon Farmer.'" She opened to the printing history and read the date. "2135. Our calendar?"

"Yes."

"Are they talking about the Little Death?" she asked hopefully.

"No."

"Something else," she murmured. She read the chronology heading the first chapter. "'From December 1993 to May 2005.'" She closed the book on her thumb. "Before I read any more, I want to ask a question."

"Ask away." He waited, but it took her some time to phrase it properly in her head.

"These are history books about *a* future, not necessarily our own, correct?"

"Yes."

"But if this chronology is . . . right, appropriate . . . if it could possibly be our future . . . then there's going to be a catastrophe in less than a month."

He nodded.

100

"I'm supposed to prevent it? How? What the hell can I do?"

"I don't know what any of us can do. We're already working on that angle. If . . . a big *if* . . . it's going to happen at all. At any rate, it should be obvious to you, as you read these books, that the Stone's universe is not the same as ours in at least one important respect."

"And that is . . . ?"

"In the Stone's past, no giant asteroid starship returned to the Earth–Moon vicinity."

"That might make a difference?"

"I'd think so, wouldn't you?"

She turned the page. "How long do I have?"

"I'm leaving tomorrow for Earth. You'll be going to the first circuit the day after."

"Two days."

He nodded.

"I'll be staying here?"

"If you find it acceptable. There's an office behind the stacks outfitted as a sleeping area, with food and hot plate. Porta-potty. The guards will check on you every couple of hours. You're not to tell any of them what you're reading. But if you feel any sort of distress, let them know immediately. *Any* sort of distress. Even just getting sick to your stomach. Understand?"

"Yes."

"I'll stay here with you this first time." He squeezed her shoulder gently. "Take a break with me in a couple of hours, okay?"

"Sure," she said.

She watched him settle into a cubicle seat. He took a slate out of his pocket and quietly typed on it.

She turned the page on the first chapter and began. She did not read in a linear fashion, instead skipping from the middle of the book to the beginning, then to the end, looking for pages where the major events were synopsized, or conclusions were drawn.

Page 15 In the last years of the 1980s, it became apparent to the Soviet Union and its client states that the Western world was winning—or would soon win—the war of technology and therefore ideology both on Earth and in space, with consequences unforeseen for the future of their nations and their system. They contemplated several ways of overcoming this technological superiority; none seemed practical. In the late 1980s, with the deployment of the first United States space-based defense systems, the Soviet states stepped up their efforts to obtain technological "fixes" through espionage and importing of embargoed goods—computers and other high-technology equipment—but this was soon shown to be inadequate. In 1991, the space-based defense systems they themselves had deployed were shown to be inferior in design and ability, and it became obvious to the Soviet leadership that what had been predicted for years was in fact happening; the Soviet Union could not compete with the free world in technology.

Most Soviet computer systems were centralized; privately owned or noncentralized systems were illegal (with a few exceptions—namely, the Agatha experiments), and the laws were rigorously enforced. Young Soviet citizens could not match the technological "savvy" of their counterparts in the Western bloc nations. The Soviet Union was soon going to suffocate under the weight of its own tyranny, remaining a twentieth- (or nineteenth-) century nation in a twenty-first-century world. They had no choice but to attempt, in the football (q.v.) terminology of the time, an "end run." They had to test the courage and resolve of the Western bloc nations. If the Soviets failed, then by the turn of the century, they would be far weaker than their adversaries. The Little Death was inevitable.

Patricia took a deep breath. She hadn't seen reports of the Little Death handled from quite so distant—so historical—a perspective. She remembered nightmares as a girl, after living through the incredible tension and fear, and then seeing the results on television. She had learned to cope since, but these cold, critical evaluations—ingested in such an authoritative environment—brought back the shivers all too effectively.

Page 20   By comparison, the Little Death of 1993 was a low-technology bungle. A minor contretemps causing embarrassment as much as horror, it resulted in an insincere international resolve that resembled the mocking promises of young children. Afraid of their weapons, during that first conflict, the Western bloc and Soviet forces constantly "pulled their punches," relying on the tactics and technology of past decades. When the engagements became nuclear—as all in command knew in their hearts they would—the space-based defense systems, still young and unproven, showed themselves to be remarkably effective. They could not, however, stop the near-shore submarine launches of the three missiles which destroyed Atlanta, Brighton and part of the coast of Brittany. The Russians could not protect their city of Kiev. The nuclear exchange was limited, and the Soviets and Western bloc countries capitulated almost simultaneously. But the rehearsal had already been conducted, and the Soviets had emerged with less "hits" than their adversaries. They had gained nothing but a deadly resolve: that they would not be defeated under any circumstances, nor would history overtake their outmoded system.

     The Death, when it came, was completely earnest and open. Every weapon was used as it had been designed to be used. There seemed to be no compunction about consequences.

Page 35   In retrospect, it seems completely logical that once a weapon is invented, it will be used. But we forget the blindness and obfuscation of the late twentieth and early twenty-first centuries, when the most destructive weapons were regarded as walls of protection, and when the horror of Armageddon was seen as a deterrent no sane society would risk. But the nations were not sane—rational, composed, aware, but not sane. In each nation, the arsenal included potent distrust and even hatred. . . .

Page 3   The Little Death resulted in 4 million casualties, most in Western Europe and England. The Death resulted in approximately 2½ billion casualties, and the numbers will always be uncertain, for by the time the body counts were "completed," it is possible that as many bodies had rotted as had been counted. And, of course, as many more had been completely vaporized.

Patricia wiped her eyes. "This is awful," she murmured.

"You can take a break if you want," Lanier said solicitously.

"No . . . not yet." She continued skimming, back and forth. . . .

Page 345   In summation, the naval battles were hideous jokes of technology. During the Little Death, submarines were hunted (and in some cases, sunk) up to and even after capitulation, but the great fleets only skirmished. In the major conflict, once the war began in earnest, about two hours after the first hostile actions, the navies of East and West went "in harm's way." In the Persian Gulf, the Northwestern Pacific, the North Atlantic and the Mediterranean (Libya had provided the

104

Soviets with a Mediterranean base in 1997) the battles were fierce and quick. There were few victors. Sea battles during the Death lasted an average of half an hour, and many took less than five minutes. On the first day, while strategic intentions were being tested and before the large-scale escalations, the navies of the Eastern and Western blocs destroyed each other. They were the last great navies allowed on the oceans of the Earth, and their radioactive scrap still pollutes the waters, 130 years later.

Page 400 A peculiar phenomenon of the latter half of the twentieth century was the increase in "retreatists." These people—usually in groups of fifty or less—staked out isolated country tracts as their territory, expecting a disaster of major proportions to destroy civilization, resulting in anarchy. With their stores of food and weapons and their "strictly survival" attitude—a willingness to isolate themselves morally as well as physically—they embodied the worst aspects of what Orson Hamill has called "the conservative sickness of the twentieth century." There is no room here to analyze the causes of this sickness, where individual power and survival counted above all other moral considerations and where the ability to destroy was emphasized over any nobility of spirit, but the ironies of the outcome are rich.

The "retreatists" were right—and wrong. The catastrophe had come, and much of the world was destroyed, but even in the Long Winter that followed, civilization did not crumble into complete anarchy. Indeed, within a year, highly cooperative societies emerged. The lives of one's fellows became almost infinitely precious—and all of the Death's survivors became fellows. Love

105

and support of neighborings groups were essential, for no single group had the means—or the stamina—to survive long without aid. The retreatist enclaves—heavily armed and viciously indiscriminate about how they defended themselves or whom they killed—soon became targets of hatred and fear, the sole exceptions to this new perception of brotherhood.

Within five years after the end of the Death, most of the retreatist enclaves had been sought out and their half-crazed members killed or captured. (Unfortunately, many isolated "survivalist" [q.v.] communities were also included in the sweep. The distinction made between these branches with similar inclinations is a historical one, and was ignored by the authorities of that time.) Many of the retreatists were put on trial for crimes against humanity—specifically, for refusing to participate in the recovery of civilization. In time, these purges extended to all who advocated the right to bear weapons, and even, in some communities, to all who favored high technologies.

Those military personnel who had survived were forced to undergo social reconditioning.

The landmark trial of 2015—where high-ranking politicians and military officers of both the Eastern and Western blocs were accused of crimes against humanity—capped this grim but not-unexpected reaction against the horrors of the Death.

It didn't seem real. She closed her book and shut her eyes. Here she was, reading a book about events that hadn't taken place—yet—and had happened in another universe.

She swallowed the lump in her throat. If it *was* real, and if it was going to happen, then something should be done. She leafed through the appendices.

On page 567, she found what she was looking for. Every city in the world that had been bombed was listed in the next two hundred pages, with approximate casualties and deaths. She searched for California and found it: twenty-five cities, each receiving from two to twenty-three warheads. Los Angeles, twenty-three, spaced over a two-week period. ("Spasm," an asterisked footnote commented.) Santa Barbara, two. San Francisco—including Oakland, San Jose and Sunnyvale—twenty over a three-day period. San Diego, fifteen. Long Beach, ten. Sacramento, one, Fresno, one. Vandenberg Space Operations Center, twelve evenly spaced along the coastal strip.

Air bases hit in or near the cities, including civilian airports which could be used for military purposes: fifty-three. All space centers around the world had been destroyed, even in noncombatant countries (again the footnote: "Spasm").

Patricia felt dizzy. The book seemed to recede from her. There was no tunnel vision, no loss of sensation, just a kind of isolation. She was Patricia Luisa Vasquez, twenty-four, and because she was young she would have a long time to live. Her parents, because she had known them all her life, would not die for a very long time—an inconceivably long time. And Paul—because they had just begun knowing each other, because he was the one man she had met who had even tried to know what she was about—Paul would be safe, too.

And all of them lived in zones that would· be (*might be*) vaporized from the face of the Earth.

It was simple, really. She would take this book with her when she left, which would be soon, days perhaps. She would take it back to Earth and show people. (Perhaps something like that had already been done.)

And if the universes were close enough that a similarity in immediate futures was possible, then people would be forced to act. Faced with the prospect of nuclear war, people would start disarming, start apologizing, *Jesus, I'm sorry we came so close; let's take this as a blessing and*—

"Oh, CHRIST!" She closed the book and stood.

Lanier walked with her through the decrepit park near the library. She cried for five minutes, then pulled herself together. The questions she wanted to ask were so difficult to express in words. And if she knew the answers, she might go mad. . . .

"Has anyone made comparisons? I mean, between their history and our own?" she asked.

"Yes," Lanier said. "I have, and so has Takahashi."

"He knows as much as we do?"

Lanier nodded.

"What did you find? I mean, are the universes similar?"

"The differences in the history records are small enough that they can be interpreted as differences of fact between two sources. No major differences. Until the Stone."

"And the situations these books describe—they sound like what's happening on Earth, now, don't they?"

"Yes."

"The Little Death didn't teach anybody a thing?"

"Perhaps not."

She sat beneath a dead tree, on a concrete planter wall. "Do they know, down on Earth?"

"Eleven people know, here and there."

"What are they doing about it?"

"All that they can," Lanier said.

"But the Stone can change things. It's the crucial difference. Isn't it?"

"We hope so. In the next few weeks, we'll need all the answers we can get—to questions about alternate time-lines, universes, where the Stone came from. Can you help?"

"You need to know why the Stone is here, and how similar the universes might be, to decide whether we're going to have a war on Earth?"

Lanier nodded. "Very important."

"I don't see how any results I get can be detailed enough."

"Hoffman believes that if anyone can tell us, you can."

Patricia nodded and looked away. "Okay. Can I make conditions?"

"What sort of conditions?"

"I want my family evacuated. I want some friends taken into the countryside, put under protection. Put where the generals and politicians will be."

"No." He walked around the tree slowly. "I'm not angry with you for asking, but no. None of us has asked for anything like that. Thought about it, certainly."

"Do you have family?"

"A brother and a sister. My parents are dead."

"Wife? No. You're single. A girl friend, fiancée?"

"No major attachments."

"So you can be more objective than I can," Patricia said angrily.

"You know that has nothing to do with it."

"I'm going to work up here, for you people, and wait until my parents, my boyfriend, my sister, all the people I love die in a disaster I already know about?"

Lanier stopped before her. "Think it through, Patricia."

"I know, I know. There are hundreds of people aboard the Stone. If we all know and ask, things go haywire. That's why the libraries are off limits."

"That's one reason," Lanier said.

"And to keep the Russians from knowing?"

"That too."

"How smart." Her voice was soft, just the opposite of what he had expected. She sounded rational and if not calm, not terribly upset, either. "What happens when I get mail from home?" she asked. "What if I don't write back?"

"It won't matter much, will it? The dates are only a few weeks away."

"How will I feel, getting letters? How will I be able to work?"

"You'll work," Lanier said, "knowing that if we get the answer soon enough, we might be able to do something about it."

She stared hard at the ground with its dry, yellow grass. "They said shuttle landing areas were bombed. In that book."

"Yes."

"If it happens, we'll be stuck up here, won't we?"

"Yes. Most of us. We won't want to go back soon, anyway."

"That's why you've started farming. We won't get anything from Earth for . . . how long?"

"If there's a war, and it's as described, perhaps thirty years."

"I . . . I can't go into the library now. Is that all right, if I stay out here for a while?"

"Sure. Let's return to the first chamber and have dinner. And remember—I've had to live with this information for some time now. There's no reason you can't, as well."

She got to her feet without responding. Her legs and hands were steady. She was in amazingly good shape, considering. "Let's go," she said.

Chapter Eleven

The travelers gathered by the truck two hours into the morning shift, looking like nothing so much as a bunch of backpackers about to set off on a hike. The truck was very full after loading.

Patricia sat between Takahashi and a brawny mohawked marine named Reynolds. Reynolds was armed with an Apple and a compact machine pistol. Carrolson sat beside the driver, American navy lieutenant Jerry Lake, a tall outdoorsy-looking fellow with sand-colored hair. Lake glanced over the back of his seat to see that everything was in order, nodded to Takahashi and smiled at Patricia. "My men have orders to protect Miss Vasquez at all costs. So don't run away without permission."

"Yes, sir," Patricia said quietly. Takahashi—short, half Japanese, well muscled, with close-cropped black hair and large self-assured green eyes, returned Lake's nod. Takahashi was the only one wearing Earthside clothes—a cotton shirt, windbreaker and denim pants. "Dispensation," he had explained back by the tent. "I'm allergic to the dye in the overalls."

Lake urged the truck forward. Carrolson checked off their equipment as Farley read a slate list.

The truck carried a total of eight passengers, four military men and four "principals," as Carrolson referred to the scientists and Patricia.

Patricia kept her eyes on the seat in front of her. In her pocket was a letter from Paul, delivered to her in the first chamber the shift before.

Dear Patricia,

Wherever you are, my mystery woman, I hope all is well. Life here is mundane—especially when I think of where you *might* be—but it goes. I keep in touch with your folks—Rita's a doll and Ramon and I have had some pretty good conversations. I've learned a lot about you behind your back. Hope you don't mind. My applications to Prester and Minton (two software manufacturers) have been processed, I hear, but things are on hold until the Defense Platform appropriations bill passes. There's some talk about a filibuster and that could screw things up for months.

Enough talk of that. I miss you *desperately*. Rita asked me if we were going to get married and I kept mum, just as you want. I do want to; you know that. I don't care how weird you are, or where you are right now; just come back and give me a nod. We'll find our own home. Don't be too stubborn this time. Well, enough of this; you probably have other fish to fry, and my particular floppings and slappings on the bank—where you have beached me with your line—are just distractions. (Now, you know I can't end a letter without something clumsy and confusing.) I love you. Neat, prim kisses.

Paul

111

She had typed up a long, self-censored reply, showed it to Carrolson for approval, and had it sent Earthside on the next OTV.

Surprisingly, writing the letter had been easy. In it, she said all the things she knew Paul would want to hear, all the things she thought needed to be said if, indeed, Paul was going to be dead in a few weeks. Not that she had really accepted that possibility. If she had, she wouldn't be as calm as she was.

Lanier was on his way to Earth by now. Patricia envied him. She would rather be on Earth, waiting to die, than up here, facing what she knew.

No, that wasn't really true. She closed her eyes and cursed herself. This was the most responsibility she had ever had. She had to overcome her crazy grief and fear and work as best she could to *prevent*.

And—she almost hated herself for it—she *was* working. Her mind was in the state, finally. Solutions were starting to come to her, presenting themselves like suitors, all formally dressed in equations, each rejected when its inadequacies became apparent.

Takahashi seemed a bright and conscientious fellow, but Patricia hadn't felt like talking as the expedition had gathered, and so she knew little about him. Takahashi and Carrolson would be her seconds in almost everything from now on, Lanier had said.

The road ended fifty kilometers from the base camp. The truck lurched into a shallow gully, its rubber-tired band-metal-spoke wheels making their queer singing noise on the dirt. The forward aspect of the corridor didn't change as they advanced. The southern cap receded slowly, steadily, and became less overwhelming. Patricia didn't feel comfortable angling for a view, however, so she caught only brief glimpses as they traveled. Carrolson, Farley and Takahashi played chess on a slate as Patricia watched inattentively.

"Halfway," Lake said two hours later. The chess players recorded their moves and cleared the slate as the truck slowed and came to a smooth stop. The doors slid aside and the

112

marines climbed down with groans of relief. Patricia slid after them and stood on the dry dirt, stretching and yawning. Carrolson came around from the opposite side of the truck, water cooler in hand, and poured drinks into their cups. "All the luxuries," she said.

"Beer?" Reynolds asked.

"Sacrificed to science," Carrolson said. "Anybody hungry?"

Patricia removed a sandwich from the kit and walked with Takahashi a few dozen meters away from the truck. For a time, she had felt a floating sense of anxiety and nausea, but that had dissipated. How could there be anything to fear in an endless stretch of desert, devoid even of insects? The very blandness was comforting, a blank slate.

" 'The sea was wet as wet could be, the sand was dry as dry,' " she said.

"Indeed," Takahashi agreed. She squatted on the dirt and he sat beside her, folding his legs into an easy lotus. "Do you know why I'm along on this trip?"

His approach was awkwardly direct. She looked away from him. "No doubt to keep an eye on me."

"Yes. Lanier said you should be observed diligently. How are you holding up?"

"Well enough."

"The library . . ." He lowered his voice and stared back at the cap. "It isn't easy."

"Pretty soon I'm going to feel like a royal princess, surrounded by retainers."

Takahashi chuckled. "It won't get that bad. I'll keep Lanier's worries in check. But I have to ask one important question. Can you work?"

Patricia knew precisely what he meant. "I *am* working. Right this minute."

"Good." No more needed to be said on that topic.

She plucked a branch of scrub to see if the growth differed from the variety near the camp. It didn't—small leaves, waxy surfaces. Even the dry grass was the same. "Not a garden spot," she said. "At least I expected some more dwarf forests."

"It gets worse," Takahashi said.

"Have you ever considered how much dirt they had to bring into the corridor?" she asked, standing up. She had taken only a few bites from her sandwich. She hadn't been hungry for two days. "If the dirt is about a quarter kilometer deep—"

"So we estimate from sounding," Takahashi said.

"And let's say the corridor is a billion kilometers long . . ."

"Why that figure?"

"Just a guess," she said. "That makes about forty billion kilometers of dirt."

"If we broke the Earth down and paved the corridor with it—crust, magma and core—we could cover about thirty billion kilometers." Takahashi poked his finger into a sandy patch.

"What if they have mountains farther on? Even more dirt and rock required, then."

"That's possible," Takahashi said. "But the big question is, Where did they get it all? And don't forget the air. It's about twenty kilometers deep, so that would make . . . one point six trillion cubic kilometers of air, at just over a gram a liter—"

"You've worked all this out before."

"Of course. Many times. Rimskaya started it, and the statistics people carried on. I kibitzed. So many questions about logistics and design. How does the air get renewed in the corridor? The Stone's regeneration ponds couldn't possibly keep up with it, not if there's any sizable population of animals farther on. So maybe there's just enough air to last a few thousand years."

"That doesn't seem right," Patricia said. "Whoever—or whatever—set this up, designed it for eternity. Don't you get that feeling?"

"Sometimes. Doesn't mean it's a valid assumption."

"Still, there must be some kind of corridor maintenance system."

114

Takahashi nodded. "Rimskaya theorized there would be openings in the corridor even before we discovered the wells."

Carrolson joined them. "Ever notice what the corridor smells like?" she asked.

Patricia and Takahashi shook their heads.

"Smells just like before a storm. All the time. But the ozone levels aren't very high. Another mystery."

Patricia sniffed the air. It smelled fresh, but not like a brewing storm.

"I was *raised* in storm country," Carrolson said defensively. "That's the smell, all right."

Back in the truck, continuing the journey, Patricia spent much of the time doing problems on the processor, figuring volumes and masses and putting them all into a small table.

An hour later, Takahashi pointed out the first circuit, four wells at the quadrilateral points of a ring. Each well sat in the middle of a dimple about half a kilometer in diameter and twenty meters deep. In the center of the dimple was an inverted bronze-colored dish fifteen meters wide, suspended eight meters above the bowl. The dish hovered in empty air, unsupported.

The truck slowed near the rim of the dimple. At Takahashi's request, Lake drove them around the well before stopping. They climbed down and approached the rim.

"We've made about twenty trips to this circuit," Takahashi said. "Beaten a path, almost."

Patricia held her multi-meter before her. The value of *pi* held steady. She knelt down and hung the instrument over the rim. The readout remained the same.

"Now step into the depression," Takahashi suggested. The marines, Farley, Carrolson and Takahashi stood beyond the rim in a group. She wrinkled her nose at them. "Another initiation? You first, then."

"That would spoil the fun," Carrolson said. "Go ahead."

Patricia pushed one foot forward, then put her weight onto the sloping, sandy soil.

"All the way," Lake urged.

115

She sighed and walked into the dimple. Ten meters from the rim, feeling peculiar, she looked back. Her body was not inclined at the same angle as the others. Dizzy, she tried to right herself and almost fell over. The natural stance was along the radius of curvature, as if the corridor force followed the curve of the bowl. Yet there was no local distortion of space registering on the multi-meter. The rest of the group followed after.

In the shadow of the floating dish was a slightly protruding bronze-colored plug about half as wide. Takahashi walked across the plug to show it was safe. Patricia followed, multi-meter again at the fore. No change.

"Any idea what holds the dish up?" she asked. Farley and Carrolson shrugged. The marines sat in the sand around the well, looking bored.

"That may not be an appropriate question," Takahashi said. "Look at the material of the dish and plug—up close. As far as we can tell, it's the same stuff as the corridor walls."

Patricia kneeled and ran her hands along the plug's surface. The color was not uniformly bronze. There seemed to be red and green streaks, even spots of black, merging, separating and twisting in the surface like worms.

"This stuff is geometry, too, then?" Patricia asked.

"It isn't matter," Carrolson said. "We ruled that out just after the wells were discovered."

"It took us all some time to get used to the idea of using space as a building material," Takahashi said. Farley nodded emphatically.

"Not at all," Patricia said coolly. "I wrote about it four years ago. If nested universes are somehow kept from assuming one definite state, a barrier against penetration will form due to continous opposed spacial transforms."

Takahashi smiled but Carrolson and Farley simply stared. "So," Takahashi said, "nothing supports the dish. It doesn't have any real existence. It's simply a shaped jam-up of probabilities. Makes perfect sense."

116

"Oh," Farley said.

Lake sat in the middle of the plug, Apple lying across his knees. "I'm just a small-town boy from Michigan," he said. "But it sure feels solid. It isn't even slippery."

"Good point," Patricia said. She reached down to feel it with her palms. "There apparently isn't total separation of probabilistic states. Some interaction between matter and the surface is allowed, besides resistance to intrusion." She put her multi-meter directly on the surface. The value of *pi* fluctuated wildly, then stabilized: *3.141487233 continuous*. "*Pi*'s down," she said. She invoked the other constants. "Gravitational constant is nominal, speed of electromagnetic radiation is nominal and stable."

"Slash aitch?" Carrolson asked.

"The same. What purpose do the wells serve?"

"This circuit is capped, so it serves no purpose we can determine."

"The wells may give access to something outside the corridor," Takahashi said. "We decided against finding out where they lead. But the wells were not plugged, and the sand was kept out of the central hole by a spongy field of force, nature unknown. The only thing we could see was red light coming up out of each well. We sent a little drone helicopter into one well. It didn't come back. Our viewing angle was such that we couldn't see it after it traveled about ten meters. We decided against sending anybody after it."

"Wisely," Carrolson said.

Lake, still sitting, said laconically, "My men are ready to go as far as you'd like, any time you like."

"We appreciate that, Lieutenant," Carrolson said. "But we have good reasons for taking these things slowly."

"Give me an all-environment suit and a weapon, a couple of backups . . ." He grinned.

"You'd really go down?" Patricia asked, turning to the officer with an incredulous expression.

Lake grimaced. "If we were reasonably sure about the

117

general category of things to see and experience, I'd go. We'd all go." The marines nodded in unison. "Duty here hasn't been all that exciting. Outside of the obvious scenic values."

"We dug all around the dimple," Takahashi said, edging up the slope and pointing with extended arms to indicate placement of the holes. He picked up a handful of dirt and let it sift between his fingers. "The dirt in all the wells is dry. No microorganisms, no large life forms, no plants."

"No living things . . . except us," Farley said.

"And no radiation," Takahashi continued. "No traces of unusual chemistry. So maybe these closed wells are just survey markers."

"Benchmarks of the gods," Carrolson intoned.

"Each well is alike?" Patricia asked.

"As far as we know," Takahashi said. "We've only examined two circuits."

Reynolds stood and brushed sand from his overalls. "Hey, Lieutenant. Maybe this is where boojums come from."

Lake rolled his eyes.

"Have you ever seen a boojum?" Patricia asked, looking intently at the marine.

"I don't think anyone has," Carrolson said.

"Mr. Reynolds?"

Reynolds glanced between Lake and Patricia. "Am I really being asked?"

"Yes," Patricia said. "I'm asking." She tapped her badge, uncertain whether that carried any weight with the marines.

"I've never seen one," Reynolds admitted. "But others have, others that I trust."

"We've all heard about 'em," another marine named Huckle said. "Some guys are full of stories."

"Still," Lake said, "these men aren't prone to seeing things that aren't there. The reports are few, but interesting."

Patricia nodded. "Are there any plans to descend into a well?"

"Not so far," Takahashi said. "We have other problems to face."

She looked down at the plug, rubbing her boot across the surface. "I'd like to see the complete expedition report when we get back," she said.

For the first time, a solution had presented itself—even as they talked—that had survived the first level of criticism. She looked up at the inverted dish, at the minutely active colors.

"Shall we return, then?" Takahashi asked.

"I think so," Patricia said.

The Frant used an adapted pictor to project the objects and landscapes around them and camouflage their activity in and about the tent. The two guards, dressed in black, might hear Olmy if he was especially noisy, but they wouldn't see him. He walked within a few dozen centimeters of one guard on his way to the box that served Patricia Luisa Vasquez as a desk.

He was particularly interested in the young woman; from what he had heard, she was becoming central to the group's endeavors. And if she was the same woman he had heard the Engineer speak of . . .

On the box, notes filled perhaps fifty sheets of paper, arranged in no apparent order. Many of the notes were scribbled over or heavily blacked out; sometimes entire pages, except for a few square centimeters of equations or diagrams, were obscured by hard-pressed pencil marks. He leafed through the sheets quietly, puzzling over Patricia's private notation.

A slate lay on one corner, its silver-gray screen blank. A memory block had been plugged into the aperture in the right side of the slate, just above the small keyboard. Olmy glanced around, checking for the position of the guards, and kneeled beside the slate, turning it on. Learning how to use the antique was not difficult; in a few minutes, he had it rapidly scrolling up the contents of the memory block. He recorded the series of files in his implant for later analysis; this took about four minutes.

From what he could see and understand of her work, she was quite advanced for her century.

He was arranging the papers into their previous order when a guard came around the corner of the tent and stared in his direction. Olmy stood slowly, certain the picted camouflage was still effective.

"You hear anything, Norman?" Sergeant Jack Teague asked his colleague.

"No."

"Puff of wind or something? I could have sworn I heard these papers moving."

"Just another boojum, Jack."

Teague approached the box and looked down at the papers. "Jesus," he murmured. "Wonder what this stuff is." He bent and ran his fingers just above the line of symbols. There were cursive letters mixed with bold black lowercase letters; double upright bars reminiscent of the matrix symbols he had studied in flight school, integral signs, exponents containing German gothic letters and Greek letters, squiggles and triangles and lopsided circles with double dots in the middle, letters with single and double dots like umlauts over them . . .

"What a mess," Sergeant Teague said, rising again. His neck hair bristled and he sniffed the air, twisting suddenly.

Of course, nothing was there. What did he expect?

Chapter Twelve

Lanier had slept through most of the two-day OTV ride, head full of weightless dreams indiscriminately mixing the Stone and Earth, past and future.

He looked at his watch and then at the face of the secret service agent sitting beside him in the limousine. There was an eighteen-hour lag between the time he had landed at Vandenberg and the time he would report to Hoffman's office at the Jet

Propulsion Laboratory. Outside the smoke-colored car window, desert flashed by. The air pressure was high and the gravitation oppressive. Even through the dark windows, the sun was hot and yellow.

He missed the Stone.

"I have some spare time," he said.

"Yessir." The agent looked straight ahead, face pleasantly bland.

"You fellows are discreet."

"Oh, yessir. We are that," the driver said. The agent seated beside the driver glanced back at Lanier.

"Ms. Hoffman says we're at your disposal, but we're to have you in Pasadena, alive and sober, by eight o'clock tomorrow morning."

Lanier wondered how Hoffman would react to being called "Ms." "Gentlemen," he said. "I've been celibate for more months than I care to count. Rank hath its responsibilities. Is there a safe place in Los Angeles where one can get . . ." He searched for a phrase as antique as "Ms." ". . . one's ashes hauled? Discreetly, charmingly, cleanly."

"Yessir," said the driver.

He was allowed two drinks in a fancy but ancient hangout known as the Polo Lounge, surrounded by aged relics of the bad old days of network television. By three o'clock in the afternoon, two suites in the Beverly Hills Hotel—directly opposite one another—were checked out. The agents efficiently inspected the suite where he would stay and pronounced the rooms safe with a nod to each other.

He finally had some illusion of privacy. He took a shower, lay on the bed, almost drifted off. How long would it take for him to get used to the extra weight? How would it affect his performance?

The woman who arrived at five was stunningly beautiful, very friendly, and ultimately—through no fault of her own—unsatisfying. He judged his performance as adequate, but the act brought little joy. She left at ten.

121

Lanier had never resorted to a prostitute before. His physical passions, with a few notable exceptions, had never been as persistent as those of other men.

At ten-fifteen, there was a light knock on his door. He opened it, and the agent who had driven the limousine from the desert landing site passed him information on two memory blocks. "Ms. Hoffman sends these to you with her compliments," he said. "We'll be just across the hall, if you need anything."

The memory blocks he had brought with him from the Stone—more precious than Lanier himself—had been transferred to separate, more secure vehicles and driven carefully into Pasadena that day. No doubt, the Advisor would be going over the blocks even now.

He shut out all the lights and lay on the bed, staring at the ceiling, wondering how many of the aged executives in the Polo lounge the call girl had serviced in her young life.

He had never been comfortable with desire. This time, he had not felt desire as much as obligation to the flesh. After so many months of deprivation—more like a year, actually—it seemed likely the body had requirements it was no longer communicating to him.

That at least would have hinted at normality. He had always felt vaguely guilty at his coolness—if that was the right word. Guilty and grateful. It gave him much more time to think, without constant distraction or diversion of purpose.

The coolness had also kept him a bachelor. He had had his share of lovers, but work and accomplishment had always won out. Lovers had become friends more often than not—and had married other friends.

A very civilized situation.

Sleep. Gravid dreams, heavy and dark. He was captain of a huge luxury liner on a black ocean, and each time he peered over the side to check the water level, the ship dropped a meter or two. By the end of the dream he was in a panic. The Earth's gravity was dragging the ship beneath the sea, and he was the

122

captain, and the ship was the most beautiful he had ever commanded. He was losing it, and he simply could not abandon it by waking up. . . .

At eight o'clock the next morning, Lanier walked across the concrete quadrangle of the Jet Propulsion Laboratory, briefcase in hand, accompanied by two new agents. He enjoyed the bright sun and the increased weight more now and almost regretted the thought of spending the day in air-conditioned offices. The first of two, perhaps three scheduled sessions would take place in the VIP conference room.

He popped a pill to knock down a runny nose, drank from a bronze fountain in a newly planted park, and slowed to a saunter past the broad black-background panel displaying JPL projects. Mars development activity schedules vied with Solar Sail reports and a hologram of the proposed Proxima Centauri probe.

There was no mention of the second ABE—asteroid belt explorer—launched two years ago.

Lanier and his gray-suited shadows climbed the steps slowly, allowing for his gravity fatigue, and passed through heavy-glass security doors. He presented his card to a monitor, and the steel gate swung wide with a pleasant hum. The agents did not enter with him. Beyond was a hallway lined by display cases. Intricate small-scale replicas of the Jet Propulsion Laboratory's past triumphs glittered in their plastic boxes: *Voyager, Galileo,* the Drake and the Solar Sail. There were also OTV models and diagrams explaining the Star Probe concept.

He took an aging elevator to the sixth floor, staring up at the glowing blue numbers.

Another secret service agent awaited him and asked for his ID again as the elevator door opened. Lanier took the card from his pocket and lined it up beside his badge. The agent thanked him and smiled as he walked on, unaccompanied, to the conference room.

Hoffman sat at the end of a long black table. Piles of paper, two slates and a clutter of memory blocks were arranged before her. To her left sat Peter Hague, the President's representative to ISCCOM, and on the other side, Alice Cronberry, advisor on aerospace security and project manager of the second ABE. Lanier walked around the table and shook hands, Hoffman's first—warmly cupping her hand in both of his—then Cronberry's and Hague's.

"I see Joint Space Command and the Joint Chiefs have no representatives here," he said, sitting at the opposite end of the table.

"We'll get to that in a moment," Hoffman said. She had aged since he last saw her; her hair was grayer, she looked more matronly and her wrinkles had transformed from smile to frown. "You're looking fit, Garry." She was being polite.

"Feeling less fit."

"How is Patricia Vasquez doing?"

"As well as can be expected. I was called away before I had much chance to see her at work, or before she came up with any results."

"I take it," Hoffman said, "that means you're uncertain about her."

"I am," Lanier said. "Not because I don't think she's capable, or the best in her field—whatever that may be—but because she's young. The library was quite a shock to her."

Cronberry put her right hand flat on the table, leaning away from him slightly. "It was a shock to all of us," she said.

Hoffman passed a sheet of paper down to him. "We've studied the material you brought with you. We've already made our final report to the President."

"Before Vasquez tells us anything?"

"I doubt she'll tell us what we'd like to hear. Call it instinct, but I think we're in deep trouble." Hoffman's eyes focused on an empty space over Lanier's shoulder. "We've verified some of the information from the library."

Lanier inspected their faces intently. They were all unhappy; even trying to hide their emotions, they revealed that much. "And?"

"There are divergencies."

"Thank God," he said. Hoffman raised a hand.

"Not broad divergencies. The consensus here is, given the information from the library and what we've discovered since—from the second ABE and elsewhere—war is a definite possibility. We've verified the historical references to Party Secretary Vasiliev. He has restructured the Defense Council just as the library said he would. The Russians are deploying SS-45's on their Kiev-class carriers and Kirov-class guided missile cruisers, and of course the Typhoon and Delta IV supersubs, to match our Sea Dragon program. They do indeed know how to foil our multi-spectra laser communication systems, which puts them in violation of the 1996 Arms Elimination Accords . . . not that that is in itself important, since no arms were ever eliminated."

Lanier nodded.

"We had to get tough to pry the information about the multi-spectra systems out of the Joint Space Force," Cronberry said. "That's one reason why the DOD and Joint Chiefs have no rep here."

"That's not the worst," Hoffman continued. "Congress is beginning inquiries on our budget. We've been well within appropriations, so that doesn't make sense, unless we take into account a push to discredit the library, the Stone, all of us. The President is convinced—has been convinced by several members of his cabinet—that the Stone is either fraudulent or irrelevant."

Lanier's clenched his jaw tightly, making his cheeks ache. "Why?"

"I suspect the President is incapable of understanding what you've found on the Stone. He's a solid midwestern liberal, very weak on science and technology. An administrator, no imagination. He's never been comfortable with space matters, and this is simply beyond him."

Cronberry pulled a copy of a letter on White House stationery out of her briefcase and handed it to Lanier. It said, in effect, that the President was considering launching an investigation into the way research was being conducted on the Stone. "That was written after we began passing reports to the White House from the Second ABE imaging team, and after confirmation of the library evidence."

"We wanted to get the Vice-President up to the Stone by week's end, but he's declined the invitation," Hoffman said.

"What's the Russian position on the Stone?" Lanier asked.

"They secretly launched their own asteroid belt probe two years ago. That probe returned confirmation to them before or about the same time as ABE. They know that there is indeed a very large asteroid which precisely matches the Stone."

"Juno?"

"Yes. The imaging match is perfect, allowing for the excavations."

Lanier hadn't heard about the confirmation from the second ABE until now. "So Juno and the Stone really are the same."

Hoffman passed down a file of ABE and near-Earth surveillance photos. One ABE picture showed Juno, a sweet-potato-shaped chunk of primordial planetary material covered with craters and rills. The Stone was identical, but lined with excavations and dimpled with the bore-hole depressions. "God," Lanier said.

"I don't think He's the one to blame," Hoffman said. "Perhaps your Konrad Korzenowski is."

"At any rate," Hague said, "the Russians are going to pull their team out within three weeks, perhaps sooner. They're upset because we deny them complete access, when we allow the Chinese as far as the seventh chamber. That's their excuse, and frankly, it's a good one. I'd be pissed, too. But it doesn't explain everything."

"They agreed to those divisions a year ago, when we set up team responsibilities," Lanier said, frowning.

"Yes, but apparently there have been more leaks," Hague said.

"Oh, Christ." *Who?*

"And," Hague continued, "they are now claiming that we misled them as to the contents of the libraries."

126

"Which we did," Hoffman said, smiling faintly.

"Can the science team get along without the Russians?" Cronberry asked.

"Yes. They're mostly working on inner-chamber plasma tube power-supply theory. We can get along without them, but a lot of important research will slow way down, perhaps come to a stop. What about Beijing?"

Cronberry leafed through a folder of personnel papers. Hague reached across and drew one out. "Karen Farley is a Chinese citizen, and she's working for you on theoretical physics, correct?"

"Yes. She's made herself useful in all sorts of areas." *Oh, please, not Farley—not Wu and Chang—*

"She and her colleagues are to be withdrawn if the Russians leave."

"Why the coordination?" Lanier asked.

"The Chinese smell a rat," Hoffman said. "Or a rout. If the Russians feel they are being misled and kept out of important decisions, the Chinese have similar grounds for complaint. Their own presence might be more advantageous to us than to them."

"I can't believe either group would give up a place on the Stone. I wouldn't."

"They won't," Hoffman said. "We have evidence that both the Russians and the Chinese have clandestine operatives in the security team, perhaps even in the science team. And there have been interesting activities in Russian orbital space and on the Moon. Not to mention heightened activity at Tyuratam and the Indian Ocean launch site."

"Invasion from Earth and Moon?"

Hoffman shook her head. "Look, this is all chickenshit compared to the big question. Has Vasquez come up with *anything*? What does she have to say about parallel worlds, alternate histories?"

"She hasn't had time to say much of anything," Lanier said quietly. "In a few weeks, we might know."

"I understand the President's point of view. I find this very hard to believe," Cronberry said. "Is it your opinion that the Stone comes from *our* future?"

"No," Lanier said. "The Stone comes from another universe, not precisely our own. That much is certain. There's one obvious difference."

"No Stone in the Stone's past," Hague said.

"Exactly."

"And we have no way of knowing how much the Stone is affecting the course of our history."

"It's changing things a lot, I'd say," Hoffman remarked. "If anything, the Stone has made things worse." She held up a memory block marked "Plant Physiology Changes under Plasma Tube Conditions." "You made this copy yourself?" She passed it to Cronberry, then to Hague.

Lanier nodded. "It's in S-code," he said. "It's a summary from the best sources, mostly from the third chamber library. Vasquez should be going into the third chamber in a few days."

"What does it summarize?" Hague asked, hefting it.

"The first two weeks of the war."

Cronberry flinched.

Hoffman took a slate, programmed it for reading S-code, plugged in the block and skimmed over the material. Her face went ashen. "I haven't looked at this before," she said.

"It's mostly historical photographic records made by the armed forces on both sides. Some of the stuff toward the end chronicles the Long Winter."

"So that's not just theory anymore," Hague said.

Lanier shook his head.

"How long was . . . will . . . the winter be?" Cronberry asked, reluctantly accepting the slate from Hoffman.

"One or two years in its major effects."

Hague took the slate from Cronberry. "You guarantee this material is from the third chamber library?"

Lanier swallowed before answering, irritated. "I could hardly have conjured it out of thin air."

"Of course not," Hoffman said. "If the libraries are

128

correct—if our universes coincide in this one way—then we have about sixteen days?"

"One way or another, we'll know by then," Lanier said. "Although the knowledge of the events will almost certainly shape the results. If. If they happen at all."

"We're scheduling a meeting with the Russians tomorrow at noon," Hoffman said. "Strictly informal. They've asked that you be there. Mr. Hague's department has pushed very hard for State Department and DOD approval of the meeting. If those talks succeed, there will be other meetings below the cabinet level. And if we can convince the President before next week, perhaps a summit will be arranged." She blinked slowly in his direction, still focusing somewhere over his shoulder—not quite the thousand-yard stare of a battle-weary veteran, but very nearly.

Chapter Thirteen

The third chamber city was the next step.

Having made the trip to the first circuit of wells, and having absorbed as much as she could from the books in the Alexandria library selected for her by Lanier, Patricia felt herself numbing nicely to the whole subject. It was a game, an exercise, no more real than the odd mathematical exercises she had made up as a teenager.

She had ridden the trains *beneath* Thistledown City so many times in the past two weeks, but the third chamber was the most closely guarded of the first five. The trains had never stopped—until now.

Rupert Takahashi escorted her from the subway station to the ground-level walkways.

Takahashi served the science team in an unusual capacity. His title of mathematician was hardly sufficient description of what he did; he seemed to move from interest to interest, working with one group on one day and another the next. He was more than a generalist—he was a generalist with a specific purpose, to oversee the mathematical and statistical rigor of the various groups within the science team. That explained how he had come to work with Rimskaya on preliminary corridor theory; they had discussed the topic while Takahashi double-checked Rimskaya's population studies.

Thistledown City was astonishing, newer than Alexandria by two centuries; it had been built after the Stone's launch, incorporating designs not thought of until the inhabitants had had long experience with their environment. Here the Stone architects had allowed themselves complete freedom. Treating the chamber as a giant valley, they had strung cables from cap to cap and hung buildings from them in graceful curves. Taking advantage of the upward slope of the floor, they had built arched structures fully ten kilometers long, bands of steel and processed Stone material interacting in patterns of silver and white, casting soft-edged shadows over the neighborhoods below. Some of the structures rose to the very limits of the chamber's atmosphere; these were actually thicker at the top than the bottom, like golf tees.

Even empty, Thistledown City seemed alive. It would take only the merest suggestion of people to come to life, Patricia thought; a few hundred citizens, moving from building to building, dressed in outrageous clothes—colorful, flowing garments suited to the curves and vaults and arches, bright colors to contrast with the muted creams, whites and metallics of the city.

The main library was practically hidden beneath a sprawling annex of one of the smaller golf-tee structures. Takahashi had said it was within easy walking distance, so they strolled across plazas, over pedestrian bridges, alongside service roads that at one time would have teemed with traffic—mostly computer-controlled and unoccupied vehicles. "All the vehicles are gone," Takahashi said. "We only know what they looked like through the records. They must have been put to use in the exodus."

She tried to imagine tens of millions of Stoners—such a population could easily have been accommodated by Thistle-

130

down City alone—tooling off down the corridor in their robot cars.

The library entrance was a solid sheet of a material resembling black marble. As they approached, an amplified voice asked them to halt for identification. They stood for a full two minutes before being cleared to enter.

A broad half-ellipse flowed aside in the black expanse. Beyond waited the ubiquitous security team in gray and black, passing them through after more ritual. The interior of the library was fully illuminated; no additional strip lighting was necessary. "No circuit breakers in Thistledown," Takahashi said. "We're not even sure how the power gets to the lights, much less where it comes from."

The library proper was smaller in overall volume than its cousin—or ancestor—in Alexandria and had no visible stores of records. The main floor was a pastel-blue-carpeted plaza beneath a sheet of softly glowing white material which stretched without support for a hundred meters. The plaza was dotted with at least a thousand lime-green padded seats. In front of each seat was a chromium teardrop on a slate-gray pedestal.

The fabrics and materials in the library showed no sign of wear or decay.

Takahashi led her to a seat. Recording and monitoring equipment surrounded the seat, looking out-of-place and obviously rigged by the investigators. "We use this one normally, but the choice is yours."

She shook her head, "I don't like all this stuff," she said, indicating the equipment. Moving through the ranks of seats, she chose one about twenty meters from the edge of the array and sat.

Takahashi followed. "You can show yourself the entire Stone from here—as it used to be," he said. "Would you like a tour of the cities when they were occupied?" He pushed aside a fabric-covered lid on her seat arm and showed her how to use the simple controls on the panel beneath. "These are just the basics. There are hundreds of other tricks possible. Feel free to experiment. Think of it as a vacation. It's no fun to watch, and I have no real business here except to show you the ropes, so I'll wait outside. Join me when you're done—say in an hour or so?"

She didn't feel easy about being on the plaza alone, and she had deeply appreciated Lanier's staying with her in the Alexandria library. Still, she agreed with a nod and settled into the seat, manipulating the controls with one hand. A simple circular graphic display hovered before her, as crisp and clear as something solid. Takahashi had misinformed her on one point, and her fumbling triggered a tutorial. It corrected her errors and informed her—in only slightly accented American English—how to operate the equipment properly. Then it provided her with call numbers and codes for other types of information.

She called up a student's basic guide to the second chamber city. In an instant, Alexandria surrounded her. She appeared to be standing on the portico of an apartment in the lower floors of one of the megas, looking down on the busy streets. The illusion was perfect—even providing her with a memory of what "her" apartment looked like. She could turn her head and look completely behind her if she wished—indeed, she could walk around, even though she knew she was sitting down.

In both her ears—or somewhere in the middle of her head—a voice explained what she was seeing.

She spent half an hour in Alexandria, observing the clothes the people wore, their faces, their hair styles and expressions and ways of moving. Some of the outfits attracted her. Others were positively puritanical—in a slinky sort of way. One of the most popular styles at the time of the record, for women, was an opaque robe—usually in pink or dusty orange—with hood, capped by a small crimson disk of some feathery material. Some women wore hexagonal blue designs on their left shoulder blades—

("?"

(*For information on insignia of office and rank, positively and silently vocalize the following code string. . . .*)

132

—and others red ribbons draped over the right shoulder, terminating in gold beads. Men's clothing was no less flamboyant, or somber; the distinctions seemed to point up sexual attitudes quite different from those in her time, her world.

She heard them speaking. It was a peculiar speech, resembling Welsh but occasionally understandable as English or French.

("What language did you—this unit—speak to me, and how did you know?"

(*Late twenty-first-century English, the earliest accessible without specific code, selected because of your conversation before access to data.*)

While ethnic populations still retained versions of their mother tongues, many of the languages had mutated into a common tongue—though she was informed subliminally that fashions in language were much more variable over shorter periods of time. Rapid changes were possible because learning had been accelerated by tutorial devices such as those in the library. One could learn any new language or variation in a few hours, or mere minutes.

For the written languages she understood, many of the spellings had been simplified or—paradoxically—made more complex. Had there been a time when flowery spelling was in vogue?

(*This is the famous Nader Plaza, which won awards for architectural excellence before the Thistledown vessel left Earth behind. . . .*)

She listened attentively, completely lost in the experience. Some men wore kilt-like skirts and unyoked sleeves, others wore business suits that would not have been out of place in twenty-first-century Los Angeles. Shoes seemed to have gone completely out of fashion, perhaps because automated sanitation kept everything spotless.

(What about social deviation? Ghettos and tenements?)

The scene shifted dizzily.

(*Social unease in Alexandria and the rest of the Stone is not*

133

unknown. Certain districts have been kept free of constant city maintenance. The citizens living in these districts have chosen to avoid all modern conveniences, and shirk any equipment invented after the twentieth century. Their wishes are strictly observed; they are often honored citizens, and they are entitled to their belief that technology led to the Death, and that God wishes us to live with no supports not mentioned in the works of the Gentle Nader and his Apostles of the Mountain.)

She had heard the name *Nader* mentioned several times, but it took her some time to get around to toggling a different branch of the "footnote" function. As she did so, she asked for explanations of several other things any Stoner would have taken for granted. That triggered an elementary, synopsized history of the Stone, and of the time between the Death and the construction of the Thistledown.

She was more than a little shocked to discover that the Gentle Nader was, in fact, Ralph Nader, the consumer advocate and independent investigator who had made a big stir in the 1960s and 1970s. He was still alive, back on Earth—her Earth, her time—but in the library records his name was always used reverently. He was always "Gentle Nader" or "the Good Man." Those who took his name—the Naderites— were a powerful political force, and had been for centuries. Or . . . *would be.* She vowed to use the physicist's concept of time from here on, with events strung along a line, and no particular breakdown into past, present or future.

After the Death, the hideous Long Winter and the Recovery Revolutions, a Spaniard named Diego Garcia de Santillana rose to power in the remains of Western Europe, under the banner of the Return to Life movement. He initiated a tentative push for world government. The next year, in 2010 (*just five years from now*, she thought, breaking her vow) the first Naderite coalitions formed in North America. Nader—"martyred" during the Death—had been chosen for his stand against nuclear energy and excessive technology; however just or unjust the elevation, he became a saintly figure, a hero in a wasteland still filled with fear and rage against what the human

134

race had done to itself. In 2011, the Naderites absorbed the Return to Lifers, and the re-emerging governments of North America and Western Europe made pacts of exchange and cooperation. Naderite governments were put into office by landslide elections and immediate curbs were sought on high technology and nuclear research. "Agrarianize!" became the rallying cry of a third of the world economy, and the Raiders— an elite, somewhat shadowy organization—fanned out around the world to "persuade" reluctant governments to join in. In Russia, the revolution of 2012, staged by Naderite sympathizers, brought down the last Council government of the USSR, which had already retreated into its center of power, the Russian Soviet Federal Socialist Republic. Nations throughout the Eastern bloc regained their political sovereignty, and most of them went over to the Naderites.

That, at least, explained the prevalance of Nader's name in the records. Between 2015 and 2100, the followers of the Good Man consolidated their power over two-thirds of the world. The only dogged resistance in those decades was in Asia, where the Greater Asian Cooperative—made up of Japan, China, Southeast Asia (occasionally) and Malaysia— renounced Naderism and returned enthusiastically to scientific research and high technology, including nuclear energy. The first real opposition to the Naderites in the West began in 2100 with the Volks movement in Gross Deutschland—

She switched off the machine and lay back in the chair, rubbing her eyes. The information had come in printed displays, selected visuals and even more selected sounds. Where documentation of the multimedia sort was lacking, print took over, but with subtle and clear vocal accompaniment. Compared to this, simple reading was torture and current video methods as archaic as cave paintings.

If she were so inclined, she could pleasantly spend the rest of her life here, an eternal scholar parasitizing the knowledge of centuries neither she nor her ancestors had lived through.

Considering the alternatives she faced, that prospect was very attractive.

The hour was almost up.

She returned to the system briefly to look up information on the corridor, the exodus of the Stoners and the desertion of the cities. In each instance she was met with a very graphic floating spiked ball signaling no access.

Meeting Takahashi outside, where he was calmly smoking a cigarette—the first she had seen on the Stone—Patricia stretched her arms and neck. "I'm going to have to come back."

"Of course."

"Where to next?"

"A short tour. We can't walk to where we're going in any reasonable time, so we'll use a truck."

The garage for the third chamber trucks was a sheet metal shed nestled incongruously at the base of one of the chamber-spanning arches. A subway entrance opened nearby; the transit lines that had once served Thistledown City were no longer operative, however, and to get from one subway junction to anywhere else in the city, it was necessary to drive trucks along the narrow service roads.

"I can't access anything in the libraries on the exodus," Patricia said as Takahashi inspected a truck. He bent down to peer beneath the chassis, then stood straight and brushed his hands together.

"The archaeology group is working that out now. We should be back in time for their weekly report; that's at eleven hundred hours." He glanced at his watch. "It's oh nine hundred now. Everything seems to be shipshape. Shall we be off?"

He held the driver's door open for her. "Had your truck lessons yet?"

Patricia shook her head.

"It's about time, then, don't you think?"

She shrugged nervously.

"Not hard at all. Especially here. The service roads are easy to follow. We've learned the code for the signs on the walls that service machines used—not that different from bar codes on Earth. Replaces street signs. I just shine a pen reader on the signs near the corners and we know where we are. I tell you when to turn . . . you turn. All the service roads are surrounded by walls; you can't fall off anything even if you try. Okay?"

"Okay."

He climbed into the shotgun seat and showed her the column guidance system. "It's like an airplane in one respect—push the column forward and the truck moves forward; the farther you push, the faster it goes, up to a hundred klicks. Slow down by pulling the stick back to upright; reverse by pulling the stick toward you. Maximum speed in reverse is about ten klicks. Gear shifting is automatic. Grip the handles on the horizontal bar and twist the bar the direction you want to go. If you want to make a complete about-face without moving forward or back, just hold the column on the center line and twist the bar as far as it will go. The truck will rotate around its center line. Want to practice?"

"Of course." She maneuvered the truck back and forth around the garage. Using the stick as a brake took some getting used to. When she felt she was reasonably proficient, she smiled at Takahashi. "Let's go," she said.

"Catch on fast, don't you?"

"Don't speak too soon," she warned.

"Okay. Spin us around." He pointed out the nearest service entrance.

The walled service roads wound through and under the city's buildings, usually avoiding grades steeper than ten or fifteen degrees. In one section, however, the ride resembled a roller coaster. Takahashi coaxed her up and down the slopes. "We just passed over the main plumbing for this neighborhood," he explained.

Where the service roads became tunnels, and where the arches and other structures blocked out most of the tubelight, large milky panels cast a soft illumination. The city was without appreciable shadow; everything was cast in a rich and even light.

Takahashi suggested she slow down as they approached a

branch in the serviceway. He took a pen reader from his pocket and pointed it at a squiggle of lines of uneven thicknesses near the end of the left-hand wall. The pen was hooked to his slate, which displayed a map, a digital coordinate and directions to nearby points. "Left," he said. "We'll be entering the apartment building soon. By the back door, so to speak."

The serviceway soon passed beneath the plaza of a dazzling gold-surfaced cylindrical tower. Lights flashed at them as they passed, but the shape of the truck—or their presence within— did not trigger any automatic responses.

"Stop at that open door ahead," Takahashi said.

A sign mounted on a chain blocked the passageway to vehicle traffic. Patricia read the sign after stopping the truck and setting the parking brake.

NO TRUCKS OR PEDESTRIANS BEYOND THIS
POINT BY ORDER OF Y. JACOB
DIRECTOR ARCHAEOLOGY TEAM

"And he means it, too," Takahashi said dryly. "That's virgin territory beyond that sign. They've checked over this building, and that's why we're allowed in—but don't touch."

They climbed up a meter-high ledge and stooped over to enter the hatchway. Recently installed locks and chains held more doors open. Patricia noticed other sensing devices— some covered with silvery tape—mounted on the walls, floor and ceiling.

"The machines would offload food, equipment, whatever the building needed through these halls. Automatic carts would deliver the goods to the appropriate chutes and they would lift them to different parts of the building. From this point on, though, we're not cargo; we're people."

Another open hatchway gave access to a large ground-floor reception area. Free-form seats and couches—apparently made of natural wood—furnished a sunken conversation pit near a broad, one-piece window that stretched at least twenty meters to the ceiling. A well-maintained flower garden

138

stretched beyond the window. She was completely taken in by the illusion until she realized the garden was illuminated by sunlight and that blue sky showed through the trees. She stopped to stare and Takahashi waited patiently with hands folded.

"That's lovely," she said.

"The garden's real; the sunlight and sky are fake," he said noncommittally.

"I was wondering how they got along without sunshine and blue skies."

"If you went outside, you'd see the window's having us on."

"It looks very real."

The floor resembled shiny stonework but felt carpeted. Patricia shuffled her feet experimentally but her efforts produced no sound.

"Going up will take some will power," Takahashi warned. At the far end of the reception area were two open shafts sunk into the wall. "Not recommended for those with vertigo." They entered the left-hand shaft. Takahashi pointed down and reached out with his foot to tap a red circle on the floor. The circle glowed. "Seven," he said. "Both of us."

The floor receded. With no visible support, they flew up the shaft. Except for the appearance of motion there was no sensation whatsoever. Patricia's eyes widened and she reached for Takahashi's arm. Above the reception area, the shaft was featureless. There was no way of telling how many floors were passing.

"Only takes a second," he said. "Don't you love it? I don't know how many novels I've read with this sort of thing in them. In Thistledown City, it's real." This was the first time Patricia had heard him express delight. He seemed intensely interested in her reaction: *Another spaghetti worm mystery,* she thought. *See how the girl screams.*

She let go of his arm just as a portion of the shaft became transparent in front of them. They were smoothly, gently deposited on the floor beyond.

Patricia swallowed hard. "I am amazed," she said with some effort, "how well everything is working here, while nothing much works in the second chamber."

Takahashi nodded, as if acknowledging that was an interesting problem, but he was unable or unwilling to provide the answer. "Follow me, please."

The hallway curved off to either side. It was round in cross section, and its color varied smoothly from rich forest green to dark maple. Always they seemed to walk in a circle of warm light. Patricia looked down and noticed that their feet touched an invisible plane above the floor of the hallway. "We're walking on air," she said, suppressing a nervous tremor.

"Favorite illusion for the Stoners. Gets dull after a time." They stopped and Takahashi pointed down at the floor to their right. "756" glowed in red beneath a faint leaf-green line. "This is a door, and it happens to be the door we want. Now, you do the honors. Hold your hand up to the wall and press anywhere."

She reached out and did as he suggested. A seven-foot-high oval vanished from the wall, revealing a white room beyond.

"The archaeologists found this one by accident. Apparently it was vacant before the exodus and this is the way prospective tenants checked out the apartments. All the other doors in the building are personality coded or otherwise blocked to visitors. And—as you know if you tried—information on interiors of private spaces in Thistledown City is not available in the libraries. Welcome."

Patricia entered the foyer ahead of him. The quarters were pristine white, furnished with ungraceful white blocks barely suggestive of couches and chairs and tables. "It's ugly," she said, taking a turn around the windowless living room. Oval doors led off to two equally white and blocky bedrooms—at least that was what she assumed they were. The beds could have been settees.

The only object in the apartment that was not white was a chromium teardrop on a pedestal. Patricia paused next to it. "Like the ones in the library."

Takahashi nodded. "Off limits." He indicated the little box attached to the base of the pedestal. "Any tampering and alarms go off in the security offices."

"It's a home library unit?"

"We assume so."

"It works?"

"As far as I know, nobody's tried. You might ask Garry."

"Why no windows? Is this an inner apartment?"

"None of the apartments had simple windows."

"And why so ugly?"

"If you mean plain, that's because nobody has chosen an environment. No design because nobody's living here. Vacant, you see."

"Yes. What would it take to decorate it?"

"Some sort of rental contract, I assume," Takahashi said. "Then it might respond like everything else around here. You could decorate by voice."

"Wonderful," Patricia said. "Nobody's entered any other living quarters?"

"Not in the third chamber. Locked up tight as a drum."

"Then how did they find this one? Just by accident?"

"Yitshak Jacob went from floor to floor, alone, and walked around the circumference of the building on each floor. This was the only apartment that had a number glowing."

"How would anyone know when they were home?"

"Maybe their number would glow and the door would open as they approached. Maybe they had other ways. We're far from understanding such basic things."

If we don't know the basics, Patricia thought, *how can I ever hope to understand the embellishments . . . the sixth chamber, the corridor?*

"We'll go back the way we came," Takahashi said, "and try to get to that meeting before it begins."

They barely made it. The cafeteria in the first science team compound had been rearranged, and a low stage, lectern and rows of seats now occupied the dining area. Rimskaya stood near the stage as interested team members entered the cafeteria, talking and looking for good vantage points in the rows.

Patricia and Takahashi entered at precisely 1100. Most of the seats were filled, so they sat in the back. Karen Farley turned in her seat and waved at them. Patricia returned the wave and then Rimskaya came to the lectern.

"Ladies and gentlemen, colleagues, our report this morning has to do with the exodus from the Stone. We have made substantial progress with this problem and can now present our conclusions with some degree of confidence." He introduced a slight man with wispy light brown hair and delicate Apollonian features. "Dr. Wallace Rainer of the University of Oklahoma will present our conclusions. Today's meeting should not last more than thirty minutes."

Rainer looked to the back of the room, received an affirmative nod from a woman on the projection system and stepped up to the lectern, brandishing a collapsable metal pointer. "All of the archaeology group has worked on this report, and several members of the sociology group as well. Dr. Jacob is indisposed, and I drew the short straw."

Amused chuckles from the audience. "Jacob never delivers reports," Takahashi said. "Very shy. He prefers deserted ruins."

"There has always been some puzzlement as to the coexistence of the second chamber city, known as Alexandria, and the far more advanced Thistledown City in the third chamber. We've all asked the question at one time or another: Why did the Stoners keep Alexandria in its earlier state, rather than rebuilding and modernizing? Certainly people with our present-day temperament would feel awkward living in comparatively primitive surroundings when more modern facilities could be had for the price of a little urban renewal.

"We know a great deal now about living conditions in Alexandria but substantially less about Thistledown City. As you know, security—Stoner security—is very tight at Thistledown City, and unless we want to do some extensive breaking

142

and entering, we have only one location where we have access to living quarters. Alexandria is more open, in some ways more friendly, if I may be excused a very unanthropological judgment.

"All of us here have level two security; we are aware the Stoners were humans, and that they came from a culture remarkably similar to our own. In fact, they come from a future version of the Earth. We know that there were at one time two major social categories: the Geshels, or technically and scientifically oriented peoples, and the Naderites. I'm wondering, by the way, who's going to tell Ralph about this."

Weary laughter from the audience. "Old joke," Takahashi whispered to Patricia.

"We now know that Alexandria, before the exodus of the Stoners, was occupied largely by orthodox Naderites. They seemed to cling to technologies and styles predating the twenty-first century."

Patricia, with something of a jolt, realized none of these people except herself, Takahashi and Rimskaya would know the reason why that particular dividing line was important.

"In this way, they were something like the Amish. And like the Amish, they made concessions—the megas and other architectural innovations among them. But their aim was clear; they chose to retain the style of Alexandria and rejected the more advanced style of Thistledown City. We are not at all sure when this division of the orthodox Naderites and their more liberal fellows and Geshels occurred, but it was not early in the Stone's voyage.

"We are fairly certain now that Thistledown City had been evacuated and locked up at least a century before Alexandria. In other words, the exodus had occurred in the third chamber almost a hundred years before the final evacuation of the second chamber. There is substantial evidence that the second chamber was finally emptied by force.

"The Stone was emptied, then, not simply because of a mass social migration, but to fulfill a definite plan. The people behind the plan apparently gave their more conservative fellows a century to comply, and when they still proved reluctant, moved them out against their will. Oddly enough, we have evidence that some of the orthodox Naderites were forced to live in Thistledown City for a few years.

"We assume that all the Stoners exited by way of the corridor. We have no physical proof of this, and no knowledge yet why the exodus occurred, or why the powers behind the exodus wished the Stone to be completely deserted."

The presentation ended with a series of projected pictures showing living quarters in Alexandria and diagrams of theorized population levels for different centuries in the second and third chambers. To scattered applause, Rainer returned the lectern to Rimskaya.

"The anthropology and archaeology groups have done a wonderful job, don't you agree?" he prompted, gesturing to those in the front row of seats.

Patricia stood as there was more applause. Takahashi followed her out of the cafeteria and into the tubelight.

"That's fascinating," she said, "and I appreciate the tour today. They're working in the dark, aren't they?"

Takahashi shrugged, then nodded. "Yes. The sosh and anthro groups don't have level three clearances. Rimskaya guides them as best as he can without breaching security."

"Don't you get sick of this charade?"

Takahashi shook his head vigorously. "No. It is essential."

"Maybe," Patricia said doubtfully. "I have a lot of work to do before Lanier returns."

"Certainly. Do you wish an escort?"

"No. I'm going back to Alexandria for a while. Then I'll be in the seventh chamber if you need me for anything."

Takahashi paused, hands in his pockets, and nodded, then returned to the cafeteria.

Farley came out seconds later and caught up with her by the garage outside the compound. "Hitch a ride?" she asked.

"Rupert's given me driving lessons. I think it would relax me to drive for a while."

"Certainly," Farley said. They signed out a truck and climbed aboard.

144

Chapter Fourteen

The room smelled of stale smoke, air conditioning and nervous labor. When Lanier and Hoffman entered, there were four others already inside, all men. Two wore silver-gray polyester suits; bulky, balding, comic-opera Russians. The other two wore tailored wool worsteds; their styled hair and their girths were just barely respectable. Hoffman smiled at all as amenities were exchanged, after which everyone sat around an oval conference table. An awkward silence drew out through several minutes as they waited for Hague and Cronberry to arrive.

When the groups were evenly matched, the senior Russian official, Grigori Feodorovski, removed a single sheet of paper from a cardboard folder and laid it on the table. He then pulled a pair of wire-frame glasses over his nose and behind his ears with one smooth sweep of a hand gripping the temple piece.

"Our governments have some necessary points of discussion concerning the Stone or, as we call it, the Potato." His English was excellent. His expression was calm and unhurried. "We have presented these objections to ISCCOM, and now we must hear what you have to say.

"While we concede under protest that primary exploration rights go to those who first visited the Stone—"

That, Lanier recalled, had been a concession two years in coming.

"—we feel that the Soviet Union and our allied sovereign states have been cheated of their rights. While Soviet scientists have been allowed on the Stone, they have been constantly harassed and not allowed to conduct their work. They have been denied access to important information. In light of these and other grievances, which are at this moment being presented to your President and the Senate Space Advisory Council, we feel that ISCCOM has been compromised, and that the

Soviet Union and sovereign ally states have been . . ." he cleared his throat, as if embarrassed—"treated most malignantly. Our fellow states have been advised that further participation in the multinational Stone investigation, dominated as it is by the United States and NATO–Eurospace, will serve no purpose. Therefore we will soon withdraw our personnel and support for this enterprise."

Hoffman nodded, her lips pressed tightly together. Cronberry waited for the requisite ten seconds to consider the statement, then spoke. "We regret your decision. We feel that allegations made against ISCCOM, NATO–Eurospace and the Stone personnel in the past have proven unfounded, based on unfortunate rumors. Is the decision of your superiors final?"

Feodorovski nodded. "The ISCCOM agreements made with regard to the Stone demand the withdrawal of all Stone investigators until these issues are resolved."

"That's completely impractical," Hoffman said.

Feodorovski shrugged, pursing his lips. "Nevertheless, that is what the agreements stipulate."

"Mr. Feodorovski," Hague said, putting both hands on the table, palms up, a gesture which Lanier studied closely, "we believe there are other reasons, not yet stated, for the withdrawal of your personnel. May we discuss these things?"

Feodorovski nodded. "With the warning that none of us are empowered to negotiate or make formal statements."

"Understood. Neither are we. I think we all need to relax a bit, to see our way clear to . . . deal honestly, forthrightly, with each other." He looked at Feodorovski and the others, eyebrows raised in query. They nodded. "Our President has been informed that the USSR believes dangerous information of a technological, weapons-oriented nature has been discovered on the Stone," Hague said.

Feodorovski's face was blank, held in an attitude of polite attention.

"While it is true that NATO–Eurospace has begun the investigation of certain heretofore neglected aspects of the Stone's second and third chambers—"

"Against our wishes and protests," Feodorovski said.

"Yes, but with your final agreement."

"Under duress."

"Indeed," Hague said, again raising his brows and looking down at the desk. "While this has been our ceded area of investigation, there has been no such information discovered aboard the Stone."

And indeed, there had not. The libraries contained no specific information on weapons.

"Under the agreements, any such discovery would be reported immediately to the arbitration board in Geneva."

"That may be so," Feodorovski said. Lanier wondered what purpose the other three served—place-keepers? Back-ups? Overseers keeping tabs on Feodorovski? "But we are not concerned with such reports. Let me speak frankly." Now he, too, placed both hands on the table, palms up. "I cannot speak formally, remember. As a private citizen, allow me to express my concern in this matter." He took a deep breath, full of worry. "We are all, in a sense, colleagues. We have many of the same interests. Let me say that this report about new weapons technology, this is not an important issue. My government, and the governments of our sovereign ally states, are far more concerned about reports that libraries on the Stone, in the second and third chamber cities, to be specific, contain accounts of a future war between our countries."

Lanier was stunned. He had thought security aboard the Stone—certainly around the libraries—was extremely tight. Would he be held responsible for such a hideous leak—or was the leak from another source, perhaps the President's office, or Hoffman's?

"This is a highly unusual situation," Feodorovski continued. "Frankly, my colleagues and I have a difficult time believing we are not living a fairy tale." The other three nodded, not quite in unison. "But these reports are reliable. What do you have to say about them?"

"The libraries have been approached cautiously," Hague

said. "We've just begun to process the information stored there."

Feodorovski looked up at the ceiling, exasperated. "We have pledged to speak frankly with each other. My government *knows* such information exists in the libraries. In fact, we are certain that the accounts of this future war are already in the hands of your President."

He looked around the table. Lanier met his gaze steadily and noticed a flicker of smile on his lips. "Yes," Feodorovski said. "We know, of course, that humans built the Stone, or will build it, centuries from now. We know that it will be constructed from the asteroid known as Juno. We know this because in every particular the asteroid Juno and the Stone are identical. Our spacecraft in the asteroid belt has confirmed this."

"Mr. Feodorovski, we are dealing with a very unusual problem," Hoffman said. "We are certain that the Stone does not come from our universe, but from an alternate universe. We strongly believe that the information contained in the libraries could be misinterpreted. They may not predict conditions in our world in any way. The scientific data could be useful, and we are studying that closely, but releasing information haphazardly could be disastrous."

"Nevertheless, there is such a history."

Cronberry said, "If there is, we are not privy to it."

Lanier felt his heart sink. He hated lies, even necessary lies. He hated being a party to lies. Yet he no more wanted the Russians to get the information in the libraries than Cronberry and Hague. That made him a liar.

The Russian seated closest to Feodorovski—Yuri Kerzhinsky—leaned over to whisper in his ear. Feodorovski nodded. "Mr. Lanier," he said, "do you deny the existence of this information?"

"I don't know anything about it," Lanier said smoothly.

"But you concede, do you not, that if such information exists, being aware of it, knowing certain dates, even certain hours, knowing the situations and consequences in advance

148

would be of great strategic value, and also would put a very great strain on you individually?"

"I imagine it would," Lanier said.

Hague interrupted. "Mr. Lanier is not to be badgered—"

"Very sorry," Feodorovski said. "My apologies. But our concern is larger than individual politenesses."

Kerzhinsky stood up abruptly. "Gentlemen. You realize there is now very grave tension between our nations, perhaps the gravest since the 1990s. It is our opinion that troubles aboard the Stone are jeopardizing world peace. The Stone is increasing tensions, particularly with regard to this issue about libraries. It is obvious that we cannot resolve these difficulties at this level of dialogue. Therefore, I see no further need for discussion here."

"Mr. Kerzhinsky," Hoffman said. "I have a paper here I believe your Party Secretary should see. It states the position of all the scientists aboard the Stone with regard to cooperation. And I think it clarifies the rumors of harassment."

Kerzhinsky shook his head and tapped his forefinger on the table several times. "We are no longer interested in such posturings. Harassment is not the issue. The libraries are the issue. Talks are proceeding at a formal level right now. We can only hope for better results there." The four stood and Hague escorted them to the door.

Outside the door, a secret service agent took them in charge. Hague closed the door and turned back to the others. "That," he said, "is that."

"Makes me sick," Lanier said in an undertone.

"Oh?" Cronberry said, rising halfway from her seat. "And what would you have us do, Mr. Lanier? You're the one responsible, you know that? You didn't keep a tight rein on security, and now we have this mess . . . this goddamn diplomatic catastrophe. Why did you ever open the libraries in the first place? Couldn't you just *smell* the trouble they'd cause? I would have smelled it, by God. The whole place must *reek*."

"Shut up, Alice," Hoffman said quietly. "Stop behaving like an ass."

Cronberry glared at them all, then sat down and lit a cigarette. The way she fumbled at the lighter and clenched the cigarette between tight fingers made Lanier queasy. *We're way out of our depth here,* he thought. *Children playing with real guns, real bullets.*

"The President called yesterday," Hoffman said. "He's very angry about the libraries. He wants them closed and all research halted. He says we've let things get out of control, and I can't really disagree with him. Garry is no more to blame than any of us. At any rate, the President is going to order the Stone Congressional Oversight Committee to put all research on hold until further notice. The Russians are going to get what they want."

"How long do we have?" Lanier asked.

"Until the order goes through channels? A week, probably."

Lanier grinned and shook his head.

"What's there to be amused about?" Cronberry asked coldly, wrapped in a loose shell of smoke.

"The records say we have two weeks before the war."

Hoffman invited Lanier to her office for drinks that evening. He arrived at seven, after a quick dinner in the JPL cafeteria, and again checked his agents at the door. Hoffman's JPL office was as spare and utilitarian as the one in her home in New York, the major difference being more shelves of memory blocks.

"We tried," she said, handing him a Scotch neat. "Well." She toasted him with a raised Dubonnet on the rocks.

"We did," he said.

"You look tired."

"I am tired."

"Weight of the world on your shoulders," she said, looking at him cautiously.

150

"Weight of a couple of universes," he said. "I'm discovering how tough a bastard I am, Judith."

"Me too. I talked to the President again this afternoon."

"Oh?"

"Yes. I'm afraid I called him an idiot. I'll very likely be fired or forced to resign by the time you're in orbit."

"Good for you," Lanier said.

"Sit. Talk to me. Tell me what it's like. I want to get up there so badly. . . ." She pulled out chairs and they sat across from each other.

"Why?" Lanier asked. "You've seen the blocks, all the information."

"That's a stupid question."

"It is," Lanier admitted. They were both getting slightly tipsy before the alcohol could possible have had time to take effect. Lanier had noticed the condition before, in times of stress.

"Goddamn, I sure understand what the Russians are worried about," Hoffman said after a moment's silence. "For the last ten years we've been beating the pants off of them in every area—diplomatically, technologically. In space and on Earth. Hares to their tortoise. They're dinosaurs and they hate anything faster and more adaptable. Why, young Ivan doesn't know a computer terminal from a tractor wheel. Even the Chinese are beating them."

"The Chinese might edge ahead of us in a generation or two."

"Good. Serve us right." Hoffman said. "Now the Stone comes down, and we intercept it, claim it, let them have little useless nibbles of it in the interests of international cooperation. . . . And whatever's on the Stone, it might just as well be a tombstone for the Eastern bloc. We'll be in control of unimagined technology. Jesus. I wish we could sit down with them and reason . . . but they're too scared, and our President is too damned stupid."

"I don't think stupid is the right word. Shell-shocked, perhaps."

151

"He knew a little about the Stone when he ran for office."

"He knew it was coming," Lanier said. "None of us knew much more than that."

"Well, fuck him if he can't take a joke," Hoffman said, staring at the shutters on the window. "When you were a pilot, way back when," she continued, "you crashed once. Where did you want to be before your plane went down?"

"At the controls," Lanier said without hesitation. "I wanted to save the plane so badly I couldn't even think about punching out. I thought it—the plane—was absolutely beautiful, and I wanted to save it. I also wanted to keep it from killing other people. So we both landed in a lake."

"I'm not nearly so brave," Hoffman said. "I think the Earth is beautiful, and I want to save it. I've been working my buns off to do so. Now all I get is shit. Your airplane didn't thumb its nose at you. It didn't call you on the carpet for your best work, did it?"

Lanier shook his head.

"That's what's happening here. So now I'm saying to myself, 'The hell with 'em.' I want to be up on the Stone when it happens."

"If everything goes to hell on Earth, we're not going to get down from the Stone for years. Not even the lunar settlement will be able to help us."

"Earth will survive?"

"Barely," Lanier said. "A year of sub-zero temperatures throughout the northern hemisphere, plagues and starvation, revolutions. If the libraries reflect our reality, maybe three or four billion people will die overall."

"But it isn't the end of the world."

"No. It may not even happen."

"Do you believe that?"

Lanier kept his silence for a long moment. Hoffman waited, hardly blinking. "No. Not now. Perhaps if the Stone had never arrived."

Hoffman put down her drink and ran her fingers around the rim of the glass. "Well. I'm going to try to get up there. Don't

152

ask how. If I make it, I'll see you on the Stone. If I don't . . . You've been good to work with. I'd enjoy working with you more." She reached out and drew him to her, kissing him on the forehead. "Thank you."

A half hour later, after they had drained three drinks apiece, she escorted him to the door. She took a folded piece of paper and pressed it into his hand.

"Now take this and use it however you will. You can give it to Gerhardt if you want, or you can destroy it. It's probably not that important now."

"What is it?" he asked.

"The name of the Russian operative on the Stone."

Lanier's hand tightened on the paper, but he did not unfold it.

"The President is moving quicker than I thought he would," Hoffman said. "Sometime tomorrow, you're going to be ordered to close the libraries. He wants to convince the Soviets we're on the up-and-up."

"That's insane," Lanier said.

"Not very. It's politics. He's got big problems. Did I just say that? Yes. I even understand the President now. I must be drunk. Anyway, does it matter?"

"It sure as hell could."

"Then do what you wish. It'll take them a couple of weeks to find out and mount an effort to remove you." She smiled. "As soon as Vasquez does her stuff, you let me know somehow, okay? Not all the cards have been played yet. There are senators and a couple of members of the Joint Chiefs still on my side."

"I'll do that," he said. He took the paper and put it in his pocket.

She opened the door for him. "Good-bye, Garry."

The agent several steps down the hall regarded him with a deadpan expression.

Do I really want to know?

He had to know.

He had to get the Stone ready for whatever would come.

Chapter Fifteen

Heineman piloted the V/STOL alone, using the aircraft's rocket to push the tuberider along the axis from the first chamber bore hole. It had been only forty minutes since he had linked the tuberider and V/STOL in the south polar bore hole. The "ground" surrounded him on all sides, giving him a peculiar sensation of vertigo at first; which way should he orient? But he adapted quickly.

Using radio beacons set up in each chamber, coordinating through the V/STOL's guidance computers, he could tell his position within a few centimeters. Cautiously and lovingly, he eased the assembly from chamber to chamber, using temporary propulsion packs on the tuberider and the aircraft, coordinated through the aircraft's own customized guidance system.

Coming up on each bore hole was a thrill that raised the hair on his neck. In the center of the massive gray caps, that tiny hole—wider than a football field, no challenge really, but from a distance almost invisible . . .

He flew steadily over the fifth chamber's darkly Gothic landscape of clouds, mountains and chasms. Entering the bore hole between the fifth and sixth chambers, he issued a terse instruction to a crew of his engineers waiting near the seventh chamber singularity: "Take 'er down. I'm coming through in a few minutes." They acknowledged and began to dismantle the top of the research scaffold.

It was Heineman's intention to thread the needle without readjustment, slowly but expertly.

The mated vehicles were monstrous from an aerodynamic viewpoint, and cumbersome from any perspective, but the flight was not difficult. The near-vacuum of the Stone axis offered no resistance.

Even concentrating on the last phase of the delivery, Heineman couldn't stop thinking about flying the aircraft.

Reentry was the uncertain part. Once the tuberider was threaded and steady on the singularity, Heineman would test the clamps by moving thirty-one kilometers down the axis. Descent would be much less complicated—so he was told— that far down the corridor; he could descend in almost a straight line instead of the spiral necessary within the rotating chamber.

The V/STOL would unlink and propel itself away from the axis with short bursts from hydrogen peroxide motors. Then it would fall steadily, encountering resistance at the level of the atmosphere field barrier and plasma tube, about twenty-two kilometers above the chamber floor, three kilometers from the axis. Jets and upwellings from coriolis and compressional heating made the first thin kilometer of air tricky; the V/STOL's pilot would have to forget a lot of the truisms learned on Earth.

The designers had estimated the aircraft's fuel use. It could make twenty ascents and descents, and fly approximately four thousand kilometers at cruising speed in the air, before having to tap the tuberider fuel, oxygen and hydrogen peroxide tanks. Fully loaded, the tuberider could refuel the V/STOL five times. And when it was clamped to the singularity, the tuberider could travel indefinitely using the spacial transform effect.

Now, both plane and tuberider were traveling light. Once they were threaded, crews could load them with fuel and oxygen from the staging area of the seventh chamber bore hole.

The sixth chamber rotated around him, a cylindrical cloudscape with broken patches revealing the machines he had only learned about three days before.

He was half-convinced the archaeologists and physicists had conspired to keep him away from the most interesting parts of the Stone out of sheer spite. "No moving parts," Carrolson had said. "We didn't think you'd be interested." He gritted his teeth, then blew out his breath with a whistle. The sixth chamber machinery was overawing. He had never dreamed he would see anything like it, even on the Stone. It almost took his attention away from piloting the tuberider and V/STOL.

The last bore hole approached rapidly. He slowed the assembly and nudged the craft one last time. Allowing for some mid-hole corrections and drifts caused by irregularities imposed on the Stone by its Earth–Moon orbit, he would be able to slide right onto the singularity, slow the assembly with the clamps and then proceed with the tuberider test.

"There it is," Carrolson said, pointing. She stared through the polarized and filtered binoculars at the plasma tube where it joined the southern cap, then handed the glasses to Farley. Farley squinted through them and clearly saw the mated vehicles, seemingly poised without support; the singularity was impossible to make out from this distance.

"He's going to fly it down today?"

Carrolson nodded. "Heineman will try it out and stay here until Lanier returns."

Rimskaya walked up behind them and stood silent while they passed the glasses back and forth. "Ladies," he said some moments later, "we have work to do."

"Certainly," Farley said. Carrolson grinned behind Rimskaya's back. They returned to the tent.

Chapter Sixteen

Vasquez continued her tour of the third chamber city by way of the library simulation. She discovered she could wander at will through the record, taking any route she chose, although she was still unable to enter private spaces.

Mostly, she used the tours to relax between long periods of heavy brainwork. She also made tours on foot; the independence she felt, going from place to place in the Stone with a pocket map or slate and memory blocks—no one questioning her about her intentions—was exhilarating. She could almost shut out the dark thoughts—but not quite.

She rode the trains from the sixth to the third chamber at least once every twenty-four hours. Occasionally, she used the second chamber library, sometimes staying over and sleeping on the cot in the darkened reading room. That wasn't her favorite place to sleep—she much preferred the tent in the seventh chamber, near people—but it was the most private. Not even Takahashi used the second chamber library often.

The libraries were the two foci of her work. As the problems moved from point to point on their routes through her mind, she occupied herself with gathering more information than she actually needed, and reveled in the intellectual luxury.

When she asked for reference materials having to do with Stone design, the library displayed its solid-looking and convincing black sphere surrounded by an outward-facing circle of spikes. A pleasant voice would announce: "There is no current access to that material. Please consult an active librarian."

Early on, she sensed a pattern, and it proved very frustrating. Virtually all material dealing with the theory and construction of the sixth chamber was inaccessible. There was no material on the seventh chamber and the corridor—the response for her queries in that area was simply, "Not in records," accompanied by a black bar.

While fuming over these rebuffs, it occurred to her that she might go back through the records and look up her own papers—even future papers—to see if she had a counterpart, and if that counterpart had made a mark in the Stone's universe.

But she had an almost superstitious reluctance to probe that deeply. When she finally did come across her own name, it was by accident.

The only real clues to the sixth chamber were in the Alexandria library, bound into a seventy-five-volume set of basic instruction manuals that looked as if it had been

157

printed for handymen and engineers as a collector's edition, or a testimonial for retirees.

It was in the forty-fifth volume, a hefty tome of two thousand pages containing theory of early sixth chamber machinery and inertial damping, that she found her name in a footnote.

In the dark reading room, with the desk lamps and strip lighting providing the only illumination, she stared at the reference, her back stiffening.

"Patricia Luisa Vasquez," she read, as if the sounds were magic, *"Theory of n-Spatial Geodesics as Applied to Newtonian Physics with a Special Discourse on ρ-Simplon World Lines."* She had never written a paper with that title—not yet, at any rate.

It would be published in 2023, in an issue of the *Post-Death Journal of Accepted Physics*.

She would survive the Death.

And contribute, at least in this small way, to the construction of the Stone.

She found the article in the Thistledown City library, where it was apparently regarded as too archaic to be interdicted. She read it, palms damp, and found much of it very difficult. Weaving her way through the unfamiliar symbols and obscure terminology, trying to get the gist of what her counterpart would write, eighteen years from now—or had written, centuries past—a ghost of an explanation occurred to her.

In the Stone's revised original plans, the sole purpose of the sixth chamber machinery had been to damp the momentum of selected objects within the Stone, in directions roughly parallel to the axis. This function had eliminated the need for banked channels of rivers, special architecture for buildings, even for a different design in the chambers themselves.

At the beginning of the Stone's construction, an upward limit had been placed on the Stone's acceleration and deceleration of 3 percent g. With the sixth chamber machinery, there was no need to limit the acceleration at all. The Stone's chambers became part of a controlled and separate reference frame, independent of outside influence.

Chapters in the manuals explained how the damping system did not operate universally; if it had, the Stone's rotation would have been useless, and everything within the chambers would have floated around weightless. The damping was highly selective.

And *that* was super-science. The implications were astonishing. What the sixth chamber machinery did, in effect, was alter the mass-space-time character of everything in the Stone.

That was little short of being able to manipulate space and time in such a way as to create the corridor.

Yet the Stone did not travel faster than light, and it did not possess artificial gravity—not in the first six chambers, at any rate. Those achievements could also have been expected in light of the theory of inertial damping. Why hadn't the Stone's engineers and physicists been able to close the conceptual loop?

She returned to the Alexandria library and skimmed the manuals, but in themselves they provided no answer, concerned as they were with theory and maintenance of specific Stone machinery.

On her cot in the reading room, she buried her face in her palms, squeezing the bridge of her nose and rubbing her eyes. Her brain felt tight. Too much concentration. Too little time, trying to force the queued problems, trying to emerge with answers ahead of schedule.

She had to have a break. She stood and followed the strip lighting to the lower floor, emerging in the tubelight and sitting on a bench surrounding a treeless concrete planter.

She tried to shut out all conscious thought, to get back into the state, but she couldn't.

Thoughts of Paul and her family kept interposing.

"I am losing myself," she murmured, shaking her head. She was becoming nothing but a series of thoughts floating in gray void, a cerebral point. Overworking.

Then—a gap in the void.

She had once studied fraction spaces—individual dimensions operating without counterparts, and dimensions of less than unit numbers. Time without space; length without breadth, depth or time. Probability without extension. Half-spaces, quarter-spaces, spaces composed of irrational fractions. All to be handled by fractional transforms and fractal geometric analysis. She had even begun to chart the geodesics of higher fractional spaces, and the way these geodesics might project in five- and four-space.

She dropped her head between her knees. Her thoughts were zagging. No order, no discipline.

The corridor—just an extension of the sixth chamber machinery, designed for inertial damping.

On a journey of centuries, the Stoners had changed their minds, or perhaps lost sight of the original goals. A world unto itself, the Stone had impressed upon succeeding generations its own character, until it seemed perfectly natural to live in rotating cylinders, hollowed out of asteroid rock. In time, perhaps even the asteroid had seemed to fade out of immediate awareness, leaving only life within cylinders.

Squeezed and confined across centuries, nurtured by the perceptions of the Stone, the Stoners' genius erupted. They became nothing short of godlike, making their own universe, and shaping it in the image of the world they were most familiar with.

When they found a way out of the Stone without compromising the ultimate mission—

When they found they could create an incredible *extension* of their world—

Would any of the Stoners have been able to resist the temptation? (Yes . . . the orthodox Naderites—and they had stayed behind for a century.)

So the sixth chamber engineers, headed by the enigmatic Konrad Korzenowski, had created the corridor, imbued it with certain properties, played with its potentials. They had created the wells and found some way to fill the corridor with air and soil, with landscapes equal if not superior to the valley floors of their everyday lives.

Her body relaxed. She sat up. Some of the symbols in her as-yet-unwritten article made sense to her now; she could riddle their meaning. Her mind unfogged and she seemed to see all the problems interacting at once, like workers in a skyscraper with glass walls and floors.

The Stoners had created the corridor to relieve cramped conditions, confinement of the mind if not any real confinement of their personal space. (The records made it clear that the Stone had never become overcrowded.)

But the corridor—and this came to her abruptly, without precedent—the corridor carried a certain unexpected liability, a side effect they might not have been aware of at first. . . .

Or never became aware of.

By creating the corridor, they had knocked the Stone out of its own continuum. The image that came to mind—all too irritatingly specific, since she wasn't at all sure it was accurate—was that of the corridor as a length of whip, and the Stone as the tip. With the creation of the whip, and its inevitable uncoiling in superspace, the tip had been snapped out of one universe—

And into hers.

Four hours later, she woke up, her body stiff and her mouth tasting like mud. She lifted her aching back from the bench and blinked in the tubelight. Her head ached abominably.

But she was on to something.

Discovering they had made it impossible to fulfill the Stone's original mission, in time all the Stoners had migrated down the corridor.

She stood and brushed down her jumpsuit. Now she had to go back and put foundations beneath all the hypothetical air castles she had built.

And find some aspirin.

161

Chapter Seventeen

Lanier had kept the paper unread in his pocket on the shuttle and OTV, dreading that moment when he would have to know and have to act against a colleague, even a friend.

The OTV had docked with the Stone and he had disembarked, made a brief report to Roberta Pickney and the staging area communications team, and passed on his recommendation to Kirchner that Stone external security should be especially watchful.

As for internal security—

It wasn't really supposed to be his job. Had Gerhardt already received the same information awaiting him in the folded paper? How had Hoffman come across the name, and why had she given it to him?

He received reports from the various team leaders by way of a messenger bearing a slate. He floated in a small anteroom adjacent to the staging area, wrapped in one of the mesh cylindrical slings that served as bunks for axis-bound workers; he read, and absorbed, and realized he was only delaying the inevitable.

Boarding the zero elevator, accompanied by a taciturn marine guard, he removed the paper from his pocket and unfolded it.

"As soon as possible, I'd like to take a truck to the second well circuit," Patricia said. Takahashi held open the tent flap for her and she entered. Carrolson and Farley napped in one corner of the central room; Wu and Chang worked over slates and processors in another. Takahashi followed her inside.

"On a mental roll?" he asked. Carrolson and Farley grumbled awake simultaneously and blinked at the intrusion and noise.

"We have to make space-time spot checks," Patricia said.

162

Her face was drawn and there were pastel purple smudges of fatigue under her eyes. "I've asked Mr. Heineman to help. There's a directional beacon on the airplane and we can pick up that signal with some security team equipment, feed it into a frequency analyzer, find out if we're moving faster or slower in time by comparing our readings as the plane passes overhead."

"You've reached some conclusions?" Carrolson asked, sitting up on her cot.

"I think so," Patricia said. "But nothing's definite without evidence. I've made some predictions and if they're corroborated, then I might hypothesize."

"Want to tell us about the predictions?" Takahashi asked, sitting beside Carrolson on the cot.

Patricia shrugged. "Okay. The corridor could be dimpled. Each dimple is a fluctuation in the corridor's space-time, marking some point of potential entry into another universe. The dimples should reflect a minor change in geometric constants like *pi*; maybe in physical constants as well. Wherever there's a dimple—or a potential for a dimple—we may also find time fluctuations."

"Does that mean the corridor is full of potential wells?"

"I think so. Only a few have been selected—tuned, as it were." She looked up at the roof of the tent, trying to find a way to explain what she saw in her head. "The dimples butt up against each other. There could be an infinite number of them. And a well opened in a dimple—potential or already tuned—could lead to another universe."

Takahashi shook his head. "This is getting entirely too weird."

"Yeah," Patricia said. "I'd like to hold off on more explanations until Garry returns."

"He's coming down any time now. He entered the bore hole a few hours ago," Carrolson said. She slapped her knee and stood up. "Which reminds me. We're having a dance tomorrow in the first chamber. All are invited. It's not exactly

Garry's homecoming, but it will serve as such. We all need to let down our hair a little bit."

"I'm a good dancer," Wu said. "Foxtrot, twist, swim."

"Listen to him! You think we thirty years behind the times," Chang said.

"Forty," Wu corrected.

"And if we can peel Heineman away from his toy," Carrolson said, "I'll teach the old coot a few hot steps."

Lanier dropped the paper on his desk in the science team compound office and reached for the com button. He hesitated before pressing it.

He thought he had figured out why Hoffman had given him the name. "Ann," he said. "I want to see Rupert Takahashi in the compound as soon as possible."

He hoped he was doing what Hoffman had hinted he should do: defusing the bomb the Stone had become. . . .

Lance Corporal Thomas Oldfield, twenty-four, had spent the last six months on the Stone, and he regarded them as the most exciting time of his life, though in fact there wasn't much overt excitement. Most of the time he stood guard duty in the second chamber, just outside the tunnel to the first chamber. He spent many of his hours alternately keeping an eye on the road, the zero bridge and near city, and examining the distant curve of the opposite side. He was usually accompanied by at least one colleague, but today a special detail had been ordered to accompany a scientist into the first chamber from the subway terminal in the city, and now he was left alone. He didn't expect any trouble. In the entire time he had spent on the Stone, nothing untoward had happened. He had never even seen a boojum.

He didn't believe they existed.

Oldfield whistled to himself as he stepped outside the booth and looked down the length of the bridge. Deserted. "Fine day, Private," he said briskly, saluting ceremoniously. "Yes, *sir. Fine* day, sir. Always a *fine* day."

He wondered if technically speaking it had been the very same day since he had arrived. One long-drawn-out day, no intervening night. The weather changed now and then—rain, sometimes mist from the river. Did that serve to divide the time?

He inspected his Apple and tested it behind the booth on a cement block lined with foil ration packages. Each invisible tooth of light blew a foil package off the block. When he was relieved, he would line up the pierced foil packages for the next watch to test their weapons. It had become a ritual.

He walked around the booth to the door, stopped and turned.

He couldn't begin to describe what he saw.

He didn't even think about the Apple. He thought about reports and making a fool of himself.

It stood about seven feet high, skinny, narrow head like a sidewise board with two jutting and unblinking eyes regarding him calmly. Its two long arms emerged from the torso well below where the shoulders should have been and were covered with something similar to the foil ration packets. The legs were short and powerful looking. Its skin was smooth and reflective—not shiny or slimy, but polished like old wood.

It acknowledged his presence with a polite nod.

He nodded back, and then, under the pressure of all his past training, raised the Apple and said, "Identify yourself."

But by that time it was gone.

Oldfield had the impression it had entered the tunnel, but he couldn't be sure.

His face reddened with anger and frustration. He had had his chance. He had seen a boojum and he hadn't buzzed it down so others could see it. He had followed the pattern of everyone who had ever claimed—officially or unofficially—to have seen one.

Oldfield had always thought he was made of sterner stuff. He pounded his fist against the booth and punched the emergency button on the com.

Chapter Eighteen

Lanier met Takahashi in a conference cubicle at the end of the second floor hall. Carrolson had joined Takahashi and the escort, unaware of Lanier's purpose. That wouldn't cause any problem, Lanier decided; best to keep up an atmosphere of normality. He asked for lunch to be brought to his office and they ate quietly before he outlined his new orders. When he was finished, Carrolson shook her head and sighed.

"Vasquez wants to mount another expedition, this time to the second circuit," she said. "I'm sure she won't like being barred from the libraries."

"Nobody goes into the libraries," Lanier said. "They're strictly off limits. And no second expedition. We freeze all activity on the Stone. I want the archaeologists back at the compounds, and the bore-hole studies shut down, too."

Takahashi regarded him dourly. "What happened with Hoffman?" he asked. Lanier didn't look at him; eating lunch together, he thought, was the last amenity in their relationship. But now was the time. As gracefully as he could manage, he asked Carrolson to leave. She gave him a puzzled look, but he barely noticed her going out the door. All his attention was focused on Takahashi.

"I'm going to defuse a very bad situation," Lanier said when they were alone. "I want you to help me with the defusing, and I want you to report it to your bosses."

"Pardon?" Takahashi asked. The mathematician's hand was a little less steady around the glass of orange juice he had been drinking.

"I want you to report it to your superiors, however you've been doing that."

"I don't understand."

"Nor do I," Lanier said, unmoving in his seat. "I'm not informing Gerhardt, though my instincts tell me I should. You

166

will remain free to observe that we are shutting everything down until negotiations have resolved our differences. You will personally investigate and verify that we have found no information about weapons in the libraries."

"Garry, what are you talking about?"

"I know you are an agent for the Soviets."

Takahashi's jaw muscles tightened and he regarded Lanier from under straight, tense brows.

"There's a dance tonight," Lanier said. "Carrolson will expect all of us to attend. And we will. Gerhardt will be there. He won't be told, because he'd slap you in the bore-hole detention center and ship you back on the next OTV run, in irons, so to speak. I don't want that."

"Out of respect?" Takahashi asked, blinking.

"No," Lanier said. "I don't fall for that old shit about just doing our jobs. You're a goddamned traitor. I don't know where it all began, but it ends here, and I want it to end well. The information you fed back to Earth has damned near started a war. Inform your superiors that everything is cooling off, that we are backing away from the libraries and that in the long run, we may evacuate the Stone. Pull out, let everybody settle their differences. Understood?"

Takahashi said nothing.

"Do you know what's happening on Earth?" Lanier asked.

"No, not precisely," Takahashi said solemnly. "Perhaps we should explain a few things to each other. To help defuse the situation, as you say. Their stake in this is as big as ours."

"Ours?"

"I am an American, Garry. I did this to protect us as well."

Lanier felt his stomach go sour. He clenched his teeth together and turned his chair away from Takahashi. He fought back an urge to ask Takahashi if there had been a lot of money involved; he did not want to know.

"Right. Here's how we stand."

And he told Takahashi what he had learned on Earth.

He hoped to hell this was what Hoffman had intended.

* * *

167

Late in the afternoon, the sociology group presented another team report in the main compound lecture hall. About twenty team members were in the audience; not many more than sat on the low stage, behind the lectern. Rimskaya stood to one side while Wallace Rainer introduced the first of four sociologists.

Lanier watched and listened from the back, slumped in the seat. Ten minutes into the first presentation, Patricia sat beside him and folded her arms.

The first speaker outlined a brief hypothesis of Stone family groupings. She went into some depth on triad families, chiefly found among the Naderites.

Patricia glanced at Lanier. "Why am I barred from the libraries?" she asked in an undertone.

"Everybody is," he said. "As of today."

"Yes, but why?"

"It's very complicated. I can explain later."

Patricia turned away and sighed. "Okay," she said. "I'll do as much as I can outside. That's still allowed."

He nodded and felt a sharp surge of empathy for her.

The second speaker was Tanya Smith—no relation to Robert Smith—and she briskly elaborated on the previously presented report on the evacuation of the Stone.

Patricia half listened.

"It now seems apparent that a resettlement committee handled applications for corridor migration and coordinated transportation—"

Patricia glanced at Lanier again. His eyes met hers.

It was all crazy, no way to run a railroad, much less a huge research effort.

In its most crucial hour, the human race was represented by a team of blindly searching, hog-tied and gagged intellectuals. Thinking of Takahashi, and how useless all the security had been, Lanier's stomach went sour again.

The plan, of course, had been to allow researchers on the lower levels of security clearance and badge status to do their work as best they could, watched over by a senior member

168

with almost full clearance. Their findings would then be filtered and collated and assembled into final statements, checked with corresponding documents in the libraries. It had to be that way. With so few people cleared to do research in the libraries, and with lifetimes of information stored away, decades would have passed before substantial overviews emerged.

That had been the reasoning, at any rate. Lanier had gone along because he was still, after all, a military man at heart, obeying if not implicitly trusting those beyond Hoffman in the chain of command.

Not that it mattered.

Not that it mattered one goddamn bit, because it was all being shut down anyway. They were going to pack up and go home and Takahashi would (if all went well) report that a good-faith effort was being made to placate the worried Soviets.

But the Soviets would still not be allowed into the libraries. Unless the President was totally mad. Only one hand in Pandora's box at a time.

He had seen some of the material on the Stoners' technological advances. He had experienced the education system used in the library. He had touched on the ways the Stoners had tampered with biology and psychology. (*Tampered*—did that betray a prejudice? Yes. Some of it had shaken him to his core and contributed to his worst bouts of being Stoned.) He was uncertain what his own beloved country would do with such power, much less the Soviets.

Patricia sat in on the charade a few more minutes, then left. He stood to follow after her and caught up near the corner of the women's bungalow.

"Just a minute," he said. She halted and half turned, not looking at him but at a potted lime tree growing in a wide space between two buildings. "I don't intend for you to stop your work. Not at all."

"I won't," she said.

"I just wanted to make that clear."

169

"It's clear." Now she faced him directly, hands slipping into her pockets. "You can't be happy with the way things are going."

His eyes widened, and he drew his head back, feeling a sudden anger at her presumption, obtuseness, whatever it was she rolled up into one short sentence.

"You can't be a happy man, keeping us here, knowing all that."

"I'm not keeping you here."

"You've never talked to me, to any of us that I've seen. You say things but you don't talk *with* us."

The anger evaporated and left behind an equally sudden pit of lostness, aloneness. "Rank hath its privileges," he said softly.

"I don't think so." Squinting at him. She wanted to challenge, to provoke. "What kind of person are you? You seem kind of . . . solid. Frozen. Are you really, or is that just a privilege?"

Lanier lifted a pointed finger and waggled it at her, his face creasing with a grim smile. "You do your job," he said. "I'll do mine."

"You still aren't talking."

"What the hell do you want?" he said in a harsh undertone, stepping closer to her, shoulders hunched forward and chin drawn back almost into his neck, an incredibly tense and uncomfortable posture, Patricia thought. She was startled by the sudden breakthrough.

"I want somebody else to tell me what to feel," she said.

"Well, I can't do that." Lanier's shoulders corrected themselves and he extended his jaw. "If we start thinking about anything—"

"But the work, the work," Patricia completed, on the edge of mockery. "Jesus, I'm doing the work, Garry. I'm working all the time." There were tears in her eyes, and to her further shock, she saw tears in his. Lanier's hand moved to his face but he held them back and one tear fell to his cheek, then down the furrow at the side of his mouth.

"Okay," he said. He wanted to leave but he couldn't. "So we're both human. Is that what you wanted to know?"

"I'm working," Patricia said, "but inside I'm just bloody. Maybe that's it."

Quickly, he wiped his eyes. "I'm not a snowball," he said defensively. "And it isn't fair to expect anything more from me, right now, than what I'm giving. Do you see that?"

"This is really peculiar," Patricia said, lifting her hands to her face, as if to mimic him. Her fingers went no higher than her cheeks, which were hot. "I'm sorry. But you followed me."

"I followed you. Shall we leave it at this?"

Patricia nodded, ashamed. "I never thought you were cold."

"Fine," Lanier said. He turned and walked quickly toward the cafeteria.

In her room, she pressed her fists into her eyes, now dry, and tried to mouth the words to a song she had dearly loved as a child. She couldn't quite remember them—or wasn't certain she remembered correctly. *But wherever you go,* she ventured to accompany the tune, *whatever you do, I'll be watching you. . . .*

Chapter Nineteen

Patricia sat in a director's chair on the roof of the women's barracks. She glanced at the date on her watch as those attending the dance gathered in the science team compound. The war was scheduled to begin in seven days.

Everything was coming down on her too quickly. She could render opinions but she could not convince herself of their accuracy. She could, for example, tell Lanier that the Stone could not have been shunted very far from its original continuum. Stone history and their current reality would not differ substantially. Perhaps not enough to prevent war.

171

Perhaps the Soviet knowledge that a war was imminent would turn them around, make them back off, prevent the war. . . .

Perhaps the presence of the Stone, and the clear technological advantage that it gave to the Western bloc countries, would push the Soviets over the edge anyway. . . .

Perhaps the Stone simply made an effect and canceled that effect, and would leave hardly a ripple on the immediate future of the Earth. . . .

Carrolson and Lanier entered the compound. Patricia could see them greeting team members as they arrived from the other chambers.

The ragged, bloody feeling inside had passed. She didn't feel angry or sad. She didn't really even feel alive. The only thing that gave her any joy now was sinking into the state, continuing her work, bathing in the brilliance and majesty of the corridor.

She would have to make an appearance, however. She expected it of herself. Patricia had always resisted playing the reclusive genius and avoiding contact with others. Resisting was not the same as denial of the urge's existence; she *did* want to stay away, to go to her quarters and work. The thought of dancing under the eternal tubelight (the dance was being held in the open) and making small talk—essentially, of going on the social roster, if only for a few hours—frightened her. She wasn't sure she could maintain her temper, the balance that kept her from dissolving into tears of rage and frustration.

She descended the stairs and left the barracks, hands in pockets, forcing her chin higher as she approached the milling crowd.

Two soldiers, two biologists and two engineers had built their own synthesizer and electric guitars out of discarded electronics. The story had been circulating for some weeks that the band was tolerable—perhaps even good. This was their first time in front of an audience, and they seemed coolly professional as they tuned and adjusted the amplifiers.

Loudspeakers of a peculiar design had been cadged by

172

archaeologists working in Alexandria and offered up for the dance as a kind of goodwill sacrifice, an atonement for their fussy protectiveness. The speakers had been set up at corners of the rectangular dance area, an unused acre reserved for future buildings. No wires went to the speakers; the music was broadcast to them on a special frequency through a low-power transmitter. The sound coming out of them was somewhat metallic, but they were serviceable. Heineman inspected one casually and said, "I'm not sure *what* this is. It isn't a loudspeaker."

"It's working, isn't it?" Carrolson said, sticking close to her intended dance partner.

Heineman agreed that it was producing sound from the beamed signal, but went no further than that. The question was never satisfactorily settled.

Beneath the steady tubelight, security team members took turns dancing with the scientists and technicians. The Soviet group stood together to one side, playing wallflowers. Hua Ling, Wu, Chang and Farley joined in energetically, though they had already been informed of the shutdown.

The band switched to older acid rock for a few selections, but that didn't suit the mood and they reluctantly returned to more modern music.

Patricia danced once with Lanier, one of the Japanese waltzes that had become popular in the last few years. At the conclusion, as they held hands at arm's length and bobbed around one another, Lanier nodded mysteriously and smiled at Patricia. She felt a flush work up her neck to her face. At the dance's conclusion, he held her close and said, "Not your fault, Patricia. You've done great. A real team member."

They separated and Patricia retreated to the sidelines, confused, her sensation of nullity broken. Had she *really* expected or wanted approval from Lanier? Apparently; his words pleased her.

Wu asked her to dance and proved to be a capable partner. She then sat out the rest of the festivities. Lanier rejoined her during a break; he had been dancing rather feverishly with a number of partners, Farley and Chang among them.

"Enjoying yourself?" he asked.

She nodded. Then she said, "No, not really."

"Neither am I, if the truth be known."

"You're a good dancer, though," Patricia said.

Lanier shrugged. "Have to stop thinking sometime, right?"

She couldn't agree with that. There was so little time. "I have to talk to you," she said.

"On recreation time?"

"Is here okay?" she asked, simultaneously. The noise was loud enough that they could hardly be overheard.

"As good a place as any, I suppose," Lanier said. He looked around for Takahashi; he was on the opposite side of the dance quad, nowhere near the Russians.

She nodded and again her eyes filled with tears. Because he had said something nice to her, now she would open up and express her worst fears, her darkest opinions. "I've tried to calculate how big a snap the corridor's creation would have given the Stone."

"How big?" Lanier asked, keeping an eye on people passing close enough to hear.

"Not very big," she said. "It's a complicated question. But not big at all."

"We're on, then?"

Her throat tightened. "It's possible. Is that why you really wanted me on the Stone? Just to say that?"

He shook his head. "Hoffman wanted you here. She told me I was responsible for you. I just put you to work." He reached into his pocket and brought out an envelope, opening it and withdrawing two letters. "I haven't been able to give you these before. No, amend that. It slipped my mind until now. I brought them back with me on the shuttle."

She took the letters from his hand and looked at them. One was from her parents, the other from Paul. "May I write back?" she asked.

"Say anything you like," he said. "Within reason."

The postmarks were a week old.

* * *

174

A week passed. The day scheduled for Armaggedon passed.

Patricia stayed in her quarters, working harder than ever with the resources left to her.

She could not change her initial opinion.

Each day, then, was a victory, with reality showing her how wrong she could be.

Chapter Twenty

Lanier exited the elevator and took hold of the cable, maneuvering into the cart. The slightly built driver—a woman in air force blue coveralls—moved the cart off its normal route and followed a track into Kirchner's staging and practice area. Lanier had been there only twice before, each time to meet with the admiral. He clung to the cart handgrips and tried to prepare an answer for the questions he knew would be asked.

Hoffman had hinted in her last communication that the information she had given him had finally reached the Joint Chiefs. That meant Kirchner and Gerhardt had it now.

Gerhardt's aide met him in the short tunnel before the converted cargo storage area where Kirchner's bore-hole team practiced. He led Lanier into a bare-rock cubicle lined with makeshift file cabinets. One wide vein of nickel-iron had been polished and wire-brushed to serve as a projection screen. Kirchner floated into a harness, viewing readouts on a slate, as Lanier was escorted in and announced. Gerhardt pushed himself along the hall and entered after him.

Kirchner nodded at them both. The admiral did not appear comfortable.

"Mr. Lanier—used to be lieutenant commander, did it not?" Gerhardt asked bruskly. He was a squat, trim man with wiry black hair and a broad squashed nose. His dress differed little from that of his internal defense marines: green uniform, black boots with soft rubber soles for traction.

"Yes, sir." Lanier waited out the pause.

175

"You did not inform us that Takahashi is a Soviet operative, Mr. Lanier," Kirchner said.

"No, I did not."

"You learned of this almost two weeks ago and did not inform your security team leaders of the breach?"

Lanier said nothing.

"You had your reasons," Kirchner offered.

"Yes."

"May we be informed?" Gerhardt asked, his tenor voice tightening slightly.

"It was our intention to give the Russians a little breathing space, to let them see we were backing off. We could not do that if Takahashi was locked up."

"Which I would have done," Gerhardt said.

Lanier nodded.

"You're right. I would have. Do you realize this could put our whole operation in jeopardy? Takahashi could have witnessed our maneuvers here, our preparations for the assault—"

"No, sir. He's kept to the compound except to send messages." Kirchner, his usual taciturn self, was letting Gerhardt administer the dressing-down.

"And he's been sending those messages right over our heads, right along with our alignment beams for OTV docking. Wonderful. I am arranging for his arrest now. I want him shipped back to Earth immediately and I want him tried for treason. Christ, Garry." Gerhardt shook his head vigorously, as if to frighten away insects. "Hoffman wanted this?"

"She implied it."

"She gave you the name. Any results? I mean, have the Russians decided to negotiate yet?"

"No, not that I've heard."

"You're damned right they haven't. They know what we're holding here. You expected them to believe we would just pull back and share it all with them?"

"I thought we needed a breather. Chance to reassess."

176

"Did Hoffman know what information Takahashi was passing along?" Kirchner asked.

"Yes. Material about the libraries."

"Jesus, Garry, the clown had access to places *Kirchner and I* can't go. If you ask me, you've screwed this operation up royally. Is there anything I should know that *he* knows? Or that your sweet little female student has learned?"

"Yes, undoubtedly," Lanier said, keeping calm, letting the general blow off steam. "And you know I won't tell you. You'll have to ask your superiors."

Gerhardt smiled. "Yes. A President—off the record, Garry?—a President who's living in some antebellum dream of democracy, can't even talk about space much less think about it; a Senate composed of his stooges and ass-backwards Republicans grinding out bills on southern reapportionment . . ." He glanced at Kirchner, who shook his head, smiling slightly and looked off at the asteroid rock wall. "Nobody's giving half the attention to the Stone they should—or am I wrong?"

"You're right and wrong. At this moment, I don't think there's any more important topic to the governments of the world than the Stone. Everybody's speculating. The Russians are scared shitless we'll have a technological drop on them. We already do, but the Stone cinches it, doesn't it?"

"What are Kirchner and I doing up here, Garry? Why aren't we kept informed, like you? The Stone's security relies on the Captain and me, but those bastards have pulled curtains around us. We can't get into the libraries, can't see documents. . . . I don't understand . . . some of the weirdest things I've been hearing. It's going to drive me nuts. Isn't it time we cooperate with each other?"

"They have their reasons," Lanier said.

"I've watched you, Garry. You've gone downhill the past year. I don't want to know your secrets for my health's sake. What in hell have we got here?"

Lanier pulled himself into a second harness and gripped the straps. "What are your orders from Earth, Oliver?"

177

"I am to prepare for imminent assault on the Stone and for the possibility of nuclear confrontation on Earth."

"Can the Russians take the Stone?"

"If they put everything they have in space against us, yes," Kirchner said.

"Do you think they will?"

"Yes," Kirchner said. "How, I don't know. But we're thinking day and night trying to second-guess. On our next close approach, they'll use little skirmishes on Earth—at sea and in Europe—to distract attention from the Stone. They they'll come at us and try to take it from us. Or they'll try the Stone first. I don't know."

"Can they succeed?"

Gerhardt raised his hand to interrupt. "Will you level with me on what we're facing, Garry? And let me lock the bastard away?"

Takahashi had probably served his usefulness.

"Yes," Lanier said. "Get him off the Stone as soon as you can. Let the State Department take care of him once he reaches Florida."

"You'll let us into the libraries?" Gerhardt asked.

"No. They're closed. I'll tell you what you need to know."

"Then I'll answer your question," Kirchner said. "The Russians can succeed. They can take us over. If they put eveything they have into it, we can't really stop them short of sealing off the bore hole, and we can't do that without sealing ourselves in. We've been ordered not to do that."

"Of course," Lanier said. That would have ended all doubts for the Russians.

"Good talking with you, Garry," Gerhardt said sharply. "Now, let's get busy and move those sons of bitches off the Stone."

"Only Takahashi. Don't touch the Russian team."

"God, no," Gerhardt said. "We won't do that until it's too damned late for anyone to be sensitve."

Chapter Twenty-one

Within the belly of the ocean-launched heavy-lift cargo vehicle, battalion commander Colonel Pavel Mirsky listened to the technicians of Orbital Sentry Platform Three refueling the tanks surrounding and below the cramped aft compartment, preparing them for the next step of the journey.

Mirsky had learned to enjoy weightlessness; it reminded him of skydiving. He had spent so much time falling from airplanes (and floating in the bellies of falling airplanes) in Mongolia and near Tyuratam—and experiencing the real thing during his training in orbit—that weightlessness seemed only natural.

The same could not be said for many of his men. Fully a third were in the throes of desperate space sickness. The three tight, stuffy compartments, stacked atop one another along the heavy-lifter's centerline, had not been designed for comfort. The orange bulkheads and dark green quilted pads snapped over most surfaces did little to make anyone feel secure.

The troops had already spent twenty hours in confinement. In that time they had been subjected to the stress of lift-off and now weightlessness. The motion sickness medicines had turned out to be long past their shelf life, pharmaceutical antiques in plastic bottles.

Mirsky took such things in stride and offered what support to his men that he could.

"What do you think of history now, eh, Viktor?" he asked his depty commander, Major Viktor Garabedian.

"Fuck history," Garabedian said, waving his hand listlessly. "Shoot me now and get it over with."

"You'll be fine."

"Fuck health."

"Drink some water. Yes, and fuck it, too, if you wish." They hung in their slings in the forward compartment,

179

surrounded by the smells of sickness and tension and the sounds of men trying to be quiet, lying in their slings, some eating out of ration pouches and tubes, most not.

When they had launched out of the Indian Ocean, just over the southern extremity of the Carpenter Ridge, they had used a slot scheduled for resupply of a near-earth Sentry platform. They were the fourth of seven heavy-lifters, one launched from the Moon. The seven bore the code names Zil, Chaika, Zhiguli, Volga, Rolls–Royce, Chevy and Cadillac. Three of the heavy-lifters, including Volga, their own, carried generals—code-named Zev, Lev, and Nev, after a popular comedy dance troup. Six of the ships carried two hundred men and the small arms and contingency supplies they would need if they succeeded in the first part of their mission. The seventh—Zhiguli—carried heavy artillery, extra supplies and fifty technicians.

If they did not succeed, there would be no need for more supplies. If they did, they would be able to live for years without support from Earth or Moon. So the tacticians had claimed, based on their intelligence.

Mirsky wondered about details that had not been included in his briefings. The method of entry seemed logical enough; there was only one way in, and one way out, both the same. The heavy-lifters were masked, supposedly difficult to detect—great dark bloated cones topped by three blisters containing the cockpit and weapons. Leading surfaces of the vehicles were armored beneath their disposable heat-diffusing panels. The armor had been covered with reflective anti-laser shields. How much that would help them as they entered the very throat of the beast—best not to think about that.

He shut his eyes to review their actions once they had entered. Each of them carried a lightweight spacesuit in a plastic bag; bulky helmet strapped to one side with coiled and tied connectors; backpack with two hours' oxygen and battery power; and in another bag, a parachute and a folded aerodynamic shield. Each also had a kit containing small vapor propellant rocket. The rockets had three nozzles only a few

180

centimeters across, aimed radially outward when attached to the bottom of the backpacks. They were controlled by buttons on flexible cords that laced through loops and fit into pockets just below the gloves. The nozzles in their plastic packages were folded inward and the propellant sloshed gently when moved.

So equipped, clutching their laser rifles and Kalashnikov AKV-297 vacuum projectile weapons (just machine guns with bigger clips and folding stocks, modified not to jam in airless condition) they proposed to win back the honor and historical place of the Soviet Union and its concerned allies. Not that their briefings had included such phrases—no leader would ever admit that honor and place had been lost.

Mirsky was a practical man, however.

In the half-darkness, another man began retching miserably. Perhaps they would be over it in a day or so. That is what the medical experts had told them; no worse than the first few days on a troop ship. Russians had spent enough time in space that what the experts said had to be based in fact.

He tugged on his sling. When the time came, it would convert into a harness. They would all be hitched to the dispersal trolley and pushed, one by one, out of the ship. From that point on, they would be free agents until they gathered within the Potato—the Stone.

Mirsky wondered how the bore hole was defended, and what lay beyond. Details were tantalizingly specific while the overview remained sketchy; they had been told the absolute minimum necessary to let them do their work.

No objective in orbit had ever been assaulted by troops before.

There was no way of knowing or even guessing everything that could go wrong.

Not that any soldier had ever expected to live through a battle. In the Great War, his grandfather had died along the river Bug when Hitler's troops had made their first crossing, and of course there was Kiev. . . .

Russians knew how to die.

Chapter Twenty-two

Hoffman had taken only the most essential items; seven high-density memory blocks out of perhaps two thousand, a few personal effects and two pieces of jewelry given to her by her late husband, ten years before. She had left the Taos home with the doors open; should any vagabonds chance upon it, she would let them have a few days of pleasure.

There was nothing more she could do. She had asked for a few return favors. There was no doubt what was going to happen within the next four days; no one she had talked to had ever seen tensions so high.

Operating on the instinct which had served her so well in the past, Judith Hoffman was on her way to the Stone. She hoped she hadn't started out too late.

She drove the innocuous second car—a leased Buick—for hours across the desert and open countryside, through small towns and medium-sized towns, trying not to think or feel guilty. There was nothing more she could do.

She had been stripped of all authority by an angry and foolish Chief Executive. Three cabinet members had accused her of actually starting this entire mess.

"The hell with them," she whispered.

Beside the turnoff to Vandenberg Launch Center, in a small complex of civilian stores serving the base personnel, she saw a garden shop. Without hesitating, she pulled into the parking lot.

Inside the store, she found a skinny young male clerk in a leaf-green apron and a Robin Hood hat. She asked where the seed racks were. "Vegetable or flower?" he asked.

"Both."

"Aisle H, just across from hand tools, next to mulch."

"Thank you." She found the racks and took one package of everything she could see, two or three of some of the vegetables and fruits. When she was done, her basket was filled with about ten pounds of seed packages. The clerk looked at the pile in bewilderment.

Hoffman threw two hundred-dollar bills down on the counter. "Will that be enough?" she asked.

"I think so—"

"Keep what's left over," she said. "I'm in a hurry and I don't have time to count them all."

"Let me get the manager—"

"I don't have time," she repeated, and she took out another bill and laid it next to the two.

"I'm sure that will cover it," the clerk said quickly, swallowing.

"Thank you. Put them in a box for me?"

Hoffman picked up the box and returned to the car.

Lanier was asleep in his cubicle when the comline chimed. He reached over to press the button, but no message awaited, only silence.

He rubbed his eyes clear, blinking. Then he heard the other comlines in other rooms throughout the barracks, all chiming. Footsteps sounded in the hallway.

He punched a number into the unit. A shaky voice answered, "First chamber communications."

"This is Garry Lanier. Are we having a central alert?"

"Yes, Mr. Lanier."

"Why?" Lanier's voice was infinitely patient.

"I'm not sure, sir."

"I want to speak with axis communications right now."

"Yes, sir."

When a woman's voice answered some seconds later, he requested a briefing.

"We have DefCon three from London and Moscow," the woman said. "Radar activity is up, especially orbital tracking. There's been some action against communications and navigation satellites."

183

"Any messages from Florida or Sunnyvale?"

"None, sir."

"Messages from the lunar settlement?"

"Nothing to us, sir. They're farside to us now."

"I'm coming up to the axis now. Tell Link and Pickney to set up a special situation room with seating for about fifteen people."

Roberta Pickney's voice interrupted. "Garry, is that you? Everything's already set up, Kirchner's orders. He wants science and security coordinating on this. Get up here immediately."

In the elevator, surrounded by security personnel and baffled engineers who hadn't heard details yet, Lanier tried to think of all the things left to be done, all the preparations yet to be made. He felt his rough, unshaven chin.

It had all been hypothetical, a long-running nightmare. Down below, where he had spent most of his life, where most of the people he loved—and how few they were!—still lived, it was probably beginning.

He couldn't block images of what people back home were doing at this moment. He had lived through it as a pilot, but never as a civilian. Listening to radios, to sirens, to civil defense instructions never comprehensive enough to be of real value. Orders to evacuate, issued over cable communications from neighborhood to neighborhood. People afraid, people throwing things into automobiles or scrambling for buses or trains or Civil Defense trucks . . .

He tried to quell such thoughts. He needed his wits about him.

At the axis chambers, the security guards organized the people into priority tram groups. He was plucked from the crowd by three young marines and ushered almost forcibly into a special car.

The center of Stone external communications was a walled-off area about twenty meters square in one corner of the prime dock staging area. Six marine corporals stood by the door, rifles at ready, their boots hooked into special loops to brace them in case they needed to aim and fire. Lanier passed between them. Inside the room, ten people had gathered. They watched him closely as he pulled himself into a seat.

Four video screens were mounted in one wall. Innumerable repeaters had been wired into most of the consoles. Only one of the big screens was on, showing a fuzzy picture of the Stone itself surrounded by data readouts. That was a picture from the Drake: just as he had first seen the Stone, four years ago.

Pickney handed him a pair of Velcro galoshes. "It hasn't started yet," she said. "But there's been an alert. Something's hit the fan but we're not sure what it is. Put this on." She wrapped earphones and mike around his head. "I've been getting everything coordinated for the past half hour."

"Orders yet?"

"Nothing specific. Just the alert."

He sat where he was told and a bank of keyboards and viewers was moved near to him. Captain Kirchner and his aide, a young mustachioed lieutenant commander dressed in khakis, entered a few minutes later and were seated a few meters away in similar accommodations.

Kirchner, in charge of external Stone defense, was really the central figure now. Gerhardt was in the first chamber, making preparations; but for the moment, what happened in the chambers was incidental. "Get fifteen men outside the bore hole with portable detection systems," Kirchner said. "I want them hidden behind those honey-comb walls, out of sight—no heat signatures. And get those goddamned Gatling guns in position."

Quiet descended. Pickney, earphones clamped over her short, bobbed hair, listened intently. A burst of static issued from a speaker on the other side of the room.

On the largest screen before Lanier, a picture flicked on, wavered and steadied into crystal clarity. The source was a camera just outside the bore hole, in the honeycombed dimple. The camera was oriented toward the Earth at that moment. The limb of the Earth, still in darkness, came into focus. The picture shuffled twice as enhancers did their work. Lanier

185

could then make out continents, cloud patterns, city lights in the night. They were within a few minutes of being nearest in their orbital path to Earth—less than three thousand kilometers.

A crackly radio voice came over their headphones. "Heavensent, Heavensent, this is Red Cube. Alert situation Remarkable."

"Shit," Kirchner murmured.

"Bears have just announced their end run. Captain Kirchner, we are devising responses now. Your situation is unknown. Please advise."

"We are secure and making preparations," Kirchner said.

Red Cube—the Joint Space Command western headquarters in Colorado—came back with, "You are now out of our response pattern, Captain. We must conduct affairs as if you did not exist. The steam in the sweatbox is thick. Looks like they're going to take out our near-Earth capability. Understood?"

"Understood. Hope to God you can keep them in line, Red Cube."

"Heavensent is now on its own, Captain."

"Yes, sir."

The transmission ended.

"My screen shows an OTV approach," Kirchner said. "Is it identified?"

"OTV forty-five, carrying supplies and reinforcement personnel, launched nine hours ago from Station Sixteen," Pickney said. "We've been monitoring."

Kirchner's aide confirmed that the marines in the dimple had picked up a blip on their scanners.

"Take it aboard," Kirchner said. "We're going to be getting a lot more in a day or so if this goes all-out."

"Yessir—several more launching already."

A screen before Lanier rolled up a picture of the OTV approaching the bore hole. Suddenly, the OTV expanded into a glowing sphere. Silently, quickly, the sphere dissolved at its edges and darkened to dull orange. Debris scattered in silhouette against the diffuse shells of gas.

186

"Sir," Kirchner's aide said, "they're seeing dark transits out there, blocking stars. Behind the OTV."

"The OTV's gone," Lanier said. "Captain, they've snuck in behind our ship."

"My God," exclaimed a voice over a the hissing and crackling loudspeaker. Pickney had opened the marines' frequency to all in the room. "Something's taken out our ship. Am I seeing—"

"Transits, transits! No blips."

"Durban here. I'm getting dark spots but they have to be retinal."

"No way. I didn't see the flash and I'm getting four, five, six transits blocking stars. Big suckers."

"They're going to come down the pipe," Kirchner said. "Get the OTV tanks rigged to block them. Team A, release your cables."

Cameras in the bore hole showed ghostly infrared- and low-light-enhanced images of men in suits moving behind the first rotating dock. Mortar-like cannon fired coiled steel cable across the hundred-meter diameter of the bore hole. Harpoons fixed the cables in the opposite wall. Seven were fired in rapid succession, making a web in the bore hole. Three discarded OTV tanks were maneuvered up from the sides and fixed in position with more cables. All this was done in less then ten minutes.

"They won't come into the staging areas," Kirchner said confidently. "It would be a waste of time. If they come down the pipe, they'll go for the chambers. They can mop us up later. I hope Oliver's soldiers are prepared."

In the commotion, Lanier had directed his eyes away from the screens displaying the Earth. He returned his attention to them.

Tiny orange spots blossomed along the Soviet coast west of Japan, simple suborbital rockets deploying solid debris to bring down low-orbit satellites and battle stations. "Pop-ups," Kirchner said.

One of the marines outside the bore hole said something

garbled. Then, as Pickney enhanced the reception, the voice continued, "Sir, they're blowing the masks."

The large screen switched to a view down the bore hole. Stars twinkled beyond the flare-lit rotating dock and the outer lip of the bore hole. Three shadows moved against the stars. Then, fire rimmed the shadows and pie slices of black material drifted away, revealing shapes difficult for the eye to define. The mirrored noses of the intruders were reflecting the dark interior of the bore hole and the illuminated prime dock. "Signature," Kirchener's aide said. "They're Russian, ocean-launched heavy-lift cargo vehicles. First is in the pipe."

Twenty meters wide, the Russian ships resembled Christmas decorations as they entered the bore hole. Invisible beams of energy from guns hidden beyond the rotating dock were already making parts of the leading heavy-lifter glow orange. Lanier could not begin to keep track of what was happening. His eye moved from screen to screen; Kirchner spoke rarely now. The procedures had already been outlined; his men were doing all they had been trained to do, all they could do.

"Pickney, patch me through to seventh chamber," Lanier said.

"Everyone's in first and fourth chambers by now," Gerhardt said.

"Then get me fourth chamber. Wherever. I want Heineman."

"Lead ship returning fire," said an anonymous voice from within the bore hole. "Looks like they're aiming for the tanks, maybe the cables."

"Maybe they don't see the cables," another voice suggested. The tone of both soldiers was calm, expectant.

Lanier noticed a monitor showing the tiny star of Station Sixteen, in low Earth orbit of one thousand kilometers. As he watched, the star became a glowing smudge of white light. The light winked out.

"Heineman on your button five," Pickney told Lanier. He punched the button.

"Lawrence, this is Garry."

"I was almost out the door and they pulled me back in. I'm in fourth chamber, Garry. I was on my way—"

"Lawrence, we're in—we're being attacked. Just get to the V/STOL and take it up. Hitch to the tuberider and take it down the line. Stay there until we call you back."

"Got you. I was on my way."

The button popped up and dimmed.

More brilliant white flowers grew from pinpoints to blue-white smudges over Japan and China—four in all. These were orbital nuclear bursts, designed to incapacitate communications and power nets with intense flashes of electromagnetic interference—the source of more static over the speakers. As the Stone moved in its counterclockwise orbit, and as the Earth turned beneath them, he saw more bursts over the Soviet Union and Europe—fourteen in all. A veritable nuclear springtime. They had upped the ante since the Little Death. No strategic exchanges yet—but no unshielded electronics or communications systems would survive these preliminary steps in the dance.

The smaller viewscreens showed pictures intercepted from those scanning satellites still intact and broadcasting.

The coast of North America, southern and Baja California prominent, came into dawn, high-altitude glows casting an eerie light across the ocean and land, like penlights on a relief map. The carnage still hadn't begun. What was the plan— bluff? Deception?

The negotiations would have begun already. *What has been done, what will be done unless . . . How to scale back, defuse, settle for a limited confrontation . . . Who was bluffing whom, and how far they would go.*

Who would surrender.

Chapter Twenty-three

Colonel Mirsky gripped the edge of the hatch leading to the ship's cockpit. There was no direct view of the bore hole; the laser shield and armored outer hull covered the forward windows. He couldn't understand the displays before the two pilots; they were a confusion of vague lines, spinning circles, things like Easter eggs rolling and precessing in a grid pattern. "Get your men ready," the ship's commander said, glancing over his shoulder. "Tell them to stay close to the bore-hole walls until they exit into the first chamber. They have men with lasers waiting. Sting like bees."

Heavy fists seemed to slam on the outside of the hull in a rapid tattoo. Alarms went off. "Naughty fellows; that was a Gatling gun," the copilot said. "Laser shields penetrated. Minor outer hull breach."

Mirsky backed out and closed the hatch behind him, the commander's comment about bees still echoing in his mind. Mirsky had once tended bees on a city co-op in Leningrad as a student project. *We invade the hive,* he thought. *Naturally, they try to sting.*

He floated across the first compartment, picked up his helmet and issued terse instructions. The sergeants—squad leaders for the second and third compartments—pulled themselves through the hatches to alert their men. Minutes and it would begin.

"Why so glum, Alexei?" he chided a soldier inspecting his helmet. "Friends, are your weapons charged?"

They pulled their rifles out of a charging rack and checked the glowing LEDs.

"Line up," Mirsky said. In the second and third compartments, he heard orders being barked. The first company commander, stationed in the first compartment, Major Konstantin Ulopov, was already in his helmet, with the cannon-bearer Zhadov tugging experimentally at the connections and seals on his suit. When he was given the okay, Ulopov would in turn assist Mirsky.

None of them had much protection against laser or projectile hits. In this sort of warfare, an AKV or even a pistol— prepared for the vacuum, but with standard-issue bullets—was as effective against a soldier as antipersonnel lasers.

Mirsky approached the small group surrounding "Zev," Major General Sosnitsky. "Our battalion is prepared, Comrade General," he reported.

Sosnitsky's staff of three officers—with the *Zampolit*, Major Belozersky, standing nearby—were checking and re-checking the general's suit, like chicks around a hen. Sosnitsky lifted a gloved hand over the commotion and offered it to Mirsky. Mirsky grasped it firmly. "The Marshall would be proud of you and your men," Sosnitsky said. "Today—or tonight or whatever it is—will be glorious."

"Yes, sir," Mirsky said. Even though his thoughts about the command structure bordered on the cynical, Sosnitsky had the power to make him feel emotion.

"We will give them something back for Kiev, won't we, Comrade?"

"That we will, Comrade General."

He glanced up at Belozersky. The political officer's expression was a mix of exaltation and borderline panic. His eyes were wide and his upper lip was damp.

Mirsky wiped his own upper lip. Moist. His whole face was moist. Then he backed away from the group and resumed his position.

The queuing lights near the three circular exit hatches came on and the craft began its erratic tumbling, designed to offer unpredictable targets for marksman as the soldiers leaped forth. It would also scatter them like chaff inside the bore hole; the partners would grip each other's harnesses and jump as a group to stay together until they had their bearings.

They would not fire randomly; there was more chance of hitting one another than an antagonist. Only in direct combat

191

with clearly seen opponents would they fire, and they were not to waste their time even with that if it could be avoided.

Everyone was suited and lined up. The emergency airlock surrounding number two exit hatch had been dismantled and stowed against the bulkhead. The pumps began to evacuate the compartments with throaty grumbles and a high *pud-pud*. The connecting hatches between the compartments slid shut. The lights were extinguished. The only thing Mirsky's soldiers could see now were the queuing lights above the exit hatches and the luminous glows of their guide ropes.

"Check radios and locators," he said. Each soldier performed a quick diagnostic on his communications gear and the all-important beacon locator.

The queuing lights flashed at half-second intervals. Everyone made sure they were connected to the trolley which would guide and tug them around the compartments until it brought them to their exit hatch.

Ten seconds until hatch opening. The motion of the ship—jerking, pitching and rolling as its maneuvering jets fired unevenly—was beginning to affect even Mirsky.

He could no longer hear the pumps. They were in vacuum.

The hatches slid open abruptly and the queues began to spill out into darkness and silence.

Two squads destined for the first chamber—twenty men in all—went out in the first queue.

Mirsky was third in his queue. Ulopov went ahead and Mirsky held him by a strap attached to his thigh. Mirsky in turn was held by Zhadov, who kept the laser cannon strapped to his side. The trio gripped the hatch edge and kicked away in unison, as they had been trained, flying from the craft like a precision skydiving team, a little star of six legs in the vast darkness.

His eyes adjusted quickly and he switched on his locator. For a heart-stopping moment he thought all was lost; he could not hear even a whisper of signal. Then came the steady high-frequency *CHUFF-chuff-chuff* of the beacon, placed by some unknown compatriot—perhaps dead already, murdered by the Americans—in the bore hole leading into the second chamber.

192

And he could make out the tiny spot of light that was the opening to the first chamber.

Stuff floating around. Bumping, smearing. Dark drops fuzzing out. Large chunks of metal in his helmet beam, sections of torn bulkhead and rippling sheets of steel . . . a ship!

Tangled in something invisible ahead, the wreckage of one of the heavy-lifters vibrated ponderously, fly caught in a web, surrounded by drifting bodies, most without helmets. Pieces of limbs and trunks drifted past.

A blinding nimbus surrounded them all. High-intensity spotlights played around the ships and their disgorged soldiers, dead and alive. Zhadov let go of Mirsky's strap, and Mirsky instinctively reached for the man's weapon but caught his arm instead. The suit squirmed in his grip and the body twisted fiercely, almost dragging Mirsky away from Ulopov. Zhadov's suit had been holed and the venting gas whirled him about like a released balloon. Mirsky reached out as far as he could and gripped the cannon. He handed it to Ulopov.

(As clear as reality—clearer, at the moment—he stood in a grassy field and contemplated this nightmare. He gathered his chute up from the yellow grass and shook his head, grinning at his imagination.)

Soldiers filled the bore hole, hundreds of them, and all around he could instinctively feel the invisible laser needles and projectiles searching, piercing, picking away.

Mirsky pulled Ulopov to him and swung his helmet beam around, looking for the wall they should be approaching. It was not visible. Zhadov's death had knocked them off course.

"Use your rocket pack," he told the major. "We break up now."

"*Spshh*ome potato," the Major commented dryly, the voice-activated microphone cutting off the first sound of each phrase. "*Sphshh*otter than an oven. *Spshh*ust be baked. *Shhp*ood luck, Colonel!"

Mirsky let go of the strap and fired his thruster. He swung outward, away from the entangled wreckage and awful corpses. He cut the thruster and switched on his helmet display. Before his eyes, the beacon and his relation to it appeared on a small luminous stage. He adjusted with another thrust, as did hundreds of his comrades—how many hundreds he could not say.

He suddenly remembered the number of the entangled wreckage, now far behind. That had been the lunar ship— filled with those most recently and thoroughly trained for low-gravity combat. Their best.

Mirsky, alone now with his signal and his thruster— unconcerned for the moment about how many of his men were behind or ahead—flew down the bore hole toward the tiny circle of light.

"They've broken through," Kirchner said, slamming the side of his palm against the chair arm. "There's nothing in the bore hole but bodies and wreckage. About three heavy-lifters have backed out; we must have disabled the rest. Nobody's getting away, though—they can't go home."

"The pilots will wait until we're taken," Gerhardt said wearily on the comlink. He was now overseeing evacuation of the civilian teams to the fourth chamber.

"You don't sound in the best of spirits, Oliver," Kirchner said. "Your turn now."

"We have some transmissions from the Persian Gulf," Pickney said. "We can unscramble them. Captain, would you like to listen in?"

"Let's hear them," Kirchner said.

A man's voice, sounding almost mechanical after the processing of the signal, said, "One K that is Kill Seven, One K that is Kill Seven, have smoked the circle; repeat, have smoked the circle. Vampires, fourteen count, range fifty klicks, source Turgenev small platform. Repeat, fourteen vampires. Six down. Sweep two commencing. Smoking circle, up with directed fry, nine down, up with knives, eleven down. Three vampires, twenty-klicks. Priests out. Priests and vampires engage. Advising salamander crews. Starfish launched.

194

Sea Dragons alerted. Two vampires, six klicks. Sweep three commencing. Foaming now. Short eyes out, blades out, Guardians out, knives inboard." A pause. "Two vampires, three klicks." Another pause, then, softly, "Good-bye, Shirley."

"That's the cruiser *House*," Kirchner said quietly, rubbing his eyes with his hands. "She's gone."

"Another," Pickney said. "Coast of Oman."

"Let's have it," Kirchner said, glancing at Lanier.

"—CVN ninety-six, group Hairball," the signal commenced, "second launch Feather Two; repeat, Feather Two, commencing Chigger, repeat, Chigger. Special fourth class nuke, postal authorities will advise."

"The carrier *Fletcher* is sending in strategic aircraft for a midrange coast sortie," Kirchner translated.

"CVN eighty-five, code Zorro Doctor Betty, Postal authorities withdraw your permit. Claws will scratch Chiggers. Sea Dragons alerted. Slow wall up and Turkey Feathers down. Repeat, slow wall up and—"

"Group Hairball, Leading Man, Groom, and Alpha Delta Victor . . . Best Man, Chambermaid, luncheon postponed—"

"CVN ninety-six, I count thirty-eight vampires, source deep-blue Turgenev-class platform, range ten klicks, knives up, short eyes, Sea Dragons alerted. Priests and vampires engage angels two, Jesus Christ"—an obvious expletive, not code—"they're at two klicks—"

Kirchner flinched as the message was cut off. "I should be down there," he said. "Right in the middle of the barbecue."

"How many OTVs did Station Sixteen get off?" Lanier asked.

"Besides OTV 45, five. Three are coming for us. Two for the Moon."

"Warn the three we are under attack and may not be able to receive them. Suggest they divert to the Moon."

"If they can make it," Pickney said.

The evacuation of the low Earth orbit platforms and other

stations had already begun. The war was expanding now; not just beam defense platforms, but research and industrial stations were becoming targets.

"Some diversion," Pickney said bitterly. "Looks like it's getting out of control."

"Of course it is," Gerhardt said on the comlink. "Only an idiot or somebody very desperate would have thought otherwise. Garry, you done done all you can there. I'll need you in the first chamber in a few minutes. I'm on my way back now."

Chapter Twenty-four

Vasquez slept on a bunk beneath the tent, exhausted after seven hours of intense work. Two slates, an expanded processor and several dozen sheets of paper littered the tent floor around the cot.

Patricia, Carrolson, Farley, Wu and Chang—and of course Heineman in the V/STOL—made up the only group not confined to the first and fourth chambers. Lanier had decided her work was too important to stop completely.

She dreamed about a drugstore on Earth. She was being refused the opportunity to buy an ice cream cone. The dream transformed and she stood by a blackboard in a large classroom, trying to explain abstruse problems to a sea of unruly students. They began throwing pieces of chalk at her. With an absolute conviction of reality, she watched the chalk hit the equations on the board. Hold it, she cried, Stop! The class ceased its commotion. She picked a piece of chalk off the floor and circled the areas of the equations that had been marked by hits. Of course, she said, these would show—

Carrolson grabbed her shoulder and shook her awake. Patricia pulled aside wisps of black hair and looked up at the woman through sleep-puffy eyes.

"We have to get to the fourth chamber," Carrolson said.

"Why? I'm working—"

"Work's over, honey. There's a truck waiting. The Chinese are going, too. All of us. Move!" Her tone was acid. Patricia picked up her bag and stuffed the slate, memory blocks, multi-meter and processor into it. Carrolson made as if to knock the bag out of her hands, then pulled back, arms clutching her own shoulders. "We don't need those now," she said. "We really don't."

Tears slid down Carrolson's cheeks and spotted the breast of her coveralls. "Everyone's saying it," she continued. "I haven't seen, but there's stuff coming in on that hookup—the one for filching satellite broadcasts."

Patricia clutched the bag to her breast and ran ahead of Carrolson to the truck, cursing under her breath.

How funny she was behaving, she thought in a part of her mind where reality had not yet penetrated. How hysterical. After all, she had known. She should have been prepared.

Carrolson, Wu and Chang climbed into the truck behind her. Farley drove them up the ramp and into the tunnel.

Chapter Twenty-five

Mirsky was terrified. Pushed ahead by the vapor thrusters, periodically trailing a thin and quickly dissipating cloud of hydrogen peroxide, he aimed along the beacon. On every side, ground awaited him; his stomach told him he was falling in all directions. Ahead was a gray-black expanse. Clouds drifted in curving sheaths above, below, behind, before. He could not close his eyes; he had to keep the helmet display centered on the beacon signal.

He caught sight of several fellows, their thruster bursts resembling contrails from the wings of a jet drifting in and out of moist air. *How many?* he asked. What countermeasures would the Americans have taken?

He had to cross this beautiful horror, this place without top or bottom, and fly down a second bore hole. Only in the second chamber would he be able to drop away from the center and unfold his airfoil/shield, following the simple map that would be projected on his helmet display.

Slowly his fear turned into exhilaration. The longest jump he had ever made on Earth had lasted for six minutes, better than lovemaking, better than the day he received his wings. But here he had been flying steadily, accelerating with each new burst, for ten minutes, fifteen.

If he died upon landing, it would be worth it. To have seen a place where the land was the sky, where he could dive any direction and come to ground. Worth it all. Worth even the nightmare of the bore hole and the drifting, torn bodies of his comrades, faces bloated and livid in the vacuum, eyes protruding beyond their lids and ghastly white.

"*Pss*olonel Mirsky, is that you?"

"Yes! Identify."

"*Psh*lopov. I've seen others from our ship—and hundreds more! *Psh*are like angels, Colonel. *PshCHKCHK*irst squads have dropped away, look behind *PSCKHH*olonel."

He carefully inclined his neck, keeping his eye on the beacon alignment, then looked behind and below. He could see tiny white dots—parachutes—in the bluish haze above the floor of the chamber. He twisted smoothly and saw more at another quadrant—coming down, as planned, to take control of elevator entrances in the first chamber's southern wall. Pride swelled in him. Who else could have even succeeded this far? History!

He could see the darker hole in the center of the forward wall. None of them had more than two hours of air in their suit tanks—how much longer until he could drop away?

In the fourth chamber compound, Carrolson had given up trying to organize the members of the science team. Most of the security team had been deployed, leaving the barracks, cafeteria and grounds to the evacuees.

Patricia sat in the cafeteria, numb, snot crusted under her nose, half-listening to the sporadic radio signals coming over the cafeteria loudspeakers. The signals from the external satellite feed was still being directed down the bore hole to transponders at the entrance of each chamber. Electronic chatter of robots calmly sacrificing themselves in orbit, seeking orbiting outposts and battle stations, or going silent as they reentered the atmosphere to search out a few million more human beings, enacting a deterrence policy now guaranteeing only more and more death.

Out of control, Patricia thought.

Spasm. The motions a dying person makes, or the twitches in a corpse. San Diego, Long Beach, Los Angeles, Santa Barbara. *Spasm.*

Farley and Chang wept in each other's arms. Wu was silent and stolid, sitting on a table like a piece of sculpture. Rimskaya stood in a corner with a bottle of Scotch, almost certainly contraband, taking a gulp every few seconds until he fell down.

A few ex-defense workers, reverting to the old banter, the old assessments and guesses, conducted a calm analysis of who was winning, who was still capable of fighting, which hardened weapons sites would open next. "Submarines under the ice caps?" "No—both sides will hold those in reserve for after." "What after?" "Who cares?" "What about those trucks—you know, the reverse ground-effect vehicles, hug the ground when the shock wave passes over." "Fuck 'em all."

Spasm.

She closed her eyes as if to block an image of her home absorbing the sudden burst of light and radiation, becoming a carbonized mockery of walls and roof.

And within, slightly protected by the shadow of the house— roasted alive, but not quite carbonized—and then being blasted to fine ash by the shock wave—

Rita and Ramon.

Farley approached Patricia and tapped her on the shoulder, disrupting her reverie. "We can't go back," she said. "The engineers say none of the spaceports are left by now. Vandenberg, the cosmodromes—Kennedy Space Center, even

199

Edwards—gone. We can't get to the Moon, either. Not enough ships or fuel. Nobody'll come up for ten, maybe twenty years. That's what the engineers are saying. We might have a few good fields left in China, but there aren't going to be any shuttles in orbit to rendezvous with the OTVs even if we could go back."

Wu joined them. "Nothing out of China now," he said. "Russia still throwing things. Every city I live in, gone by now. We used to get civil defense instruction in school. We knew where bombs would drop. Russian bombs and maybe even American bombs. Every city had its bombs."

"When's the funeral?" someone asked in the background. There was no laughter, only silence. It was an extraordinarily insensitive joke. Except that it couldn't be a joke. There had to be a funeral when somebody died.

But when billions of people were dead or dying?

Carrolson sat down beside Patricia. "Office ink is all there is," she said laconically. "Wayne is gone, and our son. They're dead by now, I'm sure. You know, in a little while this is going to hurt like hell. Adjusting is going to be . . ." Her cheeks twitched, spotted red as if she were breaking out in a rash. "Rimskaya drank all the booze, the bastard."

"I'm going to the library," Patricia said.

"Can't," Carrolson said. "Off limits."

"I need something to do."

"Of course." But she offered no suggestions.

"Hey, we have more pictures from the external cameras!" someone yelled. The wide-screen video was wheeled out and connected to the central cafeteria hookup.

Patricia did not look at the video screen. She had seen satellite and lunar telescope pictures of the conflagration in the Thistledown City library. Somewhere on Earth—in Washington or in Pasadena in Hoffman's office—copies of those pictures were being embraced by the destruction they depicted, an ouroboros of doom.

Carrolson watched, however, eyes narrowed, lips drawn back.

200

One by one, the cities blossomed. The atmosphere rippled over each explosion, as if a giant steel ball had been dropped in a pond.

Over the western limb, beyond the Atlantic, a brighter-than-dawn glow was creeping, now yellow, now purple, now green.

The whole world was being swept by a crown fire, with the flames leaping not from tree to tree, but from city to city, continent to continent.

People were no more substantial than pine needles.

Chapter Twenty-six

Gerhardt and Lanier stood near several squads of soldiers guarding the entrance to the zero elevator. Gerhardt held up the field glasses. "Little specks," he said. "Mosquitos. Most of them are coming down in this chamber. But quite a few appear to be crossing over." He handed the glasses to Lanier.

"Into the second chamber." The cool wind sliding down from the cap played with Lanier's hair. Lanier kept track of two of the specks in the glasses, following their contrails along the axis. He lowered the glasses to inspect the defenses around the two science team compounds.

"Yeah. Expecting us to have a bigger force here, which we do."

He raised his glasses again and saw broader white dots at a much lower angle, near the southern cap. "Parachutes," Lanier said. "Some are in the atmosphere now."

"Jesus, what an effort," Gerhardt said in admiration. He picked up his radio. "Zero south tunnels, forces coming your way. Bore hole, keep your eyes open."

Lanier could not concentrate. He kept thinking of the diversion; had they set fire to the world just to gain an advantage here? Hoping they could control the results with negotiation, keeping the casualties close to those of the Little

Death? He suddenly grew sick of all the thousands of artificial modes of behavior conjured up by representatives of government, by military men, by patriots and traitors and fighters and—

He wanted to crawl away and sleep.

He could not keep from seeing in his imagination an image of Hoffman, on the road to Vandenberg in her limousine, hoping to escape the madness, to leave the dying aircraft and bail out—to come here, where the madness had spread, and not making it anyway; facing the blasts over Vandenberg.

"Do they know?" he asked.

"Know what?" Gerhardt said.

"Do the Russians know the Death has come?"

Gerhardt, who had never been in the library and had had none of Lanier's forewarning, frowned at him. "What are you asking, Garry?"

Lanier pointed up. "They're about to engage us in battle, but do they know neither of us have supreme commanders anymore?"

"Some leadership will survive," Gerhardt said.

"Oliver, does it matter?"

"You're goddamn fucking right it matters!" Gerhardt screamed at him, spittle beading on his chin. He wiped it away with the sleeve of his overalls, shaking his head and turning away, face reddening. "Don't go under now, Garry. We need everybody we can get."

"I'm going to fight," Lanier said.

"It won't be the first time, will it?" Gerhardt asked, his voice strained and harsh.

"On the ground, yes." *Modes of behavior. No rest, no end, even after doomsday.* "Where's my weapon?"

They had made it through the second bore hole, despite sporadic fire from troops stationed there. More had died, but not many. . . .

Would he ever stop falling?

Mirsky spun in his path to survey the city—

202

He had never seen *such a city!*

—as his thrusters pushed him a hundred meters away from the bore hole, then two hundred, then three. He spotted the landmark he was after—the zero bridge spanning the chamber-circling river—and pushed himself away from the Potato's axis, toward the thin glow of the plasma tube.

Other soldiers had already fallen free through the atmosphere barrier and the plasma tube. Their informant had assured them passage was safe, as long as they did not linger—but Mirsky trusted only experience and survival. He could not see whether his comrades were alive or dead—when he saw them at all, they were too tiny to make out details. *They were dwarfed—how could a few hundred soldiers command an object as big as a republic?*

The perspective changed very slowly as he fell away from the axis.

He felt no wonder whatsoever at how selfish his emotions were now, and how much hate filled him. Mirsky had felt these emotions many times before, during training or the horrid endurance tests. These were the emotions of soldiers in battle, hard and bitter, touched with fear but mostly with overwhelming self-interest.

He could not have cared less about the state, the Motherland, the revolution. There was no shame in him.

Only falling. Spiraling outward as the great cylinder turned around him. He kept pace with the landmarks using his thrusters. Silence, not even the sound of wind yet. He prepared his air-sled, fanning out and locking its segments.

Then he noticed he was drifting some degrees away from the bridge. He corrected with another thruster burst. There was so little sensation he might go mad . . . and yet he had been falling for only a minute or so, very slowly. . . .

He felt—perhaps only in his mind—a tingle and knew he was passing through the plasma tube. Below that, but only by a few hundred meters, lay the upper limits of the atmosphere, beyond the restraining barrier. He braced himself behind the sled and strapped his arms and legs to the concave inner surface. Whatever angle he first brushed the atmosphere, the sled would flip him around to the shape of least resistance. He would plummet through the upper air until he could hear the whistle of its passage, then he would kick free of the sled and begin his fifteen- or sixteen-kilometer dive, releasing the chute only two or three kilometers from the floor of the chamber. He would be lighter, falling; the impact would not be very hard at all.

Another soldier came close enough to wave—one he didn't recognize, with the insignia of Sixth Battalion, from Rolls–Royce. Mirsky waved back and motioned for him to prepare his sled. The soldier held it up—folded, in tatters from a projectile impact—and shrugged, flipping it aside. They were to maintain radio silence, but the soldier used his rockets to approach close enough that they could read lips.

—Can I survive without?

—I don't know. Tuck up into a ball and present your back to the air . . . if you can.

That was difficult to convey with lip movements, so Mirsky mimed by folded himself up as best he could behind the shield, drawing up his knees and wrapping his arms around him.

The soldier nodded and signaled okay with his thumb and index finger. They drifted apart—the soldier falling more slowly because of his thrust toward Mirsky. Mirsky watched the soldier thrust again to move away from the cap surface, toward which he was drifting, and then busied himself preparing for the entry.

He checked his position with relation to the bridge. One more adjustment with the thrusters. He could feel some pressure now against the sled. A vibration, weak nudges.

He made one more thrust and then unfastened and discarded the rocket pack. Where it fell he did not care, so long as it didn't land on *him*.

For an instant, through the preparations and the near-fury of anticipation, he looked again at the city and wondered what the Potato's secret actually was. Why were they fighting for it? What could it bring them?

How would the West react, facing the theft of its greatest prize? Or the attempt (he had heard rumors) to take out its orbital platforms and spy satellites?

How would Russia react in the same circumstances?

He shuddered.

The sled jerked and whirled around. He blacked out for a moment, then came awake to a bone-crushing slam and a high-pitched, wavering scream.

Coming down.

The sled swung around again and bucked but was now committed to one orientation. He was pressed against its inner surface, padded elbows and knees braced, hoping he had broken no bones. It had been more violent than the falls from three meters in training. He tasted blood in his mouth. He had bitten almost through his inner cheek—he could flap the tissue with his tongue. He closed his eyes against the pain—

(And gathered up his chute in the golden grassy field, smiling at the burning sun, looking for his comrades, shielding his eyes to spot the distant specks of the transport plane—)

And fell. He hastily unbuckled from the sled. The air roared around him. Then he grasped the straps loosely in his hands. He flipped the sled over and it was torn from his fingers.

Made it!

From here on it was a simple freefall and parachute exercise. He tucked to roll, and spread his arms and legs to flatten out and stabilize. The bridge was still only a line of white over the blue-black river. Was it really the right bridge— really the zero bridge?

Yes—he could spot the tiny speck of a guard shack nearby and make out lines of defense and sandbag emplacements. And he couldn't have fallen so far wrong as to traverse a third of the chamber's arc. . . . He was right on, too close in fact—he would have to drift away some.

The wind hummed mildly past his helmet now. He checked his laser and Kalashnikov and made quick surveys of his equipment belt.

Chute release had to be gauged purely by eye. There was no sense counting from the axis, since everyone would fall at a

205

different rate. He held out his thumb. It covered the length of the bridge.

He pulled the rip cord and the chute leaped away, billowed, collapsed and billowed again, spreading wide in the shape of a package of small sausages.

Mirsky jerked and dangled and gathered his guidelines in both hands, pulling one, then the other, spilling a little air from one side of the chute to move in one direction, then from the other side.

He saw with relief that he would land some five kilometers from the objective. Unless they had far more men than reported—and radar-aimed automatic guns within the chambers, which their informant had told them they did not—they would probably not bring him down.

He saw others coming down beside him and above him, only a few below. In all, hundreds of them.

Mirsky tried to hold back tears and could not.

Chapter Twenty-seven

"Where's Patricia?" Carrolson looked around the mess.

"I don't know," Farley said. "She was here a few minutes ago."

"We should go find her."

"I'll go," Carrolson said. She had to get outside anyway; she wasn't sure she could stand the scene in the cafeteria any longer.

She stepped out under the tubelight and looked back and forth across the compound. Her eyes fixed on something astonishing. Against the dark gray southern cap, tiny points of white were falling like snow—dozens, then hundreds of them. A marine ran by carrying two Apples. "Look!" she cried, pointing and turning a half-circle. No one paid her any attention. The marine jumped onto the tailgate of one of the fully loaded troop trucks rumbling out of the compound.

Carrolson shook her head to clear it. She was drunk with grief and anger; any solid thought seemed to be vomited away by a nauseated mind. She couldn't afford such a handicap now. She had to think clearly and she had to find Vasquez.

On the opposite side of the compound, a train pulled away from the elevated station. She glanced at her watch; as scheduled, the fourth chamber stop, 1400 hours. The platform was empty; none of the trains were being used for troops, only trucks. The trains were doing their automatic best to keep everything normal.

"Jesus," she said, suddenly realizing. Vasquez had wanted to return to the library. Which one did she mean?

Farley ran up beside her. "We're being invaded," she said, astonished. "Paratroopers. Russian soldiers. Cosmonauts. Whatever they are, they've come down in the first and second chambers. They're coming down here, too."

"I've seen them," Carrolson said. "Patricia's gone to the library. We have to find her—"

"How? The train's gone. Not another for half an hour. We can't take a truck—they're all in use."

Carrolson had never felt so helpless and out of place. She stood with fists clenched, facing the southern cap. Most of the parachutes had descended below their line of sight.

Patricia stared at the seat ahead of her, biting her lower lip. Nobody was guarding the train; that was either an oversight, or providential.

She had been in a dream ever since leaving Earth. Was it possible to be trapped in a dream?

In a dream, you can do anything, if you learn how to control, to shape and command.

And the equations hit by the chalk . . .

If what she had seen in the equations was correct, then at this very moment, there was a place—a *curve*—where Father sat in his chair, reading *Tiempos de Los Angeles*, and the corridor would pass right near it. She only had to search for the right door, the right section of the corridor, and she could find Rita and Ramon, Paul and Julia.

She could hardly wait to tell Lanier. He would be pleased. Rimskaya would be proud he had recommended her. She had solved the secret of the corridor—the last pieces of the puzzle falling into place in a dream, no less.

She could take them all home again.

The train came to her stop and she exited, climbing the stair to the ground level.

"Miss Vasquez?"

Patricia turned to face a man she had never met before. He sat on the concrete edge of the underground entrance. His hair was black and short and he wore a close-fitting black suit.

"Excuse me," she said, her eyes not really focusing on him. She was in the grip of a powerful working state. "I don't know who you are. I can't stay."

"Nor can we. You must come with us."

A tall creature with a head almost as narrow as a board and jutting eyes rose from behind the ceiling. Its shoulders were wrapped in silvery fabric; otherwise it wore nothing. Its skin was smooth as fine leather and just as brown.

She stared, inner concentration evaporating.

"Things are in quite a riot here, aren't they?" the man said. Patricia realized that he had a nose but no nostrils. His eyes were pale blue, almost blank, and his ears were large and round.

"Excuse me," she said more softly. "I don't know who your are."

"My name is Olmy. My companion is a Frant; they don't have names. I hope you don't mind our intruding. We've been watching everybody very closely."

"Who are you?" Patricia asked.

"I lived here, centuries ago," Olmy said. "And my ancestors before me. For that matter, *you* could be one of my ancestors. Please. We don't have time to talk. We must leave."

"Where?"

"Down the corridor."

"Really?"

"That's where my home is. The Frant and his people come

208

from elsewhere. They . . . well, working for us doesn't quite describe it."

The Frant shook its head solemnly. "Please don't be frightened," it said, its voice like a large bird's, low and warbling.

A breeze from the northern cap pushed through the outskirts of the third chamber city, rustling the nearby trees. Following the breeze came a slender craft about ten meters long, shaped like a cone flattened lengthwise, with the nose truncated. It drifted gracefully around a tower and landed on the point of a single central pylon.

"You're done some remarkable work," Olmy said. "There are people where I live who will be very interested."

"I'm trying to go home," Patricia said. She realized she sounded like a lost child speaking to a policeman. "Are you a policeman? Do you guard the cities?"

"Not always," Olmy answered.

"Please come with us," the Frant said, stepping forward on long and oddly bent legs.

"You'll kidnap me?"

Olmy held out his hand, whether supplicating or indicating the situation was not his to control, she could not say.

"If I don't go willingly, you'll make me?"

"Make you?" He seemed puzzled, then said, "You mean, force you?" Olmy and the Frant exchanged glances. "Yes," Olmy said.

"Then I had better go with you, hadn't I?" Her words seemed to be spoken by a distant and heretofore unknown Patricia, calm and better versed in the analysis of nightmare.

"Please," the Frant said. "Until things are better here."

"Things are never going to be better *here*," she said. Olmy took her hand with a courtly bow and led her to the open oval hatchway in the craft's flat nose.

The interior of the craft was confined, a T expanding at the rear, the walls like abstract billows of polished marble, all white curves. Olmy took hold of a soft bulkhead and stretched it out to form a couch. "Please lie here." She lay in the softness. The substance firmed up beneath her, molding to her body.

The narrow-headed, knock-kneed brown Frant climbed farther back through the whiteness and nestled into its own couch. Olmy pulled out a section across the aisle from Patricia and sat in it, again touching his torque.

He smoothed his hand over a bulge before him and the curved surface erupted into an intaglio of black lines and red circles. Beside her, the whiteness faded to an elongated transparency, forming a long elliptical window. The edges of the window remained milky, like frosted glass.

"We're going to leave now."

The third chamber city glided away beneath her. As the craft banked, the window filled with the austere grayness of the northern cap.

"I believe you'll truly enjoy where we're going," Olmy said. "I've grown to admire you. You have a remarkable mentality. The Hexamon will be impressed, too, I'm sure."

"Why don't you have a nose?" the distant Patricia asked.

Behind them, the Frant made a sound like an elephant grinding its teeth.

Chapter Twenty-eight

The Soviet troops assigned to the second chamber had come down on a two-hundred-meter-wide strip of parkland separating the river from the southern cap. The squads had regrouped at two points on opposite sides of the zero bridge, each about three kilometers from that objective. Communications with the squads on the opposite side of the bridge were good.

Mirsky's group had taken shelter in a dense forest of gnarled pines; they had determined the bridge was heavily guarded and would soon be reinforced; they had to strike now. The equipment had not yet been dropped from Zhiguli, heavy-lifter seven, and fully three-fourths of the thirty squads were not up to full strength. Attrition in the bore hole had been hideous, and of those who survived the bore hole, about one out of twenty had not completed the journey and para-sail drop.

The squads were designed for flexibility; surviving sergeants shepherded broken squads together to form new ones. Mirsky had only 210 soldiers in his immediate command and, of course, little hope of getting more. Nobody knew how many had survived the drops in the other chambers.

Twenty SPETSNAZ diversionary troops assigned to Mirsky's battalion, communicating by radio after swimming the river, had established lookouts in the second chamber city.

They had been in the chamber for two hours now. The NATO troops at the bridge had not made an offensive move; this worried Mirsky. He knew that in the defenders' situation, the best plan would be an immediate and devastating offensive. They could conceivably have attacked as his men came down from the axis; apparently, they had been confused and not yet up to strength.

Between his group and the objective, there was the forest and several broad concrete foundations of unknown utility. While there was sufficient cover for his troops, momentarily, the cover could easily be turned into a series of disastrous pin-downs.

General "Zev"—Major General I. Sosnitsky—had survived his descent into the second chamber but had been injured on landing, breaking both legs when his para-sail ripped at a hundred meters. He was now sedated, lying concealed in a copse of trees and guarded by four soldiers Mirsky could ill afford to do without. The political officer Belozersky had—of course—survived also, and stayed very close to the general, like a hopeful vulture.

Mirsky had spent a few weeks training with Sosnitsky in Moscow. He respected the major general. Sosnitsky, about fifty-five but as fit as any thirty-year-old in the training regiments, had taken a shine to Mirsky and no doubt had had something to do with his rapid promotion on the Moon.

No one of higher rank than colonel had come down in the

second chamber besides "Zev." Effectively, that meant Mirsky was in control. Garabedian had survived the drop—and that gave Mirsky some assurance. He could hope for no better deputy commander.

Mirsky led three squads to the forward concrete structure, still a kilometer from the bridge. The top of the foundation was flat and covered about three hundred square meters. The upper surface offered no protection. The concrete was two meters high, practically a wall behind which they could walk upright. Even such protection wasn't enough, however; Mirsky worried about the firing angles and opportunities offered by the chamber's curve. Did the enemy have lasers or small projectile weapons that could penetrate twenty or thirty kilometers of air? If they did, his men could be picked off easily wherever they hid.

He aimed the radio at the southern bore hole and searched for the transponder signal. Finding it, he transmitted a message to Lieutenant Colonel Pogodin in the first chamber, asking how many troops he had and what his situation was. Pogodin had been aboard Chaika with "Nev."

"I have four hundred," Pogodin returned. "Nev is missing. Colonel Smirdin is badly wounded. He probably won't live. Have captured two compounds and taken ten prisoners. We control zero elevator."

From the fourth chamber, Major Rogov reported a hundred men in position, but no objectives taken; the tunnels were heavily defended. He was contemplating moving his men to an island by rubber rafts captured at a recreation site. "Lev" had not survived the collision of Chevy with obstacles in the bore hole. Colonel Eugen was dead, and there was no sign of battalion commander Lieutenant Colonel Nikolaev.

Their command structure was in a shambles.

The hatred rose in him again, making his throat clutch and his stomach burn. "Fan out and pick your targets," he ordered the squad leaders on the near side of the bridge. He waved his arm to both sides and stayed behind the concrete to direct the other squads.

A rattle of small-arms fire greeted his men as they broke cover and spread in groups of twenty for trees and other foundations to either side of Mirsky. There was no way of telling how many laser weapons were being used; they were silent and invisible except in moist or dusty air. He lifted his radio and spoke with the captain in command of the squads on the far side of the bridge.

"Cross fire," he said. "Rush and divert."

Then he called up another three squads and ran them in a different pattern toward the river shore, where they took firing positions in the woods and behind a circular foundation.

With his binoculars, he could make out the faces of the defenders behind their plastic shields. His men had no such shields; only his binoculars were proofed against laser blinding, if the defenders possessed such systems; almost any laser cannon could be converted to spread a barrage of blinding beams. There were any number of weapons the NATO troops *could* have and *could* use, which he did not. . . .

The defenders had set up sandbags in lines paralleling the bridge road. Not all the positions were manned; if he could get his troops to the lines before the positions were up to strength, they would have almost a clear run to the bridge.

He popped up to sweep the positions again with his binoculars and then dropped down to pass instructions to the opposite squads. The air was broken by a hideous crackle; Mirsky's eyes widened and he subconsciously prepared for death. He should have known the Americans would have something advanced and deadly up their sleeves; they were fiends for surprise weapons—

The crackle sounded again and was followed by an extremely loud voice. The voice spoke Russian with a strong German accent, but the words were clear.

"There is no need for fighting. We repeat, there is no need for fighting. You may hold your present positions for the moment, but do not advance any farther. It is imperative you listen. There has been a disastrous exchange of nuclear weapons on Earth."

Mirsky shook his head and switched on the radio again. He could not waste time listening—

"We have sufficient weapons and personnel to annihilate you. There is no need. You have compatriots among us already—the Russian science team. And there is corroboration from your comrades in the heavy-lifters. Your communications can be fed through to them; they are waiting outside the bore hole."

Mirsky pressed the transmit button and ordered the attack forward. He then ordered his remaining squads to take the river shore and join up with their opposites beneath the bridge abutment. The cover looked good to that point—and once beneath the bridge, they could fire along the Americans' lanes of sandbags and prevent them from being manned.

"Fighting us is useless. Our supreme commanders are dead or out of communication, perhaps for years. Your deaths would be meaningless. You may hold present positions, but signify your acceptance or we will open fire."

Then another voice identified itself, distorted but familiar to Mirsky—Lieutenant Colonel Pletnev, squadron commander of the heavy-lifters. Either he had capitulated or he was still outside the bore hole; there was no way he could have been captured; he would have died in the bore hole entry, not been taken alive.

"Comrades. Our countries are at war on Earth. There is devastation in both the Soviet Union and the United States. Our plan is no longer effective. . . ."

The hell with him. Mirsky moved his men up from both sides. Take this objective, and then the next, and then perhaps talk—

"*Psshk*ommander Mirsky," his radio hissed. "Enemy reinforcements crossing the bridge."

The gunfire started again and Mirsky, for the first time in his life, heard the screams of dying men.

Chapter Twenty-nine

Heineman squirmed in the V/STOL's pilot seat, listening to the exchanges in Russian, English and German. Transponders in the bore holes were automatically carrying radio signals from chamber to chamber and down the corridor; why hadn't they been switched off? Perhaps they had—perhaps he was picking up signals from *Russian* transponders.

He had propelled the tuberider beyond any conceivable danger; he was now a thousand kilometers down the corridor, stationary on the singularity, feeling useless. He had programmed communications processors to track on multiple bands and retrieve all messages, storing concurrent messages for separate playback. He had a ringside seat; there was even some video coming down the bore hole.

He witnessed the crown fire sweeping the Earth before the signal gave out.

It was purely by accident that he looked over his shoulder and spotted the moving glimmer of white. It swung smoothly over his head and to the opposite side. Whatever it was, it seemed to be spiraling around the plasma tube, staying within the plasma layer; its wake was a visible shadow within the general glow.

There were no other aircraft within the Stone—none that he had heard of, at any rate. He doubted the Russians had anything sophisticated enough to follow such a difficult course.

What was it, then?

A boojum. In the middle of all the excitement, he had seen his first boojum. *That's always the way, isn't it?* He switched on the aircraft's tracking systems.

For a moment, he had a clear blip on the screens and even a computer-enhanced magnification of the craft's general outline. It was sleek and resembled a blunted arrowhead. He

215

recorded about five seconds of information on it before the trackers suddenly wheeped and lost the target.

Patricia felt icy cold inside. She stared through the transparency in the side of Olmy's craft, watching the even tan and pale gray landscape passing below. Two personalities conflicted within her; one, by far the stronger, forbade any motion or outward reaction. The second was a normal, fascinated, even slightly amused Patricia. If she spoke, she knew the second Patricia—the distant, uninvolved one—would try to be funny and make light of what was happening. But the first had grown to a position of control and she did not speak. She did not even move her head. She simply stared at the walls of the corridor turning and passing behind them.

"Are you hungry or thirsty?" Olmy asked. She did not answer. "Are you tired, do you need to sleep?"

Nothing.

"We'll be some time. Several days. The Axis City is a million kilometers along the Way—the corridor—now. Please let us know if you're in need. . . ."

He glanced back at the Frant but recieved only an outward-turning of one eye, indicating nothing to suggest.

Patricia could feel it all coming apart; all the tight-wound ambition and hope could not hold back this inevitable shattering. Her shoulders began to shake. She looked around at Olmy and quickly turned away. Her eyes seemed to float; tears gathered and broke away when she shook her head, drifting around her. She slowly raised her hands and held them before her face; the teardrops touched and spread on her fingers and palms.

All going now, all the glue going—

Her chest heaved. "Please," she whispered.

They're dead. Really gone. You didn't save them.

"Please."

"Miss Vasquez—" Olmy reached across to touch her, then drew his hand back as she flinched away.

"Ah, *Jesus y Maria.*" Her body jerked and her legs shook

216

with the force of her sobs. Each tore something out of her chest and pierced the dark behind her eyelids with jagged red. She clutched her shoulders with her hands and rocked back and forth in the couch, back arched, teeth clenched and lips drawn back.

Her spine reversed of its own will and she curled her chest and knees together. *Is this a fit?*

This is grief.

This is loss. This is awareness. This is not fooling yourself.

Olmy did not try to restrain her. He watched the woman weeping for a world lost—to his kind—for thirteen centuries. Ancient woman, ancient agony.

Patricia Luisa Vasquez grieved for dead billions and ways of living unknown to him.

"She is an open wound," the Frant said, moving forward to crouch by Olmy's shoulder. "I wish to help, but I can't."

"Nobody can help," Olmy said. Even across thirteen hundred years, the Death bent and hobbled his people with scar tissue. That became clear to him, looking at her, gauging her differences; the Nexus had been forged in the Death, the Naderites had come to power as a result. . . . And how many of their prejudices, how much of their willful blindness, was a drawn-out echo of Patricia's pain?

"If help is impossible for her, then it hurts me to think," the Frant said.

Chapter Thirty

Gerhardt carried the roll of maps from his makeshift command headquarters.

"They control the southern end of the first chamber—including the science team compounds—and the elevators to the south polar bore hole. They're still fighting us in the second chamber, but it looks like a stand-off—Berenson sent half his troops from the fourth chamber as soon as the alert was sounded. They crossed the bridge under heavy fire. The Russians didn't try anything in the third chamber—and they're scattered in the fourth, not very effective." Gerhardt smoothed the map down with a sweep of one hand. "We don't have the strength to wipe them out, but they don't have the strength to take more ground than they already have. And so far they haven't responded to our overtures."

"We still have people in the staging areas?" Lanier asked.

"Yes, and they can hold out there for months—we hadn't shipped down the last load of food and supplies. Fourth chamber is self-sufficient, and Berenson's troops are definitely in control there, so it looks like the only problem will be the first and second chambers. Our soldiers have supplies for about two weeks. Unless we drop supplies to them from the axis—we're studying that proposal now—they'll run out."

"How are we handling the heavy-lifters outside?"

"Still haven't let them in. There's one we suspect is carrying heavy equipment to be dropped into the second chamber from the axis. We don't want them breaking through the barricade. They don't sound happy, but they can cool their heels for a few days without any problems."

"They've offered to surrender?"

Gerhardt shook his head. "No. Pletnev broadcast his little speech, but he's not going to turn his ships over yet. He's offered to try to negotiate an end to hostilities. The heavy-lifter crews want to join their comrades. They know they can't go home, and I suspect they know their troops inside are under strength because of the carnage in the bore hole."

"Such a goddamn desperate maneuver . . ."

"It didn't work . . . anywhere," Gerhardt said grimly. "But it's put us in an uncomfortable position. The Stone is a capped bottle as far as we're concerned. Not that we particularly want to leave, or could go anywhere if we did. I'm worried about SPETSNAZ, myself. They could have assassins and sappers spread throughout the second chamber by now, and they'll find their way to us in a few days; we don't have the troop strength to keep them out of the third chamber, or the fourth. They're nasty individuals, Garry. Dedicated and well trained. The longer we wait, the more they'll drain us.''

"So we're at an impasse in the second chamber?" Lanier asked, his eyes darting nervously to the maps.

"Everywhere. Nobody's going to move. The only thing progressing will be casualty counts.''

"Do you think they know that? I mean, will they acknowledge it to themselves?''

"Having come all this way, with all the training that would require, I think we can safely say their COs aren't fools.''

"What about the grunts?''

"Like us, I doubt they have any grunts.''

"How long before they start listening to reason?''

"Hell, Garry, they may be listening *now*. They're just not showing any sign. We stick our heads up, they start shooting, and vice versa.''

The sergeant stood before his superiors with a troubled expression. His face was covered with scratches from crawling through undergrowth in the patches of forest. He saluted and bowed in Mirsky's direction.

"Colonel, they have found our transponders in the bore holes. We cannot communicate with any other chambers.''

"Now I ask you," Mirsky said, "is that a sign they want to lay down their arms and welcome the wolves into the sheep pen?'' Garabedian took his binoculars and surveyed the forests and fields between them and the bridge, a kilometer away. He then looked at the shell-pocked, laser-scored bridge—marred but still very much functional—and returned the glasses.

"Pavel," Garabedian said, "we should cut that bridge, don't you think?''

Mirsky looked at his deputy commander disapprovingly. "And what other way do we have to cross? We can walk fifty kilometers or more to the next bridge, or we can swim.''

"Then they cannot cross, and they cannot get any more reinforcements from this chamber—''

"No, but they can be reinforced from the first chamber. We have no idea how many there are in there.''

219

"Trapped like pigs—"

"We keep this bridge intact," Mirsky said. "Besides, we can ill afford to lose more men on a desperation move. Or to lose them from snipers while we swim!"

"It was an idea," Garabedian said.

"I am not short on ideas, Viktor. I am short of laser cannon and artillery. We can assume Zhiguli with all our artillery and supplies did not make it through, and will not now, since they have obviously reinforced the bore holes enough to find our transponders. We can assume our operative has been captured and the Russian science team is ineffective, either by choice or because they are in stockade. And we can also assume that our heavy-lifter pilots and crew do not relish staying outside for weeks while we get ourselves killed in here."

"What are you saying, Pavel? Be blunt." Garabedian smiled. With his undershot jaw, he had always reminded Mirsky of a sturgeon.

"We are not getting the support we need."

"Do you believe the war has been fought on Earth—and lost?"

Mirsky shook his head. "I believe we have taken out their orbital capability. That would make quite a show from up here—"

"Pavel, they surely can tell the difference between an orbital showdown and holocaust."

Mirsky clamped his jaw and shook his head stubbornly. "We are here to fight and take an objective. There must be a reason."

"Ask the *Zampolit*s. We are here to spread Socialism and safeguard the future of our State and our country."

"Shit," Mirsky said, surprised at his vehemence. He hated the *Zampolit*s. He had always hated all *Zampolit*s wherever he had served. As usual, the company's political officer—Major Belozersky—was in the rear, issuing orders that sometimes conflicted with Mirsky's own. "Yes, fine, they've cooked the Earth. So what are we to do, abandon the fight and—*what?* Go home to ashes? This time, it would not be a little exercise in

220

the schoolyard between hero and bully. It would be a flaming rubber-stamp skull and crossbones across the northern hemisphere!''

"That's what they're saying has happened. Pletnev backs them up. Surely we couldn't expect to take out their orbital defenses and have them kick their heels in the air and scream for mercy.''

"They are corrupt,'' Mirsky said. "Weak and fearful.''

"Pavel, I do not like playing your Armenian voice of reality. You, of all people, should face facts and their implications. Do not underestimate the enemy. Do weak and decadent people march ahead of you in almost every sphere?''

"Oh, shut up and let me babble,'' Mirsky said, cradling his head between his hands. He glanced up at the sergeant. "Get out of here,'' he said wearily. "Bring me good news or none at all.''

"Yes, sir,'' the sergeant said.

"Pity we don't have any penal battalions to send on ahead to glorious sacrifice,'' Garabedian said. "That's how we've won wars in the past.''

"Don't let Belozersky hear you say that. I have enough trouble with him—and with you—as is. We keep the bridge intact,'' Mirsky said. "That's final. And we make our move in the next hour.''

There was no arguing with Mirsky when he used that tone of voice. Garabedian paled slightly, then pulled out a stick of stale gum and inserted it into his mouth, savoring the sugar.

Mirsky's radio clicked softly. He keyed the receiver and acknowledged. "Comrade Commander, this is Belozersky. 'Zev' wishes to speak with you . . . in person.''

Mirsky swore and replied that he would be there immediately. "More shambles, I think,'' he said to Garabedian.

Twenty-six hours into the stalemate, the results of the survey were brought into Gerhardt's makeshift command post. The lieutenant who had conducted the survey, a thin-faced man with deep-set eyes, delivered his findings in an Appalachian drawl.

221

"We've peeped on every one of their positions and counted them from some distance—from the bore holes and from positions up the curve. They have six hundred or so men still alive and moving, maybe fifty or a hundred more we can't be positive about. They've lost a lot of senior officers—one general wounded or dead and several colonels. That leaves one colonel in the second chamber and two lieutenant colonels and a colonel in the first. There may be other generals—we've been hearing radio talk about 'Zev,' 'Nev,' and 'Lev.' Some of us think they're talking about three generals."

"Can you identify them?" Lanier asked.

"No, sir. They don't exactly have name badges on. But we think someone in the Russian science team might recognize a few. These troops have to be pretty highly trained, with lots of cosmonaut background, and they must have brushed up against some of the space people in the science team."

"Do you have photos of the officers?" Gerhardt asked the lieutenant.

"Yessir, most of them, pretty clear ones, too. Couple of good profile shots."

"Show them to the Russian science team members and see if we can get an identification. Garry, I think you should mediate. We'll talk to Pritikin on the Russian team—he's a straightforward fellow. We'll let one of those heavy-lifters dock—the one with Pletnev. If he or Pritikin can get through to their senior officer by radio, and if he can arrange a meeting, maybe they'll do more than just listen to reason."

"If I mediate, then I should know how to speak Russian," Lanier said.

"One of our fellows can help. Rimskaya, or that German lieutenant, Rudolph—or whatever—Jaeger."

"Rimskaya's good, but perhaps not good enough for diplomatic nuances. Jaeger could be useful. But I won't take the job unless I work with the Russians directly, no insulation. I can take the ninety train into the third chamber and learn while you're arranging for Pletnev to come aboard."

"We don't have weeks, Garry."

222

Lanier shook his head. "It won't be that long. Hours, perhaps." He took a deep breath and leaned forward. "Do you see any reason not to put a stop to all the secrecy?"

Gerhardt thought for a moment. "Internally? I'm not sure."

"Wouldn't you like to know what all this is about?"

"Of course. I mean, I'm not sure who would authorize relaxing the restrictions."

"Kirchner was told we were no longer part of Earth's military strategy; we're on our own. Can't we assume the same is true politically?"

"We're our own masters, you mean."

"Exactly," Lanier said.

"That's a can of worms I don't even want to peek into right now."

"Well, I'll take responsibility for making one move, at least. The libraries are no longer closed. The information contained in them is available to everyone."

"Even the Russians?"

"Even the Russians, if they negotiate for peace with us," Lanier said. "I'll learn Russian, you straighten out the negotiating procedures and we'll offer them a share of all we have left."

"Kirchner won't like letting the bastards dock. And he certainly won't like making concessions."

"Who's in charge of internal security?" Lanier asked pointedly. "And do we have any choice?"

Patricia awoke to find the cabin in semidarkness. She had rolled to face the window. More than twenty kilometers below, the corridor's surface was dark and scarred. Great gashes crisscrossed the mottled ground, the edges shining dully.

She rolled to look across the cabin. Her captor lay wrapped in a net of twinkling blue and green lights. Sparks shot between each light in the net, and within, his body was enveloped in a translucent greenish fog.

She had enough weight in the cabin to feel the difference between up and down. Slipping out of her molded berth, she

223

reached across to touch the net of lights and see if it was real. Before her fingers made contact, a voice stopped her.

"Please do not disturb." Olmy stood at the front of the cabin. Patricia looked between the figure in the couch and the Olmy that had just addressed her. "I am a partial personality, an assigned ghost. Olmy is resting, performing Talsit meditation. If you have any business with him, please allow me to substitute."

"What are you?" Patricia asked.

"An assigned ghost. While he rests, I perform any duties he may have which do not require physical activity. I have no substance. I am a projection."

"Oh." She frowned at the image. "What's he . . . doing? What's happening to him?"

"Talsit meditation is the process of being surrounded by carriers of Talsit data. His body is cleansed of impurities and his mind of obstacles to clear thought. Talsit data informs, reorganizes, criticizes the mental functions. It is a kind of dreaming."

"Are you just a recording?"

"No. I am connected with his thought processes, but in a way that does not interfere with rest."

"Where's the—" She was about to say, "boojum." She looked to the rear and saw the flat-headed, knock-kneed brown creature curled in its own berth, watching her with calm, slowly blinking eyes.

"Hello," it said musically.

Patricia swallowed and nodded. "What was your name again?"

"I have no name. I am a Frant."

"Who's piloting?"

"The ship controls itself at the moment. Surely you people have craft that can do that," the Frant said, its tone admonishing.

"Yes. Of course." She turned back to the image. "Why has the corridor changed?"

"Centuries ago, there was a war here. The surface material

224

brought into the Way—the corridor—was severely disturbed. In places you can see the Way itself."

"A war?" Patricia peered down at the mottled landscape.

"Where Jarts occupied the Way. They had traveled from gates hundreds of thousands of kilometers farther down. Those gates have since been blocked or tightly regulated. When the Axis City attempted to pass, and to regain control of the Way, the Jarts resisted. They were driven out, and this stretch of the Way, the entire distance to the Thistledown, is now blocked and deserted."

"Oh." She lay back and watched the lights twinkle around Olmy. She was exhausted. Her eyes were sandy and her throat scratchy; her chest ached and her arm and leg muscles were tense and sore. "I've been crying," she said.

"You have slept for the last twelve hours," the Frant said. "You seemed at peace while you slept. We did not disturb you."

"Thank you," she said. "This Axis City—that's where we're going?"

"Yes," the Frant said.

"What will happen to me there?"

"You will be honored," Olmy's image answered. "You are from our past, after all, and very brilliant."

"I don't like . . . fuss," Patricia said softly. "And I want to go back and help my friends. They need me."

"You are not crucial there, and we decided it was dangerous."

"I still want to return. I want you to know you are taking me against my will."

"We regret that. You will not be mistreated."

Patricia decided it was useless to argue with a ghost, assigned or otherwise. She wrapped her arms around her shoulders and watched the raked and blackened landscape far below. It was difficult to feel anything for the past now, for whatever had happened before she entered the craft. Did she really want to return? Was there anything so important to her, anywhere?

225

Yes. Lanier. He expected help from her. She was part of his team. And Paul, her family. *Dead.* She felt for the letters in her pocket, and then reached for the bag containing the multimeter, slate and processor. They had not been disturbed.

Sosnitsky was dying. Of the five corpsmen who had accompanied the battalion, two had made it into the second chamber, and they were in no mood to hide the facts from the general. One, a small, balding slight fellow with a bruise across half his face, took Mirsky aside as he approached the copse of trees.

"The general has internal injuries—ruptured spleen the least among them. We don't have the blood or plasma we need, and we don't have the proper conditions for operating. He will die in an hour, maybe two . . . he's strong, but he's no superman."

Sosnitsky lay on his side in a cot made out of backpack fabric and tree limbs. He blinked twice in succession every two or three seconds, and his face was pale and damp. Mirsky kneeled beside him and Sosnitsky took his hand. The general's grip was still surprisingly strong.

"My own bones have become shrapnel, Comrade Commander," he said. "I understand neither 'Lev' nor 'Nev' made it down." He grimaced, or grinned—it was difficult to tell which—then coughed. "I am about to confer a dubious honor on you, Colonel Mirsky. We need a division commander. The only other colonel left alive is Vielgorsky, and I do not want a political officer in command of our troops. I am giving you a very big field promotion, Comrade, one that may not be approved back on Earth. But then, if what we hear is correct, on Earth nobody cares now. I have witnesses—Belozersky here is one, and I will confirm the promotion by radio to other battalion commanders before I die. So I must work fast. You are now a Lieutenant General. I give you my insignia." He passed the stars to Mirsky with his right hand, face strained by the pain. "There might be trouble with . . . others in line. But these are my wishes. I trust you, General Mirsky. If what our squadron commander says is true—and it does not seem

226

impossible—then you must negotiate. We may be the last Russians. . . . Everyone else burns. In fire." He coughed again. "Until then, you hold your ground. But who am I to tell you what to do? You're a General now. Please tell Belozersky to bring the radio."

Belozersky passed with an angry look that had something else in it—a kind of pleading. *He doesn't know how to treat me yet,* Mirsky thought. The general made the announcement to his surviving staff. Belozersky gently informed him that the bore-hole transponders were inoperative, but he insisted on radioing the message anyway.

"The Americans know now that we will have a leader," he said. Minutes later, he lapsed into coma.

It took Mirsky some time to accept what had happened. He thought it best to continue as he had before, so he returned to the foundation and conferred with Garabedian.

Despite setting his deadline, Mirsky did not order any action at the end of the hour. He knew it would be suicide. He had had some vague hope of the heavy-lifter's suddenly coming through and beginning to drop, but the hope was gone now, and with it any real ambition to continue.

Major General Sosnitsky was, of course, correct.

From the very beginning it had been an extremely risky gamble. If what the enemy said was true (and surely the squadron commander Pletnev would not lie to his own men just to save his skin)—if that was all true, no victory was possible.

Garabedian approached with a tube of rations. Mirsky waved him aside. "We must eat," Garabedian said, "Comrade General."

Mirsky frowned up at him. "Why? What use is it? They will keep us here till we starve or become foxes raiding the farmer's coops. We're stuck."

Garabedian shrugged. "All right."

Mirsky turned away from his former deputy and held out his arm abruptly, making grasping motions with his hand. "Give it to me, you bastard. I don't want you eating it."

Garabedian grinned and passed him the tube.

"It's lousy," Mirsky said, squeezing the fish paste into his mouth. "Tastes like shit."

"In my hometown, we call shit sausage and fight over it," Garabedian said. "So why should you be depressed?"

"I liked Sosnitsky," Mirsky said "And then he goes and makes me a general."

Chapter Thirty-one

Lanier stood in the broad, clear luminosity of the library, face twitching. He hadn't actually sat down before one of the chromium teardrops for months. He didn't wish to, even now. The experience had not been physically unpleasant, but it seemed that all his present troubles had emerged from one of those seats—the one now festooned with inactive equipment.

Three Apple- and Uzi-armed marines stood uneasily behind him; Gerhardt had insisted they accompany Lanier, in case any of the Russian SPETSNAZ had this far infiltrated.

He walked between the seats. Like Patricia, he eschewed the cluttered seat. He stopped and turned around to survey the plaza, then sat down on the chair and flipped open the control box. At the press of his fingers, queries floating before him. The library still addressed him in clear twentieth-first-century English. Perhaps it remembered him; perhaps it knew who they were, even why they were here.

"I need to learn twenty-first-century Russian," he said. "Early twenty-first. Pre-Death. How long will that take?"

"Do you wish a reading knowledge, speaking knowledge, colloquial facility, or all of these?" the library narrator asked.

"I need speaking knowledge, colloquial, right away. I suppose the others as well, if it doesn't take much more time."

"You can be taught a command of spoken colloquial and technical Russian in two hours. An additional hour will be required to teach you to read and translate."

"Then give me all of it," he said.

"Very well. Please relax; you are a little tense. We begin first with the Cyrillic alphabet. . . ."

I am *relaxing,* he realized with some surprise. As the lessons developed, he slipped into the bath of knowledge with a deep mental sigh. *I'm enjoying this.*

He had never had a talent for languages. Nevertheless, within three hours, he spoke Russian like a native Muscovite.

Muscular, balding and florid-faced squadron commander Lieutenant Colonel Sergei Alekseivich Pletnev and his four crew disembarked the tethered heavy-lifter from the aft hatch and were guided into the first dock airlock. By the agreement negotiated several hours before, the remaining heavy-lifters maintained their positions outside the bore hole.

The Russians removed their suits and were escorted by seven Apple-bearing marines across the staging area and into the communications center. Kirchner greeted him—his words translated by Lieutenant Jaeger—and explained the procedure.

"The senior officer for your men in the Stone is in our second chamber. According to a message from your Major General Sos— Sos—"

"Sosnitsky," Jaeger finished for him, translating.

"Sosnitsky has promoted an officer named Mirsky to lieutenant general. That means we have to negotiate passage across the first chamber; your comrades have us blocked off here. Our only alternative is to fly you across the axis, and I don't think anyone relishes that thought."

Pletnev listened to Lieutenant Jaeger, and nodded vigorously. "I will speak to them again," he said. "This time directly."

"You don't have seniority over them. They may think you're a traitor."

"I can only try," Pletnev said. "Perhaps I go down alone, or with my crew, and try to convince them. . . ."

"They don't seem anxious to be convinced. Your transmissions have been broadcast to the troops and they've continued fighting."

"Yes, so?" Pletnev blustered, his face becoming even redder. "We try again."

"We try again," Kirchner agreed. "First, we'll let you transmit to the first chamber. Tell them everything; what our situation is here, what you plan on doing, what happened on Earth."

"Yes, I am no idiot. That is what I will tell them." He glared at Kirchner and then offered his hand again. "You butchered us," he said.

Kirchner hesitated, then shook the hand firmly. "Your men fight bravely."

"Show me where to go now." Pickney suggested he follow her to a communications post. She pinned a wireless microphone to his lapel and tuned the equipment to a frequency used by the Russians.

Pletnev spoke with a Lieutenant Colonel I. S. Pogodin in the first chamber. The German translated most of the rapid exchange for Kirchner.

"—You cannot have forgotten me, Pogodin. I instructed your class in Novosibirsk."

"Yes, indeed, you sound like Pletnev—"

"Lay down your fears, Pogodin! The battle is over. I need to cross your territory to speak with Colonel Mirsky—now Lieutenant General Mirsky. Will you allow—" He glanced at Kirchner.

"Yourself, one of your crew and an escort of four marines," Kirchner said.

"Two of us and four of them to cross?"

There was no reply for a moment. "We have no communication with the second chamber, or any other chamber. Our own Colonel Raksakov is dead. I am not senior officer in this chamber—there is Colonel Vielgorsky."

"Then get together with Vielgorsky and make a decision, Pogodin."

There was a few minutes' wait until Vielgorsky came back with a reply.

"You may cross unarmed. I will want to speak with you in person."

230

Pletnev cast a querying look at Kirchner. "Unarmed? Is that acceptable?"

Kirchner nodded.

"We will come down, then—"

"By the zero elevator to the science team compound," Kirchner instructed, and the German translated. "We'll need a truck released from the compound to cross the chamber."

Pletnev passed on the requirements. Vielgorsky added that one of his men must accompany them in the truck to the second chamber. After a moment's consideration, Kirchner again agreed. He then spoke with Gerhardt and confirmed the plan.

"Lanier and two of my men will be on the opposite side of the bridge as soon as we reach an agreement with whoever's in charge of the second chamber," Gerhardt said. "Lanier's learned Russian. We think one of the Russian science team should go with him, too, if everyone's aggreeable."

Pletnev pursed his lips and mumbled something the German could not understand. Then, in passable English, he asked, "Pliss, is there washroom? I have occupied suit for a week now."

Belozersky crouched beside Mirsky as the cease-fire instructions were relayed over the loudspeaker in the enemy camp.

"This could be very tricky," Belozersky said, shaking his head. "We cannot be sure what sort of misinformation they will bring."

Mirsky did not react. He listened intently, then passed orders through Garabedian for his battalion to heed the instructions. "Pletnev will be here in an hour," he said as he took a cigarette offered by Garabedian. "We can question him to our heart's content. If what he says is indeed, true, then we negotiate."

"There must be no retreat from principles," Belozersky said grimly.

"Who suggested retreat from anything?" Mirsky countered.

He disliked the little martinet with his tight-pressed lips and nervous gestures.

"If Pletnev tells the truth," Belozersky pursued, "then we must establish a stronghold of the revolution right here, on the Potato."

"They call it the Stone," Garabedian said.

"The Potato," Belozersky repeated, glaring at him.

"No one disputes you," Mirsky said with perhaps too much patience.

"We must be equal partners in this venture."

"They have all the women," Mirsky observed. Belozersky scrutinized him as if he had made a bad joke.

"Yes? Comrade General, I do not see—"

"We cannot go home—if Pletnev is correct," Mirsky said. "To carry on the ideals of the revolution, there must be . . . women. That seems obvious."

Belozersky had nothing to say to this.

"Perhaps on our science team . . ." Garabedian suggested.

"Most of them are men," Mirsky observed. "Remember the briefings? Very prestigious assignment, the Potato. Senior academicians and their assistants only. Maybe fifteen women. Spread among seven hundred soldiers." He laughed and squashed the quickly smoked cigarette butt against the concrete foundation.

Belozersky sat with his back against the concrete and stared down at his clasped hands where they rested on drawn-up knees. "Not everything in Russia has been destroyed," he murmured. "There are redoubts, fortresses. You have heard of these, Comrade General, surely."

"They reveal nothing to those who do not need to know," Mirsky said. "Rumors don't equal reality."

"But at Podlipki— the secret hangars, the helicopters and airplanes waiting . . . surely the Party Secretary, the Defense Council—"

"Perhaps," Mirsky said, more to shut the man up than to agree.

"They will communicate with us, then." Belozersky looked up, eyes bright. "We *must* have our own outside channel of communication. If we negotiate, we must demand—"

"I have thought of that already," Mirsky said. "Now please be quiet. I have a lot of thinking to do before Pletnev arrives."

The truck rolled past the lines of foxholes and the barbed wire fences scavenged from the science compound. Russians in incongruous arctic camouflage peered at them, some still wearing their spacesuit helmets. The suits themselves had long since been discarded—they littered the drop zones in the first chamber, along with the para-sails and bodies of unlucky soldiers.

"Never such an action as this," Pletnev said flatly. "Never."

Major Annenkovsky—the representative of the Russians in the first chamber—stared sadly through the truck windows and ran his hands through brick-red hair. "I am grateful to be alive," he said.

Lieutenant Rudolph Jaeger translated for the two marine escorts in a low voice. The truck passed through the checkpoint by its demolished guardhouse and headed north.

At the northern end of the zero bridge, Lanier glanced at his watch: 1400 hours. The marines nodded to each other and they began crossing on foot, as agreed.

"I just hope those damn insurgents got the word," the young sergeant said, looking back at Alexandria.

Through cameras in the first chamber bore-hole opening, Kirchner monitored the progress of the truck on the same console that had conveyed photos of Earth's death just thirty hours before. Behind him, Link jerked up in her seat and quickly tuned in a signal.

"Incoming OTV," advised one of the soldiers on watch in the exterior dimple. "Not a Russian. One of ours."

Link gestured with one hand, the other punching buttons in rapid succession. "Captain Kirchner, we have an OTV from

233

Station Sixteen. It's damaged and couldn't go to lunar settlement. . . . Sir, they say they have Judith Hoffman on board.''

Kirchner swiveled in his chair. "I'm not surprised," he said laconically. "Bring 'em in. Miss Pickney, where did I leave my jacket?''

Chapter Thirty-two

Mirsky crossed the field slowly, not so much out of caution as to display his dignity, and to gain some idea of their losses. Lanier, Lieutenant Jaeger, Major Annenkovsky and Pletnev advanced more rapidly, until only a few yards separated them. Pletnev stepped forward to grasp Mirsky's hand and upper arm, then backed away, standing alone.

Mirsky looked at the bodies spaced haphazardly on the field. Two lay half-in and half-out of an unfinished foxhole, several small burned holes and slashes of cooked flesh showing through melted gaps in their uniforms. He had counted twenty-eight corpses so far. There were at least twice that many on the field. His thoughts strayed away from tactical considerations and lingered on the unsimple fact of dead countrymen.

The forty-one wounded in the second chamber were being tended by only two corpsmen. Sosnitsky had died the day before, never emerging from coma. The wounded died two, three and four daily.

Mirsky turned to Pletnev. "What they have broadcast to us—your words, your information—it is true?''

"Yes," Pletnev said.

"Were there any instructions from Earth?''

"No.''

"And how bad?''

"It is very bad," Pletnev said softly, scratching his cheek. "There will be no victors.''

234

"No instructions from anywhere? From the Defense Council in a redoubt, from the party, a platform, from some surviving officers?"

Pletnev shook his head. "Nothing. They could not be concerned with us."

"Did you witness engagements?" Mirsky asked, his face tightening.

"We saw Russia glowing at night. All of Europe is on fire."

"Which one of you speaks Russian?" Mirsky asked sharply, glancing at Lanier and Jaeger.

"We both do," Lanier said.

"Are your countries victorious, then?"

"No," Lanier said.

"We are all *pigs*," Mirsky said.

Pletnev shook his head. "We did our duty, Comrade General. You have accomplished a marvelous—"

"How many ships survived?" Mirsky interrupted.

"Four," Pletnev said. "And how many men?"

Lanier, Jaeger and Major Annenkovsky waited for Mirsky to respond.

"Two hundred—no, about one hundred eighty here." Mirsky frowned at Lanier. "I haven't heard how many in the other chambers. Maybe seven hundred in all. General Sosnitsky died yesterday."

"Then you are the senior officer," Pletnev said.

"We should begin talks now," Lanier said. "I don't see any need to resume fighting."

"No," Mirsky said. He surveyed the field, shaking his head slowly. "If we are all that is left . . . No need to fight."

"Earth is not dead, Colonel," Lanier said. "It is very badly hurt, but it is not dead."

"You sound certain," Mirsky said. "How can you be so sure?"

"Yes," Pletnev said in English. "So you have communication with your superiors?"

"No," Lanier said. "I read about it, and watched it happen. It's a long story, General Mirsky, and I think the time has come to make it known to everybody."

While the bodies still lay where they had fallen, the Russians were guaranteed access to the first four chambers, in return for guaranteeing the Western bloc personnel access to the compounds and zero elevator in the first chamber. Promises were made that bilateral security squads would police the travel routes. With that agreed to, the debris and bodies were cleared from the southern cap and the bore hole and the remaining Russian heavy-lifters were given permission to dock.

The negotiations were conducted in the first chamber, in the first science team compound cafeteria. Half of the second compound barracks was temporarily given over to house Russian soldiers; a line drawn in white paint divided the sectors and was guarded on one side by five marines, on the other by five tired-looking Space Shock Troopers.

Eventually, the Russians indicated, they would move most of their soldiers out of the first chamber and claim a large section of the fourth chamber.

Gerhardt spoke through Lanier and Jaeger to Mirsky. Colonel Vielgorsky—a darkly handsome middle-aged man with jet-black hair and green eyes—advised Mirsky on political considerations. Major Belozersky was always lurking nearby. The third political officer, Major Yazykov, was assigned to the fourth chamber, part of a Russian survey team.

They worked through the early evening of the second day of the truce. During a break for coffee and lunch, Kirchner appeared in the cafeteria entrance with a guest and two guards. Lanier looked up at the group and slowly lowered his cup of coffee.

"Looks like you don't need much help," Judith Hoffman said. She was pale and her hair was uncharacteristically mussed; she wore an outsize jumpsuit and one of her hands was wrapped in a bandage. In the other, she carried a personal effects box from the shuttle. Without a word, Lanier pushed back his chair and crossed the room to wrap her in a tight hug. The Russians watched with mild irritation at the interruption;

236

Vielgorsky whispered something to Mirsky, and he nodded, sitting up in his seat.

"Jesus," Lanier said softly. "I was sure you hadn't made it. You don't know how good it is to see you."

"As good as it feels to be here, I hope. The President fired me and the whole board four days before . . . Before. I pulled in some favors and took a VIP tour of Station Sixteen the next day. I was arranging for an OTV flight—not easy. I was persona non grata with the politicos, and that worried the brass, but two shuttle jocks were willing to smuggle me aboard. We were all fueled and ready to go when the . . . war began, and we got away with six civilian evacuees just before they—" She swallowed. "I'm very tired, Garry, but I had to see you and let you know I'm here. Not as your boss. Just here. There are nine others—four women, two men, three crew. Let me sleep and then tell me how I can help."

"We haven't worked out chain of command yet. We don't even know whether we're an outpost or a territory or a nation," Lanier said. "There'll be plenty for you to do." His eyes were watering. He wiped them with the back of his hand and grinned at Hoffman, then pointed to the bargaining table. "We're talking. The fighting's over—for now, perhaps for good."

"I always knew you were a good administrator," Hoffman said. "Garry, I have to sleep. I haven't had a good sleep since we left the station. But . . . I brought something with me."

She put the box on the table and undid the metal clasps. Raising the top, she dumped the packets of seeds across the tabletop. Some slid over to the Russian table. Mirsky and Vielgorsky seemed stunned by the display. Mirsky picked up a packet of marigold seeds.

"Please, keep what you want," Hoffman told them. She looked up at Lanier. "They're for all of us now."

Kirchner took her by the elbow and led her away.

Lanier returned to the table and sat, feeling magnitudes better. Belozersky, standing behind Vielgorsky and Mirsky, looked down on the pile of seeds with unconcealed suspicion.

237

"My chief political officer wants to know if you have received instructions from any surviving governmental organization," Mirsky said. Jaeger translated for Gerhardt.

"No," Lanier said. "We're still operating on our own."

"We recognize the woman you spoke to," Vielgorsky said smoothly. "She is an agent of your government and the perpetrator of your policies on this asteroid."

"Yes, she is," Lanier said. "and when she's feeling better, she'll join our negotiations. But she was . . ." he searched for the word, "removed from her position before the Death."

He wondered at how easily that word came, designating past, not future.

"When did she arrive?" Mirsky asked.

"I don't know. Not too long ago."

"We insist," Belozersky said, "that any Warsaw Pact survivors be welcomed on this asteroid as well. Military and civilian."

"Of course," Lanier said. Gerhardt agreed with a nod.

"And now," Lanier said, "for perhaps the most important issues. Disarmament and territorial rights . . ."

"We will work out a rough draft of these agreements and ratify a formal document later," Mirsky said.

"We insist on sovereignty of all Warsaw Pact peoples on this asteroid," Belozersky said. Vielgorsky pursed his lips. Mirsky backed his chair away from the table sharply and led Belozersky to a corner. There, they engaged in a quiet but heated exchange, with Belozersky casting furious glances at Lanier and Gerhardt.

Mirsky returned alone. "I am in command of Soviet soldiers and citizens," he said. "I am the principal negotiator."

Lanier's office and bunkroom had been ransacked but not seriously damaged during the occupation. He slept for five hours and then took a rationed breakfast from the food vendor in the cafeteria.

Kirchner met him at the front entrance of the women's

barracks. "I'm going back to the bore hole," he said. "There's still an unholy mess up there. We're bringing down bodies now—ours and theirs. Is there a service scheduled?"

"I've suggested a single service sometime in the next twenty-four hours. More than just mourning for the dead here . . ."

Kirchner pursed his lips. "It's not going to be easy standing around those bastards."

"Has to start somewhere. How's Hoffman? Has she slept?"

"From what I've heard. Two of your astronomers took her in and kicked me and the guards out." He narrowed his eyes and nodded in the direction of the cafeteria. "What's my role going to be when you fellows are done?"

"Captain, USN, I presume," Lanier said. "In charge of external security. I'm not going to hand them the Stone on a plate."

"Have they agreed to disarm?"

Lanier shook his head. "Not yet. They want to set up a secure camp in the fourth chamber, then they'll discuss disarmament. I'm giving Mirsky a private tour later this afternoon . . . the libraries, the cities."

"Jesus, I'd like to go with you."

"You'll get your chance soon. As far as Gerhardt and I are concerned, it's all open. No monopoly."

"Even the seventh chamber?"

"In time. They haven't asked about that yet."

Kirchner raised his eyebrows. "Weren't they told?"

"I have no idea what they tell their military men. Certainly they'll know pretty soon. The Russian science team is not exactly mixing with the soldiers—military doesn't count for much in their eyes, apparently. But word will get around." He paused for a long moment. "Any word from Earth?"

"Not a thing. Some radar activity in the Arctic Ocean— maybe a few surface ships. Can't see much. Smoke is covering most of Europe, Asia, the United States. They can't be concerned with us, Garry."

Kirchner walked across the compound and climbed into a

239

truck going to the zero elevator entrance. Lanier knocked on the barracks door. Janice Polk answered.

"Come on in," she said. "She's awake and I took her some food a few minutes ago."

Hoffman sat on the couch in the small lounge. Beryl Wallace and Lieutenant Doreen Cunningham, former head of compound security, sat on chairs across from her. Cunningham's head was bandaged, evidence of the laser burn she had received before the surrender of the first compound.

They stood as Lanier entered; Cunningham made as if to salute, then smiled sheepishly and lowered her hand.

"Ladies, Mr. Lanier and I have some catching up to do," Hoffman said, placing a half-full glass of orange juice on the tank-baffle table. When they were alone, Lanier sat and pulled the chair closer.

"I think I'm ready for a briefing," Hoffman said. "I haven't heard anything since I left Earth. Was it like what the libraries showed us?"

"Yes," Lanier said. "And the Long Winter is starting."

"Okay." She pinched her nose with two fingers and rubbed it vigorously. "End of the world. All that we know." She sighed and the sigh threatened to shudder into a sob. "Shit. First things first."

Lanier held out his hand and she shook it.

"They'll think we're lovers," she said.

"A purely Druckerian relationship," Lanier said.

She laughed and wiped her eyes with a handkerchief.

"How are you doing, Garry?" she asked.

He didn't answer for a long moment. "I lost my aircraft, Judith. I was in charge—"

"Bull."

"I *was* in charge, and I did everything I could to prevent the war. I failed. So I can't really say how I am, just yet. Maybe not too well. I don't know. I'm giving them tit for tat in the negotiations. But I'm very tired."

She tapped his hand with her fingers and nodded slowly, her eyes fixed on his. "Okay. You still have my full confidence. You know that, Garry?"

"Yes."

"After things settle down, we can all take our turn sticking our heads through the hole in the Sisyphus mural. Now tell me about the invasion and everything that's happened since."

Lanier had a vague daydream of taking Mirsky to the second chamber library alone, or with at most only one bodyguard apiece. When he arrived at the cafeteria negotiating tables, Mirsky, Garabedian, two of the three surviving political officers—Belozersky and Major Yazykov—and four armed SSTs awaited him. He quickly asked Gerhardt and Jaeger to accompany him, and to balance the forces, four marines joined the group.

They rode in silence from the first chamber to the second chamber's zero bridge. One of Mirsky's troopers drove the truck for the first half of the short journey. Mirsky glanced at Lanier several times during the trip through the city, sizing him up, Lanier suspected. The Russian lieutenant general was a closed book to Lanier; not once had Mirsky revealed any of his private side. Still, Lanier had a much higher regard for Mirsky than for Belozerksy. Mirsky might listen to reason; Belozersky wouldn't even know what reason was.

Halfway across the bridge, the truck stopped and a marine took over the driving duties. They passed through the shopping district Patricia had described as "quaint" and then disembarked in the library plaza. One marine and one SST stayed behind to guard the truck. They squared off at opposite corners of the vehicle and studiously avoided conversation.

Gerhardt engaged Belozerksy in conversation through Jaeger. This gave Lanier an opportunity to lead Mirsky a few steps ahead and prepare him for what they would find.

"I'm not sure what your commanders told you about the Stone," he began, "but I doubt you had the complete story."

Mirsky stared ahead stonily. "The Stone is a better name than the Potato," he admitted, lifting his eyebrows. "Calling it the Potato makes us worms, no? I have been told the Stone was built by humans."

241

"That's not the half of it."

"Then I am interested to hear the rest."

Lanier told him the story in some detail as they entered the library and climbed the stairs to the second floor.

In the reading room, Lanier found a section of Russian volumes in the stacks and emerged with three, handing one to Mirsky—a translation of the *Brief History of the Death*—and one each to Belozersky and Yazykov.

Belozersky stood with his book firmly clutched in both hands, staring at Lanier as if he had been insulted. "What is this supposed to be?" he asked. Yazykov opened his volume hesitantly.

"Read it for yourself," Lanier suggested.

"It is Dostoevsky," Belozersky said. He traded books with Yazykov. "And Aksakov. These are supposed to interest us?"

"Perhaps if you would look at the printing dates, gentlemen," Lanier said quietly. They opened their books, read and then closed them sharply, almost together.

"We must explore these shelves thoroughly," Belozersky said. He did not sound happy at the prospect.

Mirsky held his book open in both hands, thumbing through it and returning several times to the publication notice, once touching the date with his finger. He closed the book on his thumb and tapped its spine on the surface of the reading table, looking up at Lanier. The second chamber library seemed, if anything, darker and gloomier than before.

"This tells the history of the war," Mirsky half asked, half stated. "It is an accurate translation of the English edition?"

"I believe so."

"Gentlemen, Mr. Lanier and I must be alone for a few minutes. Comrade officers, you will please wait with General Gerhardt and his men, and you will take our men with you."

Belozersky placed the book on an empty reading table and Yazykov followed suit. "You should not be long, Comrade General," Belozersky said.

"As long as it takes," Mirsky said.

Lanier had brought along a canteen half-filled with brandy,

hopeful of just such an opportunity. He now poured out a cup for each of them.

"This is much appreciated," Mirsky said, lifting the cup.

"Special service," Lanier said.

"My political officers would accuse you of trying to get me drunk and *pump me*—that is the idiom?—for information."

"There's not enough left to get drunk on," Lanier said.

"Pity. I am not strong enough for . . . this." Mirsky gave the library two widely spaced jabs with the empty cup. "Maybe you are, but I am not. It frightens me to death."

"You'll find strength after a while," Lanier said. "It's as attractive as it is frightening."

"You have known this for how long?"

"Two years."

"I think I will let others find the attraction," Mirsky said. "My people will now have access to all this—unrestricted, any of us, the soldiers and officers, too?"

"That's the agreement."

"How did you learn to speak Russian? In school?"

"In the third chamber library," Lanier said. "It took me just over three hours."

"You speak like a Muscovite. One who has been overseas for a few decades, perhaps, but still . . . a Muscovite. Could I learn English that quickly?"

"Probably."

Lanier split the last of the brandy and they toasted each other.

"You are a strange man, Garry Lanier," Mirsky said solemnly.

"Oh?"

"Yes. You are turned inside. You see others but don't let them see you."

Lanier did not react.

"There, see?" Mirsky grinned. "You are that way." The Russian's eyes suddenly resumed their sharp focus on him. "Why didn't you let the world know about this from the beginning?"

243

"After you've spent a little more time here, and in the third chamber, ask yourself what you would have done."

It was Mirsky's turn not to react. "There are bitter grievances between our people," he said, dropping the book on the table with a thump. "They will not be easily laid to rest. In the meantime, I do not understand this place. I do not understand our position here, or yours. My ignorance is dangerous, Mr. Lanier, so I will come here, or to the other library, when time permits, and educate myself. And I will learn English using your method, if that is possible. But, to prevent confusion, I do not think all my people will be allowed to come here. Would it not be wise for you to look to similar restrictions?"

Lanier shook his head, wondering if Mirsky even saw his own contradictions. "We're here to break the pattern of the past, not continue it. As far as I'm concerned, it's open to all."

Mirsky stared at him for an uncomfortably long period of time, then stood. "Perhaps," he said. "That is much easier for you to say than for me. My people are not used to being well informed. Some of my officers will find the thought frightening. Some will not believe any of this . . . they will assume it is an American trick. That would be very comforting."

"But you know it isn't."

Mirsky reached out to touch the book. "If a truth is dangerous," he said, "then perhaps it is not true enough."

The strip of parkland in the second chamber where Mirsky's battalion had landed now took the bodies of the dead. A hundred and six American, British and German soldiers had died in the battle and lay in aluminized sacks down a long trench opened by one of the anthropology team's excavators. Three hundred sixty-two Soviets lay in four more trenches. Another ninety-eight Soviets and a dozen Western bloc soldiers were missing and presumed dead, either destroyed in the battle or drifted out of the bore hole to become freeze-dried mummies in orbit around the Stone. A special marker had

244

been set up for the dead of OTV 45 and the crews of the lost heavy-lifters.

Two thousand three hundred people gathered around the trenches. Mirsky and Gerhardt spoke in Russian and English, keeping their words brief and to the point. They were burying more than just their fellows; though there was no marker yet for the dead of Earth, they were burying distant family members, friends; distant cultures, histories, dreams.

They were burying the past, or as much of it as they could part with. The Soviets stood together in ranks. Within the Soviet group, the members of their science team remained isolated, selected out.

The Soviets stood in silence as a Chaplain Cook and Yitshak Jacob, acting as a rabbi, administered last rites and kaddish. A Soviet Uzbek Moslem stepped forward to offer his prayers.

Mirsky threw the first spade of dirt into the Soviet graves. Gerhardt threw a spadeful into the NATO grave. Then, without planning or warning, Gerhardt took a shovel of dirt from the mound to be pushed over his men, and carried it to the first Soviet trench. Mirsky did the same without hesitation.

Belozersky watched with a face permanently locked in disapproval. Vielgorsky kept a silent, dignified demeanor. Yazykov seemed to be somewhere else, and his eyes were moist.

Hoffman and Farley stepped forward and laid a wreath at the head of each site.

As the crowd moved away, the archaeology team immediately began filling in the trenches. The Soviets divided to return to the first and fourth chambers. Farley, Carrolson and Hoffman joined Lanier and Heineman at the zero bridge. They watched people crossing to go to the train terminals. Carrolson edged closer to Lanier and touched his arm.

"Garry, there's something we have to talk about."

"Let's hear it," he said.

"Not here. In the compound," Carrolson said, looking to Hoffman. They gathered in the trucks and crossed the first chamber. Carrolson, Farley, Heineman and Hoffman accompanied Lanier to the deserted administration building, where they gathered around Ann Blakely's desk on the first floor.

"Sounds like bad news coming," he said. His eyes widened in prescient realization. "Oh, my God," he said. "Where's—"

Carrolson interrupted him. "You've been too busy until now. We're not sure what's happened, but Patricia can't be found anywhere. There are two reports, but one's Russian and it may not be credible. Rimskaya heard it when he was talking with the Russian science team. The other's from Larry. We thought we'd find her, that maybe she was just hiding out somewhere, but—"

Heineman nodded. "What I saw just seems to add to the mystery," he said.

"Patricia left the fourth chamber compound last Wednesday," Farley said. "Nobody saw her go, but Lenore is convinced she must have taken a train to the third chamber."

"She said she was going to a library. We were all a little crazy then, and she was taking it very hard," Carrolson said.

"The Russian team says that a Soviet soldier saw an aircraft land near one of the subway terminals in Thistledown, on the northern side—the zero line terminal," Farley said. "Two people got aboard—and something the Russian called a devil. One of the . . . humans was a man and the other a woman, and the woman fits Patricia's description. The aircraft flew off. White, spade-shaped, but with the nose blunted. It didn't make any noise."

Heineman stepped forward. "I saw a boojum go past when I was down the corridor. Arrowhead-shaped, blunt nose. It was traveling in a spiral around the plasma tube, heading north."

"There hasn't been time until now to put it all together," Carrolson said. "I'm sorry about the delay."

"It doesn't make sense," Lanier said, shaking his head. "Maybe she was just captured by the Russians. Maybe—"

"Rimskaya's asked around. He thinks not," Carrolson said. "There wasn't anybody in Thistledown but a few Soviet paratroopers off course—no diversionary troops, none of our troops—not at that time. Nobody but Patricia."

246

"And a boojum," Heineman said. "The coincidence is too close, Garry."

He continued to shake his head. "It's over. Please. I just can't handle much more," he said. "Judith, tell them. I can't do anything now. There's the negotiations, and the—"

"Of course," Hoffman said, gripping his shoulder firmly with one hand. "Let's all get some rest."

Lanier held one hand to his face, as if to smooth the deep grooves of anguish around his mouth. "I'm supposed to take care of her," he said. "She's important. Judith, you told me to take care of her."

"It's all right. There wasn't anything—"

"Goddamn this place, Judith!" He raised his fists and shook them helplessly. "I hate this fucking rock!"

Carrolson began to cry. Farley held her. "Not just you," Carrolson said. "You put her in my charge."

"Stop it," Hoffman said quietly, looking away. Heineman stood back, embarrassed and uncertain what to do.

"I'm not going to just give up on her," Lanier said, lowering his arms and opening and closing his hands. "She's not just gone. Larry, can we have the tuberider fueled and ready to go soon?"

"Any time you give the word."

"Judith, I think you chose wrong," Lanier said.

"I don't think so. What do you mean?"

"I'm not going to see it through. I'm going to run off on a foolish rescue mission, not stay here and argue with a bunch of Soviets. You know me. You know I'm going to do that."

"Okay," she said. "You'll go after her. There are other reasons."

"What?" Lanier asked.

"We're stuck here, aren't we?" Hoffman said. "We have to find out what's down there soon anyway. Larry, does the V/STOL work? The tuberider?"

"They work fine," Heineman said.

"Then we'll plan. But we'll do it carefully. Is that okay, Garry? Not right away, but soon?"

247

"Okay," Lanier said meekly.

"I think we all need to relax and eat and rest," Farley said, looking around for agreement.

They stood in silence, a bit shaken by how close to the edge Lanier had come—and by the realization of how close they all were.

"I'd like to go, too," Carrolson said.

Chapter Thirty-three

So I suppose you want to get away from it all. Feel like it's very remote.

—Yes.

Go chasing down the corridor after her. Why?

—To save my goddamn soul, that's why.

You haven't done badly.

—The Earth is in ruins, the Stone is half-occupied by surly Russians, and I've lost the one person I was specifically told to protect.

But the Stone is still here, and the situation seems to be stabilizing—

—Belozersky. Yazykov. Vielgorsky.

Old-liners, hard-liners. Yes. They're trouble, and shouldn't you stick around to blunt their particular axes?

—No.

You'll leave Hoffman with all the problems—

—She'll let me go because she knows I'm at the end of my rope. I can't take any more. I'm of no use to her or the Stone . . . except to go find Patricia.

Lanier opened his eyes and looked at his wristwatch: 0750 hours. He felt paralyzed. The voices continued in his head, back and forth. His mind was trying to cope wth the intolerable—and to find his place in a new situation.

He kept thinking of Earth, of people—friends, co-workers, perhaps the very people he had met a few weeks before—

248

crawling through the rubble. Very likely, there was not a single person alive on Earth whom he knew personally. That was good statistics but a lousy thought, lousy psychology. Most of his contacts (*his people*) had lived in cities· or worked in military centers.

One exception was Robert Tyheimer. A submarine commander, he had been married to Lanier's sister, who had died of a stroke two years before Lanier was assigned to the Stone. They hadn't talked since a year after her death. Tyheimer might still be alive, under the ice, waiting. If he hadn't already contributed to the general destruction, then Tyheimer would guard his warheads and wait . . . and wait . . . for the next exchange. For the final blows.

"I hate you," Lanier said out loud, eyes closed again. He didn't even know whom he meant. Three psychiatrists gathered in his head and discoursed; one, a cliché Freudian, always twisted the worst and most sordid interpretation out of his every fleeting glimmer of thought. *Yes . . . and your mother . . . and what did you say then? Meant yourself, didn't you?*

Another sat quietly, smiling, letting him hang himself in his own ropy confusions.

And the third—

The third nodded and recommended work therapy. The third resembled his father.

That interested the first.

He turned over in the bed and opened his eyes again. No sleep, no rest. How long would it take for the people on the Stone to crack? How many, and how seriously? Who would contend with the problem, himself or Hoffman?

But the decision had already been made. He had given Hoffman the grand tour—and had encountered Mirsky in the third chamber library, sitting before a teardrop. The Russian lieutenant general had been accompanied by three bodyguards, even though the library was otherwise empty. He had appeared exhausted, and ignored them.

Showing Hoffman to a seat some distance away from the

249

Russians, Lanier had taught her how to use the facilities. He had passed the keys to her, and she had welcomed them.

He sat up and flipped on the intercom. Ann Blakely was back at her desk and still in charge of the central switchboard. "I can't sleep," he said. "What's Heineman's schedule now?"

"He's awake, if that's what you want to know," she said.

"Fine. And in the seventh chamber, no doubt."

"No, schedule here says staging area in the southern bore hole—"

"Call him, please."

"Will do."

"Tell him I want to leave tomorrow, early, eight hundred hours."

"Yessir."

The crew of the V/STOL had already been chosen: himself, Heineman, Carrolson—perhaps the only one Hoffman would have difficulty doing without—and Karen Farley. The mission was simple and direct: they would travel a maximum of one million kilometers down the corridor, assuming it extended that far, stopping at several points along the way and descending to the floor. Who knew what the nature of the corridor would be that far north? They would then return, with or without Patricia or any evidence of her whereabouts.

There were a lot of uncertainties, but they were of a type Lanier welcomed. He had been dealing with horrors for so long that a sleek, cleanly dangerous adventure seemed like heaven.

He dressed and gathered his personal kit into a little black bag. Toothbrush, razor, change of underwear, slate with package of memory blocks.

Toothbrush.

Lanier started to laugh. The laughter seemed forced, but it gathered in waves until he was helpless. He lay on the bunk and doubled up, his face knotting painfully. Finally he stopped, gasping, and then thought of the tiny lavatory on the aircraft, with its tiny shower. He thought of taking a crap as they rode the singularity and the laughter broke out anew.

250

Minutes passed before he could control it, and then he sat up straight on the edge of the bunk, taking deep breaths and rubbing his sore jaw and cheek muscles. "God in heaven," he sighed and stuffed the toothbrush into the little black bag.

The dead Soviet trooper floated twenty meters from the research scaffold in the seventh chamber bore hole. How he had gotten so far was anybody's guess. He did not seem to have been wounded; perhaps he had feared the fall and stayed near the axis until his air gave out. He was slowly drifting back down the bore hole, toward the sixth chamber. There wasn't enough time to snag him and bring him down. He cast a tangible gloom over the farewells. He seemed to watch with great interest, his pale face visible behind the faceplate, eyes wide.

Hoffman hugged Lanier, Carrolson and then Farley, their bulky suits interfering with the intent if not the emotion. Heineman was already aboard the V/STOL, which was attached remora-like to the tuberider.

They stood around the blunt end of the singularity for a moment, silent, and Hoffman said, "Garry, this isn't a wild goose chase. You know that. We need that little Chicana. Whoever took her away from us may have known how much we need her. Of course, I'm suspicious by nature. At any rate, you folks are on a very important mission. Godspeed."

Farley turned toward Hoffman. "We reached a decision last night—Hua Ling and the rest of us, all the Chinese. It wasn't to be announced until this evening, but nobody will object if I tell you now. We are with the Western bloc. The Soviet science team made some overtures, but we decided to support you. I think the Soviet scientists wish they could follow our lead. But I just wanted you to know, before we left."

"Thank you," Hoffman said, gripping Farley's glove. "We'll be curious. No need to tell you that. Learn all you can. There's a few hundred or more of us who wish we could go along."

"That's why I volunteered first," Carrolson said.

251

"Time's a-wastin'," Heineman drawled. "All aboard."

"Shut up and let us be sentimental," Carrolson scolded him.

"Everything will be fine," Hoffman told Lanier as they hugged again and held each other back to peer through faceplates.

"Let's go," Lanier said. They hooked their safety lines to a long pole stretched out near the aircraft and kicked away one by one to enter the hatch. Two people fit into the airlock; they cycled twice, Lanier waiting until last. With the hatch sealed and air pressure restored, he removed his suit and folded it into the compartment beneath the airlock controls.

With only four passengers, the aircraft interior was spacious. The forward part of the cabin was filled with boxes of scientific equipment; Carrolson and Farley checked them out before strapping in. Lanier joined Heineman in the cockpit.

"All fuel and oxygen cables clear," Heineman said, checking the instruments. "I've run the diagnostics on the tuberider. Everything's go."

He looked expectantly at Lanier.

"Then go," Lanier said.

Heineman swung out the pylon which held the tuberider controls and locked it before him. "Hang on," he said. Then, over the intercom, "Ladies, barf bags are in the pouches of the seat in front of you. Not suggesting, you understand."

He depressed the clamp controls. Slowly, smoothly, the tuberider began to slide along the slender silver pipe of the singularity. "A little more," he said. Lanier felt himself pressed back into his seat. "And a little more still."

They were heavy now, lying on their backs in a cockpit and cabin suddenly upended. "Last bit," Heineman said, and they effectively weighed half again more than they would have on Earth. "There's a rope ladder I'll unroll down the aisle, just in case anybody has to go to the bathroom." He grinned at Lanier. "I don't recommend the lavatory in these conditions. We didn't get enough specs to design for comfort. I'll let up on the clamps if anyone gets desperate."

"Count on it," Carrolson said from the cabin.

Lanier watched the corridor moving slowly, majestically around them. Through the windscreen, the floor of the corridor merged in the distance with the pearly central glow of the plasma tube . . . stretching perhaps forever.

"The ultimate escape, isn't it?" Heineman asked, as if reading his thoughts. "Makes me feel young again."

Chapter Thirty-four

After three separate occasions where Olmy wrapped himself in his isolating net of lights, Patricia decided there was something faintly unsavory about Talsit. Perhaps it was addictive—whatever *it* was.

They had been flying for at least three days—perhaps as many as five—and while Olmy and the Frant were unfailingly polite and answered her questions with seeming sincerity, they were not exactly voluble. She spent much of her time sleeping fitfully, dreaming about Paul. She often touched his last letter, still in the breast pocket of her jumpsuit. Once she awoke screaming and saw the Frant jerk spasmodically in its berth. Olmy had half fallen from his couch and was staring at her with evident alarm.

"Sorry," she said, looking between them guiltily.

"Quite all right," Olmy said. "We wish we could help. We could, actually, but . . ."

He didn't finish. A few minutes later, when her heart had stopped racing and she realized she couldn't remember what had made her scream, she asked Olmy what he meant by saying they could help.

"Talsit," he said. "Smooths the memory, rearranges priorities without dulling memory. Blocks subconscious access to certain disturbing memories. After Talsit, such memories can only be opened by direct conscious will."

"Oh," Patricia said. "Why can't I have some of this Talsit?"

Olmy smiled and shook his head. "You're pure," he said. "I'd be reprimanded if I brought you into our culture before our scholars had a chance to study you."

"Sounds like I'm a specimen," Patricia said.

The Frant again made that sound of amplified teeth-grinding. Olmy looked at it reproachfully and swung down from his berth. "You are, of course," Olmy said. "What would you like to eat?"

"I'm not hungry," Patricia said, lying back in her couch. "I'm frightened, and I'm bored, and I'm having bad dreams."

The Frant peered down at her, its large brown eyes unblinking. It held out one hand, spread its four slender fingers and curled them again. "Please," it said, its voice like a badly tuned calliope. "I cannot help."

"A Frant always wishes to help," Olmy explained. "If it cannot help, it feels pain. I'm afraid you're quite a trial to my Frant."

"Your Frant? You own him?"

"It. No, I don't own him. For the time of our assignment, we are duty-wed. Rather like social symbionts. I share its thoughts and it shares mine."

Patricia smiled at the Frant. "I'm okay," she said.

"You are lying," the Frant judged.

"You're right." Patricia reached up hesitantly and touched the Frant's arm. The skin was smooth and warm but not resilient. She withdrew her fingers. "I'm not afraid of you, either of you," she said. "Did you drug me?"

"No!" Olmy answered, shaking his head vigorously. "You must not be interfered with."

"This is so strange. I don't even feel it's real, but I'm not afraid."

"Perhaps that is well," the Frant said solicitously. "Until such time as you awake, we are a dream."

After that exchange, they did not speak for hours. Patricia lay facing the window, noting that the corridor had changed its character yet again. Now it was covered with lines resembling densely clustered freeways. As they spiraled around the

254

plasma tube, one turn every fifteen or twenty minutes, she saw that the entire floor was covered with the designs, whatever they signified. There didn't seem to be anything moving, but across a distance of more than twenty kilometers, she couldn't be sure.

The aircraft's spiral course was hypnotic. With a start, she realized she had been staring at new phenomenon for several minutes without conscious awareness. The dense-packed patterns on the floor of the corridor now crawled with moving lights. Strung along the "freeway" lanes were lines of red and intense white beads. Lances of light swung up in arcs above the patterns and illuminated the edges of low-flying disks. Girdling walls at least two or three kilometers high broke the flow at regular intervals of about ten kilometers.

"We are nearing Axis City," Olmy said.

"What's all this?" Patricia asked, pointing.

"Metered traffic between domestic gates," Olmy said.

"What are gates?"

"You called them wells when you discovered the first and second bands. They lead to spaces beyond the Way—the corridor."

Patricia frowned. "People go between the wells, enter and leave the corridor?"

"Yes," Olmy said. "The Axis City regulates the flow along a billion kilometers."

"But the wells—the gates—they can't possibly open into our universe, not in present time."

"They don't," Olmy said. "Now please, hold your questions until after we arrive. Too much information could reduce your purity."

"Excuse me," Patricia said with false contrition.

"However, you must not miss this," Olmy said. "Please look straight ahead, at the wall over your couch."

She stared at the smooth white surface. Olmy made a few quick clicking noises and the surface rippled like a disturbed pool. The ripples spread wide into a broad rectangle and solidified. The rectangle became black, then filled with

255

colorful snow. The snow attracted her eyes and the rectangular frame blurred, passing from her notice.

She might have been flying through the corridor alone. All around, the glowing, pulsing lights traveled their complex paths along the floor. Ahead, a dark circle was strung on the singularity, stretching from one side of the plasma tube to the other. Interrupted by the circle, the plasma tube changed color from white to a vivid oceanic blue.

"The Axis City lies beyond that barrier," Olmy said nearby. "We'll be given clearance soon, and pass through."

She turned her head and the illusion dissipated.

"No, no, please," Olmy said. "Keep watching." His tone and expression were almost little-boy eager, proud. She faced the rectangle of snow again.

The barrier filled her view. It was a somber dark gray-brown, shot through with radiating pulses of red. Where the singularity intersected it, the barrier glowed like molten lava.

Voices began speaking words she couldn't understand, and Olmy responded in kind. "We've been acknowledged," he explained to her. "Keep watching."

Directly ahead, a section of the barrier bubbled toward them and dissolved in a scatter of red pulses. They passed through.

Her first impression was that they were suddenly underwater. The plasma tube had ballooned out in all directions, widening by several kilometers and glowing the oceanic blue she had seen around the circular barrier. The floor of the corridor was still visible on all sides but reduced in definition and overlaid by the plasma's new color.

Directly ahead, two broad cubes were strung in succession along the pale thread of the singularity. Each of the visible faces of the cubes were marked with a broad horizontal cleft; the front of the foremost cube welcomed the singularity through a large hemispheric dimple, marked by glimmering spokes. At the center of the indentation was a red hole, and there the singularity was engulfed.

Beyond the cubes—and several times as broad—was a cylinder, rotating around its central axis, the line of the

256

singularity. Its outer surface sparkled with thousands of lights; the side facing her was dark but for a series of five radiating arrays of beacons.

Next in line after the cylinder, three curved vanes stretched outward to the structure's maximum radius, perhaps ten kilometers. The vanes seemed to touch or support the plasma tube, making it glow blue-white around the outermost edge of each vane. Whatever else was beyond the cylinder was effectively blocked from view.

"Home," Olmy said behind her. She turned and looked at him, blinking. "The first segments are navigation and power stations, all automatic. The rotating cylinder is Axis Nader. We can't see them from this perspective, but beyond lie Central City, Axis Thoreau and Axis Euclid."

"Where are we going?" she asked.

"We'll enter a dock in Axis Nader."

"How large is the city?"

"Do you mean, how extensive, or how many people?"

"Both, I suppose."

"It stretches forty kilometers down the Way, and it has a population of about ninety million—twenty million corporeal, embodied; seventy million stored in City Memory."

"Oh." She turned back to the screen and watched in silence as the craft moved inward, past the doubled cubes and along the dark side of the rotating cylinder.

"I suppose, in your time, you would have called Axis City a necropolis, a city of the dead," Olmy continued. "But the distinction isn't so precise for us. I, for example, have died twice performing my duty to the Nexus."

"They revived you?" Patricia asked.

"They made me over again," he replied.

She did not turn away from the screen, even though her back prickled.

The Presiding Minister had advised Olmy to report to Ser Oligand Toller immediately upon his arrival. Toller, advocate for Tees van Hamphuis, the President of the Hexamon Nexus,

257

was a radical Geshel who had chosen to maintain a completely human appearance. That the appearance bore no relation to his natal design—it had been adapted for maximum leadership qualities—did not mitigate the unusual conservatism; most radical Geshels, including the President, had chosen neo-morph shapes, which bore little relation to natural human forms.

What Olmy had to say, the P.M. judged, would be of extreme interest to the President. The President himself was unavailable, involved in a long-term conference on the problem of the impending Jart offensive; Toller was a kind of unofficial replacement.

This did not please the Naderites, or even the members of van Hamphuis's immediate staff. Toller was not an easy man to deal with. Olmy had met the advocate once before, and had not liked him at all, though he had gained a healthy respect for his abilities.

Toller kept his office in the most desirable professional wedge of Central City, no more than a few minutes tracting and just a few seconds shaft ascent from the Nexus Chambers in the precinct's core. Once Olmy had made arrangements for Patricia's quarters, but before he had had a chance to confer with his own advocate, he went to Toller's office.

Toller had decorated the small rectangular space in the most simple and adaptable Geshel style. Decoration was spare; the major texture theme was platinum and steel, and the overall effect was harsh and unyielding.

The President's advocate was not pleased with the news Olmy brought.

"The P.M. had no suspicion of this when you alone were sent?" Toller picted. The symbols that flashed between the two men came from pictor torques around their necks, devices which generated and projected the graphicspeak that had developed over the centuries in the Thistledown and in the Axis City.

"His information was highly equivocated," Olmy said. "All he knew was that the Thistledown had been reoccupied."

258

Toller picted an unpleasant image of a roiling nest of snake-like creatures. "This is extraordinary news, Ser Olmy. Coming from anyone else, I would find it difficult to believe. . . . But then, you've brought one of them back with you, haven't you?"

"Her name is Patricia Luisa Vasquez."

"A genuine . . . ancestor?"

Olmy nodded.

"Why did you bring her back? As evidence?"

"I could not leave her; she was close to discovering how to modify sixth chamber machinery."

Toller raised his eyebrows and picted four orange circles of surprise. "What is this woman?"

"A young mathematician," Olmy said, "highly regarded by her superiors."

"And you did nothing else to correct this situation you found on the Thistledown?"

"The situation is highly unstable there; they will not be able to organize for some time, and I thought it best to consult with the President and the Nexus."

"I'll inform the President, but you're aware we have our own major difficulties now. This conference . . . it could determine the whole course of the Axis City. And there's been considerable unrest and speculation among the Naderites—especially the Korzenowski faction. If they learn of this . . ." The picted nest of serpent-like creatures glowed a furious orange-red. "Seclude this woman and keep your information to your immediate superiors."

"She is secluded, and of course, I perform my duties as instructed," Olmy said. "She will have to have an advocate assigned to her, however."

"If we can avoid that, we should." Toller regarded him with obvious suspicion and unease.

"It is law. All noncitizens in the city, without defined legal status, must be assigned an advocate immediately."

"There's no need for you to quote city law to me," Toller said. "I'll find an advocate and assign—"

259

"I've already assigned one," Olmy interrupted.

Toller's expression changed to deep distaste. "Who?"

"Ser Suli Ram Kikura."

"I'm not acquainted with her." By the time he had finished the statement, Toller had a complete file on Kikura on hand, ready to be picted and interpreted. He scanned the file rapidly, shifting to implant logic, and found nothing he could criticise. "She seems acceptable. She will be sworn to keep Hexamon secrets."

"She has that clearance already."

"We're sitting on political chaos as it is," Toller said. "What you've done is bring back a lit fuse for Axis City's bomb. All, of course, in the name of duty."

"You will inform the President immediately?" Olmy asked, picting a sidebar request for permission to return to his work.

"As soon as possible," Toller replied. "You'll prepare a full report for us, of course."

"It is prepared," Olmy said. "I can transfer it now."

Toller nodded, and Olmy touched his torque. High-speed transfer of the report was accomplished in less than three seconds. Toller touched his own torque in acknowledgment of receipt.

Suli Ram Kikura lived in the outer layers of Central City, in one of three million tightly packed units reserved for single young corporeals of middle social and job standing. Her rooms were smaller than they appeared; the reality of spaciousness was far less important to her than it seemed to be to Olmy, who kept more primitive and larger quarters in Axis Nader. But part of what attracted her to Olmy was his age and differing attitudes, and his habit of, every now and then, giving her something truly interesting to work on.

"This is the biggest challenge I've ever faced," Suli Ram Kikura picted at Olmy.

"I couldn't think of anyone more capable," he replied. They floated facing each other in the subdued light of her quarters' central space, surrounded by picted spheres on which

260

were projected various interesting and relaxing textures. They had just made love, as they almost always made love, without enhancement and using nothing more complicated than the quarters' traction fields.

Olmy gestured at the spheres and made a face.

"Simplicity?" Ram Kikura asked.

"Simplicity, please," he affirmed. She dimmed the lights on everything but themselves and erased the spheres from the decor.

They had first met when he had inquired into the licensing process for creating a child. He had been interested mostly in a personality meld between himself and someone unspecified. This had been thirty years ago, when Ram Kikura was just beginning her practice. She had advised him on the procedures. Permission was easy enough to obtain for a corporeal homorph of his standing. But he had not carried it to the point of making a formal request. She had gathered that Olmy was more interested in the theory than the practice.

One thing had led to another. She had pursued him—with some elegance and no small persistence—and he had acquiesced, allowing himself to be seduced in a hidden corner of Central City's forested, zero-g Wald.

Olmy's work often took him far afield for years at a time, and what they had together, to most observers, would have seemed transitory, an on-and-off thing. Indeed, she had had relationships since, none permanent, even though it was once again the fashion to have relationships for ten years or longer.

Whenever Olmy had returned, she had somehow managed to be free of commitments. They never pressured each other. What existed between them was a relaxed, but by no means trivial sensation of comfort and a high level of mutual interest. Each genuinely enjoyed hearing about the other's work and wondering where future tasks would take them. They were, after all, corporeal and usefully employed; theirs was a position of considerable privilege. Of the ninety million citizens in the Axis City, corporeal or in City Memory, only fifteen million had important work to do, and of those, only three million worked more than a tenth of their living hours.

"You seem to enjoy the task already," Olmy said.

"It's my perverse nature. This is by far the oddest thing I've found you associated with. . . . It's positively momentous."

"It could be of staggering importance," he said out loud, his tone mock-sepulchral.

"No more picting?"

"No, let's think and talk this through slowly."

"Fine," she said. "You wish me to be her advocate. How much of an advocate do you think she'll need?"

"You can imagine," Olmy said. "She's a complete innocent. She'll need complete social and psychological adjusting. She'll need protection. When her status is revealed—which is inevitable, I think, whatever the President and Presiding Minister wish—there will be a sensation."

"You're putting it mildly," she said. She ordered wine brought to them, and three static-controlled liquid spheres drifted into their light. She handed Olmy a straw and they sipped. "You've seen Earth yourself?"

He nodded. "I went down the bore hole with the Frant on my second day in the Thistledown. I didn't think remotes would convince me quite as much as seeing with my own eyes."

"Old-fashioned Olmy," Ram Kikura said, smiling. "I'm afraid I would have done the same thing. And did you see the Death?"

"Yes," he said, staring up into the darkness. He rubbed two fingers along the black fuzz dividing his three bands of hair. "Only by remote at first—there was a battle in the bore hole and I couldn't possibly have gotten through. But after the fighting stopped, I took the ship out and saw."

Ram Kikura touched his hand. "How did you feel?"

"Have you ever wanted to cry?"

She looked at him carefully, trying to gauge how serious he was. "No," she said.

"Well, I wanted to. And I've wanted to many times since, thinking about it. I tried to purge the feeling with Talsit on the way back—quite a few sessions. But Talsit couldn't cure all of

262

it. I could feel our beginnings . . . a smudged, dirty, dead and dying world." He told her about Patricia's grief. Ram Kikura turned away in distaste.

"We cannot release as she did," he said. "It isn't in us anymore, and perhaps that's something else we've lost."

"Grief is not productive. It simply represents an inefficiency in accepting change of status."

"There are orthodox Naderites who still have the capacity," he said. "They find grief a noble sentiment. Sometimes I envy them."

"You were organically conceived and born. You had the capacity at one time. You knew what it was like. Why did you give it up?"

"To fit in," Olmy said.

"You wished to conform?"

"For higher motives, yes."

Ram Kikura shuddered. "Our visitor is going to think us all very strange, you know."

"It's her privilege," Olmy said.

Chapter Thirty-five

The storm began as a series of accelerated risings and fallings of air, circular cells rubbing against each other and generating a thick, tortured layer of clouds throughout the first chamber. Western bloc scientists in the middle of the chamber along the zero road made quick measurements before retreating to their trucks. Dust and sand were kicked up in immense, slender twisters, which in turn uncoiled and gave way to thick curtains of dust. The dust clouds billowed and spread, bouncing from cap to cap like waves in a channel. Cameras at the bore hole recorded the phenomenon, but there was nothing that could be done to control it. Either the storm was a planned part of the chamber's weather system, or the chamber had no effective weather control. It had not, after all, been a steadily occupied part of the Stone. Weather control might not have been thought necessary.

In the years of the Stone's reoccupation, nothing of this violence and strength had ever happened. The dust clouds covered the valley floor and slowly settled into a soupy, opaque layer a few kilometers thick. Above the dust, water clouds became darker and darker.

By 1700 hours, 6 hours after the storm's first high winds, rain fell through the dust and landed as great drops of mud. In the first compounds, people huddled in the bungalows, both alarmed and thrilled by the sudden change.

Hoffman watched from her mud-splattered window, chewing on a knuckle with eyebrows raised. The surcease from tubelight was welcome. This was the closest to night that anyone had experienced on the Stone, and it made her feel drowsy and content.

Lightning crackled throughout the chamber and engineers and marines braved the wind and rain to fasten conducting rods to the buildings.

In the Russian command bungalow, at the middle of the second compound, the storm and darkness were ignored. The argument over the political and command structure ran late into the sleeping period, with Belozersky and Yazykov most vehement, and Vielgorsky staying in the background.

Mirsky insisted on a military organization and refused to reduce his power in any way, or to share it equally with (and he emphasized the point) *junior* officers.

Belozersky proposed a true Soviet structure, with a central party committee, led by a general secretary—Vielgorsky was suggested—and a president and premier acting through a Supreme Soviet.

Just the day before, Mirsky and Pogodin—the commanding officer in the first chamber—had supervised the beginning of construction on a Russian compound in the fourth chamber; permission had been granted to harvest wood from the thick forests. Tools were at a premium; everything was at a premium.

Negotiations over the second chamber had grown heated when NATO archaeologists protested the potential desecration of what they regarded as their site. Mirsky had brusquely informed Hoffman that the Potato was no longer a monument; it was a refuge.

That had worn him down. His long sessions in the third chamber library—often instead of sleeping—had added to his fatigue; and now, this.

"We must situate our people before we decide the final political structure," Mirsky said. "All we have are makeshift tents and this compound, and Hoffman—"

"That *bitch*," Belozersky commented dryly. "She's worse than the fool Lanier."

Vielgorsky touched Belozersky's shoulder and the martinet sat down obediently. Vielgorsky's ascendancy among the political officers did not surprise Mirsky; neither did it please him. Mirsky was sure he could handle Belozersky, but with Vielgorsky's cunning, reserve and authoritative speaking voice—and Yazykov's razor-sharp legal mind—Mirsky felt a nasty challenge brewing.

Was there some way he could "turn" Vielgorsky and Yazykov, put their talents to his own advantage?

In his favor, he felt, was his continuing education. Or, perhaps more accurately phrased, his *enlightenment*. Never before had he been able to wander at will through such a huge and diverse source of information. Soviet libraries—military and otherwise—had always been severely restricted, with books available only to those with a demonstrable need to know. Simple curiosity was frowned upon.

He had been unsure even about the geography of his own country. History had been a subject in which he had never felt much interest, other than the history of space travel; what he learned in the third chamber library was turning him around completely.

To his colleagues he revealed none of this; he took pains to conceal the fact that he now spoke English, German, and French and was working on Japanese and Chinese.

"On the contrary," Belozersky said, glancing at Vielgorsky, "political considerations must always be foremost. We must abandon neither the revolution nor its ideals; we are the last fortress of—"

"Yes, yes," Mirsky said impatiently. "Now we are all tired. Let us rest and start again tomorrow." He glanced over his shoulder at Garabedian, Pletnev and Sergei Pritikin, senior engineer from the science team. "Comrade Major Garabedian, will you escort these gentlemen to their tents and make sure our perimeters are secure?"

"There is more to be discussed than we have time for," Vielgorsky said.

Mirsky fixed his gaze on him and smiled. "True," he said. "But tired men become angry men, and frustrations make for bad thinking."

"There are other . . . things which lead to weakness and bad thinking," Vielgorsky said.

"Indeed," Belozersky concurred.

"Tomorrow, Comrades," Mirsky persisted, ignoring the barb. "We need to be fresh when we face Hoffman and continue the negotiations."

They filed out and left Pritikin and Pletnev with Mirsky. The senior engineer and former squadron commander sat down at the tank-baffle table and waited as Mirsky rubbed his eyes and squeezed the bridge of his nose. "You realize what happens if Vielgorsky and his puppets take control," Mirsky said.

"They are not reasonable men," Pritikin said.

"Yet I believe about a third of the troops supports them wholeheartedly, and another third supports nobody—general malcontents," Mirsky said. "I am the commander, so the malcontents dislike me. If it was Belozersky alone, I wouldn't worry—the malcontents hate political officers even more. But Vielgorsky has a velvet tongue. Belozersky lashes with words, Vielgorsky strokes. He can control a dangerous majority."

"What do we do then, Comrade General?" Pletnev asked.

"I want five men to guard each of you. Hand-picked by Garabedian or me. And I want four squads with AKVs around this bungalow. Pritikin, I want the science team confined to the fourth chamber by the day after tomorrow. Vielgorsky will not trust intellectuals; he may not tolerate their existence if push comes to shove."

The two left and Mirsky was alone. He sighed and wished for something to take his mind away for the rest of the evening—a bottle of vodka, a woman . . .

Or more uninterrupted hours in the library.

Never in his life had he felt more aware, and more hopeful, then he did now, even though surrounded by ignorant vipers.

Chapter Thirty-six

The tuberider was on automatic pilot and all four of them slept in the cabin.

Heineman had limited the tuberider's speed to nine kilometers per second. Something in the tuberider's construction caused a violent shudder beyond that.

Lanier lay awake, restless, strapped to his reclined seat and staring up at the softly glowing orange light overhead. Heineman was breathing steadily across the aisle from him; the women slept behind a curtain Carrolson had rigged across the middle of the cabin. Carrolson snored faintly. From Farley he heard nothing.

Sexual passion had seldom dominated Lanier; his drives were normal enough, but he had always been able to ignore them, or control them in inappropriate situations. His two-year celibacy on the Stone had been less a hardship for him than it might have been for others. Nevertheless, he had never been hornier in his life than he was at this peaceful moment.

Despite the advantages, he had always felt faintly ashamed of his lack of masculine anguish, as if it made him some sort of cold fish. Now the passion was upon him with a vengeance. It was all he could do to keep from stealing back through the curtain and fondling Farley. The desire was both funny and agonizing. He felt like a pubescent teenager, sweaty with need and unsure what to do about it.

The psychiatrists in his head worked overtime. *Death,* said the Freudian, *only strenghthens our desire to procreate*—

So he lay sleepless, erect, unable to think clearly and refusing to masturbate. The very idea was ridiculous. He hadn't masturbated in well over a year, and never except in complete privacy.

Did the others feel this way? Heineman certainly never let on. Not once, in fact, had Lanier ever heard Heineman make a sexual comment except in the most isolated and theoretical sort of joking.

Did *Farley* feel this way?

Just as a test, one hand reached up to pull aside the thin thermal blanket covering him. He forced the hand to pull it back. Madness.

Finally, after an eternity, he slept.

At 100,000 kilometers, the V/STOL's forward-looking radar reported a massive obstruction ahead in the corridor. Heineman searched the corridor bore-hole science records for any echoes from such a distance and found none. "Looks like the physics people just shot a radar beam along the singularity," he said. "And what we're looking at now is a circular wall with a gap in the middle."

The wall obstructed passage to a height of twenty-one kilometers, leaving a hole in the middle about eight kilometers across. The plasma tube and singularity were not interrupted.

"Let's pass through and see what's on the other side," Lanier suggested. "Then we'll decide where we want to come down."

At a mere six thousand kilometers per hour, Heineman eased the tuberider down the singularity. The wall was a dirty bronze color, smooth and featureless. As they approached the hole, Carrolson trained a telescope on the wall's upper surface—with some difficulty.

"It's only a meter thick at the top," she said. "Judging by the color, I'd guess it's made out of the same stuff as the wells and the corridor."

"That is, nothing," Farley said. "Patricia's spacial building blocks."

Heineman reduced speed to a few hundred kilometers an hour and they glided through the hole. On the opposite side, the view of the corridor floor was crystal clear, unobstructed by atmosphere. The floor was a chaotic mess of hundred-kilometer-long gouges, black marks and broad strips of revealed bronze corridor surface. The instruments confirmed their suspicions.

"No atmosphere," Farley said. "The wall's a plug."

Heineman decelerated until they came to a stop two thousand kilometers past the wall, now reduced in size to a tiny patch in the corridor's merciless perspective. "What'll it be?" he asked.

"We slide back and find a well circuit," Lanier said, "just like we planned. We check that out, then we proceed—and we don't waste time. Research is really secondary."

"Yessir," Heineman said. He swung the V/STOL around on the tuberider to face the opposite direction. "Hang on; full reverse coming up."

Four hundred kilometers south of the wall, they located a circuit of wells and slowed to prepare the V/STOL for its descent. All loose objects were made fast while Heineman unlocked the aircraft from the tuberider. With a gentle nudge of the attitude jets, they eased away from the singularity. Heineman oriented the craft with its nose toward the corridor floor.

Unlike in the asteroid chambers, where some sort of push was required to move away from the axis, the V/STOL began a slow, accelerating descent immediately, repelled by the singularity—or attracted by the floor, whichever way they cared to think of it. After falling four kilometers, Heineman kicked in the rocket engine for three short bursts and pointed the plane's nose north. "I wouldn't land this way in a chamber," he said, "but it's the best tactic in the corridor. We won't hit the atmosphere on a spiral course here. So I'm going to take advantage of a long glide down. Garry, take hold of your controls and get the feel of what I'm doing."

Lanier gripped the wheel and felt Heineman's motions as he pulled the nose up. A rippling series of shudders announced atmospheric buffeting; outside the walls a whimpering whine began to decrease in pitch and increase in loudness. Heineman brought down flaps to decrease their airspeed and gently swung the V/STOL to the right, lowering the nose and deploying the prop blades from their receptacles in the engine nacelles. The smooth, beautiful roar of the twin turboprops made him smile like a little boy. "Ladies and gents," he said, "we are now an airplane. Garry, like to take it down?"

"My pleasure," Lanier said. "Passengers will please keep their seatbelts on."

"Aye-aye," Carrolson said.

"That was fun. Let's do it again," Farley called forward.

"Terrain looks smooth enough, but we'll fly over and decide whether we want a short landing or a vertical touchdown," Heineman said.

Lanier banked the aircraft and circled around a well, then flew over the cupola at about fifty meters, slowing by angling the props up. Heineman peered at the prospective landing sights and signaled thumbs-up. "Short roll; it's smooth sand down there."

Lanier brought the V/STOL down on the corridor floor at fifty kilometers an hour, gently and easily, nose pointed at the dimple and cupola of the well. He then reduced the pitch on the props and taxied, nose bobbing, to the edge of the dimple, pivoting the plane until it was tangent to the well's outer circle. The engines' roar dropped rapidly to silence.

"Bravo," Heineman said.

"God, that was great," Lanier said. "I haven't flow in six years . . . and I've *never* flown like that. Jesus, you look at the ground and it seems like you're always going to fly right into it."

"If you two flyboys will give us a hand," Carrolson interrupted, "we'll get out work done faster."

Carrolson took photographs and Farley made instrument readings as they skirted the dimple. The well was open—that much was obvious even from a distance. Ten or eleven meters from the floating cupola was a platform cradling two irregular red-and-black-checked spheres, each three meters in diameter and sporting a pair of waldoes front and back.

They descended the slope of the dimple and inspected the platform. Heineman climbed a ladder built into one side of the platform and walked along a scaffold passing above the checked spheres. "Spacesuits," he said. "Tough ones, too."

"Here's a message," Farley called out. She pointed to a bronze-colored plaque mounted on a pedestal near the mouth of the well. The alphabet was Latinesque, with discernible A's, G's and E's, but none of them could decipher the words. "It's not Greek, and it's not Cyrillic," Carrolson said. "It must be Stoner. Some new language." She photographed it from three sides and beneath.

"I never encountered anything like it in the libraries," Lanier said. He stepped beyond the plaque and felt a sudden, molasses-like resistance around the lip of the well.

"WARNING," a deep, forbidding masculine voice announced out of nowhere. "WARNING to be heeded by speakers of twentieth-century English. Do not attempt to enter any gate in this region without proper environmental protection. Conditions of high gravitation and corrosive atmosphere prevail beyond the gate entrance. Suits are provided for your protection. WARNING."

Carrolson touched the plaque and whistled. "Look," she said. The letters of the plaque had reformed into Roman alphabet English and repeated what the voice had said aloud. "Now *that's* service."

Heineman ran his hands along the upper surface of one of the spheres and found a depression in a black square. He pressed it cautiously; nothing happened.

"Excuse me," Farley said to no one in particular. Lanier

271

turned toward her and she smiled, embarrassed, and held up her hand. She then addressed the underside of the cupola. "Excuse me, but if we wish to enter the well—the gate—how do we use the suits, the . . . pathoscapes—"

"Bathyscaphes," Carrolson corrected.

"Yes . . . how do we use whatever they are?"

"Vehicles respond to vocal commands and can be adjusted to your language. Do you have proper authorization for a gate excursion?"

"What sort of authorization?" Farley asked.

"Authorization from the Nexus. All gates are controlled by the Nexus. Please present authorization within thirty seconds or this band of gates will be locked against tampering."

They stared back and forth at each other as the time passed. "No authorization," the voice announced without inflection. "These gates are now closed until a survey team investigates and corrects the situation."

Lanier pulled back from the invisible barrier. The twenty-meter-wide opening at the center irised in silently and formed a smooth bronze bulge. On the scaffold, Heineman yelped and jumped clear as the spheres and cradle slowly sank into the surface of the dimple, vanishing without trace.

Farley swore in melodious Chinese.

"Oh, well," Carrolson said, sighing. "We didn't have time to be tourists anyway."

The bland landscape around the well consisted of flat stretches of sand without any sign of life. The air was dry and soon their noses and throats were parched; it was with some relief that they boarded the V/STOL, sealed the hatch and prepared to return to the tuberider.

"This is fun," Heineman said. "She works like a charm." He lifted the V/STOL from the ground and increased their speed by inclining the engine nacelles forward. They climbed steadily, until they were within a kilometer of the plasma tube and the upper limits of the atmosphere. "Abracadabra," Heineman said, withdrawing the blades into the nacelles and activating the tail rocket.

272

With a sharp surge forward, they punched through the atmosphere barrier and plasma tube and entered the vacuum surrounding the singularity. Heineman guided the V/STOL with little pushes from the attitude jets, bringing it up beneath the tuberider and completing the linkup under direction of the plane's computers.

"She's a beauty, isn't she?" he enthused, then shook his head and let out a puffed *whooo*.

Chapter Thirty-seven

"We're not going to get a disarmament agreement out of them any time soon," Gerhardt said as he preceded Hoffman down the platform steps into the fourth chamber compound. "They're more afraid of each other than they are of us, right now, and nobody's going to hand in their weapons until the situation is settled."

"Who do you think will come out on top?"

Gerhardt shrugged. "No bets. They're all tough sons of bitches; my hopes are for Mirsky."

"He's been in the third chamber library more often than any of us," Hoffman said.

"He has more to catch up on," Gerhardt said. "Russians don't want soldiers with a liberal education."

"I suppose we should be happy with a cease fire and separate camps."

Gerhardt opened the mess door for her and she passed through into the cafeteria. Four agricultural scientists—one man and three women—waited for her with charts and slates. She shook hands with all of them and took a seat. Gerhardt received a meager lunch from the vendor and sat at the next table; this was not his direct concern.

"Food programs," Hoffman said. "Farming and subsistence. Okay. Show me what we have to do."

Push came to shove barely eighteen hours after the con-

273

ference in the bungalow. The first chamber storm settled even more quickly than it started; the winds suddenly stopped, the clouds unleashed a few more drops and then dissipated. The tubelight brightened and the air felt warmer.

Belozersky ordered a platoon to surround the bungalow and capture Mirsky. The ostensive reason was Mirsky's lack of dedication to the cause of socialism; but all three *Zampolit*s felt the Lieutenant General was weak and would soon make concessions to Hoffman that the Soviets could ill afford.

The platoon moved in quickly and surrounded the command center, bringing their AKVs to bear on the twenty guards. The guards surrendered without resistance and Belozersky approached the bungalow door to place Mirsky under arrest. Three burly troopers kicked in the door and poked their rifles through, keeping their heads and bodies back.

"Comrade General!" Belozersky shouted, his voice breaking. "You have violated the confidence of your men. In the name of the newly reconstituted Supreme Soviet, you are under arrest!" The troopers swung around the door frame and into the bungalow. Pletnev sat up on a bunk, blinking sleepily.

"General Mirsky's not here," he said thickly. "Is there anything I can do for you?"

Vielgorsky had napped briefly after the conference with Mirsky, then taken advantage of the weakening storm to move three trucks with fifty soldiers out of the first chamber, and to ride the ninety tube train—reserved exclusively for Russian use—into the fourth chamber.

The plan was to have him out of the way when Belozersky arrested Mirsky, just in case something went wrong. For a few hours, then, he could enjoy the fourth chamber woods. He especially enjoyed the sight of soldiers in the Development Detail bringing down trees and hauling them to the water. Stories of the conquest of the east and the buiding of the trans-Siberian railway had enchanted him as a boy; now he visualized something similar in the Potato, a series of Soviet settlements linked by roads, clearing fields for farms and building cabins. Something good might come out of this fiasco after all, he thought—a purer, less corrupt and more tightly controlled socialist community, which could eventually take over the asteroid and return to Earth to complete the task Lenin had begun eighty-years before.

Things were moving with astonishing speed already; only nine days ago, they had made their landing, and now they had been ceded territory in the most attractive of the Potato's seven chambers. If this didn't demonstrate the weakness of their opponents, what possible could?

Three SSTs approached him. The lead trooper carried a few papers, no doubt for him to sign in his capacity as director of fourth chamber exploitation.

"Colonel," the first soldier said, pulling a pistol from behind the papers. He pointed the pistol at Vielgorsky and tipped his cap higher.

"Mirsky," Vielgorsky said, losing none of his control.

The other two soldiers were Pogodin and the scientist Pritikin. Each carried an AKV slung over his shoulder. Mirsky took Vielgorsky's arm and poked the pistol into his side, near the kidneys. "Not a word, please."

"What are you doing?" Vielgorsky whispered harshly. Mirsky thrust the pistol forward with more force.

"Quiet. Your rat is gnawing a hole in my bungalow."

They walked with measured steps to a truck waiting by the lakeshore. Pogodin unceremoniously pushed Vielgorsky into the back and threw a tarp over him, climbing in after and lightly tapping the barrel of the AKV on the bulge his head made.

Mirsky climbed behind the steering column and looked across the dark sand to the soldiers in the woods. Another group was playing *lapta*—a kind of baseball—with branches and pinecones; none seemed concerned with the truck or its occupants.

"Where are we going, General?" Vielgorsky asked from the rear, voice muffled by the tarp.

"Quiet, sir," Pogodin said, prodding him again with the AKV.

275

Chapter Thirty-eight

The chaotic and scarred section of the corridor stretched for half a million kilometers, airless and barren. Plans for a second sortie to the floor were abandoned; without an atmosphere, ascent and descent would use an exorbitant amount of fuel. If the barren segment continued past their million kilometer turnaround point, they would abandon the mission and reverse course, Lanier decided.

"Do you think all of it's like this?" Farley asked, sitting next to him. "From here on?"

Lanier shook his head. "They took Patricia somewhere."

"Have you thought about the wells? Perhaps they left the corridor, and we can't follow."

"I've thought of that—and I have a hunch they didn't use a well."

"Another wall!" Heineman announced.

They gathered in the cockpit, Carrolson sitting in the copilot's seat and Farley and Lanier jammed into the hatchway. Lanier was all too aware of the press of Farley's body.

The tuberider's passage through the corridor was dizzying; it reminded Lanier of running through a drain pipe. The corridor fled past on all sides, purple and brown and black with its scars, the revealed corridor surface dirty bronze. The Forward-Looking Radar returned a steady beep at half-second intervals.

"Seats please," Heineman said. "We're going to slow this sucker down. Reverse seats this time; I want to keep our FLR facing forward, and there'll be about two-tenths of a g. . . ."

Carrolson strapped herself into the copilot's seat with a pixie grin at Lanier. "Backseat, boss," she said. "I was here first."

Lanier and Farley crawled past the equipment boxes and sat next to each other. Lanier took a deep breath and closed his eyes; the urge was almost unbearable.

"Something wrong?" Farley asked.

276

"Not at all." He touched her hand reassuringly with his own and drew it back.

"You feeling all right?"

He smiled unconvincingly and nodded.

"Something's wrong, Garry. I've been around you long enough—"

"We'll be there in an hour or so," Heineman announced from the cockpit.

"So what is it?" Farley pursued.

He took a deep breath and his face reddened. "I can't help it, Karen. It's crazy. I've been . . . horny for the last twenty hours. It isn't going away."

She regarded him without expression, and then her eyes widened the merest fraction.

"You asked, dammit," he said.

"Just in general?"

"No."

"Someone in particular."

"Yes," he said.

"Who . . . or is that asking too much?"

He raised a finger and pointed it at her, shaking with stifled laughter. His face was red as hamburger now and he sounded like he was choking.

"That's funny?"

"No-oo-o," he said, finally controlling his laughter. "It's *crazy*."

"You've never been interested in me before?"

"No—I mean, yes, you're attractive, obviously, but—"

"Then shut up." The deceleration had already started. She unbuckled her belt and fell slowly toward the cockpit, easing herself along with the handgrips on the side of the seats and storage racks overhead.

"Wait," Lanier said, reaching for her and missing. He looked back over the neck rest. "Karen!"

Farley hung in the cockpit hatchway. "Wake us when we're at the wall," she said pointedly, sliding the partition shut with a decisive snick of the bolt. She pulled herself back along the

277

aisle and braced one knee against his seat and the seat opposite.

"I'm sorry—" Lanier began.

"Not at all," Farley said. She tugged at her jumpsuit zipper and pulled it down, revealing a T-shirt with the Chinese character

鯨

on the front, signifying "whale," the Chinese name for the Stone. She shimmied it off quickly and removed white cotton panties.

Lanier watched in shock.

"You should have said something sooner," she admonished. "Anything that keeps you from thinking straight is a detriment to our mission." She pulled the T-shirt over her head and stuffed all the clothes in a rear seat pouch.

He removed his jumpsuit, glancing nervously at the cockpit partition. She lay on the rear of the two opposite seats; the tuberider's deceleration provided an effective if skewed sense of direction. "You never did put yourself on the social roster," Farley said, taking his hand and pulling him toward her. "Not because you were shy, surely."

Lanier touched her breast, his heart hammering. He gently rubbed the knuckles and backs of his fingers along the line between her hips and stomach. "I've never needed anyone more in my life," he said.

Carrolson ascended the ladder up the middle of the aisle. Farley and Lanier had dressed and seated themselves opposite each other. "Ten minutes and we'll be there," Carrolson said, deadpan. She looked at Farley and then turned her head toward Lanier, her eyes lingering for a moment on Farley's face. "It seems like the same sort of wall as the last one, but this one rises even higher above the level of the atmosphere with a narrower clearance—no more than a hundred meters—around the singularity. We should run the same tests we did before, though."

"Agreed," Farley said.

"Garry—" Carrolson began, regarding him intently.

"What?"

"Never mind." She descended the ladder and returned to the cockpit.

"Jesus, I'm embarrassed," Lanier muttered.

"Why, because you're human?" Farley asked.

"I have responsibilites," he said.

"There isn't a person on the Stone who doesn't," she said. "And there was an awful lot of hamky-pamky going on while I was there."

Despite himself, he chuckled. "That's 'hanky-panky.' "

"Whatever. Don't tell me you didn't notice?"

He shook his head. "No, I honestly didn't. The boss is the last to know."

"Only if the boss has his eyes shut. I doubt Hoffman is letting such things escape her."

"All right, so I'm a . . . I don't know. I'm not a prude, but I'm maybe a bit innocent."

"Not innocent at all," Farley said, reaching across to touch his arm. "And don't worry. You're still the boss."

Chapter Thirty-nine

Vielgorsky had difficulty keeping his calm. He sweated profusely and smelled bad. His voice was hoarse. Mirsky almost felt sorry for him.

The black entranceway to the third chamber library opened impressively, and Pogodin and Pritikin urged the captive through with a few well-placed jabs of their AKVs. Mirsky followed at a more leisurely pace.

"This is where you've been wasting your time," Vielgorsky cried over his shoulder.

"You've never been here?" Mirsky asked, pretending surprise. "At the very least I would have thought you'd be curious."

"It's useless," Vielgorsky said. "It's filled with American propaganda. Why waste my time?"

Mirsky laughed out loud, more in anger than humor. "You poor son of a bitch," he said. "The people who built this starship were no more American than you or I." They halted before the ranks of chairs and chromium teardrops.

"If you kill me, Belozersky and Yazykov are fully capable of carrying on," Vielgorsky said.

"I'm not going to kill you," Mirsky said. "We need each other. I want you to sit down."

Vielgorsky stood his ground, shivering like a cold dog.

"The chairs won't eat you," Pogodin said, prodding him again.

"You cannot brainwash me," Vielgorsky blustered.

"No, but maybe I can *educate* you. Sit."

Vielgorsky slowly lowered himself into the nearest chair, facing the teardrop apprehensively. "You will force me to read books? That will be very silly."

Mirsky came around behind the chair and reached over to flip the control cover. "Would you like to learn how to speak English, French, German?"

Vielgorsky didn't answer.

"No? Then perhaps you'd like to learn a little about history. Not from an American point of view—from the viewpoint of our descendants. The Russians who survived the Death."

"I don't care," Vielgorsky said, his pale moist face almost all nose in the teardrop reflection.

"This is what the Americans were hiding from us," Mirsky said. "Isn't it your duty to inspect the treasure we were fighting for? Your superiors cannot. They are dead, or soon will be. The entire Earth will be covered with smoke for years to come. Millions will starve to death or freeze. By the end of this decade, there will be less than ten million of our countrymen left alive."

"You're talking nonsense," Vielgorsky said, wiping his face with his sleeve.

"Our descendants *built* this starship," Mirsky said. "That's not propaganda, it sounds like fantasy, but it's *truth*, Vielgorsky, and all our squabbling with each other cannot conceal the truth. We trained and came here and fought and died to find the *truth*. You would be a traitor to turn away from it."

"Are you proposing we share power?" Vielgorsky asked, glancing up at him. Mirsky swore under his breath and turned on the machine.

"It will speak to you in Russian," he said. "It will answer your questions and it will teach you how to use it. Now ask."

Vielgorsky stared at the floating library symbol, eyes wide. *"Ask."*

"Where do you want me to start?"

"Start with our past. What they taught us in school."

The symbol changed to a question mark.

"Teach me about . . ." Vielgorsky looked up at Mirsky.

"Go on. It isn't painful. But it is addictive."

"Teach me about Nicholas I."

"That's pretty safe," Mirsky said. "Too far back. Ask it to teach you about the grand strategic plan of the Soviet Army from 1960 to 2005." Mirsky smiled. "Weren't you ever curious?"

"Teach me . . . about that, then," Vielgorsky said.

The library silently searched and organized its presentation, numerous colorful utility symbols flickering around Vielgorsky's field of view. Then it began.

After a half hour, Mirsky turned to Pogodin and Pritikin and told them to go back to the fourth chamber. He nodded at the entranced Vielgorsky. "He'll be no trouble. I'll watch him."

"When will we get our chance?" Pritikin asked.

"Anytime you're free, Comrade," Mirsky said. "It's open to all."

Belozersky jerked the muscular Pletnev up from his chair and swung him around with surprising strength. "I know fantasies when I hear them," he growled.

"It's easily proven," Pletnev said, his head turned to one

side to avoid Belozersky's fist on his collar. "We must go there—comrades Pritikin and Sinoviev have told us as much as they know. The seventh chamber does not stop. It goes on forever."

Belozersky let him go and backed away slowly, fists clenched. "Deviationist crap. Pritikin and Sinoviev are intellectuals. Why should I believe them?"

Yazykov motioned for the three soldiers to take Pletnev by the arms. "You sold us into defeat for your own miserable skin," he said. "It was your duty to die out there, not come sniveling to the Americans."

"It was finished," Pletnev said. "We had no other choice."

"This rock can be ours!" Yazykov shouted. "Now, where is Mirsky?"

"I've told you. He's in the fourth chamber."

"Shit. He's in his beloved library," Belozersky said.

"Then that's where we'll arrest him," Yazykov said. "Now we should find Garabedian and Annenkovsky—they're Mirsky's men as well. Comrade Pletnev, I will personally execute you against the far wall of the seventh chamber. I will spread your blood and counterrevolutionary brains on solid proof of your gullibility." He threw his hands up in the air in disgust. "Keep him here until we find the others."

Rimskaya walked across the compound with the message from Belozersky in his hand. He climbed the steps to what had once been Lanier's office, and was now Hoffman's, and knocked on the door. Beryl Wallace answered.

"Message from the Soviets," he said tersely. His face was pale and he looked as if he hadn't slept in days.

"Something important?" Beryl asked.

"Beryl, don't play the protective underling with me. Where is Judith?"

"She's downstairs in conference with the medical supervisor. I'm not being officious, Joseph, but she's very busy."

"Yes, well, the Soviets are busy being Soviets, and I think

there's going to be trouble." He wiped his eyes and blinked owlishly.

"I'll get her. She'll meet you downstairs by the secretary's desk."

Rimskaya grunted and clumped back down the stairs.

Hoffman emerged from the executive conference room and took the slate from Rimskaya's hand, reading it over quickly. She also looked exhausted, though less so than Rimskaya. Her eyes were rimmed with purple and her cheeks were puffy from lack of sleep.

"What is Belozersky . . . position, rank?"

"A *Zampolit*—political officer," Rimskaya said. His hands were shaking. "Major. I've talked with him once or twice."

"What did you think of him?"

Rimskaya shook his head grimly. "Hard-liner, ignorant and unimaginative. These other two, Yazykov and Vielgorsky, they worry me. They're smarter, more dangerous. If they say they've deposed Mirsky and we have to deal with them directly, they've probably done it."

"Then arrange a meeting. We can't just stop talking because of their internal squabbles. And find out from—what's his name?—Sinoviev or Pritikin. Find out from one or the other what's going on and how this affects the Russian civilians."

"They aren't around. They may be in detention or dead."

"You think it's gone that far?" Hoffman asked.

"They're acting very Russian," Rimskaya said, spreading his hands.

"I'll be in this conference for another hour or so. Get them to meet with us in an hour and a half."

"Better to let them suggest the time, and then make them wait a while," Rimskaya suggested.

"You take care of it."

She watched the tall, dour mathematician walk out the door and then stared at a blank space on the wall over Ann's empty desk. The secretary was in the cafeteria on lunch break.

"Just thirty seconds," Hoffman said, focusing on nothing. She stood alone, breathing steadily, one finger tapping lightly on the corner of the desk, beating time to some internal meditative clock. When half a minute had passed, she closed her eyes tightly, opened them wide, took a deep breath and turned back to the hallway and the conference room door.

Chapter Forty

The tuberider slid slowly past the second wall. On the opposite side, beginning about a kilometer from the wall and paralleling it around the circumference of the corridor, a series of dark brick-colored structures squatted on the bare bronze floor. Each sat on a square base about two hundred meters on a side, rising in a series of steps, each step-level twisted slightly, creating a rounded, half-spiral pyramid.

"Bingo," Heineman said, pointing down the throat of the corridor. The floor was alive with moving lights channeled into lanes, the lanes piled many layers deep like a super-dense freeway system. "We are not alone."

"How far have we come?" Carrolson asked.

"Seven hundred and seventy thousand kilometers, give or take two," Heineman said. "Garry, could you pilot for a bit? I'm going to run more tests."

"We'll just keep moving ahead slow, ninety or a hundred kilometers an hour," Lanier said.

"That's about right. I don't feel very easy about meeting the inhabitants, whatever they may be," Heineman said, shaking his head as he climbed out of the seat. They were weightless again, moving at a steady velocity.

"Why would we worry, I mean, besides the obvious reasons?" Farley asked.

"The obvious reason would be bad enough, but frankly, I'm not happy about coming along the singularity. It's just occurred to me whoever's down there might not like people traveling this way. Maybe there are other vehicles—authorized vehicles. Maybe there's something else. Whatever, if we were to come zipping along at eight or nine klicks a second, anything we hit would be in serious trouble. That's enough to get us a moving violation, wouldn't you say?"

"I hadn't thought of that," Lanier said, settling into the pilot's seat.

"Yes, well, now that your head is more clear . . ." Heineman glanced at him sternly and then patted him on the shoulder. "Girls, let's find out what all the fuss is."

They replaced various instruments in ports along the floor of the aircraft and installed new sensors in ports so far unoccupied. Lanier stared overhead at the corridor floor, fascinated by the procession of lights. Even with binoculars, he couldn't make the lights resolve into anything but bright spots, contrasting against the black of the lanes.

Something large and gray covered his field of view in the binoculars and he pulled them down. A disk at least half a kilometer wide floated slowly above the lanes, moving south. Another disk followed a similar course twenty or thirty degrees to the west.

"Absolutely no coherent radio signals," Heineman said. "Waste microwaves and heat and a little X- and gamma-ray activity and that's it. Radar—the repeater back here shows something substantial about a quarter of a million kilometers ahead—surface area of at least fifteen square kilometers, right on the axis—dead center."

"I see it," Lanier said, looking at the primary display. "Objects moving around it, and all along the wall of the corridor."

"Don't ask me what *they* are," Heineman said, peering through the windscreen at the gray disks. He squinted in puzzled anxiety. "And don't ask me how long we're going to stay up here unmolested."

"At least we're small," Farley said. "Maybe they won't notice us."

"That big thing up ahead, whatever it is, will notice us," Heineman said. "Ten to one it's riding the singularity, too."

Five hundred kilometers past the wall, four large brick-red

285

twisted pyramids rose above the tangle of lanes. From their spacing—equidistant around the circumference, at the quadratic points—Lanier surmised they were built over wells. From this distance, they appeared the size of a commemorative postage stamp held at arm's length—which made them perhaps two kilometers on a side, and a kilometer high. Kilometer-wide clear lanes extended straight north from each structure, for as far as he could see.

"I think we're in over our head," Lanier murmured.

Farley put her hand on his shoulder and pulled herself into the copilot's seat. "We've been over our heads for years, haven't we?"

"I'd always assumed the corridor was empty—I don't know why. Perhaps because I couldn't have imagined this."

Heineman floated between them and gripped a bar on the instrument panel to steady himself while he programmed a flight plan. "We're going to accelerate to ten thousand klicks an hour, get as close as we can to that big object on the singularity—slowing down on the approach, so they won't think we're going to ram them—then reverse and hightail for home. That is, of course, if you approve." He raised an eyebrow in Lanier's direction.

Lanier weighed the risks and realized he had no idea what they were.

"If we reverse now, what can we tell the folks back home?" Heineman persisted. "It's obvious this place is important. But we have no idea what is it, or what it means to us once we're back on the Stone."

"You're stating the obvious, Larry," Lanier said. "Now tell me whether we'll survive or not."

"I don't know," Heineman said. "But I'm having the time of my life. What about the rest of you?"

Carrolson laughed. "You're crazy," she told him. "Crazy jock pilot engineer."

Heineman wagged his head back and forth and proudly lifted the breast pockets of his jumpsuit out with his thumbs. "Garry?"

"We have to find out somehow," he admitted. "Let's go, then." Heineman began the sequence on the computer pilot and the tuberider bore down on the singularity, once again putting a sense of direction into the V/STOL cabin.

When the acceleration stopped and the tuberider coasted at ten thousand kilometers an hour, Heineman distributed supper—sandwiches in foil packets and bulbs of hot tea. They ate in silence, Carrolson and Heineman strapped to the bulkhead behind the cockpit. The corridor's passage was steady and easily perceptible.

Another circuit of rectangular structures passed, and several minutes later, yet another—all connected by the four straight clear lanes and the crowded tangled lanes of lights.

Lanier vacated the seat to Carrolson and took a nap while Heineman trained the women in the fine points of tuberider control. He dropped in and out of a dream about flying a light plane over jungle and tangled rivers. Somehow, that segued into a track meet. He awoke with the aftertaste of tea in his mouth and undid the seatbelts, pulling himself forward. Farley was adjusting instruments in their ports and replacing memory blocks on the slates collecting and collating the data. She dropped full blocks into a plastic sorting tray and slipped it into a file box. Then she held up one of the auxiliary multimeters built by engineering before the Death, pointing out the display for Lanier's inspection.

"Yes?" he asked, looking down at the flickering numbers.

"It's kaput," she said. "Putting out nonsense. So are most of our instruments. We'll be lucky to interpret half the data we've gathered."

"Reasons?"

She shook her head. "Wild guesses, and that's the best I can do. Other electrical systems seem to be working—so it's possible we're passing through control fields like those that selectively damp inertia on the Stone. These fields damp other effects . . . distorted geometry's effect on activity in the nucleus, changes in slash aitch . . . Or the equipment may be crapping out all at once. Warranty expires today—surprise!"

"The equipment's fine," Heineman called out from the copilot's seat. "Don't blame my machines."

"The man's so proprietary," Farley marveled. "He gumbles everytime I question quality control."

"Grumbles, not 'gumbles,' Lanier said.

"Whatever."

"Your turn," Lanier told Heineman, indicating the rear of the plane with his thumb. "Naptime. We'll all need to be bright and cheerful."

Heineman adjusted the tuberider's roll and floated past Lanier. "Wait," Carrolson said. "What's that?"

The singularity ahead of the tuberider was no longer a shiny cylindrical surface. In intermittent pulses, it glowed orange and then white, like a hot steel wire.

"No rest for the wicked," Heineman said, replacing Lanier in the pilot's seat. He applied the tuberider clamps to the singularity to brake. The craft suddenly bucked and rolled violently, tossing Lanier and Farley against the storage rack and pinning them there until Heineman released the clamps.

"We're accelerating," Heineman shouted over the roaring shudder of the tuberider and airplane. "I'm not in control anymore."

Lanier slid toward the rear of the cabin, banging into seats with his arms and legs as he tried to grab hold of something. Farley clung to a seat tenaciously and struggled to swing around and sit in it.

The singularity now drew a long, steady red line down the middle of the plasma tube. Laner strapped himself into a seat and reached across to help Farley climb into hers. Equipment bounced and fell to the rear, striking storage racks, bulkheads and other equipment.

"Can you reverse us?" Lanier shouted over the tumult.

"No way," Heineman answered. "If I clamp down, we start bucking. Thirty thousand and still accelerating." The tuberider rolled again and Lanier and Farley shielded themselves against another onslaught of rebounding memory block racks, test kits and coiled light cables.

"Forty," Heineman said a few moments later. "Fifty."

288

The radio crackled and *chuff*ed and a genderless melodic voice began in mid-phrase:

"—violation of the Law of the Way. Your craft is in violation of the Law of the Way. Do not resist or your craft will be destroyed. You are under the direction of the Hexamon Nexus and will be removed from the flaw in six minutes. Do not attempt to either accelerate or decelerate."

The message ended with a soft burst of white noise.

Chapter Forty-one

Belozersky stood stiffly to the rear of Yazykov at the conference table, hands locked behind his back. Yazykov sat with his hands folded on the table. Hoffman looked over the demands and wrote out a quick translation on her slate for Gerhardt. Gerhardt read them quickly and shook his head.

"We reject your demands," Hoffman said flatly in Russian. She, too, had spent time in the third chamber library.

"These men are criminals," Yazykov said. "They have kidnapped one of our colleagues and hidden in one of the cities where we cannot find them."

"Whether that's true or not, we already agreed to separate governmental and judicial systems. We can't help you find these men without breaking our agreement."

"They are hiding in sectors dominated by your people," Belozersky said. "You yourself may be hiding them."

"If that's the case, then I've been told nothing about it," Hoffman said. "I doubt it."

"Surely you support our attempt to form a civilian government," Yazykov said.

"We don't support it, and we don't oppose it," Hoffman said. "That's your concern. Our concern at this table is with our peaceful coexistence. Nothing more."

Yazykov rose quickly and nodded at Hoffman. They crossed the cafeteria and exited through the rear door.

"What do you make of that?" Hoffman asked Gerhardt. The general shook his head ruefully and grinned.

"Mirsky's stolen their main man," he said. "Looks like he anticipated them and made the first move."

"What's your opinion of Mirsky?"

"Hard-line Soviet military or not, I'd rather deal with him than with Yazykov or Belozersky."

"So do we help him?"

"Help Mirsky? Hell, no. First instincts are best. We stay out of it and let them settle it themselves. Besides, Mirsky won't *ask* for help. We just have to hope it doesn't come to a fight. We might not be able to stay out of that."

Mirsky and Pogodin removed Vielgorsky from the third chamber city in the truck, following a tortuous series of service roads until they found a main artery that crossed the remaining twenty kilometers in a straight line. The artery emerged through a number of open half-moon gates onto the ninety tunnel leading to the second chamber.

Mirsky examined several buildings along the second chamber thoroughfares before picking one that suited him. It was hidden between one of the giant chandelier-skyscrapers the Americans called megas, and a long row of hundred-meter-high asteroid-rock towers of no apparent utility.

The building was only four stories tall and seemed to have once been a kind of school. Long rows of connected seats filled the three rooms on each floor, facing slate-black walls rimmed with silvery glass.

In the easternmost room of the top floor, they spread their supplies, and Mirsky sat down with a much quieter and even more somber Vielgorsky. Pogodin went to hide the truck.

"I don't thank you," Vielgorsky said. He lay back on a bench and stared at the gold stars on the dark blue ceiling. "My father died in Afghanistan. I was told nothing about his death . . . state secret. I still don't know. But that it was all a military exercise . . . to battle-test the army . . ." He shook his head wonderingly. "A ten-year exercise! To find—"

he coughed into his fist, "to find that all one has believed has been an orchestrated lie—"

"Not all," Mirsky said. "Much, but not all."

"Having one's eyes opened doesn't make one grateful."

"We've always known bits and pieces, haven't we?" Mirsky asked. "About the corruption, the inefficient and incompetent and venal superiors . . . The State preserving itself at the expense of revolutionary ideals."

"Every man must work with such things, if not accept them. But using our finest athletes and dancers as concubines—"

"Hypocrisy mixed with stupidity."

"How much worse for a government that says it is above scandal, and cannot do wrong! At least the Americans wallow in their scandal."

They talked for two hours. Pogodin returned. He listened attentively, his brow wrinkling when they discussed things that pained him. He interrupted only once, to ask, "Haven't the Americans discovered how corrupt they are?"

Mirsky nodded. "They have always known, or at least as often as their press could uncover the facts."

"Their press is not controlled?"

"Manipulated, yes," Mirsky said. "Never completely controlled. They had thousands of historians, each with his own perspective. Their history was confused, but deliberate distortions were usually found out."

Pogodin looked between Vielgorsky and Mirsky and then turned away to walk to the entrance of the room.

"What we've been told about Stalin, Khrushchev, Brezhnev, Gorbachev—" Vielgorsky let his words trail off with a shake of his head.

"Is different from what our fathers were told," Mirsky finished for him, "and their fathers before them."

And they talked for another hour, this time about life in the army. Mirsky described how he had nearly become a political officer. Vielgorsky outlined the accelerated training courses he and the other *Zampolits* had been given before being launched with the Space Shock Troops from the Indian Ocean.

291

"We are not so far apart after all," Vielgorsky said as Mirsky poured him water from a thermos. Mirsky shrugged again and handed him the cup. "You know the responsibilities of a political officer . . . the duty to party, to the revolution . . ."

"What revolution?" Mirsky asked softly.

Vielgorsky's face reddened. "We must still be loyal to the revolution. Our lives, our sanity depends on it."

"The revolution begins here, now," Mirsky said. "We are unloaded of the past."

They regarded each other for an uncomfortably long time. Pogodin returned to find them silent, and sat to one side, gripping the index finger of one hand with thumb and forefinger of the other and tugging it uneasily.

"The power must be shared," Vielgorsky said. "The party must be reestablished."

"Not by murderers and louts," Mirsky said sharply, jaw muscles tensing. "We have had enough of them. Russia has been raped by murderers and louts too long in the name of revolution and the party. No more. I will end it all here rather than bring this back to our children on Earth."

Vielgorsky fumbled at his pocket, pulling out an antique gold watch. "Belozersky and Yazykov will be frantic by now. There's no telling what they will do if they don't hear from me."

"That weakens them," Mirsky said. "Let them sit for a while, or hang themselves."

Vielgorsky grinned wolfishly and shook his finger at Mirsky. "You bastard. I know what you are. You're a visionary. A deviationist visionary."

"And I'm the only one you can be comfortable with, sharing the power," Mirsky said. "You know they will come after you eventually. You can no more trust them than you can trust a mad dog."

Vielgorsky did not look convinced.

"Maybe now we understand each other."

Vielgorsky shrugged and turned down the corners of his mouth.

At 1200 hours the next day, Pogodin aimed the truck's antenna toward the southern bore hole, and Vielgorsky sent a message to Yazykov and Belozersky:

"Our fourth chamber troops have captured Mirsky and henchmen in third chamber library. Join us there. Trial will be held in library."

Chapter Forty-two

They watched in silence as the red line of the singularity guided them toward the black shield. Lanier joined Farley and Carrolson in the rear, trying to make sense out of the instruments. They periodically registered meaningful data, but not often enough to be of much use.

"Something approaching along the singularity—It's a machine, big and black," Heineman said. "Coming up fast . . ." Lanier pushed himself forward.

Straddling the glowing red line, a machine twice as thick as the tuberider, round in cross section, bore down on them, its surface a glossy black. Bright purple lines on the machine's surface outlined squares and rectangles in symmetric arrays. Lanier watched in facination as the squares and rectangles opened to extrude grapplers and a variety of jointed arms. It now resembled a deep-ocean submersible—or a madman's Swiss Army knife. "What's it going to do?"

"It's matching speed. Looks like it's—"

Colored lights flashed in the cabin. Heineman flinched and drew back; Lanier closed his eyes and batted out with his hands. "What was that?" Carrolson called from the rear. Red and green translucent objects danced again before Lanier. He reached out to touch one, but it was insubstantial.

"They're symbols or something," Heineman said. "You see them?"

"I see them," Lanier said. "I don't know what they are, or where they're coming from."

293

The radio hissed again. "Please state your identity and reason for approaching the Axis City shield."

Lanier took the mike from Heineman. "I'm Garry Lanier." That'll clue them, he thought ruefully. "We're exploring. If there are problems—"

"Do you wish an advocate?"

"I'm sorry—what?"

"You will be assigned an advocate immediately. Are you a corporeal human claiming the appropriate rights in the Hexamon Court?"

"Say yes," Carrolson advised.

"Yes."

"You will now be removed from the flaw and escorted to Axis Nader."

The machine ran one arm down the underside of the tuberider. Flying sparks obscured the windscreen; the V/STOL rolled and vibrated. Gas hissed against the fuselage and alarms went off in the cockpit; there was a wrenching sound, and with a jerk, they floated free.

The tuberider had been cut from the singularity and cast adrift. The V/STOL had then been removed from the tuberider.

Heineman peered up at the bright red line and the dark machine, which still clung to the stern of the mangled and useless tuberider. "It's pulled us out of the mounting," he said, voice thick with anger. The aircraft had drifted thirty or thirty-five meters. "I'm going back to check integrity."

Lanier pulled himself into the copilot's seat. He methodically strapped himself in and tried to control his breathing. Just like ditching, he thought. No worse, perhaps better—

"I don't hear any leaks, but I'd still rather be down in an atmosphere," Heineman called from the cabin.

The machine abandoned the tuberider and spread its grapples wide as it drifted toward the V/STOL. Heineman came forward again, brushing between Carrolson and Farley.

"Shit," he said. It was the first time Lanier had ever heard him swear.

The machine's bulk obscured the windscreen and the plane twisted. Floating in the cockpit hatchway, Heineman did not roll with the craft. Lanier rotated around the startled engineer, then reversed. "Hang on before the next one," he shouted. Heineman grabbed for the pilot's seat with one hand. The airplane spun around again and, like a martial arts master, used Heineman's own mass to dislocate his shoulder.

The engineer screamed and let go, now rolling in the opposite direction of the cabin. Lanier watched helplessly, waiting for the motion to stop. When the lull stretched out to four seconds, he unbuckled and held Heineman around the waist, pushing him gently toward the rear. The engineer's face was a mask of pain; he opened his eyes wide like a child cruelly injured by a friend.

Carrolson and Farley had sustained bruises but no worse before grabbing handgrips. Farley held Heineman's head and Carrolson took his kicking feet while Lanier inspected the arm.

"Son of a bitch!" Heineman howled. "Leave it alone."

"The longer it's out, the longer it'll hurt," Lanier said. "I don't think anything's torn. Jesus, how do I reset in zero-g?"

"Here, brace your foot in one of these stanchions and we'll grab his torso," Carrolson said. Heineman squirmed, wild-eyed. His short hair stuck out in all directions. Lanier hitched one foot under a rung and pressed the other against Heineman's ribs. Carrolson and Farley tightened their hold on the engineer.

"Let me go," Heineman said weakly, his face slick with sweat and tears.

Lanier grabbed one arm and forearm and pulled, braced and twisted all at once. Heineman screamed again and rolled his eyes until only whites showed. There was a satisfying billiard-ball *snick*, and the arm was back in place. His head rolled limply and his mouth gaped. He had passed out.

"He'll never forgive us now," Carrolson said.

"Wrap the shoulder in a cold compress," Lanier instructed. He pushed his face against the side port again. The machine obscured the windscreen.

295

"Do not attempt to accelerate," the radio voice advised again. "Do not activate your drives. You are being taken to Axis Nader."

Farley helped Heineman into a seat. He lolled his head back to look at Carrolson, his face pasty. Carrolson inspected his eyes, prying the lids open with two fingers. "Shock," she said. She opened the first-aid pack and took out a prepackaged syringe, injecting it into his uninjured arm.

Lanier sat in the cockpit and tried to get whatever information he could from the instruments. The V/STOL was moving rapidly; that much and little else was apparent.

Olmy entered the flaw monitor room, picting his Presidential access pass at the corporeal guard. The room was a high, oval chamber filled with out-of-focus information picts directed at two neomorphs on monitors duty. He floated to their position and was surrounded by detailed readouts on the destroyed and drifting tuberider and the airplane, now in control of a flaw maintenance vehicle. "This is a security operation, by extended order of the President," Olmy picted at the senior neomorph.

"I cannot accept that," the neomorph replied. "This is a serious breach and must be reported to the courts at once. They will be assigned an advocate—"

"They already *have* an advocate. You *must* accept a direct order from a representative of the President," Olmy said. The neomorph—shaped like an egg, with traction field grappling arms extended to each side and a human face on the forward, large end of the egg—surrounded itself with a picted white circle, signaling compliance under duress. But that was not enough for Olmy.

"By order of the President of the Infinite Hexamon Nexus, authority of the Presiding Minister, you are removed from this duty," he said. The neomorph protested furiously in garbled sound and red-shifted picts as it exited the chamber.

Olmy took the position, exchanging glances with the remaining neomorph. "This will not reach the court," he stated.

296

"It has already been relayed," the second neomorph said. Olmy telepicted a message to Suli Ram Kikura's office in Central City. A stylized personal emblem appeared before him. "Ser Ram Kikura is not available at the present. This is one of her partials. May I help?"

"This is an emergency. We have more guests. They are in violation of Hexamon law, and their case needs to be suppressed in court immediately, authority of the Presiding Minister." He picted the code authority.

"Received," the partial said. Then, in a completely lifelike image, the partial shook his head. "Really, Olmy, you bring us so much trouble." The partial signed off, and Olmy opened another channel to Axis Nader, requesting that the Frant escort Patricia from her quarters to the inspection hangar. He ordered the clearing of all passageways between. That would arouse some suspicion and resentment, but he could see no way around it. "And we'll need more quarters space." The Frant also took his coded authority and signed off.

Olmy then turned his full attention to the flaw maintenance device and the aircraft. "They are uninjured?" he inquired, his picts demandingly purple-tinted.

"They have not been harmed by this station," the neomorph answered, appearing alarmed.

"You realize the secrecy of this operation?" he asked. It assented in the meekest shade of green. "Good. Then direct your vehicle and the violators to the inspection hangar."

Olmy pushed himself from the station and the chamber and found the quickest shaft to Axis Nader.

"How many individuals are there within your craft?" the voice asked.

"Four," Lanier said. "One injured."

"They are all corporeal humans?"

"We're all humans. What are you?"

"You are now in a reception area for illegal vehicles. Do not attempt escape; the area is sealed."

The machine removed its grapples and lifted away from the

aircraft. Lanier saw they were in a broad, uncluttered hangar-like enclosure, the walls smooth black and gray. Slender silver cables coiled before the cockpit windscreen. The plane hung from cables attached to a pale silver torus suspended below the hangar ceiling. Three large metallic gray mechanical workers surrounded the aircraft, pushing it along. They moved on four delicate jointed legs, their bulky bodies divided into hemispheres connected by a narrow flexible casing.

There was no sign of human life in the hangar. At two points, elliptical portals about four meters wide opened in the walls, but they gave no clue as to who was preparing to greet them.

"Will you address the person who has tentatively confirmed your identity?" the voice asked, still as pleasant and melodic as ever.

"Who is it? I mean, who identified us?"

The next voice was instantly recognizable. "Garry, it's Patricia. There are four of you? Who are they?"

"That's her—we've found her," Lanier said. "Or she's found us."

"I thought someone would come after me—it's just like I said. They're my friends." Patricia leaned forward, hoping to receive the picted images more clearly. She had spotted Lanier inside the cockpit. "They must all be terrified." She watched the black flaw patrol machine rise into its cavity above and behind the aircraft.

"They could be in serious trouble with the city authorities," Olmy said. "I'm trying to get the case cleared and suppressed, but I can't guarantee anything."

"The've come looking for me," she said. "You can't blame them for that."

"They rode the axial flaw, and that's strictly forbidden."

"Yes, but how could they know?"

Olmy didn't answer. "I know who they are," he said. "Your boss Lanier, the scientist Carrolson, the Chinese Caucasian called Farley, and the engineer, Heineman."

"You recognize them? You kept track of all of us, didn't you?"

The mechanical workers pushed and guided the aircraft into a dilated entrance to a side chamber. The iris closed behind the plane and the hangar lights darkened.

Patricia stepped out of the chamber and took Olmy's proffered hand. He led her to the inspection hangar lock.

Suli Ram Kikura entered the chamber. She had not yet met Patricia, but she had become fully acquainted with her. The advocate picted a brief conversation with Olmy. Patricia was not in line to pick up the exchanged visual symbols—not that she could have understood many of them, anyway—but she could get the gist from the woman's attitude. The woman was a corporeal advocate. She was taking Olmy's deposition and relaying it to the pre-trial court.

The V/STOL hatch opened. A worker settled on its jointed haunches a few yards away, sensors fully extended to record the disembarking of the passengers.

History, Patricia thought. *We're all history here.*

Lanier came out first. Patricia restrained an urge to wave to him; instead, she lifted up on tiptoes and nodded. He returned the nod and descended the hatch steps. Farley came next. Carrolson waited in the doorway. Lanier pointed back into the cabin and said loudly, "We have an injured man inside. He may need assistance."

Olmy and the woman conferred again and the woman touched her silver torque. As she did so, she glanced at Patricia and smiled. Her pictor projected an American flag above her left shoulder; she had American ancestors and was proud of it.

"What do we do?" Carrolson asked. "Leave him there?"

"Tell your friends a medical worker is coming," Olmy said in an undertone.

"He'll be okay. Help is coming," Patricia said. Lanier tried to approach but was blocked by a worker.

"Let him pass!" Patricia pleaded. "Olmy, what harm can they do?"

"They're in quarantine," Olmy said, pointing to the glowing red line surrounding the V/STOL at chest level.

Patricia turned to Lanier, holding up one hand. "They're not going to hurt you. Everything's okay. Just wait a moment."

"It's good to see you," Lanier said, keeping an eye on the scuttling workers. "We had no idea we'd ever find you."

Patricia swallowed back a lump in her throat. She turned to Olmy. "We have to stay together," she told him. "We have to help each other."

Olmy smiled at her, but that didn't mean assent; he picted with the woman again and she touched her necklace once more.

"A decision is being made now," he said.

"Whether they're criminals or guests?" Patricia asked.

"Oh, they will be guests," the woman said in perfect English.

"They will be sampled now," Olmy said. "Perhaps it would be best if you told them."

"Garry," Patricia said, "they're really interested in our skin cultures. One of the workers—the machines—is going to approach you and collect skin scrapings. It doesn't hurt. And the cabin's waste tank—they'll want that, too."

"Here's the medical team," Olmy said. He would have to contact everyone involved later and have them swear out statements of secrecy. Two more corporeal citizens and a smaller worker entered the chamber and approached the red line. As they passed through, red chevrons appeared over their shoulders; they were now in quarantine also.

Lanier, Carrolson and Farley allowed the medical worker to pull back the sleeves of their jumpsuits and take samples. The worker then withdrew, touching the red line. It was instantly surrounded by a lovely lilac glow; when the glow dissipated, the worker crossed the line and came to a halt.

The medical team—all homorphs—entered the aircraft hatch. A few minutes later, Heineman walked out on his own power between them. The lead homorph picted a message to Olmy.

300

"He was in pain but not seriously injured," Olmy told Patricia. "They have relieved his pain but have not yet given him healers."

"Virgin specimens, like me, right?" Patricia asked. Olmy agreed and walked with her to the line.

It vanished as they approached. "Quarantine is over," the lead medical homorph stated. He picted a few simplicities at Patricia and she acknowledged the politeness. Then she rushed forward and hugged Lanier, Carrolson and Farley, lingering with each. When Heineman's turn came, she hugged him more gingerly.

"Don't spare me—I feel pretty good," he told her. "Where in hell are we?"

"I'm receiving a judgment," said the advocate, still flying the American flag on her shoulder. She approached the group with hands extended.

"She has an implant, they all do," Patricia explained to Lanier, touching her head. "She's listening to the court decision now."

"The case is cleared from all pre-trial court records, and negated by circumstance," the woman announced. "You are all guests of the Axis Nader." With a meaningful glance at Olmy, Ram Kikura added, "By authority of the Presiding Minister."

Chapter Forty-three

Vielgorsky stood in front of the black panel which marked the entrance of the third chamber library. Across the plaza, almost shadowless in the tubelight, Belozersky and Yazykov walked cautiously toward him. Behind them followed two squads of SSTs, their rifles unslung.

Mirsky and Pogodin watched from the abandoned NATO security post, a small room in the overhang equipped with a video monitor. Mirsky toyed with the loud-hailer switches.

301

Pogodin looked at him. "We're taking a chance now," he said.

"I know."

Pogodin turned back to the screen. Mirsky aimed the American listening device at them and increased the volume.

"We won't need more soldiers," Vielgorsky said. "I have already sent Mirsky and Pogodin to the fourth chamber for detention."

"He seems to be cooperating," Pogodin said quietly.

Mirsky nodded. There was indeed a risk here; it had become apparent to him in the past couple of days that without Vielgorsky, he could not rule; he had neither the experience nor the inclination to engage in political intrigue and survive for long. Vielgorsky was the best of the political officers. If he and Mirsky could not work together, then no cooperation was possible. Mirsky doubted that he could kill all of them, which was the alternative. It would be better for him to turn himself over to the Americans or became lost in the cities and fend for himself.

"I think it is time you see what we fought for, and learn how to use it," Vielgorsky said.

"I have no desire to imitate Mirsky," Belozersky said. "I do not care for that place."

"Comrade," Vielgorsky said patiently, "knowledge is power. Do you want to be more ignorant than the rest? I have been in there, and I am still Vielgorsky, still Party Secretary."

"Yes . . ." Yazykov said. "It doesn't frighten me."

"Nor I," Belozersky said hastily. "But—"

"Then let's enter and see what Mirsky was up to, spending so much time here."

Mirsky trained the video cameras on them until they passed out of view. There was something else at stake. Was it possible to be ignorant of the character of one's own country, after having spent one's entire life within its borders? Yes; there was no basis for comparison, and however much he knew, without comparison the knowledge was dormant. Even with the library's information, he had to conduct an experiment.

However unfair the test was, he would now judge his country and all it stood for by how Vielgorsky acted.

"He'll take their weapons," Mirsky said. "We can't have them armed when I appear."

"You're going down there now?" Pogodin asked.

"Yes."

"You trust Vielgorsky that much?"

"I don't know. It's a risk."

"Not just for you," Pogodin said. "We cooperated with you—Pletnev, the scientists, myself, Annenkovsky, Garabedian."

Mirsky headed for the stairwell. His back crawled as he descended the stairs. He was more afraid now then when he had leaped from the heavy-lifter in the bore hole. Strangely, he felt like a child again. And he was tired. He had observed the same weariness in the American, Lanier.

Opening the door.

Stepping out onto library floor. Only the three *Zampolits* had entered: Vielgorsky, holding a pistol on Belozersky, Yazykov standing to one side staring at his fellow political officer in dismay. Their rifles lay scattered on the floor, kicked out of reach.

"Come forward, Comrade General," Vielgorsky said. He took several steps to one side, still pointing the pistol, and bent to pick up an AKV. Belozersky stared at Mirsky with uncomprehending hatred. Yazykov's face was blank, tightly controlled. Mirsky walked across the plaza toward them.

When he was five meters from the group, Vielgorsky turned the pistol away from Belozersky, lifted it and sighted along the barrel at Mirsky. "I do not thank you, Comrade," he said. He squeezed the trigger.

Mirsky's view of things skewed, as if the anamorphic lens on a motion picture projector were suddenly twisted. One side of his head seemed very large. He fell on his knees and leaned forward, bowed, then fell over, his cheek smacking sharply against the yielding floor. That hurt more than whatever had happened to his head. His one good eye blinked.

303

Vielgorsky lowered the pistol, handed it to Belozersky, walked toward the scattered rifles, picked up and aimed an AKV at the chairs and globes on the plaza and began firing a clip. Teardrops shattered and bullets ricocheted, the sound somewhat distant and unimpressive in the large hall, even with the echoes.

Belozersky's yell of triumph and delight was cut short by a very big sound, impossible to describe. The three political officers twitched; Vielgorsky dropped his weapon and jerked his head back. Yazykov clapped his hands to his ears and mouth. All three collapsed. White streamers jetted from the ceiling all around the plaza and untwisted into thick fog.

The fog lay down over them and Mirsky closed his eye, grateful at last for the undisturbed slumber.

Chapter Forty-four

Lanier—lying on the couch, hand gripping the African print upholstery, staring up at the featureless cream-colored ceiling, ostensibly resting—knew this much, and very little more:

Their quarters were located in the outer reaches of the rotating cylindrical precinct called Axis Nader: five apartments along a hallway, each with a bedroom, a bathroom and a living room; at the end of the hallway, a communal dining area and a large, circular lounge. The centrifugal force at this level of the precinct was just slightly less than that at the Stone's chamber floors. All the quarters were closed off and lacked real windows, though illusart windows of idyllic terrestrial scenes in the apartments and lounge provided a sensation of spaciousness which was hard to deny.

Someone had gone to considerable effort to make the accommodations pleasant and familiar. What Lanier gathered, from all the fuss, was that they were important people. Whether they were prisoners or honored guests, it was impossible to tell for the time being.

He turned his head to one side, reached over to a stack of magazines on the coffee table near the couch, picked up a copy of *STERN* and flipped through it, not really looking at the turning pages. His eyes kept tracking the apartment, lingering on little details—the art glass vase in one corner of a bureau, red and purple with overlaid gold threads; the rich-feeling couch fabric; the books that lined one shelf; and the memory cubes stacked in an ebony wood holder nearby.

He was about to put the magazines down on a frosted glass coffee table when he realized he hadn't looked at the issue's date. March 4, 2004. Over a year old. Where did they find it?

Or any of the objects in the apartments?

"May I come in?" Patricia asked. The apartment door became transparent and he saw her standing in the hallway. Judging by her attitude, she could not see in.

"Yes," he said. "Please do."

She continued standing outside. "Garry, are you home?"

He puzzled this over for a moment; she hadn't heard him. Symbols appeared in the air to one side of the door, flickering rapidly, little marvels of calligraphy—picts, Patricia had called them, statements made up of single symbols called icons. When nothing happened, he approached the door and the room voice, sexless and melodic, asked, "You have a visitor, Mr. Lanier. Would you like Patricia Luisa Vasquez to enter?"

"Yes, please, let her in," he said. The door became opaque again and then slid aside.

"Hello," she said. "We're all meeting in a half hour—getting together with the woman who was in the hangar. Olmy says she's our 'advocate.' I thought I'd talk things over with you first."

"Good idea," he said. "Let's sit."

He took a comfortable leather-upholstered chair and Patricia sat on the couch. She folded her hands in her lap and regarded him steadily, her lips pursed as if to hold back a smile.

"What in hell happened to you?" Lanier asked.

"Isn't it obvious? I was kidnapped. I think we were being invaded or something. I was half-crazy then. Maybe more than

305

half. So I took a train to the third chamber, and Olmy found me there. He had a Frant with him—a nonhuman."

"Who is Olmy?"

"You met him—the one who took us here and arranged for the quarters to be done in period."

"Yes, I met him, but *who* is he, what rank, what importance?"

"He's an agent of some sort. He does work for the Nexus— the main governing body of the Hexamon. He's been my teacher for the past few days, ever since we got here. Were we being invaded?"

"Yes," Lanier said. "By Russians." He told her what had happened and she listened intently.

"I think that's one reason Olmy wanted me out of the chambers," she said. "He thought I might be in danger. I'm not yet sure why he chose me in particular, but . . ." She shrugged. "I have some ideas. They've already put me through tests. They'll test you, too. Diagnostics, psychological, everything—all in a few minutes. It doesn't hurt. They're really interested in our bodies. We're historical curiosities."

"I'll bet. At any rate, when I heard you had been kidnapped, I went a bit crazy myself. Judith Hoffman made it up to the Stone from Station Sixteen—"

"How wonderful!" Patricia said. "Was anybody with her?"

"Yes—nobody we knew."

Patricia's expression of joy stiffened.

"She obviously decided I wasn't going to be very effective anymore. You were the last straw, I think."

"Me?"

"Hoffman told me to take care of you. I couldn't prevent what happened on Earth, and I lost you, besides. I don't take failure very well, Patricia." He rubbed his cheeks and eyes. "Failure. Yes. I suppose you could call losing the whole Earth failure."

Patricia gripped her hands tightly between her knees. "Not lost," she murmured.

"So Hoffman authorized an expedition to find you."

306

"It's good to have you all here—my friends, my helpers."
Her sudden cheeriness had an edge.

"We're really guests here, then?" he asked.

"Oh, yes. They weren't expecting you—though when Olmy
first heard, he knew it had to be the tuberider. They consulted
him right away since he had been down the corridor most
recently."

"Do they knew about the Stone—what we've been doing?"

"Yes, I suppose they do—Olmy must have told them."

"And do they plan to do anything with us? I mean, I assume
they're still interested in the Stone. . . ."

"I'm not sure. Some of them are. It's confusing, and I've
only been taking lessons steadily for the last couple of days.
It's all very political, that's what Olmy tells me."

"They're advanced, aren't they?" Lanier asked.

"Oh, yes, but not so much we can't understand a lot of
things. Our rooms, for example—they're not very different
from that apartment in the third chamber. The one Takahashi
showed me."

Lanier hadn't mentioned Takahashi's treason. He didn't
think it necessary now.

"All the decorations are illusions," Patricia said. "There's a
pictor—a kind of projector—in each room. It makes our minds
feel and see the elaborations. The furniture is here in basic
shape and function, but everything else is projected. They've
had this technology for a long time, centuries. They're as used
to it as we are to electricity."

Lanier reached out and riffled the copy of *STERN*, then
pulled a copy of *TIME* from beneath it. "These magazines,
that vase"—he pointed to the art glass—"are just records
stored somewhere, projected?"

"I suppose they must be."

"Are they watching us now?"

"No. They told me they aren't, anyway. Privacy is very
important here."

"You said you had an idea why they wanted you."

"Well . . . just a guess. Olmy might have been worried I
would find a way to change the sixth chamber machinery."

"But he wanted to keep you safe."

"Out of trouble." She stood and nodded at the decorations. "Do you like what they've done?"

"It's thorough." He shrugged. "It's comfortable."

"They're good at matching decor to people. My rooms are comfortable, too. Not very much like home, though. I'm . . ."

The edge in her cheerfulness became fully visible for an instant, making her eyes hard and determined. "I'm not taking everything well. Some parts of me are pretty messed over."

"That's . . . not unexpected," Lanier said.

"They're going to help," she said. "They're going to help me find home. They can, you know. They don't know it yet. But they will. I've learned that much since I've been here. The corridor is very twisty." She tangled her fingers and tugged her arms against them. "Let's go join the others."

Olmy stood in the center of the circular lounge, Suli Ram Kikura beside him. He introduced her to each of the five, formally and at length, telling her the functions they had served on the Thistledown. Lanier was impressed by how much Olmy knew; he seemed to have kept a dossier on all of them.

"And this is Ser Suli Ram Kikura, your advocate. Your arrival on the tuberider was highly illegal, so she's been of service to you already. She had your court case negated because of the circumstances."

"And under authority from the Presiding Minister," she added. "It's not something an advocate of my standing could have accomplished on her own."

"She may underestimate herself," Olmy said.

"Now that we know each other's names, I think we'd better get everything out in the open," Ram Kikura said. Olmy took a seat and folded his arms. "First of all, most of the citizens and clients of the Axis City and the communities along the Way—what you call the corridor—talk to each other by picting." She touched the torque around her neck and looked

308

at Heineman. Flashes of light darted before his eyes. "I'm wearing a personal pictor. You will all be given pictors in a couple of days. It won't be absolutely necessary for you to learn the graphicspeech, but it will be very helpful. Lessons should take no more than two or three days. Miss Vasquez, I understand, already has a rudimentary knowledge of picts."

"Amenities," Patricia said.

"I speak American English, and have for years, because I am proud of my ancestry, which is North American, specifically United States of America, even more specifically, California.

"When you first saw me, you might have noticed I was picting a flag from the U.S.A. over my left shoulder. This is frequently done by Ameriphiles; it symbolizes our pride. After the Death, it was considered shameful to claim either Russian or American heritage. Those who did so were persecuted. Americans were persecuted more than Russians. When South Americans and Mexicans repopulated large sections of North America, people claiming to be citizens of the United States were arrested. The Naderites of that time were trying to create a unified world government, and there was resentment against the former Superpowers."

"That's changed?" Heineman asked.

Ram Kikura nodded. "The United States gave us most of our culture, the foundations of our laws and government. We feel about America as you might feel about Rome or Greece. Citizens take considerable pride in having American ancestors. If your presence becomes generally known—"

Lanier clenched one hand tightly, worried by the implications of indefinite secrecy.

"—then I will have to act as your theatrical agent, I'm afraid." Her smile seemed to indicate both humor and confidence. Lanier released some of the tension in his fist.

Farley shook her head. "I'm Chinese. Do I miss out?"

Ram Kikura smiled. "Not in the least. Those with Chinese heritage make up at least a third of the Hexamon—far more than Americans.

309

"As for your status—for the time being, your presence here is being treated as a Hexamon secret. You will not have any further contact with citizens of the Hexamon until that situation changes. Nevertheless, you have all the rights accorded to Hexamon guests. Not even the President himself could take those rights from you. One of them is the right to have an advocate represent your interests and advise you. Should anyone here object to my being your advocate, let me know immediately, and another will be assigned." She looked from face to face. There were no objections; she hadn't expected any.

"Your status here is that of potential client innocents. That is, you may be of service to the Hexamon, and such services will gain you advantages—what you might term payment—but for the moment you are not to be disturbed. As innocents, you will be studied—unless you object—and the knowledge gained from these studies will be invested for you in certain Hexamon information banks. It will also be available to the Nexus and other governing bodies of the Hexamon, whether you object or not."

"I have some questions," Lanier said.

"Please ask them."

"What's the Hexamon . . . and the Nexus?"

"The Hexamon is the totality of human citizens. You might call it the state. The Nexus is the main lawmaking body of this city, and of the Way from the Thistledown and the forbidden territory to mark two ex nine. That is, the two-billion-kilometer point of the Way."

"You're all descended from the stoners—the people who lived in the Thistledown?" Carrolson asked.

"Yes," Ram Kikura said.

"Excuse me," Heineman said. "How many people live here? How large is this Axis City?"

Ram Kikura smiled and picted instructions to the empty walls. There were no data pillars anywhere—apparently their functions had been integrated into the inconspicuous room pictors.

A very solid looking image of the Axis City appeared next to her, rotating slowly. Heineman leaned forward in his seat, frowning in concentration.

"One hundred million humans occupy the city and the Way. Ten million live off-city, along the Way, chiefly traders and coordinators of the five hundred and seventy-one active wells. Ninety million live in the Axis City. Of these, seventy million are in City Memory. Most of those have lived out their legal two incarnations and have retired their bodies to exist as personality patterns in the City Memory environment. Under special circumstances, they may be assigned new bodies, but most often they are content in Memory. Some five million deviant personalities—those who are incomplete or deranged in such a way they cannot be redeemed, even with extreme methods of therapy—are kept inactive."

"People don't die?" Carrolson asked.

"Death and dying here usually refer to loss of corporeal states, not mental states. In a word, no, or very rarely," Ram Kikura said. "All of us are equipped with implants." She touched a spot behind her ear, then moved her finger to a spot above the bridge of her nose. "They supplement our reasoning, and should an accident occur, they retain a record of our most recent experiences and personality. The implant is almost indestructible—it is the first thing we recover from the victim of an accident. Every few days, we update our backups in City Memory with records from these implants. That way, a personality can be quickly reconstructed. All we need to do is make a final update and inhabit a new body, and the resurrection is indistinguishable from the original."

She looked around the room, ready to field more questions. There were none; implications were beginning to sink in.

"I'll use Olmy as an example," Ram Kikura said. "With his permission . . . ?"

Olmy nodded.

"He is something of a rarity because of his age and history. His original body was born five centuries ago. His first death was by accident; the destruction was not total, so he was

311

reconstructed. Since he was considered important to the Hexamon and was involved in dangerous work, he was allowed three incarnations, rather than the usual two. His present body is adapted for specialty work; it's a popular type and is completely self-contained. His waste systems are also closed. Within his abdomen there is a small power supply; all his wastes are reprocessed internally. He needs to replace his power source and bring in supplementary materials only once a year. He requires water every three months."

"Are you human?" Carrolson asked Olmy pointedly.

"I am," Olmy said. "I presume you're curious about my sexuality?"

"What . . . Yes, frankly," Carrolson admitted. Heineman squinted one eye and raised the opposite brow.

"I am fully masculine by birth and choice, and my sexual organs are functional."

"They are, indeed," Ram Kikura said. "But natal sexual orientation, even in those born naturally, is not necessarily permanent."

"You mean, once a man, not always a man?" Farley asked.

"Or a woman. Or man or woman. Many neomorphs today have no specific sexual orientation."

"You talk about those born naturally," Heineman said. "You have test-tube babies, that sort of thing?"

"At the risk of shocking you—which may be unavoidable—most people today are not born of man and woman. Their personalities are created by one or more parents through the merging of partial personalities in City Memory, with the infusion of what we call Mystery from at least one individual, usually a parent. The young personality is educated and tested in City Memory, and if it passes certain tests, it 'matures,' that is, it earns its first incarnation, most often as a mature young adult. The corpus the personality inhabits may be designed by the parents, or by the individual. If in time the corporeal citizen uses its two incarnations, it then retires to City Memory."

Carrolson started to say something, thought better of it, then

312

decided to speak anyway. "Are the people without bodies—in the computers—are they human, are they alive?" she asked.

"They believe so," Ram Kikura said. "They have specific rights, and certain duties, as well, though by necessity their say in government is less than that of corporeal citizens. But if I may suggest we are not discussing the subjects of most immediate importance . . ." She pointed toward the rotating image of the city.

"This is where you will stay. For the time being, you cannot return to the Thistledown. Your home will be in this precinct, Axis Nader, where conditions are reasonably familiar— design, culture, people. Though you may not meet them for some time, this precinct is inhabited by orthodox Naderites.

"Miss Vasquez has told Ser Olmy that some of you are aware of the basics of our history. Then you will understand that orthodox Naderites typically prefer conditions as close to those of Earth as possible. This section contains many areas of natural beauty—and as few illusions in the public thoroughfares as possible. There are two other rotating precincts— Axis Thoreau and Axis Euclid—spaced beyond the Central City. Axis Thoreau is also occupied by Naderites, though of a more liberal persuasion."

"More questions," Lanier said. "When can we return to our people?"

"I don't know. That decision isn't ours to make."

"Can we send a message to them?"

"No," Olmy said. "Technically, your people are in violation."

"Isn't the situation a little unusual?" Lanier asked. "Now that the Thistledown has returned to Earth . . ."

Olmy looked distinctly uncomfortable. "Unusual. And very complicated."

Patricia touched Lanier's hand and gave a slight shake of her head: enough for now.

"After you've eaten, you will have time to become reacquainted and learn how to use your accommodations.

313

Then you may rest. Tomorrow morning, you will be awakened in your rooms. Please return here.''

In the hallway, Patricia walked close to Lanier. "We're pawns," she said in an undertone. "We've set off alarms." She held her finger to her lips and darted into her doorway.

Chapter Forty-five

Wu and Chang walked arm-in-arm from the train station to the library plaza, saying little but obviously content with each other's company. They had decided, hours before, to go to the library together, to make the pilgrimage that so many were planning but few had time to actually do. Singly and in groups, perhaps a total of twenty members of the NATO and allied forces and the science teams had gone and had returned with awed reports of the library's potential. This impressed Wu; he had asked permission of Hua Ling, and since their studies had been reduced in scope, the leader of the Chinese team had agreed.

But something was wrong. Russian soldiers milled outside the library in some confusion. As they spotted Wu and Chang crossing the plaza, alone, they dropped prone on the pavement and raised their rifles. Wu held up his hands instinctively; Chang backed away a step and seemed ready to run.

"No, my love," Wu whispered.

"What are they doing?"

"I don't know. I recommend we make no fast moves."

She edged up beside him and raised her hands high as well, glancing at him for approval. He nodded.

They maintained this position for several long and unpleasant minutes while a few of the soldiers crawled toward each other and conferred. Then a command was barked and all but two of the Russians stood and slung their rifles.

"Can we move now?" Chang asked.

"No; we are still in danger."

Two Russians walked across the plaza toward them. Some meters distant, they stopped. "Do you speak Russian?" one asked, in Russian.

"I do," Chang replied in kind. "My English is better."

"My terrible English," the spokesman said, demonstrating his point. "You are Chinese?"

"Yes. We were on a walk," Chang said. From this point on, they spoke Russian.

"I am Corporal Rodzhensky, and this is Corporal Fremov. Something has gone wrong in the library; we are not sure what. We cannot allow anyone to pass; besides, the building is closed and will not open for us."

"Do you have any idea what the trouble is?" Chang asked, struggling to appear especially interested and polite.

"No. We heard gunfire, and then the black . . . wall closed, and would not open."

"Why was there gunfire?"

"We do not know," Rodzhensky said, glancing nervously at Fremov. "We have communicated with our superiors in the fourth chamber, but they have not arrived yet."

"We will help any way we can," Chang said. "Or, if you wish, we will leave."

"No . . . Perhaps you can approach the door, try to make it open. It may be ridiculous, but then again . . ." Rodzhensky shrugged, then suddenly realized guns were still being trained on the pair. "Do you have weapons?" he asked, looking over his shoulder at the prone riflemen.

"No. We are scientists."

Rodzhensky called out for the riflemen to put away their guns. "We are not familiar with this place," he said. "It makes us nervous. Especially now. Our officers are inside that building—searching for a fugitive." He frowned and seemed to realize he was revealing too much to outsiders. "Please, come with us and see if the door will open for you."

Chang explained what had happened to Wu, who maintained a look of intense interest as they were escorted to the library entrance. The soldiers milled around in some confusion. Wu approached the black wall, hands held up, and touched the smooth surface with his fingers and palms.

It did not dilate, as he had been told to expect. He stepped back and lowered his hands. "Sorry," he said. "It doesn't seem—"

A low, vibrating series of tones issued from the wall, and repeated, followed by a voice. "Police attention required in this precinct," the voice said in Russian. "No entrance to unauthorized personnel. Please alert medical and police authorities immediately. No entrance allowed." It then repeated its message in English and Chinese.

The soldiers backed away, AKVs unslung and pistols drawn.

"Something must have happened inside," Chang said calmly to Rodzhensky. "Perhaps we should tell our own superiors. Wouldn't that be wise?" She looked up at the Russian with her narrow almond eyes, her face a mask of persuasion and equanimity. Wu felt tremendous admiration for her. He had never seen her react to this sort of crisis.

Corporal Rodzhensky thought that over, shook his head firmly, then slumped his tension-hunched shoulders and seemed to reconsider. "What do we do if it doesn't open?" he asked.

"It doesn't open now."

"Our leaders are inside—*all* of them," he said.

Chang maintained her intent gaze.

"Yes—all right," Rodzhensky finally said. "Please go and bring your own superiors."

"Thank you," Chang said. She took Wu by the arm and walked with him back across the plaza.

"Very strange," she exclaimed, shaking her head in wonder. "Most strange."

"You were wonderful," Wu said, awestruck.

"Thank you." She smiled appreciatively.

Chapter Forty-six

He had buried his parachute and now lay down in the long, sweet-smelling dry yellow grass near the road. Hands over his eyes, he waited for a truck or car to come along, so he might hitch a ride back to Podlipki—or was it that base in Mongolia with only a number, 83?

Not that it mattered. The sun was warm, and except for a slight headache, Major Mirsky felt grand. He had fallen so far off course that he might take hours to reach the base, missing dinner, but also missing the political instruction. He would gladly trade kasha for a few hours alone to think.

At length a dusty, long black Volga came down the road and stopped beside him. The rear window rolled down and a bulky, beefy-faced man in a gray fedora stuck his head out, frowning at Mirsky.

"What are you doing here?" the man asked. He resembled Major General Sosnitsky, but he also looked a bit like poor Zhadov, who had died in the bore-hole massacre, wherever that was, and whenever. "What's your mother's name?"

"Nadia," he said. "I need a ride—"

"And what did you have for a cake on your eleventh birthday?"

"Comrade, I don't see—"

"It's very important. What did you have?"

"Something with chocolate, I think."

The man in the fedora nodded and opened the door. "Get in," he said. Mirsky squeezed in beside him. The seat was wet with blood; the man's three companions were corpses, all alike, all with their heads bloody and brains leaking. "Do you know these people?"

"No, I don't," Mirsky said, laughing. "We haven't been introduced."

317

"They are you, Comrade," the man said, and the dream faded to grayness. Once again, he buried the parachute. . . .

He began to get suspicious. Finally, after he had been picked up for the seventh or eighth time—the car minus its corpses—and the man in the fedora asked him about his Komsomol days, Mirsky decided to ask some questions of his own.

"I know I'm not dreaming, Comrade. So where am I?"

"You have been very badly injured."

"I don't seem to remember that—"

"No, but you will. You were shot in the head and suffered severe trauma. Parts of your brain are missing. You will never remember your life in quite as much detail, and you will never be quite the same person again."

"But I feel whole."

"Yes," the man in the fedora agreed. "That is normal, but it's an illusion. Together we've been exploring, finding out what you have left. There is quite a lot, actually—surprising, considering the damage—but you will never be quite the—"

"Yes, yes," Mirsky interrupted. "So will I die?"

"No, you are out of danger. Your head and brain are being repaired and you will live. But you have decisions to make."

"What sort of decisions?"

"You can live with the missing portions left blank, or you can receive prosthetic neurological programming and artificial personality segments tailored to fit those remaining to you."

"Now I'm really confused."

The man pulled a picture book out of his satchel. When he opened it, the pages were filled with beautiful complex designs, some in garish color, others muted and metallic, still others stimulating tastes and bodily sensations. He took the book and read through it. When he was finished, he asked, "Will I know what is mine and what is not?"

"If that's what you want."

"And without all these . . . prostheses? What will I be?"

"A cripple. You will have memories," the man explained, "though some will be difficult to recall clearly and others will

318

have curious gaps. It will take you weeks to learn how to see again, and you will never see very well. You will never recover your sensations of smell or the sensation of touch on the left side of your body. Your mathematical reasoning abilities will be intact, but your speech will be impaired and may never return."

Mirsky looked at the man's face until it seemed to fade into the sky beyond the car's side window. "It doesn't sound like much fun," he said.

"It is your choice."

"You're in the library, aren't you?"

"Not what you're seeing," the man said. "I am a city function shaped to be acceptable to you in your present condition. Human medical authority is not available, so the city has taken it upon itself to repair you."

"Okay," Mirsky said. "That's enough for now. I want to have nothing but darkness."

"Yes, that will come naturally after you give us your answer."

"I mean, I wish to die."

"That is not an option."

"Okay, then yes." He made the decision quickly so as not to have to consider all the possibilities, all the horrors.

"You consent to prosthetic programming?"

"I consent."

The man ordered the car to stop and smiled. "You may get out," he said.

"Thank you."

"You're welcome."

Mirsky left the Volga and closed the door. "Oh, one more thing," the man said, leaning out the window. "Did you have any plans to harm either Belozersky, Vielgorsky or Yazykov—particularly Vielgorsky?"

"No," Mirsky said. "They irritated me, and I would have rather done without all of them—except maybe Vielgorsky—but no, I didn't plan to harm them."

319

"Thank you," the man said and rolled up the window.

"You're welcome again," Mirsky turned away from the road and it was night. He lay down in the grass and stared up at the blackness.

Chapter Forty-seven

"I'd like it dark, please," Lanier said. The rooms darkened. He sat upright on the illusory couch and mentally repeated what Patricia had said after the meeting. *Alarms set off*. Did she mean that the Axis City had known they were in the Stone since their arrival? How long had self-contained, self-powered Olmy been watching them?

As he mulled, he felt the ineffable tension in the lower part of his abdomen and realized that mentally he was as uninterested in sex as he could be, but his body was disregarding his brain.

The door voice announced, "Karen Farley is in the hallway and requests entrance."

"Why?" he asked abruptly, angry at the convenience, the coincidence. "Wait—is she alone?"

"Yes."

"Send . . . let her in." He stood and smoothed down the jumpsuit he had worn on the V/STOL, now cleaned and pressed. He had ignored the robe laid out for him on the elliptical bed in the single bedroom.

Karen had not. As the door irised open, the lights came up and she entered in a very similar robe, this one a golden beige rather than midnight blue. "Pardon my comeuppance," she said, smiling and lifting her hands as if to fend off a rebuff.

"What?"

"Is that the right phrase?"

"I don't think so," Lanier said. "What can I do for you?"

"I've been talking with Patricia," she said, "or rather, she came to me, and I thought you'd like to know a few things."

He indicated a chair opposite the couch. "She and I had a conversation before the meeting, but it was more confusing than informative."

"Heineman and Carrolson are together tonight," Farley said, sitting. "Patricia didn't tell me that—Lenore did. And before we left the Stone, I noticed Wu and Chang were sneaking away together." She smiled at him, a brisk, armored smile with a touch of puzzlement and irritation.

Lanier lifted his shoulders and clapped his hands together softly, then rubbed them. "That's normal," he said.

"Yes. But I caught you when your guard was down, didn't I? I mean—"

"I appreciate what you did."

"I don't know what to say." She looked around the apartment curiously. "I've never really had a leech for you—"

"Letch," he said, grinning.

"Oh, yes, my God. Letch. I haven't. But you looked so lost. And I was feeling lost, too. Honest, you're still the boss."

"That's not important," he said. "What did Patricia—"

"It is important," Farley said flatly. "I enjoyed you. I believe you enjoyed me. It was healthy too. I just wanted you to know I thought so and don't resent you."

Lanier said nothing for a moment, regarding her with his dark, falsely Amerindian eyes. "I wish I spoke Chinese so we could really understand each other. I could learn . . ."

"That would be useful, but not necessary right away," Farley said. She smiled. "I could teach you."

"What did Patricia say?"

"She thinks we're being used by somebody—Olmy or somebody else—to some end. Olmy has been talking to her a lot, and she's even had some conversations with the Frant. She thinks there's a lot of politics in the Axis City, and we can't possibly know what any of it means. Not yet. Also, she says the data service in her apartment actually accesses less information than the ones in the third chamber city. She thinks they may be censored for us."

"That doesn't sound good," Lanier mused. "Or rather, it might not be good—it might not mean anything. They might want to treat us gently, let us get accustomed slowly."

"I told her I thought that, and she just smiled. She's behaving strangely, Garry. She also said she has a way to get us all home. There was a real tinkle in her eye when she said that."

Lanier did not correct her. "She told me that, too. Did she elaborate?"

"Pardon? Oh, yes. She did. She said the corridor moves forward in time about one year every thousand kilometers. And she said it's the most beautiful curve she's ever conceived. Garry, they kidnapped her—she believes this—they kidnapped her because they were afraid we might interfere in the sixth chamber. Remember all the people—all those Naderites in the second chamber being forced to move out, years after the third chamber exodus?"

He nodded.

"Patricia says she thinks they were forced out against their will, because the people on the Axis City wanted the Stone empty. No interference, no sabotage. That's why she thinks we're stuck in the middle of politics. There is still division between Naderites and Geshels."

"Has it occurred to anybody that no matter what we're told, these rooms are bugged?" Lanier asked. "That perhaps we shouldn't be discussing these things here?"

"Where can we discuss them?" she asked innocently. "They could follow us anywhere they wanted and listen to us, maybe even read our minds. We're children here, very ill-educated children."

Lanier looked down at the milky-translucent table between the couch and the chair. "That makes sense. I really like the way this apartment is decorated."

"Mine's nice, too."

"And how would they—the rooms, I presume—know what we like?"

Her expression became conspiratorial. "Right," she said.

322

"I've asked the room voice and it just says, 'The rooms are made to suit."

Lanier leaned forward on the couch. "This whole place is incredible. Unbelievable. Are we dreaming, Karen?"

She shook her head solemly.

"All right, then. Is Patricia dreaming she's found a way out, a way to go back to Earth?"

"Oh, she doesn't want to go back to Earth the way it is now. She says she can take us 'home,' whatever she means. And she's serious. She'll explain later, she said."

"You're a physicist. Is what she says possible?"

"I'm just another child here, Garry. I don't know."

"What else did she say?"

"That's it. And . . ." She stood. "I'll go now. But I didn't just . . . Oh." She clasped her arms around herself and looked at him. "Not just to tell you what she said. To make sure you understood I wasn't taking advantage."

"I understand."

"It's just, like you say, healthy, though I've been worrying."

He hadn't called it healthy; she had, but he found the transference acceptable.

"Don't."

"Okay," Farley said.

He stood. "In fact . . ." His face flushed again. "I feel just like a teenager when I . . . when you're here and we talk like this."

"I'm sorry," she said, her face falling.

"No, that's good. Until now, I've felt like a very old man, losing all my marbles. I would enjoy it if you stayed with me tonight."

She smiled, then abruptly frowned. "I will enjoy that, and I will stay," she said. "But it worries me about Patricia."

"Yes?"

"She is now the only one of us sleeping alone."

Chapter Forty-eight

Step by step, Patricia traced the progress of the curve through five dimensions, watching it unfold like some nightmare staircase, one part shadowing, one part a necessary negative of the primary curve. Her eyes were closed so tightly they hurt, and her face was convulsed into an expression between ecstasy and grief. She had never known an intensity of thought like this, so deep an involvement in her inner calculations. It frightened her. Even when she opened her eyes to the twilight blueness of the ceiling and rolled over on her side, one hand reaching into the emptiness beyond the bed—

Even then, her finger traced a part of the curve, a projected and living snake in the air. Clenching her fist, she saw little spots of light gather along the path her finger had made. She closed her eyes again.

And immediately slept, dreaming the curve. She was still half-aware in her sleep, and she watched from a distant vantage point as her brain continued, though at a reduced level, the work she could not put a stop to.

Only a few hours later, she came instantly awake, realizing she needed to reexamine her seminal article—the one she had yet to write, which she had found in the third chamber library. With some apprehension—the data service, in the four times she had resorted to it, had not always provided what she needed—she got out of the oval bed and donned her lavender robe, tying the belt as she walked through the dimly lit living room.

"Data, City Memory," she said. An armillary sphere appeared before her, its bands glowing red and gold. Two circlets, one above the other and twice the diameter, followed, a replacement for the antiquated question mark.

"Access to article by Patricia Luisa Vasquez . . . Oh,

Lord, I've forgotten the exact title and date. Do you need them?''

Complicated picts flashed until she deactivated them and requested spoken language only. "Do you wish to see a complete list of the short works of Patricia Luisa Vasquez?" the data service voice asked.

"Yes," she said, again touched by the prickling spookiness of what she was doing.

Roman alphabet listings appeared before her as if on an extensive sheet of white paper. About midway through the list appeared, *Theory of n-Spatial Geodesics as Applied to Newtonian Physics with a Special Discourse on Rho-Simplon World Lines.*

"That's it," she said. "Display."

She reread the paper carefully and drummed the fingers of her free hand on the edge of the seat. "It's brilliant, she said grimly, "and it's *wrong.*" It might have been an influential paper, but it was obvious to her now that it was an early and primitive work. "Please display the list again."

The service obliged and she picked out a later piece and requested that it be displayed.

The old and familiar symbol of the spiked ball appeared. "Interdicted," the voice said.

She chose another, feeling her anger rise. "Interdicted."

And another, toward the end of the list, written when she was—would be—about sixty-eight. "Interdicted."

"Why are my papers interdicted?" she asked angrily.

The spiked ball was the only reply.

"Why is this service being censored?" She suddenly experienced the neck-itching realization she was no longer alone in the room. "Olmy? Lights up." The room brightened. No answer.

She stood up and looked around slowly, her whole back tensing.

Then she saw the intruder, hovering near the ceiling, a gray baseball-sized roundness with a face in the middle. For a moment, she did nothing but return the face's scrutiny. It

325

seemed masculine, with small dark Asiatic eyes and a pug
nose. Its expression was hardly menacing; if anything, it was
intensely curious.

She backed up against the wall. The face did not move, but
its eyes followed her closely.

"Who are you?" she asked. Symbols appeared around the
room, incomprehensible to her. "I don't pict," she said.
"Please, what are you doing here?"

"True, I'm not supposed to be here," the face said. It fell a
couple of feet, the ball assuming the color of a rosy dawn.
"But then, I'm just an icon myself. Please don't be alarmed."

"I *am* alarmed. You're scaring me. Who are you?"

"I'm from City Memory. A rogue."

"I don't know you," she said. "Please go away."

"I can't possibly harm you. Irritate you, perhaps. I only
need a few questions answered."

The globe dropped and fleshed out like a vampire in an old
horror movie to form a masculine body, clothed in loose white
shirt and forest-green pants. The figure seemed to solidify. In
her room now stood a small, delicate man appearing slightly
younger than middle age, with long black hair and a weary,
thin face. Patricia's heart slowed and she moved a few inches
out from the wall.

"I pride myself in my accomplishments," the image said.
"I have access to the very best records. Forgotten records,
actually. There's such an awful clutter in the lower levels of
City Memory. And what I've found is the partially purged
record of a court case. . . . Something serious, actually.
Violation of flaw security. Bits and pieces of information
pointed here. . . . Subtle connections, I admit, but intrigu-
ing."

The figure seemed familiar, as if she had met him or seen
him somewhere else. "What are you doing here?"

"I'm a rogue. A rather violent one, actually, though you
wouldn't know it to look at me. I go where I please, and so
long as I'm careful, I maintain. I've been non-corporeal for a

326

hundred and fifty years now, supposedly condemned to inactive Memory. Of course, there's only a copy of me inactivated. Sometimes I'm hired for various jobs. Usually I duel with other rogues. I've taken down sixty in my time. Lethal chess."

"You haven't answered my question." She was close to tears now. She couldn't think who the rogue reminded her of. "Leave me alone. I just want to think."

"Rogues are never very polite. You're attracting a lot of attention in Axis Nader. I hadn't any idea where you were, though, until you used the data service just now. A tracer found you—one of my very best tracers. Based on the patterns of a mouse."

"Please!" Patricia shouted to the apartment. "Get him out of here!"

"It's no use," the rogue said. "Where are you from?"

Patricia didn't answer. She edged toward the bedroom door.

"I've been commissioned to find out where you're from. I've been paid in advantages over a very long-term adversary. I will not leave until you tell me."

"Who hired you?" she shouted, really frightened now.

"Let's see . . . I'm speaking twentieth-century English— American, actually. That's very surprising. Only the most die-hard Ameriphiles actually learn to speak the language as well as you do. But why would anybody be interested in an Ameriphile?" The image followed her into the bedroom. "They aren't paying me for guesswork. Tell me."

Patricia ran to the main door and ordered it to open. It did not. She gulped a breath of air and turned to face the image, suddenly determined not to lose control. "What . . . what do I get in return?" she asked. "If I tell you?"

"Maybe we can trade."

"Let me sit down, then."

"Oh, I wouldn't stop you from doing that. I'm not cruel, you know."

"You're a ghost," she said decisively.

327

"More so than most ghosts you meet," the image elaborated.

"What's your name?"

"I don't have one now. Spoor, but no name. Yours?"

"Patricia."

"Not a common name."

Suddenly, she retrieved the memory of the rogue's face. Just as suddenly, she rejected the clue; it was ridiculous. "I'm really an American," she said.

"What percentage? Most are happy to claim three or four percent, though statistically that has to be a pose—"

"One hundred percent. I was born in the United States of America, in California. Santa Barbara."

The image wobbled again. "Not much time, Patricia Luisa Vasquez. What you say doesn't make any sense, by itself, but you seem to believe it. How did you grow up so uncluttered and primary?"

"Where I come from—and when"—she took another deep breath to calm herself—"that's almost all the choice there is." She cocked her head to one side. "I *know* you," she said. "You look like Edgar Allan Poe."

The rogue betrayed some surprise. "Fancy you recognizing that. Fancy that indeed. Did you know Poe?"

"Of course not," Patricia said, feeling an incongruous tingle of delight beneath her fear. "I read him. He's dead."

"He's my chosen mentor. Such a mind!" The rogue surrounded itself with rapid picts of sepulchral figures, live burials, ships in whirlpools and arctic wastes. "Patricia Luisa Vasquez recognizes Poe. Claims to be a twenty-first-century American. Fascinating.

"I have to go soon. Ask me what you need to know, and then I'll ask you one more thing."

"What are they going to do with us?"

"Us? There are others?"

"Four others. What are they going to do?"

"I really don't know. I'll try to find out. Now, my last question for this visit. Why are you so special to them?"

"Because of what I just said." To her surprise, all her fear was gone. The rogue or ghost or whatever it was seemed to be willing to cooperate, and she saw no reason to be foolishly loyal to their kidnappers.

"We can help each other, I think. Did you know your data service has a block on it? They're keeping you here and they're selectively cutting off your access. If you tell them I've been here, I may not be able to come back, and I won't be able to answer your question. Think about it. Until next time," the rogue said, and vanished. The apartment suddenly found its voice.

"Ser Vasquez, are you well? There has been interference—"

"Don't I know it," Patricia said.

"Could you describe the difficulty?"

She bit on her knuckle for a moment, then shook her head. "No," she said. "It wasn't much of a problem." The image had frightened her—but it had told her a number of interesting things, too. She doubted the incident was a test or experiment. The rogue might prove a useful source of information. . . . "Must have been a short circuit or something, in your works, you know."

The room did not respond for some seconds. "Repairs will be made, if necessary. Do you need anything?"

"No, no thank you," Patricia said. She looked at the pictor, frowning, and again bit at her knuckle.

Chapter Forty-nine

The Presiding Minister of the Infinite Hexamon Nexus, Ilyin Taur Engle, kept his quarters in one of Central City's six broad ventilation shafts, buried deep in the spreading Wald. Olmy had never wished to settle into a primary home, but he envied the P.M. his quarters nonetheless. There was such an air of isolation and peace in the Wald, and such a fantasy of elegance in the quarters themselves.

The six shafts ran straight from the outermost facets of Central City to the governing spheres at the precinct's core. Within each shaft, as many as ten thousand corporeals lived among the winding paths through the Wald. Their homes varied from thick clusters of communal glass floats anchored to the broad aerial roots, to small free-moving cells adequate for one or at most two homorphs, or no more than four of the average neomorphs.

The Wald was both decoration and a nod to Naderite philsophies; about a third of Central City's atmosphere needs were taken care of in the shafts, with Geshel-designed scrubbers doing the rest. Thousands of varieties of trees and other plants—some food-bearing—had been genetically altered and adapted to weightlessness. Fully a third of the Axis City's biomass was botanical and concentrated in the Wald.

One of Olmy's great pleasures was to tarzan through the Wald, flying from root to limb, drifting down the paths without benefit of traction fields. There were designated sport paths and quickways with many exercising homorphs and a few whizzing neomorphs and virtually no vehicles; he had timed himself on a thousand different occasions on the more difficult of these and had honed his time down to as little as fifteen minutes from outer facet to shaft bottom.

Now, however, he felt no need to race. He tarzaned at a leisurely pace, arms folded behind his back, legs cocked like a skater's, kicking from broad leaf to smooth-worn root surface, following well-traveled courses down the path. More valuable than speed was the time to think.

Plastic tubes containing thick luminescent soups of bacteria, known as light-snakes or glow-worms, wound through the Wald, each a meter thick and sometimes half a kilometer long. In glades, they would macrame across one side in dazzling bright patterns, proximity making some glow peach and red, others dull down to a rich dark gold. Homorphs often gathered in the glades to bathe in the light from the patterns; Olmy

330

barely glanced into the few glades he passed, intent on his steady progress down the shaft.

It took him twenty minutes to reach the Presiding Minister's quarters. He left the main path by way of a narrow fork, and drifted through the flowering hoops formed by a tormented root. The quarters floated in the middle of the P.M.'s private glen.

The residence was designed like an old eighteenth-century terrestrial English manor house, with many modifications to allow for the lack of up and down. There were three roofs, and ways to enter the house from six different angles. Bay windows opened on three axes. Geometric cypress growths screened one window against a glow-worm pattern at the far end of the glen.

Monitors flew up to him as soon as he emerged from the flowering hoop tunnels and identified him positively, retreating to their other duties: hedge trimming, insect watch and keeping track of the P.M.'s pets.

The house voice welcomed him and requested he enter by the bright door, facing the glow-worm pattern. The P.M. would be with him directly.

Olmy braced himself into a dormier and watched with a mix of condescension and boredom a brief picting of the household's recent activities. When the pictor cleared, he saw an unfamiliar neomorph preceding the P.M. into the waiting room. The neomorph—vaguely fish-shaped, limbless—regarded Olmy with a crystalline fox face and picted casual greetings, but no ID. Olmy returned the greetings with a similar deletion, recognizing one of Toller's aids. The neomorph exited through the bright door, surrounded by its own midge-cloud of compact monitors.

"Getting more and more daring, aren't they?" the P.M. asked, extending his hand. Olmy shook it. "Now I ask you— would you trust somebody you can't shake hands with?"

"I've not trusted many I could shake hands with," Olmy said.

The P.M. regarded him with a mixed expression of humor

331

and not-quite-hidden irritation. "You've come to brief me on our newest ancestral guests." He ushered Olmy into his broad duodecahedral internal office. The P.M.'s round desk gimbaled on the single rod at the center; seven of the walls were covered by rootwood cases containing antigue books and message blocks. Other walls held fine illusart and false windows opening onto time-delayed scenes of other rooms in the house, edited to take out whatever occupants were in them.

"The President is still upset," Ingle said, tucking his elbows in to sit behind the desk. "I'm afraid most of the President's council are finding it difficult to understand why you brought the five back with you."

"I only brought one," Olmy corrected. "The others followed on their own, unexpectedly."

"Yes, well, however they got here, they're trouble. Secessionists are seeking advantages already, and concessions. They're not far from getting all their groups together—and this certainly could unite them. It could also convert the Korzenowski faction from a radical party to a popular front. The President's position could be endangered. Even so, he feels he doesn't have the time to oversee these difficulties directly, what with the Jart conferences still filling his days, so he's assigned Ser Oligand Toller—whom you've met, I believe—and myself."

"Bearers of bad news are never appreciated," Olmy said.

"Yes? Well, whether the news itself is actually good or bad depends on how we react, does it not? Frankly, I don't share all the President's misgivings—some, but not all. I feel we can turn the situation—and the news—to our advantage. Perhaps we can even achieve the consensus we need to face the Jarts effectively. Now, your message said you had more news."

"Someone has hired at least one rogue in City Memory to penetrate the guest quarters. Someone is desperate to find out what all the fuss is."

"Yes, that much I could have guessed," the P.M. said. "Well, then, perhaps it's time we released all we know. It's probably going to be common knowledge in a week or less,

332

especially if rogues are in on it. What's your opinion, Ser Olmy?"

"I've voiced it before, Ser; I should testify before the Nexus."

The P.M. considered that for a moment. "I still have my doubts as to the wisdom of that. But you may be right. If the truth must be unveiled, let us do the unveiling, no? But delicately. Millions of neomorphs are already scared silly by the secession talk. Drop a bombshell into the middle of it— saying the Thistledown has returned to Earth? Not an easy decision. At any rate, we can't call a full Nexus because of the Jart conferences. A partial will have to do." He left the desk, betraying his nerves. "I'll need a heavy session of Talsit this evening." He crossed his arms and floated in the middle of the office, his voluminous black robes assuming billows of repose. "You will testify in person, then, as an agent of the Hexamon?"

"The Frant and I," Olmy confirmed.

"The Frant won't testify; it's against their creed to take an oath."

"It will confirm my testimony. That's allowed."

"And what then, Ser Olmy? How can we restrain our curious ones—whoever hired the rogue—or the Korzenowski faction, Pneuma be kind, after that?"

"That may not be our greatest problem. There are still two thousand humans in the Thistledown; sooner or later, we have to bring them under our control. Our first guest, Vasquez, was already very close to learning how to manipulate the sixth chamber machinery. I assume others will eventually duplicate her work, despite the interdictions in the Thistledown libraries."

"Star, Fate and Pneuma never see fit to limit our troubles, do they?" the P.M. said with a sigh that upset the billows of his robe. "Logos be praised."

"Logos," Olmy echoed doubtfully.

"We share a certain Geshel incredulity, don't we?" the P.M. said, watching Olmy's reaction carefully. "Not wise to reveal it to everyone, however, not from this lofty position, anyway. Is there immediate danger of our . . . ancestors! Such a word—is there much chance of their disturbing the sixth chamber soon?"

"Not with Vasquez in the Axis City. Not in a matter of months, or even a year."

"Very well. First things first. I'd say it would be in our best interests, if we reveal at all—and that seems unavoidable now—to make a public show of our guests. They *are* extraordinary—and they might give us an advantage over the President's opposition. I'll have my secretaries plan an agitprop. Their advocate—your partner, Suli Ram Kikura—has she been useful?"

"Very," Olmy said. "But her work has hardly begun."

"Excellent," the P.M. said. "But we mustn't be too confident. If the Jarts start their offensive early—or, heaven forbid, decide to open a gate into a star's heart—then our visitors will mean next to nothing." Ingle shook his head, picting a chain of symbols—a gnat being consumed in a solar prominence.

Chapter Fifty

Corporal Rodzhensky lay with his back against the black library wall. Before him were scattered ration packets and tins, some Russian, most American. He snored lightly and regularly. Beside him, Major Garabedian had squatted to eat an American dinner of ham and potatos au gratin, imported from the fourth chamber as part of the as-yet-unratified treaty agreements.

As he ate, he kept a wary eye on the American soldiers lounging several dozen meters across the quadrangle. The forces were exactly equal; ten Russians, ten Americans, all armed with rifles but without lasers. There would be no silent assassinations.

Tensions had calmed slowly after the Americans had arrived at the behest of Corporal Rodzhensky and the Chinese man and woman. The library had been sealed ever since, with Lieutenant General Mirsky, Colonel Vielgorsky, Majors Belozersky and Yazykov and Lieutenant Colonel Pogodin held incommunicado. There had been some suspicion at first that American trickery was involved; Garabedian had decided otherwise after several hours of talks with Pritikin, Sinoviev and the American civilian leader, Hoffman.

No one knew what had happened within the library, although Hoffman had expressed an all-too-plausible theory that made no one happy. Garabedian still mulled the theory over, shifting his eyes between the implacable black wall and the American soldiers.

The *Zampolits*, Hoffman suggested, had tried to kill General Mirsky. Whether or not they succeeded, the library building had sealed itself off to prevent further violence and perhaps preserve evidence.

All they could do was wait.

It had been a week. During that time, Garabedian and Pletnev had managed to keep the Russian troops from doing anything unwise—factionalizing, spreading agitation or unfounded speculation. Work had proceeded on construction of their quarters in the fourth chamber. A few Russians—fifty-two, at last count—had simply left the camps and vanished into the fourth chamber woods. Five had been found so far, well fed—the woods were full of various edible plants. But three of those five had been fetal-curled and withdrawn in delayed shock.

American psychologists had offered to help; there had been similar cases among the Americans, most notably Joseph Rimskaya, who had been stricken just three days before. He had wandered into the main Russian camp in the fourth chamber, weeping uncontrollably, his clothes and back in shreds from self-flagellation. He had been returned to the Americans. But Garabedian did not think it wise to allow Russian soldiers access to American psychologists.

What he felt, above all, was sadness, a sense of loss which almost overwhelmed his sense of duty. He—like Mirsky and most of the young officers—had been part of the new Russian military experiment, begun to fix the problems highlighted by the manifold failures of the Little Death. They and their colleagues had worked with each other as a team, not as brutal antagonists in a throwback nineteenth-century system. They had achieved great things, increasing efficiency and decreasing alcoholism, desertion, violence and suicide.

They had been the new breed, and their successes had made them cultural heroes. The conquest of the Potato would have brought them untold glory; instead, through some error he could not yet comprehend, they had failed miserably, and their heritage was now ashes.

Garabedian understood all too well the pressures which drove his comrades to swim to the fourth chamber islands and lie down on the forest floor, pulling humus and mold over their soaking fatigues.

The director of the Infinite Hexamon Nexus, Hulane Ram Seija, could trace his ancestry back to the Greater East Asian Geshels who had first returned man to space, thirteen centuries before; yet he looked less human than the Frant. In this, he was typical of many neomorph citizens occupying Central City.

Ram Seija was round, one-half of his body brushed silvery metal, the other half an elegant black-and-green-swirled mineral shell from the worlds accessible through the 264 gate. His face, which could be projected to any of three different positions on the sphere, had large, inquiring eyes and a sharp-toothed grin which was definitely not designed to mask his basic aggressiveness. His two muscular arms had the twin advantanges of human appearance and prosthetic adaptability; they could stretch two meters if need be.

He had no legs, using his arms and the ubiquitous traction fields to get from place to place.

He was less than a century old and this was his second shape; for his first thirty years, he had been as homorphic as

336

any orthodox Naderite. It was in those years that Ram Seija had made his contacts and learned the basic political skills. To Olmy, he exemplified the quintessential Journey Century Twelve Radical Geshel.

Ram Seija was number four in the power hierarchy of the Hexamon, behind the President, the Presiding Minister of the Nexus and the Minister of the Joint Axis Council.

In the Nexus Sphere, located just outside the flaw passage near the core of Central City, Ram Seija had convened twenty-three corporeal representatives and five senators in a discovery session. Twenty of the Nexus members were present incarnate, which was a word that had lost much of its meaning centuries before; now it meant little more than being in primary physical form. Such form did not necessarily include much flesh. By law, no partial personalities were allowed in the chambers— however convenient that would have been for those still confined to the Jarts conference, being held on Timbl, the Frant home world.

Ram Seija guided himself to the middle of the sphere and took on the golden armillary bands of light to announce the meeting's start.

Olmy drifted at the outside, the Frant curled up beside him, only neck and head extended. Olmy had ended an exchange with Corprep Rosen Gardner some minutes before, on an apparently disputatious note; the New Orthodox Naderite leader of the Korzenowksi faction had wanted a little preliminary testimony, and Olmy had resisted. Gardner was one of the few corpreps who broke procedure often and was tolerated nonetheless; he was also one of the few Korzenowski factioners who was reasonable in a debate. In the eyes of the radical Geshels, this—and his large following of Naderites— made him a particularly dangerous opponent.

"In the name of Star, Fate, Pneuma and the Good Man, who sought equality and fair deals for all consumers, and who sought the end of overwhelming and inhuman technology, this meeting of the Infinite Hexamon Nexus convenes. There is news, gentlepeople," Ram Seija announced, "there is news.

337

"Our testimony is from Ser Olmy. We also have corroboration from one of our valuable allies, who helped Ser Olmy with his investigation."

Olmy and the Frant advanced to the center and received their armillary bands.

"I have spent the past year in the Thistledown, at the request of the Presiding Minister," he said. "This Frant accompanied me. Together, we investigated an unusual intrusion. Do we have permission to playback our records and to testify by picting?"

Ram Seija gave his permission.

For each of the senators and corpreps, the seven chambers of the Thistledown were displayed in considerable detail. In a few minutes, they became acquainted with the new human occupants of the Thistledown's chambers. Olmy and the Frant had managed to record some five hundred individuals on their instruments. The compounds were shown, along with a few building interiors. Olmy then demonstrated that the various languages spoken by the new occupants derived from pre-Death Earth.

The point of view of the picted testimony took a dizzying climb up the south polar cap of the first chamber and zoomed down the bore hole. The reactivated rotating docks and staging areas were briefly shown, and then the point of view emerged from the bore hole.

At a distance of some thirty thousand kilometers, the crescent Earth dominated the darkness, the sun emerging from behind its limb in the west.

The reaction in the Nexus chamber was extraordinary. Homiform corpreps gasped; all registered strong emotions in various ways.

Gardner spoke first. "Blessed Konrad," he said. "He found a way to bring us home again."

"Stricken; not testimony," Ram Seija decreed abruptly.

"It is truly Earth," Olmy said. "The Thistledown has returned to its construction orbit, automatically and without our knowledge. The creation of the Way did not remove us from all familiar spaces. It is possible that the Thistledown could have completed its intended journey. It did not. Instead, it sought out the sun and altered its course to return home.

"But we did not escape all effects of the Way's creation. The Thistledown was indeed shifted into a neighboring continuum, but also into the relative past. It entered its current orbit some three centuries before its launch."

The chamber was silent, stunned by the implications of what Olmy was saying.

The picted testimony continued. In less than four minutes, it showed the beginning of the Death and concluded with the spectacle of Earth covered with a thick gray pall of smoke, on the threshold of the Long Winter.

The stillness in the chamber was profound. Olmy quickly pushed on.

"I returned to the city with one of the new occupants, a corporeal woman named Patricia Luisa Vasquez. Subsequently, four others violated the axis flaw by riding a vehicle near the city. They have been acquitted and made guests of Axis Nader. All of them, of course, are corporeal and primitive, of primary form and unsupplemented mentality. They are our pre-Death ancestors."

The armillary bands now glowed around the first senator assigned to speak. She advanced. Olmy recognized Prescient Oyu, daughter of the still-regnal Gate Opener Ry Oyu. Senator Oyu had worked with Suli Ram Kikura, two years before, to exempt victims of sex-retrovirus from the limit of two incarnations; she was known to have Naderite sympathies, though her background was moderate Geshel. She was a homorph with elaborations designed to heighten both sexual and leadership traits.

"The Thistledown returned to Earth at the precise moment of the Death?" she asked.

"That is in testimony," Ram Seija reminded her.

"Not precisely," Olmy said. "The Thistledown entered the solar system five and a half years before the Death. I have evidence—presented in subtext—that our arrival in fact triggered the Death. It is possible that without the Thistledown's presence in orbit around the Earth and Moon, the earth in this continuum would have escaped the Death."

Gardner raised his hands in horror. "This is an abomination," he said. "Blessed Korzenowski could never have intended this."

"All credit to the Hexamon Nexus," Prescient Oyu continued, "but a question arises as I look over the précis on the agenda. Why has this news not been broadcast through the entire city? I suggest we make an unequivocal report public and convene an emergency full Nexus convention."

Her bands of light changed to amber and she receded a meter. Ram Seija extended both arms and spread his fingers wide to have Nexus attention. "The news is startling and important, but it also could have adverse social consequences. We wish to release the news in the most constructive fashion."

Corprep Enrik Smys, a moderate Geshel with past service to the Hexamon in a capacity similar to Olmy's, objected that the Jarts conference certainly held precedence. The Jarts showed every sign of preparing to advance beyond 2 ex 9. "And even our subject today, compared to that, is trivial."

"Perhaps not, Corprep Smys," said Rosen Gardner. "All these questions may yet be tangled."

"Did you find evidence of deliberate reprogramming of the Thistledown guidance system?" Ram Seija asked.

Olmy rotated to face the center. "I did not," Olmy said. "But the system erased all instructions immediately after arrival. There is no way of knowing."

Gardner formally requested the armillary bands. Ram Seija, with some hesitation, assented.

"It is time once more to ask for a search in City Memory," he said. "There is one who can tell us all we need to know—"

"The Engineer is dead!" Ram Seija objected vehemently.

"We are aware he is inactive," Gardner said with uncharacteristic control. "But Blessed Korzenowski knew of the danger to his patterns when he retired his corpus. We must authorize a search for any parts of his personality not purged by the assassins."

"Overruled," Ram Seija said.

"I request a hearing before the full Nexus," Gardner persisted.

"Disallowed."

"Procedural inquiry," Gardner said coolly. Ram Seija's face rose to the top of the mineral half of his sphere and he glowered at the corprep. Only in extremus was a procedural inquiry called for; he had played right into the corprep's hands by going beyond his jurisdiction.

"Seconded," Senator Oyu said, turning her elegant eyes to the surprised Gardner.

"Procedural inquiry," Ram Seija assented; he had no choice. But his expression—now in the middle of his sphere—made it clear Corprep Gardner's standing in the Nexus would be weakened by any means in his power.

Olmy listened to the discussion without much interest from that point on and, when his release was given, left the sphere with the Frant to return to Axis Nader. He took a rapid lift to the circle and quadrant where the terrestrials were being secluded.

Escorting the Frant into the kitchen lounge area, he credited an open meal for his companion.

"You are gracious, Ser Olmy," the Frant said, eyes narrowing as it surveyed the feast possibilities. "I assume I am to remain here for a time."

"We'll introduce you to the others a little later," Olmy said, his thoughts far away.

"I am content."

Olmy keyed open the entrance to the secluded sector. The Frant squatted at the arena of shelves which was a traditional Frant dining table, then turned to blink at Olmy.

"You did not expect so much trouble, did you?" the Frant said. Olmy smiled at the Frant from the dilated doorway. "You'd be surprised," he said and entered the sector with a wink.

341

Chapter Fifty-one

The zero elevator to the bore-hole staging areas was seldom used now. Only two people continued their work in the staging areas—Roberta Pickney and Silvia Link. Hoffman considered their work important, however, and made it a point to visit them personally at least once a week.

The broad spaces and comparatively low ceilings of the staging areas reminded her of a parking garage or convention center. With her two marine guards, she took a tracked cart to the communications and control center beneath the prime dock and walked alone into the quiet room.

Silvia Link was asleep in a sling. Roberta Pickney greeted Hoffman quietly and showed her the intercepted transmissions from Earth and the Moon.

"Lunar settlement seems to be doing well," she said. There were heavy bags under her eyes; she looked ten years older than when Hoffman had first met her. "There are still people on Earth, but they're only using low-power transmitters—working off batteries and windmill generators, I'd guess. I think one or two small cities are still transmitting these low-power signals—areas that may have been protected by orbiting platforms. I send out our own signals every now and then, but nobody's called back yet. It's only a matter of time."

"There're people, at least," Hoffman said.

"Yeah. At least. But nobody much cares about us, and why should they?"

"You should get into the fourth chamber for some R and R," Hoffman suggested. "You don't look too well."

"I feel pretty lousy, too. But this is all I have left. I'll make it as long as there're voices down there. You're not going shut us down, are you?"

"No, of course not," Hoffman said. "Don't be silly."

"My privilege to be paranoid," Pickney said, thrusting her

342

lower jaw forward and pulling it back, with an audible grind of molars. "When Heineman gets back, I'll go to work with him refurbishing the shuttle. I'd like to get to the Moon. I have friends there."

"No word on the expedition," Hoffman said. "They're late, but that's not much reason to worry . . . yet. I may get some of Heineman's fellows working on the shuttle soon. Give us all something new to think about."

"What about the missing Russians?" Link asked from her sling, blinking at them sleepily.

"Still unavailable for comment," Hoffman said. She took Pickney's hand and squeezed it. "You're needed," she said. "Both of you. Don't overdo it."

Pickney nodded without much conviction. "All right. Have Janice Polk and Beryl Wallace spell us in a day or so. We'll go get some tubelight and see the sights."

"Fine," Hoffman said. "Now show me where the signals are coming from. . . ."

Chapter Fifty-two

The rogue reappeared before Patricia as she slept and awoke her by tickling her ear. "Miss Patricia Luisa Vasquez, late of Earth—the late Earth," he said. "I'm here with some answers."

She rolled over and rubbed her eyes. The rogue's appearance had changed; he now seemed to wear baggy pants and a cardigan sweater. His hair was styled in a loose shag, and a watchless fob hung from a belt loop, terminating in a hemline pocket in the sweater. The rogue was in the height of 2005 fashion. She leaned over the bed and examined his shoes. *Huaraches* and Japanese *tabi* socks completed his wardrobe.

"They're on to me," he said. "I had to slip in a different way. I'm using the auxiliary pictor; the primary is locked. And I've reprogrammed the apartment privacy unit to edit us both out of any record while we talk. I've found there *is* a way to get into the city record. Very disappointing; to the Nexus, apparently nothing is sacred."

Patricia blinked and then got out of bed, reaching for her robe. "Do you do this all the time?"

"No," the rogue replied. "Takes a lot of effort to get this far. I'd much rather be playing games in City Memory, but my employers are handing out incredible advantages for the information. Luckily, I sent mine in just before the general release—now everybody knows you're here."

"We've been told that already."

"Right," the rogue said. The lights in the bedroom came up. Patricia examined herself in the lavatory mirror and decided there wasn't much that could be done in a hurry. She looked exhausted and her hair was tangled from restless sleep.

"Anyway, answers," the rogue said, "more answers than questions asked. You're going to testify before the full Nexus in a couple of days—nobody knows that yet but me and those who should. They you're going to be included in the Last Gate ceremony. That's not its official name, but that's what it amounts to—you'll meet the Prime Gate Opener at the one point three ex nine segment and witness the opening. They may close it just after—Jarts coming down fast."

"What are Jarts?"

"Fleas, the Nexus will tell you—parasites, monstrously aggressive and not in the least cooperative. The Way was in place a thousand years before it was finally connected to the Thistledown—Way time, of course, which wasn't congruent until the linkup. The Jarts entered through a test gate and took up residency before it was opened. They matured in the Way and we had to fight them back. They know how to open gates and they control between two ex nine and, we think, four ex nine. But look, this is all in the Memory and I don't have much time. I have news about Olmy. You know about the orthodox Naderites and the Geshels?"

"Yes," Patricia said.

"Well, they have two contingency plans should the Jarts

344

overpower us, which seems all too likely now. The Geshels want to mobilize the entire Axis City, grab the flaw and ride it at near-light-speed over the Jart territories, and at the same time blow the Thistledown off the end of the Way."

"What? Why?"

"That could seal the Way—cauterize it. And eliminate the danger of the Thistledown's being reoccupied and having the entire Way controlled by Jarts. The other alternative is to guide the Thistledown to a habitable planet and simply abandon the Way—or close it down, eliminate it. The Axis City could escape by passing through the end of the Way, blowing off the Thistledown and going into orbit around the planet. That would take time . . . or would have, until now. The Thistledown is in Earth orbit, an ideal situation for abandoning the Way. Everybody knows that. So the orthodox Naderites—especially the Korzenowski faction—"

"Who are they?" Patricia asked, all her muzziness vanishing at the rogue's mention of the familiar name.

"They're descended from the engineers who once supported the Way's designer, Konrad Korzenowski. The core is a small, conservative group—return-to-Earthers, most of them. Geshels regarded them as candidates for inactive Memory, until now. The Naderites and Korzenowski people are calling for reconsideration."

"They want to blow up the asteroid and take the Axis City into Earth–Moon orbit?"

"That's it. Now—my time's running out fast. I'm going to trigger all sorts of safeguards shortly, and I won't be able to visit you again—this is my last avenue. Olmy isn't what he seems. He's—"

What happened next, happened so fast Patricia could hardly follow it. The rogue's image wobbled violently and something fizzled in the far wall. A jagged beam of red shot from the auxiliary pictor across the room and hit her slate on the nightstand. The rogue vanished. The bedroom lights dimmed.

The furniture and walls were indistinct and gray. "Brighter, please," she said.

"Many regrets," the room voice, now harsh and dissonant, replied. "Pictors in your quarters are malfunctioning. Please be patient. Repairs are in progress."

She sat on the edge of the bed. As her eyes adjusted, she realized that all detail had gone out of the room. She sat on a basic white bed-form, surrounded by basic white furniture-forms. The walls were blank. She picked up her slate to see if it had been damaged by the flash.

On the screen, a crude line drawing of the rogue in his high-fashion togs appeared, followed by a string of numbers and then an end-of-string triangle. Beyond the triangle, in the next register, were three equations and a code equivalency. She integrated the two registers and performed a basic operation with the equations.

Words appeared on the slate, flashing: *Olmy knew Korzenowski. Knows him yet. In Thistledown City.*

Olmy's quarters were in Axis Nader most of the time; he never kept a residence beyond four months, but he did stay in that section of the Axis City more often than not. He never decorated his quarters, relying on a minimum of elaboration to make the rooms livable. He seemed, in fact, to avoid as many as he could of the services most Axis Citizens regarded as basic.

Yet he was not an ascetic. He simply had no need for such accoutrements; he did not criticize those who did.

He sat in the all-white living room, waiting for his trace to be completed. Olmy had patterned his tracer after the central mental programs of an old terrestrial species of dog known as a short-haired terrier, supplemented with several of his own partial personalities. It was a tough trace to elude, hardy and resourceful. It rarely failed him.

By Axis City law, rogues in City Memory were fair game. Citizens could not wipe the rogues they located, but they could corner them and call down an immediate inactivation.

Olmy was not interested in inactivation. He simply wanted to maintain a steady trace on the rogue—and to keep pressure on him, to heighten the sensation of illicit activity. The rogue was of very high quality; he had outlived dozens of duels, some extending across decades, which meant virtual millennia in City Memory. He kept no name, not even adequate spoor; he had designed his active persona to be efficient, elusive and only as egotistical as necessary to provide motivation for duels.

The tracer had caught the rogue in Patricia's quarters, and Olmy had then commanded it to back off, in such a way that the rogue would be led to believe it had escaped.

Olmy was well-acquainted with the personality of the average rogue. Most had been born during the final stages of City Memory construction—a task that had taken over five hundred years, beginning in Thistledown City before the creation of the Way.

A number of citizens, generally young, had found ways to create loopholes and to circumvent the ultimate penalties being put into effect to deter crime—recycling of the citizen's body and inactivation of the stored personality. The most popular method was making an illegal duplicate personality which would remain inactive in City Memory; if the citizen received the ultimate penalty, the illegal duplicate would be activated, guaranteeing continuity.

These "rogues" had then engaged in all manner of criminal activities, some of them resorting to acts of violence not seen in the Axis City since the expulsion of the orthodox Naderites from Alexandria. Most were caught, tried and sentenced, and the punishment carried out—releasing a virulently destructive group of personalities into City Memory. As time passed, some of the rogues were convinced by Hexamon agents that the best way they could spend their time would be to engage in duels—searching out and eliminating other rogues. That solved much of the problem. Dueling caught on, and within a decade, half of the rogues had been eliminated by their own confreres.

Many had survived, however—the smartest and most inventive, and therefore, ultimately the most dangerous.

In recent decades, one of the Nexus's most pressing problems was to make City Memory completely safe for all citizens. The Nexus had made little progress—a stubborn residue of resistance remained, creating mischief and occasionally disrupting important functions.

Hiring a rogue was always risky, Olmy knew. The patron could not expect complete loyalty—a rogue stayed loyal only so long as advantages and interest remained high.

To that end, Olmy rewarded the rogue richly with access to several private data banks—and made doubly sure that no one would ever discover who had done the hiring, especially the rogue himself.

Chapter Fifty-three

The dark library brightened slowly, allowing his eyes to acclimate. Pavel Mirsky stood blinking on the far side of the plaza of seats and teardrop globes.

His first impulse was to look for the damage done by Vielgorsky's spray of fire. There was none. All the globes were intact. Mirsky raised his hand to the side of his head, and then to his nose and chin. No scars. In his head, a tiny, unobtrusive signal told him he was using part of his brain that did not originally belong to him.

He walked back and forty, noticing a distinctly unpleasant sensation of *inexperience* behind his eyes. Then he circumnavigated the banks of chairs and approached the black wall, still closed and featureless. Frowning, he called out, "Hello!" Nobody responded. "Hello! Where is everybody?"

Perhaps he had been left alone. The others may have exited the library after shooting him. But there had been the white, curling mist—and he remembered the three officers with their heads jerked back, jaws slack.

"Pogodin!" he called. "Pogodin, where are you?"

Again, no answer. He crossed the dark corner of the library

to the little doorway that led to the observation booth. The door was open. He climbed the stairs and entered the booth.

Pogodin stretched on three chairs, breathing steadily, apparently sleeping. Mirsky shook his shoulder gently. "Pogodin," he said. "Time to leave now."

Pogodin's eyes opened and he regarded Mirsky with surprise. "They shot you," he said. "They took half your head away. I saw it."

"I've been dreaming," Mirsky said. "Very odd dreams. Did you see what happened to Vielgorsky—to Belozersky and Yazykov?"

"No," Pogodin said. "Just mist all over me, itching. And now this." His eyes widened and he sat up, lips quivering. "I want to leave," he said.

"Good idea. Let's find out what happened." Mirsky preceded Pogodin down the stairs to the black wall. "Open," he said.

The half-moon doorway irised open silently.

Annenkovsky stood at parade rest with his back toward Mirsky and the door, holding his rifle by the barrel with the stock on the paving.

"Excuse me, Major," Mirsky said. Annenkovski tensed and swung around on one foot, lifting his rifle and fumbling it. "Careful," Mirsky cautioned.

"Comrade Colonel—I mean, General—"

"Where are the others?" Mirsky asked, looking at the troops in the quadrangle.

"Others?"

"The political officers."

"They haven't come out. Excuse me, General, but we must go to our camp right away—we must contact them by radio and—"

"How long have I been gone?"

"Nine days, General."

"Who's in charge?" Mirsky asked. Pogodin stepped up just behind him.

349

"Major Garabedian and Lieutenant Colonel Pletnev for the moment, sir."

"Then take me to them. What are the NATO troops doing here?"

"Sir . . ." Annenkovksy seemed ready to faint. "There has been a lot of tension. Nobody knew what happened in there. What *did* happen?"

"Good question," Mirsky said. "Maybe we'll find out later. For now, I'm fine—Pogodin is fine—and we need to go to the camp . . . in the fourth chamber?"

"Yes, sir."

"Let's go. And why are our men stationed here?"

"Waiting for you, General."

"Then they'll come back with us."

"Yes, sir."

In the train, Mirsky closed his eyes and leaned his head against the wall. *I am dead,* he thought. *I can feel it—parts of me missing, replaced—fill dirt in gaping trenches. That means I'm a new person; I'm dead, come alive again. New, but stuck with the old responsibilities.*

He opened his eyes and looked at Annenkovsky. The major regarded him with an almost fearful expression, which he quickly wiped away and replaced with a wan smile.

Chapter Fifty-four

"Let's sum it up, then," Lanier said. They had gathered again in Patricia's quarters, to hear her story about the rogue and reach an agreement on their common behavior. "We're guests, but not exactly. We're protected, which means our condition bears some resemblance to being prisoners."

"Our data services are censored," Farley said.

"We can't go back to the Stone," Heineman said.

"And—if what Patricia has learned is true—we're about to become celebrities," Carrolson said.

350

"Did the rogue say whether anyone expected the Stone to return to Earth?" Lanier asked.

"No," Patricia said. "But I don't think so. If I'm right, they thought it would simply continue through space, too small to be noticed, and never end up anywhere in particular—because of the snap when they opened the corridor."

"So what's our position on all this?" Lanier asked. "Larry, Lenore?"

"What does it matter, what we want? What can we do?" Heineman asked, spreading his arms.

"Think, Larry," Carrolson said, putting a hand on his knee. "We're celebrities. They can't just ignore our wishes."

"Oh, no!" Heineman said. "They can just brainwash us. They're not even human anymore, some of them!"

"They're human," Patricia said. "Just because they can choose what shape they want to be, or what talents or abilities they'll have, doesn't mean they're no longer our descendants."

"Lord," Heineman said, shaking his head. "This is beyond me."

"No, it isn't," Carrolson insisted. "If I can handle it, you can." She pinched his knee.

"If we put forward a united front, we'll get more concessions," Lanier said. "If we're celebrities, or even curiosities, we could have some control over how we're treated—and not so incidentally, how our people on the Stone are treated."

"So what are we going to demand?" Carrolson asked.

"First, we insist that our data services be uncensored," Patricia suggested.

"I haven't even used mine," Heineman said.

"We make every attempt to get permission to communicate with the Stone." Lanier looked around the room. "Are we agreed to that?"

They were.

"We make sure that we travel in a group; we should never be separated," he continued. "If we are, we protest—"

"Hunger strike?" Farley said.

351

"Whatever works. It seems obvious to me that our hosts are not ogres, and it's not likely we'll be mistreated—dazzled a bit, perhaps, subjected to all kinds of future shock, but . . . We can handle that. We all survived our time on the Stone, so we can survive this. Right?"

"Right," Farley said, regarding Lanier with an expression of something more than respect for authority. Patricia glanced between them and put on what Lanier thought of as her sharp cheery look—a smile with an edge, her square eyes intense.

Carrolson inspected all three intently.

"Olmy's in the lounge," Patricia said. "He has Ram Kikura with him. I told him to wait until we were finished—but they want to talk to us."

"So are we united?" Lanier asked.

"Of course," Heineman said softly.

Olmy and Ram Kikura entered Patricia's quarters and sat in the middle of the group, legs crossed. Ram Kikura smiled happily; to Lanier, she looked hardly more than Patricia's age, though she had to be much older.

Lanier presented their demands. To his surprise, Olmy agreed to almost everything, excluding only communication with the Thistledown. "That I cannot grant you right now. Perhaps later. We can allow you uncensored access to data, but that will require some education," he said. "Full access to data is very complicated, a great responsibility. There is potential for abuse. For a start, would you accept the help of a pedagog? Ram Kikura could assign a ghost—a partial personality based on her own. This pedagog will perform searches for you, as well as instruct. Our younger citizens use them all the time."

"It will let us research anything?" Patricia asked.

"That is a difficult request," Ram Kikura said. "Not even a citizen has access to everything in City Memory. There is much that could be dangerous for the untrained—"

"Like what?" Heineman asked.

"Programs that alter personality, or merge different personalities. Psyche enhancement. Various high-level fictions and theoretical programs. You may wish to explore these later, but for now a pedagog will protect you from inadvertently . . . let's say, getting in over your head."

"Or under," Carrolson said.

"Are we still being kept pure?" Patricia asked.

"To a certain extent," Olmy admitted. "But the tests have been performed—"

"They have?" Heineman betrayed his shock.

"Yes. While you slept."

"I think we should have been advised what was happening," Lanier said, frowning.

"You were. Your sleep personas guided our inquiries, and we did nothing they did not agree with."

"Jesus," Carrolson said. "What in the hell are sleep personas?"

Ram Kikura raised her hands. "Perhaps now you see why your legal status is that of children, or at best adolescents. You are simply unprepared for full exposure to all the Axis City has to offer. Please don't be offended. I'm here to help whenever possible—not to hinder or frustrate you. I'm also here to protect, and I will do that over whatever objections you may have."

"Is that what advocates do?" Heineman asked. "I mean, are they lawyers, or what?"

"An advocate is both a guide and a legal representative," Ram Kikura said. "We advise on courses of action, based on researches our assigned ghosts perform in City Memory and elsewhere. We have many advantages—access to private memory collections, for example. While we cannot divulge the contents of those collections, we can act on what we learn—within limits. Some advocates—myself included—offer what in your time might have been called psychological counseling."

"Basically," Olmy said, "Ser Ram Kikura will provide another layer of protection—against abuse from higher authorities. Do you have any other questions?"

"Yes," Carrolson said, looking to Lanier. He nodded and

353

she continued. "What's going to happen to our people on the Stone—in the Thistledown?"

"We don't know yet," Olmy said. "That decision hasn't been made."

"Will they be treated properly?" Farley asked. "Americans and others?"

"I can guarantee they won't be harmed," Olmy said.

"Do you have any idea when we can communicate with them?" Lanier asked.

Olmy tapped his index fingers together before his chest and said nothing.

"Well?"

"As I said, that question has not been decided. There is no immediate answer."

"We'd like to know as soon as you learn," Lanier said.

"You will," Olmy assured them. "You have been protected and isolated. That will change somewhat now that your presence is no longer secret. You recognize your potential popularity; there will be ceremonies and tours. You'll probably be quite worn out by the attention."

"I'm sure," Lanier said dubiously. "Now, Ser Olmy, just between the seven of us—if you're just one person, as you seem to be, and there's nobody peering over your shoulder—what stake do you have in us?"

"Mr. Lanier," Olmy said, "you know as well as I that now is not the time to be perfectly frank. Frustrating as it may be, you simply do not understand, and if I were to try to explain, I would only confuse you. I *will* explain, eventually, but first you must experience our city, our cultures. Since you are now free to use the data services—"

"Relatively free," Lanier said.

"Yes, free with protections . . . You may wish to spend the next twenty-four hours 'boning up,' if that's the right idiom."

"Do we face any other restrictions?"

"Yes," Olmy said. "You cannot leave these living areas. Not until your schedule has been made up and the Nexus has arranged for your . . . let's call it a debut. And before that happens, we suggest you become fully informed about the Axis City and learn at least a little of the ways we live."

He looked from face to face, his eyebrows raised to solicit any more questions, but none were asked. Lanier clasped his hands behind his neck and leaned back on the couch.

Ram Kikura programmed the pictors from where she stood. "There is now a pedagog, based on my personality," she said. "You may use the data services from any of your apartments and the pedagog will help you. It would be best to begin with the city and Way description . . . agreed?"

The seven of them watched in silence as the Axis City was projected before them in hypnotic detail. They seemed to approach the city from out of the north, swooping along very close to the singularity—the flaw—and passing through several dark shields.

Their point of view then fell to very near the wall of the Way, until they seemed to hover a few hundred meters over the flowing lanes of traffic. Heineman twitched when he saw rushing tank-like cylinders conveyed along multiple tracks below them, each cylinder equipped with a circle of brilliant forward-facing searchlights on the nose and three bands of running lights along the side. In the distance, a four-kilometer-wide gate terminal accepted thousands of the cylinders from all directions. (A visual appendix briefly showed them the interior of the terminal—a maze of multilevel switching yards, cylinders being rerouted, guided into sheds to be loaded or unloaded, the contents being transferred to different containers for their trips into the gate. The gate itself was much wider than the ones they had encountered—a stepped hole at least two kilometers wide, resembling an open-pit mine but more regular and much more crowded with machinery.)

The Axis City was awesome from any angle, but from near the surface of the Way, it was overwhelming. The pictor highlighted the northernmost parts of the city and explained their functions, then their point of view moved south.

The farthest southern extension of the city was a broad

Maltese cross, extended from two cubes mounted one behind the other on the flaw. The center of the cross accepted the flaw, which then extended through the cubes. Here was the machinery which powered, propelled and guided the city along the singularity. The same effect that could move the city along the flaw, and had propelled the tuberider, also provided much of the city's energy. Generators within the cubes were spun by turbines whose "blades" intersected the singularity and were subjected to the spatial transform.

(*Where does the energy ultimately come from?* Patricia asked herself. Did the question even have meaning?)

Beyond the two cubes was a wineglass-shaped buffer, the broad end placed flush against the first spinning cylinder, Axis Nader, where their quarters were located. Axis Nader was the oldest section of the city. After the final transfer of the orthodox Naderites from the Thistledown, they had been moved into Axis Nader, which became a kind of Naderite ghetto.

The then-expanding populations of neomorphs had moved north to Central City and the other rotating cylinders, newer and therefore more desirable in terms of real estate. Axis Nader rotated to produce a centrifugal force at its outermost levels about equal to the force in the Way. Its population was still largely orthodox Naderites, which, it went without saying, were almost entirely homorphic.

Beyond Axis Nader was Central City. The geometry of Central City's architecture was dazzling by itself. Lanier's curiosity triggered a graphic breakdown of the shape, beginning with a cube. Each face of the cube supported a squat pyramid, the "steps" rotated slightly with respect to each other, creating a half-spiral. The overall shape could fit within a sphere about ten kilometers across and was rather like a Tower of Babel, as conceived by the twentieth-century artist M. C. Escher if he had collaborated with architect Paolo Soleri; in all respects, Central City was the showpiece of Axis City. The "twisted pyramid" motif seemed to be universal; it was also the shape of the gate terminals.

Beyond Central City was Axis Euclid, which contained a mixed population of neomorphs and homorphs of both Geshel and Naderite sympathies. Axis Thoreau and Axis Euclid counter-rotated to offset the rotation of Axis Nader, which was slightly larger than either of them.

The projected point of view returned to the Maltese cross at the southern end of the city. Within the center of the cross they found themselves in a docking facility, witnessing the outfitting of a much larger, much more sophisticated version of their own destroyed tuberider. Called a flawship, the craft was about a hundred meters long, shaped like an ocarina pinched in the middle. The two segments of the spindle were almost featureless, one shiny gray-black, the other blue-violet.

Facts and figures accompanied the display. The flawship—one of a fleet of more than a hundred—could travel at five thousand kilometers a second. It could disengage from the flaw to allow other traffic to pass—though Heineman confessed he didn't see how this was done, since the flaw passed right down the center of the ship—and it could also send out smaller craft for landing parties and reconnaissance.

Near the surface of the Way, the immense disks they had seen on their approach provided transportation for cargo and passengers on less extensive trips. The picted tour ended with a gold-and-silver armillary sphere whirling before them.

"Ser Olmy," Lanier said.

"Yes?"

"Are we guests, or prisoners?"

"Neither, actually," Olmy said. "Depending on who you ask—and how honestly they answer—you are assets, or you are liabilities. Please remember that. We have three receptions planned," he said. "One before the Hexamon Nexus, the second on the Frant homeworld, Timbl, where we may be able to meet with the President, and the third at one point three ex nine, where a new gate is to be opened."

Lanier stood slowly and pinched the bridge of his nose. "All right," he said. "We've gone public and now we're being used for purposes of propaganda. It'll take us years to

357

sophisticated here—maybe we'll never make it, since we don't have implants. But at least you're showing us more than before. We're no longer unblemished specimens of pre-Death Homo sapiens." He paused, uncertain where he was heading. "But—"

"You'll never be completely happy with my explanations," Olmy interrupted. "You sense however much we tell you, there's a subtext you cannot understand. And you're right. You'll notice that I have never asked you to trust me. That would be more than I could reasonably expect. But for this once, it should be obvious that we can help each other enormously. You want to communicate with your fellows—and the Nexus must come to grips with your very presence, and what that implies. In the next few days, you're going to learn more about the Way, and our mission here—more than even the data pillar could tell you. I'll escort you, and Suli Ram Kikura and I will do everything in our power to plead your case—first, because it is just, and then because I believe that what is in your best interest, also serves the Nexus."

Lanier looked at the other four, his gaze lingering on Farley and then Patricia. Farley smiled encouragement; Patricia's expression was less clear.

"You have our cooperation, within reason, for seven more days," Lanier said. "If it isn't obvious to me that our interests are being mutually served, and if we haven't been allowed to communicate with the Thistledown, the cooperation stops. I don't know how much of a threat that is," he said, taking a deep breath. "For all I know, you can create computer-generated images of us and make them do whatever you want, or even manufacture look-alike androids. But that's our position."

"Agreed," Olmy said. "Seven days."

Olmy and Ram Kikura left them. Heineman swung his head back and forth slowly, then looked at Lanier. "Well?"

"We keep on studying," Lanier said. "And we bide our time."

* * *

Hoffman stood before the small mirror in her "cardboard condo," as she had come to call the room in the women's bungalow. She decided she didn't look too bad. She had been sleeping better the past few days.

The suicide rate had declined; her people—Hoffman always thought of them that way, soldiers and civilians—seemed to be accepting their fate, and plans were under way to re-outfit the shuttle and some of the Russian heavy-lifters and see if a trek to the Moon was possible. A few were even discussing an expedition to Earth—Gerhardt and Rimskaya leading that group.

Rimskaya had recovered with remarkable speed from his "lapse," as he referred to it. He had been acutely embarrassed, and had finally requested—somewhat paradoxically—that people stop being so understanding. "Be as hard on me as I would be on you," he had demanded.

Hoffman had immediately put him in charge of logistics, an area she knew he would handle well. Always put a tough (but very smart) sonofabitch in front of the food and supply lockers. He would coordinate well with the Russians and he would take *that* load from her back. In his spare time—what little there was of it—he could confer with Gerhardt on their Earth plans. Hoffman had her own unique ways of being hard on people. Rimskaya seemed to flourish under the new and extensive work load.

Her only major worry, for now, was the fate of the tuberider expedition.

With the return of Mirsky, and the disappearance of the three political officers, the Russians were becoming more and more cooperative. There was the problem of a shortage of women—there had been two rapes and several near instances, but that was fewer than she had expected. Many soldiers—NATO and Russian—had donated small arms to the women. They had not had to use them yet.

Hoffman had an appointment to meet with Mirsky in the fourth chamber in an hour. It would be their second meeting since his return, and the agenda up for discussion was long but not riddled with crises.

With Beryl Wallace and two marines, she rode the zero train from the first chamber to the fourth, then transferred to a truck in the NATO compound. The Russian compound had split into three during Mirsky's absence; it now occupied a long stretch of shore and two offshore islands. Two large rafts had been slung together out of logs, and boats were being constructed slowly and painstakingly; there were no facilities for processing lumber yet, though it seemed there might be in a couple of months, and the materials available to the boatbuilders were primitive.

The spinward trip through the forest was pure pleasure for Hoffman. The Russian "mainland" compound was near the ninety train platform, about forty kilometers from the NATO compound. Some of the most rugged terrain and deepest woods surrounded the Stoner-built road. There was even a gentle rain that beaded the truck windows.

Wallace talked about the resumption of science in the sixth and seventh chambers; Hoffman listened and nodded, but found the subject somehow uninteresting. Wallace sensed this after a few minutes and allowed her to sink deeper into her reverie.

The Russian mainland compound resembled an old Western fort. Tall saplings had been stripped of branches and bark and erected to form a secondary wall of defense beyond a high rampart of dirt. Russian soldiers swung wide the gates at their approach, and swung them shut behind.

The first thing that caught Hoffman's eye was a gallows. It stood—unoccupied, she thanked God—in the center of a quadrangle cleared of all grass and foliage and demarcated by head-sized boulders.

Other log buildings were under construction; the most ambitious was going to be three stories tall, designed along the lines of an old Russian country house.

Soldiers motioned them to park the truck behind a long, narrow building made of split logs. Mirsky received them

360

informally at a desk in the east end of the long building. There were no walls; other work areas and sleeping slings were open for all to see. Hoffman and Wallace shook his hand and he motioned for them to sit in the canvas chairs. The marines stood outside, solemnly flanked by two Russian troopers.

He offered them tea. "Part of our allotment from your commissary, I'm afraid," he said. "But it is good tea."

"You're making progress with the camp," Hoffman said.

"Let's speak English," Mirsky suggested. "I need to practice." He poured the dark amber tea into three lightweight plastic cups.

"Fine," Hoffman said.

"I can't take credit for the progress," Mirsky said. "You know I was not here when most of this work was done."

"Everybody has been curious. . . ." Hoffman said.

"Oh? About what?"

Hoffman smiled and shook her head. "Never mind," she said.

"No, I insist." Mirsky's eyes widened. "What?"

"Your disappearance."

He looked between them. "I was dead," he said. "Then I was made well again. Does that answer your question?" Before she could reply, he said, "No, I wouldn't think so. Well then, I don't know. It's as much a mystery to me as to you."

"Well, whatever," Hoffman said, relaxing her smile. "We're glad you're back. There's a lot of work to be done."

First on the agenda was a discussion of the unloading of the heavy-lifter carrying equipment and supplies. It had remained docked in the bore hole since the Death; the crew had been allowed to evacuate, but no agreement had yet been reached on disposition of the cargo. In a few minutes, Hoffman and Mirsky negotiated a satisfactory procedure. All armaments would be left in a locked chamber in the staging area, guarded by Russians and NATO personnel; other materials would be delivered to the Russian fourth chamber compound. "We need material to barter as much as we need the supplies," Mirsky said.

361

The status of the Russian science team was next. Hoffman maintained that team members who wished to remain with the NATO group should be allowed to do so; Mirsky thought in silence for a moment, then nodded. "I need no more people uncertain about my rule," he said, regarding them both with eyes wide and facial muscles taut. He blinked twice, rapidly.

Hoffman glanced down at her notes. "This is going even more smoothly than last time," she said.

Mirsky leaned toward her, elbows on his knees, hands clasped. "I am tired of disputes," he said. "I have the calm of a dead man, Miss Hoffman. I'm afraid I unsettle some of my comrades."

"You keep saying you were killed. That doesn't make sense, General."

"Perhaps not. But it is true. I do not remember everything. But I remember I was shot in the head. Pogodin tells me they—" He held up his hands. "You can deduce who killed me. Half my head." He waved his hand away from the right half of his skull. "Killed, and then I was brought back to life again. I am thankful I was unarmed, or I might be where Belozersky, Vielgorsky and Yazykov are even now."

"And where is that?"

"I'm not positive," Mirsky said. "In detention, perhaps. It seems Thistledown City still has the means to carry out its own law."

"I thought that might be what happened. That means Thistledown City is still capable of making decisions and judgments, and acting on them."

"We must watch our behavior there, no?" Mirsky suggested.

Hoffman nodded and returned to the agenda. One by one, within forty-five minutes, all the items were covered, negotiated and agreed to.

"It's been a pleasure," Mirsky said, standing and offering her his hand. Hoffman shook it firmly and he escorted them to the truck.

"What about the gallows?" Wallace asked as they back-

362

tracked anti-spinward to the zero compound. "What are we going to make of that?"

"No more Mr. Nice Guy," Hoffman suggested idly. "Maybe it's just a warning."

"He's spooky," Wallace said.

Hoffman agreed. "Very," she said.

Chapter Fifty-five

From their quarters in Axis Nader, the five were taken by Suli Ram Kikura and the Frant to the flaw passage, around which the cylindrical precinct rotated. Their transportation was an empty shaft three kilometers long; their fall was similar to a ride in the apartment building elevator in Thistledown City, and therefore—mercifully—not too unexpected.

Carrolson enjoyed it the least of them; she had a distinct fear of precipices; not of heights per se, but of edges. She managed, however, with both Lanier's and Ram Kikura's encouragement. "I'm not a goddamned old woman," she said resentfully as they fell.

The flaw passage was a half-kilometer-wide pipe through the Axis City, with the singularity at its center. Hundreds of thousands of citizens lined the walls and floated in clutching, roiling yet very coordinated clusters along their path. Ram Kikura and the Frant conferred with the passage engineer, a female homorph who, like Olmy, was also self-contained and lacked nostrils.

The five were then introduced to the first of many city officials, the Minister of Axis Nader, a gray-haired, distinguished and hale-looking orthodox Naderite who flew a Japanese rising sun over his left shoulder. He seemed to have not an ounce of Oriental blood, but then, his form could have been artificial—probably was—and no one had time or much inclination to inquire. "You may call me Mayor, if you like," he said in perfect English and Chinese. These languages were

363

now the rage of the four precincts, extending even beyond those who claimed specific ancestry.

On the flaw was a beetle-like, black maintenance vehicle not dissimilar to the one that had dismantled the tuberider. It was larger, however, equipped with a wide and well-appointed cabin, liberally decorated with rare (and genuine) red bunting. Pictors projected very convincing fireworks around the vehicle and the flaw as Ram Kikura, the mayor and the Frant stood aside, allowing them to enter first. They took seats in a half-circle behind the controls and were gently clamped in by something they could not see.

The mayor took the controls—a Y-shaped black pillar with receptacles for the fingers of two hands—and the hatch irised shut silently.

They moved down the flaw, preceded by a faint pulse of red. Fireworks still blossomed on all sides, sometimes harmlessly intersecting parts of the crowd.

"It's not enough just to see you on the pictors," Ram Kikura said. "People haven't changed much. I'd guess that maybe a third of those out there are ghosts—picted themselves, with monitors at the center of their images. See and be seen."

"Where's Alice?" Heineman grumbled.

"Alice who?" Ram Kikura asked.

"Just Alice," Heineman said. "I can't help feeling we're in Wonderland."

"Are we missing someone?" the mayor asked, turning his head and appearing concerned.

"No," the Frant said, making its tooth-grinding noise.

The journey took a half hour, covering fifteen kilometers from the vicinty of Axis Nader to the Central City. Here, the crowds were even more dense—and more disorderly. Individuals—neomorphs predominating—tried to block the slow progress of the maintenance vehicle and were gently brushed aside by the uncurling sheets of traction fields rippling ahead of the craft.

Patricia sat patiently, saying little, occasionally stealing a glance at Lanier. Lanier's face wore a constant half-puzzled frown. He lifted his lip slightly at the appearance of some of the neomorphs—elongated snake-like curls, shiny as chrome; fish, birds and radiolarian spheres like the silicate shells of plankton; varieties of human shape that went beyond the basic descripton of homorph. Farley absorbed it all with gape-jawed fascination.

"I'll bet I look like a rude," she said at one point, then glanced at her companions, realizing nobody understood her. "What's the word I'm looking for?" she asked Lanier.

"I haven't the faintest idea," he replied, grinning affectionately. She put her hand on his. Patricia withdrew a little into her seat.

So what is this? she asked herself. *A little jealousy? Being unfaithful to Paul? Why should Garry pay any attention to you to at all? He came to find you—out a sense of duty.*

She shut off that area of inquiry, seeing no need to invade a territory of great pain and uncertainty and guilt.

They left the maintenance vehicle—and the mayor of Axis Nader—behind, escorted now by the neomorph Minister of Central City and Senator Prescient Oyu. Olmy greeted them at the broad circular entrance to the Hexamon Nexus Chamber. Within the chamber, there was confusion on all sides; homorphs, neomorphs, some with American flags picted over their shoulders—and at the center, near the podium, two wide and vibrantly living images of the flags of the Republic of China and the United States.

Cheers and music, boisterous and welcoming.

Heineman blinked and Carrolson took his arm as they were pushed along a traction field by Olmy and Ram Kikura. Prescient Oyu, as beautiful and graceful as any woman Lanier had ever seen, took his arm and Patricia's, and the Minister of Central City entered beside Farley.

Lanier saw several senators—or were they corpreps?—wearing the Soviet hammer and sickle. And then they were in the center of the Nexus Chamber. The senators and corpreps became quiet and all displays faded.

Director Hulane Ram Seija came to the podium and told the

365

Nexus that their guests would soon be going to the Frant gate, to see the workings of commerce in the Way. And after that, they would be taken by Senator Prescient Oyu to meet with her father, who even now presided over the preliminaries to a gate opening at 1.3 ex 9.

Lanier had been elected spokesperson for the group. Suli Ram Kikura had suggested—against Olmy's mild objections—that he might use this opportunity to state his case.

He moved unsteadily along a traction field to the podium and received the armillary bands of light.

He looked to all sides—and behind—before starting.

"It's not an easy thing talking to one's descendants," he said. "Though . . . I never had children, so I doubt if any of you are even remotely related to me. And of course, there's the matter of different universes. Discussing these things makes me feel like a Stone Age tribesman seeing his first airplane—or spaceship. We are completely out of our element, and while we have been welcomed here, we cannot call this place home. . . ."

He caught Patricia's eye and her brief expression between fear and expectation. Of what?

"But the one place we can call home is now in ruins. This is our tragedy—our mutual tragedy. For you, the history of the Death is remote, but for us it is immediate and very real. We still suffer from our memories, our experiences, and we will grieve for years to come, probably for the rest of our lives." What he needed to say came clear to him then, as if he had been thinking about it for days—and perhaps he had, but not consciously.

"Earth is *our* home—your home, your cradle, as well as my own. It is now a place of death and misery, and it is beyond the power of my friends and colleagues to remedy that. . . .

"But it is not beyond your power. If you would celebrate us, and celebrate our unlikely presence in this chamber, then would it not be appropriate to help us? Earth needs your help desperately. Perhaps we can rewrite history, and correct it.

"Let us go home together," he said, feeling his throat catch.

366

In the first ring of seats, Olmy listened and nodded only once. Just beyond, in the second ring, Oligand Toller, the President's advocate and representative in this session, locked the fingers of his two hands in his lap, his face impassive.

"Let us go home," Lanier repeated. "Your ancestors need you."

Chapter Fifty-six

Pletnev blew out his breath and wiped his red face with a scrap of towel, dropping the ax into a tree stump. A few meters away, a stack of notched logs waited assembly into a cabin. Pletnev had also made a trough for mixing mud to daub into the cracks between the logs, and cleared a site in the woods near the beach.

Beside him, Garabedian and Annenkovsky stood with arms crossed, faces intently surveying the ground.

"Are you saying," Pletnev began, after blowing out again, "that he has changed so much we can no longer rely on him?"

"He isn't concentrating on his command," Annenkovsky said. "He holds us back."

"Holds you back from doing what?"

"For one thing," Annenkovsky continued, "he treats Vielgorsky's followers as if they were merely errant children, and not dangerous subversives."

"Well, perhaps that's wise. There are too few of us to purge willy-nilly."

"That is not the only problem," Annenkovksy said. "He frequently leaves the compound, takes the train and a truck to the library, and just sits there, looking confused. We think his brain is addled."

Pletnev looked to Garabedian. "What do you think, Comrade Major?"

"He is not the same man," Garabedian said. "He himself

admits it. And he keeps claiming he is dead. Resurrected. It isn't . . . appropriate."

"Is he still General Pavel Mirsky?"

"Why ask that? Ask if he is a good leader," Annenkovsky said. "Any of us could do better."

"He's been negotiating with the Americans . . . has he negotiated badly?" Pletnev asked.

"No," Garabedian said. "Smoothly, if anything."

"Then I don't understand what we have to complain about. He'll return to normal. He's had a traumatic experience—and a mysterious one. We can't expect it not to change him some."

Annenkovsky frowned and shook his head. "I disagree that he's negotiated well for us. He's made many concessions he shouldn't have."

"And he's gained concessions very useful to us," Pletnev said. "I know. Because of the agreements, we may be able to move into the cities soon."

"He is no longer in his right mind!" Annenkovsky said heatedly. "He talks about not being the same person—he does not have the . . . the touch a commanding general should have!"

Pletnev looked between the two majors and then glanced up at the plasma tube, squinting. "What would Vielgorsky and Yazykov and Belozersky have done for us? Nothing. Made things worse. Killed all three of us, more than likely. I say, do not trade the devil you know for the devil you don't. Mirsky's a mild sort of devil."

"He's a lamb, not a devil," Garabedian said dubiously. "I regard him as a friend, but . . ."

Pletnev raised his eyebrow in query.

"Well, in a crisis, I do not know how he would behave."

"I think the crises are over," Pletnev said. "Now forget this talk. Go. Do not rock the boat. Let me build my cabin in peace."

Garabedian nodded, stuck his hands in his pockets and turned to walk away. Annenkovsky stayed for a moment, watching Pletnev trim a notch in a log.

"We were thinking of making you our leader," Annenkovsky said quietly. "We would not harm General Mirsky."

"I do not accept," Pletnev said without looking up.

"What if he goes completely crazy?"

"He won't," Pletnev said.

"Where *are* you?" Mirsky shouted for the dozenth time.

He stood in the middle of the array of library seats and data pillars, fists raised in the air. His cheeks were red and wet and his neck was ribbed with anger and frustration.

"Are you dead, like me? Did they execute you?"

Still no answer.

"You murdered me!"

He clenched his jaw and struggled to control his breathing. He knew if he tried to say anything more, the words would come out in mangled fragments. The little signal in his mind— a brief, explanatory warning, *You are now using material not native to your personality,* was about to drive him over the edge. So much of what he thought and did was punctuated by this message. He had explored those boundaries thoroughly— lying in his sling at night, trying to sleep, realizing he did not *need* to sleep.

He had the sensation that much of what he remembered about his life consisted of logical reconstructions. The entire left side of his body felt fresh and new, had a different odor, as it were. He realized it wasn't the body that was new, but the corresponding section of his head.

The first few days, Mirsky had thought all might go well. He believed he could become used to his status as a Lazarus; he made it seem like a joke, that he was back from the dead, this to gently discredit Pogodin's testimony that Vielgorsky had blown Mirsky's brains out. But the joke had not worked.

To the soldiers who had stood guard outside the library, it had seemed as tightly sealed and oppressive as a tomb. And what did you find in a tomb . . . ?

His joke had then become a grim evaluation of reality. Nobody dared flout his rule now; he was a ghost, not the

369

freshly-promoted Colonel suddenly made Lieutenant General, not Pavel Mirsky, but a stranger from the depths of the third chamber city.

Superstition. An incredible force among soldiers.

And so, after a week of rule, of struggling to be what his past demanded he be, he had returned to the library. He had been afraid to come back until now, worried that the three political officers would be there to greet him, shoot him all over again.

Superstition.

He had waited for those inside to leave—first, the Chinese man and woman, and then a single Russian, Corporal Rodhzhensky. Only when the library was empty had he entered.

And he had shouted himself hoarse.

He sat in a chair, hand fumbling at the data pillar controls, lifting the lid and dropping it. Finally, he inserted his fingertips into the five hollows. "Law," he demanded. "Law in a deserted city."

The library asked more questions, narrowing his search to a manageable subject.

"Murder," he said.

The material was rich and detailed. Murder was an offense punishable by psychological evaluation and retailoring of the personality, if such was called for.

"What if there is nobody to carry out the punishment?"

It is not punishment, the research voice said, *it is redemption, a refitting for society.*

"What if there's no law, no police, no judges, or courts or psychologists?"

Suspects can be detained for nineteen days. If that time passes and no judgment is made, or charges specified, suspects are released to the custody of a reintegration counseling clinic.

"And if there's no clinic?"

Suspects are released on their own recognizance.

"Where will they be released?"

Unless otherwise requested, at the scene of their incarceration.

"Where are they taken after capture?"

If they are captured in a structure of adequate size for an emergency medical facility—

He saw a portion of the library, behind a seamless door in the north wall, used as an example: two small, equipment-packed rooms.

—then they are held under sedation until authorities retrieve them or nineteen days have passed. Medical workers serve as police units in emergency.

He had two more days.

Mirsky returned to the fourth chamber and made a pretence of being the commander for a few hours. He met with Hoffman and Rimskaya to continue discussions about opening the second and third chamber city spaces to "settlers."

He then sneaked away, picked up an AKV and returned to the third chamber. Five people were in the library, Rodhzhensky again and four NATO people, one of them a United States Marine. Mirsky patiently waited for them to go, and entered the library with rifle in hand.

He had given the political officers one chance. If they were released, they would only come for him again. He would stay in the library for the next two days, waiting patiently. . . .

The library remained deserted for several hours. In that time, he realized that his plan was uselss. The library would not stay deserted for long. He had to carry out his executions—murders—in secret, or they would be worse than useless. Unless he destroyed the three political officers even more thoroughly than they had destroyed him, they would be resurrected, and he would be incarcerated for nineteen days, and it would all begin again—a cycle of insanity and violence beyond the dreams even of Gogol.

He walked to the wall behind which the three political officers waited, unconscious, and lowered the rifle to the floor at the northern edge of the array of seats, blinking rapidly.

"I'm not the same person you killed," he said. "Why should I take revenge?"

371

Even if he felt that he *was* the same person, this could be an excuse. He could do what he realized he had wanted to do for years. Perhaps the clarity had been brought on by the destruction of some irrational section of his thinking, releasing another impulse, truer and cleaner.

Mirsky had always wanted the stars, but not at the price of his soul. And working within a Soviet system—even one such as he would have tried to establish—would always mean working against people like Belozersky, Yazykov and Vielgorsky. Their faces kept reappearing throughout Russian history: the vicious lackeys and the capable but cruel and slightly askew leader.

He would break from the cycle. He had the chance now. His homeland was gone. His duty was over; he had already died for his men once. Perhaps if Major General Sosnitsky had survived . . . But then, if the Major General were still alive, Mirsky wouldn't be in this position. Sosnitsky would be.

He left the library and rode the train to the fourth chamber fort. There, he gathered supplies into a truck—nobody questioning his intentions, not even Pletnev, who regarded him from some meters away with a look of mild puzzlement.

"They'll be glad to be rid of me," Mirsky thought. "They can get on with their intrigues and cruelties. The political triumvirate will return to take their rightful places. I've been an impediment all along. . . ."

His last duty was to write a message for Garabedian.

Viktor:
The three political officers will return. They will be in the third chamber library sometime within the next forty hours. Accept them as your leaders if you wish; I will no longer impede them.

Pavel

He left the message in an envelope in Garabedian's tent.

Mirsky drove the truck into the woods, heading for the as-yet-unexplored 180 point. There he could be alone, perhaps

372

build a raft and pole across a shallow lake to a tree-covered island, or just explore the thick woods visible fifty kilometers directly overhead.

And he would decide what to do next.

He did not think he would return.

Chapter Fifty-seven

The flawship's interior, crowded with privileged citizens and dignitaries, was even more free-form than Olmy's craft. The surfaces varied from oyster pearl to abalone gray, and there seemed to be no edge or corner; only one spacious, long cabin, wrapped around the three-meter-wide flaw passage and propulsion machinery. People of a bewildering variety of body styles tracted from point to point in the cabin, exchanging picts or conversing in English or Chinese. Some sipped drinks from free-floating charged globules of fluid, which somehow managed to avoid passersby with both grace and anticipatory intelligence.

Lanier had barely gotten the hang of maneuvering with the traction fields. Farley seemed more adept—a natural gymnast, which caused him some chagrin. He applied himself more diligently to learning the skill. "This is lovely," she confessed, spinning slowly next to him, then reaching out and braking against the gently glowing violet sheet of a field.

Heineman and Carrolson helped each other along between the homorphs and neomorphs, smiling stiffly and nodding, hoping that—as Olmy had told them—they would find it almost impossible to do something socially unacceptable. Anything they did, any mistake they made, would be considered charming. They were, after all, "quaint."

Patricia tried to keep to herself, clutching her bag containing slate, processor and multi-meter. She was not in the least successful at being inconspicuous.

Suli Ram Kikura tracted toward Patricia and intercepted the

373

rapid pictings of a man whose skin had the sheen of black hematite. The man apologized in a few simple picts for his assumption that Patricia knew the highest degrees of graphic-speak. Then, in moderately accomplished English—no doubt picked up in a quick gloss a few minutes before boarding—he launched into a complicated discussion of early terrestrial economics. Kikura had wandered off to smooth over another complication—Lanier was being determinedly, if slowly, pushed into a broad dimple by two lean and striking women. The women were dressed in full-length leotards with long, alternately stiff and supple fantails of fabric stretched between their legs and under their arms. They resembled fancy goldfish; there was little he or Farley could do to discourage them.

Patricia listened to the man's discourse for several minutes before saying, "I'm pretty ignorant about that. My specialty is physics."

The man stared at her and she could almost hear him switching over to a recently programmed portion of his implant. "Yes, that's fascinating. So much of physics was in ferment in your time—"

Olmy moved in quickly and picted something Patricia did not understand. The man moved away resentfully, a thin circle of red around his face.

"Perhaps this wasn't such a good idea," Olmy said, escorting her to where the Frant was engaged in conversation with two neomorphs, one a radiolarian, the other recognizable as the Director of the Nexus, Hulane Ram Seija.

"I suppose we have to get used to it," Patricia said. *Why get used to it?* she asked herself. She didn't plan on staying forever.

"Ser Ram Seija," the Frant said, turning toward her, "here is our first guest." The Frant's wide-extended eyes seemed to naturally convey humor and good spirits. Though she found the word *guest* euphemistic, at best, she did not resent the Frant's using it.

"I've been looking forward to a chance to talk with you,

374

someplace out of chambers," Ram Seija said. "Though this hardly seems the best time . . ."

Patricia focused on his face, projected at mid-level on the sphere that was his body. She had a distinct impression she was on a ride in Disneyland, seeing something extraordinary with a perfectly mundane explanation. She didn't answer for some time, and then snapped herself out of her reverie, saying, "Yes, certainly."

"You'll enjoy Timbl, our world," the Frant said. "We've been long-time clients of the Hexamon. It's a very tame gate, long established."

"We'll go there first," Ram Seija said. "A journey of four hours to the Frant gate at four ex six, and then a leisurely two-day rest stop. We're hoping the President can break away from his conference to meet us."

Four ex six—four million kilometers down the corridor— merely a hop, skip and jump, she thought. And for every thousand kilometers, an advance of one year in time; for every fraction of a millimeter, entry into an alternate universe . . .

How much closer to home?

"I look forward to meeting it—him, and to visiting Timbl," she said, acquiescing to the spirit of the occasion.

"We're requested at the bow," Lanier said, brushing by with Farley. Heineman and Carrolson were already on their way. The crowds parted before them; she had never seen so many smiling faces, or felt so much interest in her person. She hated it. She wanted to run and hide.

Feeling through her jumpsuit for the letter from Paul, finding it and pressing it, she followed the Frant and Olmy toward the bow of the flawship.

Senator Oyu was there, with three Naderite homorphs from Axis Thoreau, all historians. They smiled and made room for the five. The flawship captain, a neomorph with a masculine human trunk and a serpentine body from the waist down, fully three meters in length, joined them last.

"The honor for starting our short journey goes to the first guest to arrive at the Axis City," the captain said. Patricia took his hand and tracted into position at the bow, near the flaw passage. "Miss Vasquez, would you like to do the honors? Simply ask the flawship to begin."

"Let's go," Patricia said softly.

A sharp-edged circle about five meters in diameter cleared to one side of the flaw passage, offering them a view of the Way. They seemed to float high above the lanes of traffic and the gate terminals. The ineffably glistening line of the singularity glowed hot pink just beyond the bow; for the moment, there was no sensation of motion.

Patricia turned to look back at Olmy, Lanier and Farley. Lanier smiled at her; she smiled back. Despite everything, this was kind of exciting. She felt like an indulged and pampered child, visiting a party of very peculiar adults.

We're the larvae, they're the butterflies, she thought.

Within a half hour, the flawship was moving so rapidly— just over 104 kilometers per second—that the walls of the Way became a slick blur of black and gold. They had already traveled some 94,000 kilometers and were still accelerating. Ahead, the flaw pulsed deep red. Patricia felt Farley's hand on her shoulder.

"It's amazing how much this is like a party on Earth," Farley said. "Not in Hopeh, but in Los Angeles or Tokyo. I went through Tokyo to get to Los Angeles, and then on to Florida. . . . There were quite a few receptions. The embassy party . . ." She shook her head and grinned. "Where the hell—what the hell are we, Patricia? I am very confused."

"They're people, just like us," Patricia said.

"I just don't—can't always believe what's happening. Inside, I go back to when I was a little girl in Hopeh, listening to my father teach. I escape."

Bringing Ramon Tiempos de Los Angeles *to read* . . .

"All parties get boring after a while. I'd rather be working," Patricia said, "but that wouldn't be sociable. Olmy wants us to be sociable."

Suli Ram Kikura approached them, looking concerned.

"Has anybody offended you?" she asked. "Or made improper offers?"

"No," Farley said. "Patricia and I are just watching."

"Of course . . . you're getting tired. Even Olmy forgets these necessities—sleep and rest."

"I'm not tired," Patricia said. "I'm very alert, in fact."

"I, as well," Farley agreed. "Perhaps 'dazed' is a better word."

"You may seclude yourselves any time you wish," Ram Kikura said.

"We'll just stay in the bow and watch," Patricia said. She floated with legs crossed in a lotus, and Farley did likewise.

"We're fine," Farley said to the advocate. "We'll rejoin everybody shortly."

Ram Kikura tracted aft to a group of neomorphs challenging each other with complex puzzle-picts.

"It's not a bad place to be," Farley offered after a few minutes of silence. "These people aren't cruel."

"Oh, no," Patricia said, shaking her head. "Olmy is helpful, and I like Kikura."

"Before we left, she was talking to Garry and me about our rights in selling historical information. Or exchanging for advantage, she called it. Apparently we can access all sorts of valuable private data banks for what we have in our memories."

"So I've heard," Patricia said.

After an hour, Patricia, Heineman and Carrolson secluded themselves at the rear of the cabin. The Frant fended off the curious as they napped. Lanier and Farley were too wired to relax; they remained at the bow, watching the corridor race by. At the midpoint of their journey, after accelerating at just under six g's, the flawship was traveling some 416 kilometers per second; it then began to decelerate.

In another two hours, the flawship had slowed to what seemed a crawl, only a few dozen kilometers an hour. Below, many of the broad silver-gray disks flew majestically above the lanes. Four large twisted-pyramid structures were discernible in the distance: the terminals covering the four gates to Timbl.

Two homorphs joined them—slightly more radical models of Olmy's ilk, self-contained and largely artificial. They were dressed in blue-and-white body-suits that ballooned dramatically around the calves and forearms; one was female, though her hair was cut much like Olmy's, and the other was indeterminate. They smiled at Patricia and Farley and exchanged simple picts. Patricia touched her torque and replied; Farley flubbed her answer and made them laugh goodnaturedly. The indeterminate one stepped forward, a Chinese flag suddenly picted above the left shoulder.

"We have not met," it began. "I am Sama Ula Rixor, special assistant to the President. My ancestors were Chinese. We have been discussing morphology of those times. Miss Farley, you are rare, are you not? You are Chinese, yet you have Caucasian features. Is it that you have had . . . what they called cosmetic surgery, available even then?"

"No . . ." Farley said with some embarrassment. "I was born in China," she said, "But my parents were Caucasian—"

Patricia tracted away from the stern, toward Lanier, Carrolson and Heineman. Ram Kikura glided up to them and indicated they would be leaving the flawship soon; a VIP disk shuttle was already leaving the gate terminal to take them aboard.

Heineman was questioning Olmy about the identity of the Frant that had accompanied them, suspicious that it might have changed places with one of the nine other Frants riding with them. "It looks different. Are you sure it's the same Frant?"

"They all look alike when they're mature," Olmy said. "Why does it matter?"

"I just want to know where I stand with somebody," Heineman responded, reddening.

"It's really not important," Olmy said. "Once they've

homogenized and passed current memory to each other, one can take up where the other leaves off.''

Heineman wasn't convinced, but he decided it wasn't worth pursuing.

The VIP transportation disk was as wide as the flawship was long. It ascended to within thirty meters of the axis, surface crawling with glowing sheets of charge picked up in the plasma field. The glow slipped away from the disk's upper surface like phosphorescent sea foam, and a circular opening appeared in the center.

The flawship's hatches opened then, and the guests leaped out through the connecting fields in orderly pairs and triplets, hanging on to each other, tracting to the opening in the disk. Olmy took hold of Farley and Lanier and Lanier held Patricia; Ram Kikura took Carrolson's and Heineman's hands. Together, they flew with the rest of the group.

The disk was little more than an enlarged version of the cupolas that had covered the gates just beyond the seventh chamber; except for a webwork of glowing lines, it had no visible lower half, and to Heineman's consternation, no platform or support to rest on. The party simply floated in the space immediately beneath, suspended in an invisible and all-enveloping traction field which was in turn shot through with smaller visible fields. All that separated them from the vacuum—all that lay between them and the walls of the Way, twenty-five kilometers below—was a barrier of subtle energies.

Lanier saw several homorph and many more neomorph pilots and workers at the edges of the disk, segregated from the entourage. He watched a spindle-shaped neomorph weaving its way through purple traction sheets, followed by boxes from another section of the flawship. On the opposite side, the eight Frants also waited to disembark. Their own Frant had returned to its fellows and had already homogenized with them, rendering Heineman's question academic.

Lanier reached out for a tenuous purple traction line and twisted around to look at Heineman.

"How're you feeling?" he asked.

"Lousy," Heineman said.

"He's a sissy," Carrolson said, a little pale herself.

"You should love this," Lanier chided him. "You've always been in love with machinery."

"Yeah, machines!" Heineman growled. "Show me any machines! Everything works without moving parts. It's unnatural."

The disk began its descent as they spoke. The clusters of passengers excitedly exchanged picts; Patricia floated with arms and legs spread, one hand grasping the same traction line as Lanier.

She stared down at the terminal, watching the disks enter and exit ports near the base from four directions. Many more disks waited in stacks like so many pancakes, or fanned out in spirals within a holding column.

The disk descended slowly, giving them plenty of time to inspect the wall traffic around the terminal. Most of the lanes were filled with the cylindrical container-vehicles of many diverse shapes—spheres, eggs, pyramids and some of a blobby appearance, composed of many complex curves. Lanier tried to make sense out of it all, using what the data pillar had taught them, but couldn't—there was apparent order, but no easily discerned purpose. Patricia tracted in his direction.

"Do you understand all that we're seeing?" he asked her.

She shook her head. "Not all."

Ram Kikura broke from a cluster of brightly dressed homorphs and came their way. "We'll pass through the gate in just a few minutes," she said. "You must know, if Olmy and the Nexus allow it, that I can make you very wealthy people."

"Wealth still means that much?" Carrolson asked dubiously.

"Information does," Ram Kikura replied. "And I've already picted with four or five powerful information distributors."

"Send us on tour like circus freaks," Heineman grumbled.

"Oh, give me some credit, Larry," Ram Kikura said, touching his shoulder. "You won't be abused. I wouldn't stand for it, and even if I turned out to be—what did you call them?—a *scheister*, Olmy would protect you. You know that."

"Do we?" Heineman undertoned as she departed.

"Don't be a grouch," Carrolson scolded.

"I'm being on my guard," Heineman said testily. "When in Rome, watch out for public restrooms."

Lanier laughed, then shook his head. "Hell, I don't even know what he means," he confided to Patricia. "But I admire his caution."

The disk was now level with a broad, low port in the eastern side of the terminal. The surface of the building was coated by a material resembling opalescent milk glass, with bands of brassy orange metal spaced at seemingly random intervals on the horizontal planes.

"It's beautiful," Farley said. Patricia agreed and then felt her eyes grow warm and moist; she couldn't be sure why. Her throat clutched and she wiped her cheeks as drops broke free.

"What's wrong?" Lanier said, edging closer to her.

"It *is* beautiful," she said, stifling a sob. Involuntarily, Lanier felt his own eyes moistening.

"We can't forget them, can we?" he asked. "Wherever we go, whatever we see—they're with us. All four billion of them."

She nodded rapidly. Olmy came up behind them and held an archaic and unexpected handkerchief over her shoulder. She took it, surprised, and thanked him.

"If you keep this up," he warned in a whisper, "you might be surrounded in a few minutes. We are not used to seeing people cry."

"Jesus," Carrolson said.

"Don't judge us on that basis," Olmy said. "Our people feel as strongly, but we differ in how we express ourselves."

"I'm fine," Patricia said, dabbing ineffectually at her eyes. "You carried this just in case we . . . ?"

Olmy smiled. "For emergencies."

Lanier took the handkerchief and finished wiping her face for her, then waved the cloth through the air to catch a few stray drops. "Thank you," he said, returning it to Olmy.

"Not at all."

They entered the terminal. Within the hollow structure, beams of light outlined paths for vehicles to take. In the center, still perhaps a kilometer below them, was the gate itself—a vast, smooth-lipped hole leading into a featureless blueness.

"This is our second biggest gate, five kilometers in diameter," Olmy said. "The largest is seven kilometers wide and leads to the Talsit world at one point three ex seven."

"We're going down—through this one?" Heineman asked. The disk was already resuming its descent.

"Yes. There's no danger."

"Except to my mental health," Heineman said. "Garry, I wish I'd been a house painter."

They were directly over the gate now, but no detail was visible beyond the blueness. Five smaller disks moved in a squadron below, clearing a path for them. At the rim of the gate, hundreds of cylinders and other vehicles cascaded from the lanes in majestic, controlled fall.

Light guidelines rearranged to surround their disk in a column. When they had descended to a point where they were approximately level with the edge of the gate, Lanier suddenly made out details in the bottom, directly beneath. The Frant world was actually visible in the blueness, as if distorted in an old painting-on-a-cylinder that could only be seen when placed on a circular mirror. He could make out oceans, distant mountains black against an ultramarine sky, the elongated and brilliant orb of a sun.

"Jesus," Carrolson said again. "Look at it."

"I wish I wasn't," Heineman said. "Do you think Olmy has any Dramamine?"

The floating clusters of homorphs and neomorphs picted bright circles and bursts of color in appreciation. The disk vibrated, and the landscape slid smoothly into proper perspective. The guiding column of light beams vanished and they completed their gate passage, suddenly sweeping low over a dazzling white surface.

Lanier, Carrolson and Patricia tracted to a lower point of the disk, near the boundary of the webwork lines of force, so that they could see the horizon of the Frant world. To each side, lines of cylinders and other vehicles were spaced between hovering disks disgorging cargo. Lanier turned full circle, surveying the mountains and sea beyond the white-paved gate reception area. He had never seen a sky so intensely blue.

Like a blowtorch describing an arc in the sky, a meteor plummeted toward the distant sea's surface. Before it struck, a web of pulsed orange rays lanced out from the horizon and shattered the meteor. More beams sought out and destroyed the crazily weaving fragments. Only dust remained to hit the ocean or land.

"That's the story of their life, in a nutshell," Ram Kikura said, pointing to where the meteor had met its end. "That's why the Frants are Frants." She took Lanier's hand and then reached for Patricia. Olmy gathered the other three around them. "Come. We'll disembark soon. It's a bit heavier here; you'll need belts at first."

The disk came to its assigned landing area. The transparent fields beneath them rearranged as they approached the white pavement, and the webwork of bright lines reformed into a vortex.

"The President's advocate and the Director of the Nexus will go down first," Ram Kikura said. "We follow, and then the Frants, and then the rest."

Oligand Toller, Hulane Ram Seija and their aides—two fish-shaped neomorphs and three homomorphs—drifted toward the center of the vortex and were smoothly deposited on the pavement beneath the disk. Olmy urged his group down, and they tracted along the same path, feet touching ground a few meters from the President's party.

After months in Thistledown and the Way, Timbl's pull was something of a shock, like suddenly being saddled with heavy bricks. Patricia's knees sagged and her leg muscles protested. Heineman groaned and Carrolson's face looked strained.

Bus-sized, square, low-slung vehicles rolled up on large white wheels. As each person entered, Frants wrapped lift belts around them to lessen the effect of the heavier gravitation. Neomorphs, practically helpless without traction fields, were given special full-float belts that could be adjusted to fit their wide range of shapes.

"You should enjoy this," Ram Kikura told them as the bus rolled off the white pavement onto a broad, brick-colored road. "We're going to the beach."

The Frant world, she explained, served as a resort for humans and several other oxygen-breathing beings in the Way. Because the level of ultraviolet from the bright yellow-dwarf star was higher than humans were used to, an atmospheric shield had been erected over several thousand square kilometers. The resort lay in the shield's shadow.

"The ocean has few large carnivorous life forms—none that would want to eat humans, anyway—and the environment is clean. It's ideal. The vacation spot of choice for all who can afford to go—which is virtually any corporeal citizen."

The resort's long, low main building was in an ideal location, fronting a broad white quartz-sand beach on one side of a half-moon harbor. Each room had a patio and transparent doors with a choice of undisguised real scenery or various illusart displays. The furniture, in keeping with the Old Terrestrial motif of the resort, was real and unchangeable.

They ate lunch, their first meal on the Frant world, in a restaurant decorated in late-twentieth-century style, the food served by homorphs. Mechanical workers were not in evidence. After lunch, they walked to the resort buildings and Ram Kikura inspected their rooms carefully before letting them enter. They still wore their belts, though Lanier felt he was up to doing without. He would only remove his when Heineman did, however, and Heineman seemed content to leave it on.

Patricia looked around her room, then joined the others on

Lanier's patio. Ram Kikura told them they could rest and swim for a few hours, and that she and Olmy would be nearby if they were needed. "They're taking a room for themselves upstairs," Carrolson said in a confidential tone after she had left. "I think they're lovers."

Patricia opened the patio's metal gate. "I'm going to take a walk," she said. She glanced at Lanier. "Unless you think we should stick together all the time."

"No, We're probably safe enough here. Go ahead."

Lanier watched her walk down the beach, stiff-legging through the sand past homorphs and even a few belted neomorphs. Nobody paid her much attention. He shook his head, smiling. "Could be Acapulco," he said, "with a few odd balloons drifting around."

Farley put her arm around him. "I've never been to Acapulco, but I don't think it had a sky that color."

"Lovebirds," Carrolson sniffed, glanced reproachfully at Heineman. "You never treat me that way."

"I'm an engineer," Heineman said. "I don't pamper, I just make things run right."

"You do indeed," Carrolson said.

"My God, listen to us, we're cheerful," Lanier said.

"Patricia isn't," Carrolson said. "I've seen her putting on her stern look when she sees you two. I think she's jealous, Garry."

"Christ." Lanier sat down in a patio chair and stared across the dazzling beach and intense green-blue sea to the knife-sharp horizon. "She's been an enigma since I first met her."

"Not to me," Farley said. All faces turned to her. "I understand her at least a little," she continued. "I was like her—less brilliant, but inner-directed. Stubborn. My life was miserable until I was twenty-five or twenty-six, and I decided to be more normal—exterior normal, anyway."

"She'll be twenty-four tomorrow," Carrolson said.

"That's her birthday?" Farley asked.

Carrolson nodded. "I've told Olmy and explained about birthday parties. He thinks it's a good idea. Apparently they

385

don't have birthdays here—so few people are actually born, biologically speaking. There are naming days, maturity celebrations—mostly in Axis Nader. I gather that age doesn't mean as much to them as it does to us."

"So what kind of party will it be?"

"I suggested we keep it small—ourselves, Olmy, Ram Kikura. He agreed."

"Lenore, you're a marvel," Lanier said, unconsciously adopting Hoffman's tone of voice. Carrolson curtsied and dimpled her cheeks with her twisting index fingers.

"We're more than cheerful," Heineman said, staring at her. "We're absolutely nuts."

Patricia had gone about half a kilometer down the beach when she saw Oligand Toller standing on the sand ahead of her. He wore shorts, revealing blond-haired, well-shaped legs slightly bowed, and a loud Hawaiian-print shirt. "Do you like it?" he asked, modeling for her.

She gawped, not knowing what to say.

"Well, I tried," he said, seeming chagrined. "I'd like to talk with you, if you don't mind."

"I'm not sure—" she said.

"It might be important. For all of you."

She stood her ground, head bowed slightly, staring up at him, but said nothing.

"We can keep on walking," Toller said. "I'd like to explain some things before you meet with the President—if he can make time for us."

"Let's talk, then," she said, walking past him. He took two running strides to catch up with her.

"We're not your enemies, Patricia," Toller admonished. "Whatever Olmy may have told you—"

"Olmy's said nothing against anybody," Patricia said. "This is just my way," she said. "We're—I'm not very happy these days, for obvious reasons."

"Most understandable," the advocate said, keeping pace with her. None of the other bathers or floating neomorphs seemed to find it unusual for the President's advocate and a woman from centuries in their past to be walking together. They were casually ignored. "I find the resort here wonderful—I come often. Reminds me of what it is to be human . . . do you understand?"

"To see things that are real," Patricia said.

"Yes. And to get away from the problems for a while. Well, this is obviously a working vacation, and brief at that—we can't stay more than two local days. But we thought it worthwhile to show you how our system works. We are trying to enlist your support—Patricia? May I call you that?"

She nodded.

"Because of the way things have worked out, you people can be very influential. We won't force you into our ways or opinions—that's not how our government works. Modeled on your own, after all."

They stopped at a natural basalt breakwater pointing out to sea. Patricia turned and saw a small, bright meteor pass across a few degrees of the horizon. No beams reached out to destroy it—it was small enough to disintegrate harmlessly on its own.

"We helped the Frants install their Sky Lance," Toller said. "When we opened the gate, they were still in the early atomic age. We arranged for some exchanges of information, set up a client-patron relationship and gave them what they needed to protect their world against the millennial comet sweeps."

"What did you get in return?"

"Oh, they received much more than Sky Lance for what they gave. We opened the Way to them. They're full partners in three gates now, commerce with three worlds and the normal-space trading systems around them. In return, they leased raw material and information rights to us. But the most valuable commodity they contribute is themselves. You met Olmy's partner. We find them ideal to work with—resourceful, reliable, unfailingly pleasant. And as far as anyone can tell, they genuinely enjoy working with us."

"Makes them sound like good pets," Patricia said.

"Yes, there is that aspect," Toller admitted. "But they're at

least as intelligent as we are—unsupplemented, of course—
and nobody treats them as if they were second-class citizens,
or pets. You may have to drop some of your past prejudices to
see our situation clearly, Patricia."

"My prejudices are dropped," she said. "I'm just being . . ." She raised her hands and shook her head. Not once
since their meeting had she looked directly at Toller's face.

"Before we came, every thousand years, Timbl would pass
through a sweep of old comets. They'd regularly lose more
than half their population. All this ocean is cometary water—
gathered across billions of years. Apparently, there was a long
lull about a million years ago, and in that time the Frants
evolved to their current form and built up basic cultures. Then
the sweeps began again. Gradually, the individual Frants
became more and more alike, passing information and
personality traits on through chemical messengers, then
through cultural means. They became a holographic society,
the better to absorb the shock of the sweeps. But they had
never realized their potential, and weren't about to, until our
gate was opened. Now they have some of our own technologies—using high-speed pictors to update each other, or
even exchanging partial personalities. All in all, I'm not sure
who was the more lucky—the Frants, or ourselves. We might
have lost to the Jarts centuries ago if the Frants hadn't helped
us."

Patricia listened intently, filling in what she hadn't had time
to research in the data service. "Why can't you establish some
sort of client-patron relationship with the Jarts?" she asked.

"Ah! The Jarts are quite another story. You know, of course,
that we found them occupying the Way when we first
connected it to the seventh chamber."

"So I've heard," she said, remembering what the rogue had
told her.

"The Engineer had the misfortune of opening an experimental gate on the Jart home world. Time in the Way was not
yet matched with our own time. They were able to spend about
three centuries in the incomplete Way, making it their home,

388

even learning to open crude gates. When the Way was connected and opened, there they were—much as they are today. Strong, intelligent, aggressive, absolutely convinced they're destined to populate all universes. We fought a violent war with them and pushed them back in the first decades. Then we opened selected gates and filled the first segment of the Way—down to one ex five—with soil and air. All the time we were building the Axis City, we fought skirmishes with them, pushing them back farther and farther, closing their gates. Finally, they retreated to two ex nine, and we established a barrier at that point. We tried reasoning, making exchanges. They wouldn't have it. We knew we couldn't rid the Way of them—we weren't strong enough."

Patricia sat on the lowest step of a stairway leading to the top of the breakwater. "And how can we help you?"

"That's a complicated question, actually," Toller said. "You can best help us by supporting us. Or—by not opposing us."

"You can all go home now," Patricia said. "Such as it is."

Toller paused for a moment, puzzled by the abruptness of her leap of ideas. "Exactly." He sat beside her, and she edged a few centimeters away. "Such as it is. Personally, despite Ser Lanier's most heartfelt plea, I see little reason to return to Earth now."

"You could help the survivors."

"Patricia, *they*—you—become *us*. I see nothing iniquitous with letting a world heal itself. The fact that we've made a causal loop—that we can return to the worst point in our world-line—is not what I would consider an opportunity. At the moment, it's a handicap. Has Olmy explained how we hope to push the Jarts from the Way? For good?"

She shook her head.

"It's an ambitious plan. You've heard rumors about secession—having the Axis City divide in two?"

She decided to play dumb and shook her head again.

"Our flaw research group discovered, years ago, that the Axis City could be accelerated to near c—to near light-speed. There would be no damage to the city itself, and the citizens would experience only minor discomfort—"

"I think we should all hear about this," Patricia decided suddenly, standing up. "I mean, all of my group. Not just me."

"They can learn as much as they want. You can guide them when they get back to the Axis City—it's all available in City Memory. Or Olmy can explain it to you."

"Why hasn't he told us already?"

"Patricia, our world is extremely complex, as you know perhaps better than I. I doubt Olmy has had the opportunity to educate you on a thousandth of the more important things there are to know about us."

"Okay," Patricia said, stepping onto the sand and facing Toller. "I'm listening."

"It would take over a day to approach that velocity, accelerating at about three hundred g's—which is very close to the theoretical limit for the inertial damping systems, and for something as large as the Axis City, traveling on the flaw. The flaw would be seriously stressed, producing hard radiation and heavy particles. . . . But within the Way, even a velocity of one-third light-speed would create a space-time shock wave. We would reach that velocity at about one point seven ex nine. We would pass through the territories held by the Jarts with devastating effect. The relativistic distortions within the Way would be incredible. The shape of the Way itself would be altered as we passed, and whatever gates the Jarts have opened would be *smoothed* out of existence"—he slid his hand in a flat-out gesture—"like ironing a piece of fabric in one of your world's laundries."

Patricia's eyes became distant. Her mind was racing now to absorb the idea of a relativistic object within the Way—and the realization that within the Way, an object traveling at only one-third c would be relativistic.

"A grand scheme, don't you think?"

She nodded abstractedly. "How far would you travel down the Way?"

"That's still being debated."

"And what are the alternatives?"

"The conference is considering the alternatives even now—and have been for over three weeks. We believe the Jarts will break though our barriers in a matter of years, perhaps months. They'll overrun our most extended gates—we'll shut them down and withdraw, of course—and eventually, by the end of the decade, they'll push us back into the Thistledown. We'll have to evacuate, and to keep them from following us, we'll have to destroy the Way. That would be an incredible calamity."

"You're certain about this?"

Toller nodded once. "We cannot hold them for long. They've grown quite strong, and they've enlisted the help of other worlds—by opening gates all up and down their segment of the Way."

"Couldn't you do the same?"

"As I said, they've occupied the Way for several centuries longer than we have. They're more familiar with it, in some ways, than we are, even though we created it."

Toller wasn't telling her about one of the alternatives the rogue had mentioned—blowing the Thistledown from the end of the Way and "cauterizing" it, sealing it closed so it would continue to exist, independently of the sixth chamber machinery. She decided not to ask him about that possibility. "It's fascinating," she said. "Gives me a lot to think about."

"Yes, well, I'm sure I've violated all the rules of etiquette, Patricia. You've been very kind to listen to me. Our time is quite limited, as you see, and you've brought an additional element into the equation. . . ."

"I'm sure we have," Patricia said. *Perhaps more than you know* . . . "I'd like to walk back now."

"Certainly. I'll accompany you."

She smiled at him, eyes still distant. Toller said very little as they retraced their steps up the beach to the resort buildings, and that suited Patricia.

She was already slipping into the state, her mind working, conjuring up her personal notation. Passing quickly through Lanier's room, she made a few excuses and retired to her own quarters, lying down on the bed and closing her eyes tightly.

Toller greeted the others and spoke with them for several minutes, explaining he had had a good conversation with Patricia concerning subjects of importance to all of them. After he left, Lanier knocked on Patricia's door, and received no answer.

"Patricia?" he called.

"Yes," she said softly, scrunching up her face.

"Are you all right?"

"I'm resting," she said. "I'll join you for dinner."

He looked at his watch; their second meal on the Frant World, ostensibly supper, would begin in an hour. He returned to his room.

"How is she?" Carrolson asked.

"Fine, she says. She's napping."

"Not likely," Farley said. "I wonder what Toller told her?"

Chapter Fifty-eight

The meeting between the three men who had taken Mirsky's mantle of authority began and ended in half an hour. It was held in Pletnev's private cabin, with Annenkovsky standing guard outside to make sure nobody listened in.

The topic was Mirsky's message to Garabedian. The solution to the problem they now faced, Pletnev insisted, was simple.

At first, Garabedian and Pogodin were hesitant. Pletnev had insisted they had no other choice, however. "Look, they tried to kill Mirsky, and they were locked away," he said. "Now they'll be released. Isn't it obvious? It's what the American woman thought. It makes sense to me."

"So what do we do?"

Pletnev hefted his Kalashnikov. Most of the laser weapons had long since run out of charge, and besides, he had always preferred bullets.

"Won't we be locked up?" Garabedian asked.

"Was anyone locked up after all the fighting?" Pletnev asked. Pogodin shook his head.

"Then we'll just kill them away from the city."

"I don't like the idea of killing them without a trial."

"We don't have any choice," Pletnev said. "Shit, Mirsky left *you* the message, but *I'm* the one who understands what he was really saying. Vielgorsky still has his supporters. Without Mirsky, the three of us can rule reasonably, but if the *Zampolit*s return, we'll all be shot. We meet them, and we do what we must. Agreed?"

Pogodin and Garabedian agreed.

"Then let's go," Pletnev said. "We'll wait them out. Better to be early than to miss them."

Mirsky had abandoned the truck on the water's edge and walked inland with his backpack filled with dry rations. Fingerlakes were plentiful in this area of the fourth chamber, and the fishing everywhere was excellent. He had little doubt he could survive. These forests were not meant to be harsh environments. In the regions where it snowed—roughly one-fourth of the chamber, in an area whose outer boundary was the 180 line—the snow was light, and it rained just often enough all over to maintain the chamber's plant life.

He would hardly be "roughing it."

The first few days he had spent peacefully, doing little besides making an adequate fishing pole. He had read the American biologist's reports on the fourth chamber and knew there would be earthworms and grubs to use as bait. His anxiety tapered off, and he wondered why he hadn't bothered to leave sooner.

393

He seldom encountered the boundary markers of his new mentality now. Either they were fading with use, or he had learned to ignore them.

On his fifth day in the 180 woods, he found signs that he was not alone. A Russian ration packet and an American plastic container revealed that one or more Russian soldiers had found their way here. The discovery didn't bother him. There was room enough for virtually everybody, and in privacy besides.

On the seventh day, he met a Russian at the edge of a grassy clearing. He did not recognize him, but the soldier knew Mirsky and quickly faded back into the woods.

On the eighth day, they saw each other again across a narrow lake, and the soldier did not run away.

"You're alone, aren't you?" the soldier asked.

"Until now," Mirsky said.

"But you're the commander," the soldier said resentfully.

"No more," Mirsky said. "What's the fishing like here?"

"Not so good. You notice there are mosquitos and flies everywhere, but they don't bite?"

"Yes, I've noticed."

"I wonder why?"

"Good design," Mirsky suggested.

"I wonder if it ever snows."

"I think it does, once every year or so," Mirsky said. "But it doesn't get very cold. Not like Moscow."

"I would like for it to snow," the soldier said. Mirsky agreed, and they met at one end of the lake and walked through the woods together, in search of a better fishing spot.

"The Americans would say we were Huckleberry Finn and Tom Sawyer," the soldier observed as they dipped their threadlines into a stream. "You know, the Americans aren't as bad as they were on Earth. I thought about defecting before I decided to leave for the woods."

"Why didn't you?" Mirsky asked.

"I didn't want to be around anybody. But I'm not sorry you're here, General." The soldier bobbed the tip of his pole, hoping to entice a trout. "Restores my faith in humanity. Even a general wants to get away from it all."

The soldier, who never told Mirsky his name, had left the compound weeks ago, before Mirsky's death in the library. He knew nothing of what had happened, and Mirsky did not tell him.

He was beginning to feel like a normal human being again and not a freak or a ghost. Having the time to sit and admire a drop of water on a leaf, or the way water rippled outward from a fish rising for an insect, was wonderful. It no longer mattered *who* he was, simply *that* he was.

Two more days passed, and Mirsky began to wonder if anybody would come searching for them. High-power telescopes could spot them easily, and with infrared sensors, it wouldn't matter whether they were hidden under trees or not. By now, he suspected, the *Zampolit*s were free again, consolidating their position of power—if Pletnev and the others hadn't acted on his warning.

He was only faintly curious about what had happened.

What he missed most of all was night. He would have given anything to spend a few hours in pitch darkness, to be able to close his eyes and see nothing, not even the faint brown glow of shadowy forest light through his eyelids. He also missed the stars and moon.

"Do you think anybody we know on Earth is alive?" the soldier asked one morning as they cooked trout in a flat press of stripped branches over a small fire.

"No," Mirsky said.

The soldier bobbed his head, and then shook it in wonder. "You think not?"

"It's not very probable," Mirsky said.

"Not even in the high command?"

"Maybe. But I never really knew any of them."

"Mmm," the soldier said. Then, as if it was relevant, he said, "You knew Sosnitsky."

"Not really."

"He was a good man, I think," the soldier said, removing

the trout and filleting it expertly with his shroud-cutting knife. He handed half to Mirsky and threw the head and bones into the bushes.

Mirsky nodded and ate his fish, skin and all, chewing thoughtfully until he spotted a silvery glint in the trees behind the soldier. His chewing stopped. The soldier saw him staring and turned his head.

A long metal object floated between the trees and stopped a few meters away. Mirsky's eyes widened; it resembled a chromium Russian Orthodox barred cross, with a heavy teardrop on its lower extremity. At the junction of the angled bar and the horizontal post of the cross was an intense glowing red spot.

The soldier stood. "Is it American?" he asked.

"I don't think so," Mirsky said, also standing.

"Gentlemen," a female voice said, speaking English. "Do not be alarmed. We intend you no hurt. Our detectors tell us there is a corporeal individual here who has undergone supplementary surgery."

"It *is* American," the soldier said, backing away and preparing to run.

"What are you?" Mirsky asked, also in English.

"You are the one who has received supplementary surgery?"

"I think so," Mirsky said. "Yes."

The soldier made a peculiar grunt deep in his throat and crashed off through the trees.

"I'm the one, don't bother about him."

A woman dressed in black walked slowly between the trees. Mirsky thought for a moment that she had to be American, because of the uniform—but he noticed the style was quite different. And her hair—shorn to fuzz at the sides, with a sweep of crown hair cascading behind her head—was certainly not American. It took him some seconds to see she had no nostrils, and her ears were small and round. She stood beside the chromium cross and held up her hand.

"You're not a citizen of the Axis City, are you?" she asked. "Not an Orthodox Naderite?"

"No," Mirsky said. "I'm a Russian. Who are you?"

She touched the bar of the cross and flashes of light passed through the air between them. "Will you accompany me? We are gathering all the occupants of these chambers. No harm will come to you."

"Do I have any choice?" he asked, still calm. Could a man who had died once already feel any fear?

"I'm sorry, no," the woman said, smiling pleasantly.

Judith Hoffman had just completed a marathon nine-hour session on the restructuring of the legal system for the NATO personnel on the Stone. Beryl Wallace had insisted she return to the women's bungalow afterward. Hoffman had fallen asleep in her room immediately, so exhausted that it took her some time to crawl up to awareness, and a few seconds more to realize what had awakened her. The comline alarm was chiming. She hit her switch. "Hoffman," she said, her tongue thick and unwieldy.

"Joseph Rimskaya in the fourth chamber. Judith, we're having a rash of boojum sightings—I've seen two myself."

"So?"

"They're metal, cross-shaped, zipping over our compound and over the Russian territories, too. We've followed some of them with our trackers. There must be twenty or thirty of them in this chamber alone. They're all over."

Hoffman gritted her teeth and rubbed her eyes before glancing at her watch. She had been asleep less than an hour. "You're at the zero compound in the fourth chamber now?"

"That I am."

"I'm on my way."

She shut off the comline just as she received another call. This time, Ann cut in and was dickering with the voice on the other end as Hoffman answered.

"Judith, I'm sorry," Ann said hastily. "Beryl told me to let you sleep and I was away for just a second—"

"Miss Hoffman, this is Colonel Berenson in the seventh chamber—"

"Please, Colonel," Ann cut in.

"This is an emergency—"

"Ann, let him talk," Hoffman said.

"Miss Hoffman, our sensors are picking up dozens—maybe hundreds—of objects, large and small. Some have entered the bore hole, almost certainly, and are in the sixth chamber by now—"

"They're in the fourth chamber, at least," Hoffman said. "Colonel, coordinate with Rimskaya. He's made sightings, too. I'll be in fourth chamber on the next train."

She packed her small emergency case and ran down the hall, stumbling and almost falling at the head of the stairs. She grabbed a railing until her dizzy fatigue passed, then pumped down the stairs as fast as she could without breaking her neck. Ann met her at the bottom with a mug of water and stimulant tablets.

"Shit, what are these?" Hoffman asked, downing them.

"Hyper-caffeine," Ann said. "Lanier used them all the time."

Hoffman slugged back two pills and the water.

"What is it this time?" Ann asked, her face pale. "Not another attack?"

"Not from outside, honey," Hoffman said. "Where are Wallace and Polk?"

"Second chamber."

"Tell them to be in fourth chamber, zero compound; tell them to meet me there or at the zero train."

Hoffman ran from the bungalow, shouting for a truck to take her to the second chamber. General Gerhardt ran on his stubby legs from the cafeteria, radio in hand, calling for marines, and waved for her to follow him. Doreen Cunningham met them at the security fence and pointed wordlessly to two trucks idling beyond the ramparts.

They were climbing into the nearest truck when the science compound alarms went off. Hoffman stepped away from the

398

truck hatch and jerked her head back instinctively. Overhead, a barred silvery cross drifted at leisure. The heavy lobe on its end gave it a sinister and silly appearance at the same time. It reminded Hoffman of some outlandish weapon in an eighties martial arts movie.

"That's not Russian, is it?" she asked, still slightly addled from interrupted sleep.

"No way, ma'am," Gerhardt said, hand shielding his eyes from the tubelight. The cross circled the compound, then rose to a needle-point speck against the plasma tube and vanished. "It's a real one. A boojum."

With sunset, the sky dimmed to midnight blue overhead. Where the final flat reddened edge of the sun was being swallowed by the ocean, a dark brown shadow line of cloud began, twisting and veering from the horizon to zenith, where it broke down into frothy streaks, the edge of each streak catching an electric purple gleam. Farley and Carrolson had retired an hour earlier; Frant world days were about forty hours long. Lanier was thinking steadily and was not ready for sleep. He watched the sunset from the patio, Heineman by his side. Patricia had not yet come out of her room after the conversation with Toller.

Barefoot, dressed in shorts and a long-sleeve blue jacket, Olmy walked across the sand a few meters away, spotted them and approached. "Mr. Heineman, Mr. Lanier," he said, and they greeted him with nods, for all the world like upper-class gentlemen lacking only pipes, formal wear and evening drinks to complete the picture. "Enjoying our stay here?"

"Very much," Lanier said. "The first real weather I've seen in a couple of months."

"A year, myself," Heineman said.

"Much longer for me," Olmy said. "I haven't had duty on an outside world in"—he seemed to look inward—"fifteen years. And I haven't visited this world in fifty."

"They keep you busy, Mr. Olmy?" Heineman asked, squinting at him.

"Very. How is Patricia? I understand Ser Toller had a talk with her, and she's been in her room since."

"Yes," Lanier said. "I'm going to check up on her in a few minutes. See if she'll eat some food."

"She has been under strain for some time now, hasn't she?"

"Ever since she came to the Stone—the Thistledown," Lanier said. "We put an awful lot of responsibility on her shoulders—too much, really."

"You thought she might riddle the mystery of the Thistledown?"

"We thought she might tell us whether what was in the libraries would also hold true for our world. As it turned out—"

"It did, and it didn't," Olmy finished for him.

Lanier stared at him, then nodded again, looking back at the declining twilight. "She's been acting strangely—even considering the circumstances."

Olmy leaned on the patio rail. "After we arrived in the Axis City, she and I had a very long and interesting conversation. She was eager to learn about the city, about us, and she was eager to fit in. She especially wanted to learn about gate opening. That's one of the reasons we're attending a gate-opening soon. Had she told you about her ultimate plans?"

"I don't think so," Lanier said. Heineman leaned forward, meeting Olmy's gaze earnestly.

"Before she was captured, she was going to the library to do some final work. She had a hypothesis that she could proceed down the Way and find a place between the gates, in what we call the geometry stack regions. It fascinated me that she knew about such regions—that she had calculated their existence, because to understand the rudiments of Way theory is not necessarily to understand all the implications. She believed that she might be able to construct a gate opening device and probe the geometry stacks."

"What are geometry stacks?" Heineman asked, his voice froggy. He cleared his throat and glanced at Lanier.

"Gate regions are placed in specific rhythm along the Way.

400

They open onto clearly defined locations in universes slightly different from our origin. Each gate opening, heading down the Way, will advance in time by approximately half a year in each universe. Patricia understood this very early, from what she tells me. But it took her some time to realize that the infinity of alternate worlds must be bunched by the existence of such clearly marked gate regions. The bunching occurs in the regions of stack geometry, and the distortion caused by the bunching leads to gross displacement of some universes, both in superspace and in Way time.''

"I'm not following you," Lanier said softly.

"She believed she could open a gate into an alternate universe, an alternate Earth, where the Death did not take place, yet where things were very little different from her world. She understood that gate-opening devices are tunable to a certain extent. It is her theory that with one of our devices, she can open a precise path to an alternate and hospitable Earth.''

"Can she?" Lanier asked.

Olmy didn't say anything for a moment. "We will consult with two gate openers. One is here on Timbl, the other is the prime opener, Ser Ry Oyu, father of Senator Prescient Oyu, and he awaits us at one point three ex nine.''

"Is that another reason why we've been removed from the Axis City?"

Olmy smiled and nodded. "My reasons for bringing Patricia back with me were quite sound. But your arrival has caused no end of trouble. One visitor we might have been able to keep secret—though that seems doubtful now. Five visitors, impossible. The President hopes to make you assets rather than liabilities.''

"Thirteen hundred years, and people are still people," Heineman mused with an edge of bitterness. "Still squabbling.''

"True, and not entirely true," Olmy said. "In your day, many people were so severely handicapped by personality disorders or faulty thinking structures that they often acted against their own best interests. If they had clearly defined goals, they could not reason or even intuit the clear paths to attain those goals. Often adversaries had the same goals, even very similar belief systems, yet hated each other bitterly. Now, no human has the excuse of ignorance or mental malfunction, or even lack of ability. Incompetence is inexcusable, because it can be remedied. One of Ser Ram Kikura's services is to guide people in selecting appropriate skills and attitudes for their work. They can assimilate the necessary adjuncts, whether it be a set of memories or even a personality supplement."

"So why do they still disagree?" Heineman asked.

Olmy shook his head. "Know that, and you understand the ultimate root of all conflict in the realm of Star, Fate and Pneuma. In all the universes accessible to us."

"It's unknowable, then," Lanier said.

"Not at all. It's all too clear. There can be more than one ultimately desirable goal, and many equally valid ways to achieve those goals. Unfortunately, there are limited resources, and not everyone can follow the paths they want. That is true even for us. Our citizens are for the most part good-hearted, capable and diverse. I say for the most part, because the Axis City system is by no means perfect. . . ."

"What you're saying is, the gods themselves would have war. . . ."

Olmy agreed. "Interesting how the crude myths of our youth come back as eternal truths, no?"

Lanier knocked on Patricia's door and called her name. A few minutes, and several more knocks later, Patricia opened the door and motioned for him to come in. Her hair had been mussed into twisted strands. She wore the same clothing she had worn at the beach.

"Just checking to see how you're feeling," Lanier said, standing awkwardly in the main room, not sure whether to fold his arms or let his hands hang down at his sides.

"I'm thinking," Patricia said, turning to look at him. Her eyes were plaintive. "How long has it been?"

"Since you left the beach?"

"Yes. How long?"

"Twelve hours. It's dark outside."

"I know. I turned on the lights before letting you in. This place is just like a hotel room. That's what it's supposed to be, I guess. Quaint. Back to basics. That's what the President said."

"You don't sound right," Lanier said. "Something's wrong."

"I can't stop thinking. I've been in the state—that's what I call it, deep thinking—I've been here for twelve hours now. I'm in it now. I can just barely talk to you, you know."

"Thinking about what?"

"Going home. It all comes down to that."

"Olmy said—"

"Garry, I'm losing touch. I'm going to end up like that rogue, all distorted and unreal. I can't stop thinking. The President's advocate said . . . Garry, I need help. I need something distracting."

"What?" Lanier asked. She extended one arm and spread her hand, gesturing with her fingers. He gripped the hand.

"I'm human, aren't I? I'm real. I'm not just some toy or program."

"You're real," Lanier affirmed. "I'm touching you."

"I can't be sure of that now. You wouldn't believe what's in my head. I'm seeing . . . I mean, it's not artificial, not an adjunct or anything. It's from inside me, all the calculations, theorizing. I'm seeing universes bunched up like Bible leaves, and I know the page numbers. Olmy didn't believe me, not completely. But I still think I'm right. They have these gate-opening devices, some big, some small. If I could get one of those, I could take all of us home right now. Back to where everything is all right. I know the page number."

"Patricia—"

"Let me talk!" she said fiercely. "Back to where there is no nuclear war. Where my father reads *Tiempos de Los Angeles*. Where Paul waits for me. So I'm thinking, but not just about

403

those things. The President said they could send the Axis City down the corridor, the Way, at relativistic speeds. Relativistic. Wipe out their enemies. It would work. But . . .''

"Slow down, Patricia."

"I *can't,* Garry. I need touch. I need Paul, but he's still dead until I find him." She gripped his hand tighter. "You'll help. Please."

"How?"

She scrunched her eyes up as if facing into a wind and forced an uncertain smile. "The Way would expand like a bugle. If there was a large relativistic object traveling the singularity. It would balloon. It would shut gates, just fuse them closed."

"How can I help? I'll get Carrolson—"

"No, please. Just you. I've been making notes." She held up her slate. The screen was covered with figures that made absolutely no sense to Lanier. "I have the proof. Let me go to the point in the stack geometry . . . and I can take us out. But I can't stop this."

"Patricia, you said I could help."

"Make love to me," she said abruptly.

Lanier stared at her in shock.

"I'm just a thought right now. Give me a body."

"Don't be ridiculous," he said, angry—doubly angry because he felt a sympathetic response.

She flinched. "Paul's dead. It won't be cheating on him. When I open the gate, he'll be alive again, but right now he's nowhere. I know you've been staying with Farley. . . . And Hoffman . . ."

She had almost said the wrong thing, almost brought up the question of his responsibility for her, and both of them knew it. "I am jealous, and I'm not," she said. "I like Karen. I like all of you. I've felt apart from you, different, but I've wanted to be . . . with all of you. I've wanted you to like me."

"I will not take advantage when you're vulnerable," Lanier said.

"Advantage? I need you. I'd be taking advantage of you. I

404

am taking advantage, I know, but—I just know what would help. I'm not a little girl. Right now, I have thoughts in my head even *these* people haven't come up with. Olmy knows that. But if I think any more, I'm going to loose all of it. Snap."

She clicked the fingers of her free hand.

"I'm probably not very good in bed," she said.

"Patricia," Lanier said, trying to remove his hand from hers, yet not wanting to.

She stepped closer to him and laid her hand on his stomach. "I'll be unfair if I have to be. Body's a tiger, brain's a dragon. Feed one to keep the other."

"You'll drive me over the edge, too," Lanier said quietly.

She lowered her hand to his erection. "I'm not just an awkward little genius."

"No," he said.

Patricia leaned her head back, feeling him, and smiled ecstatically, eyes closed. There was no more resistance left in Lanier. She let go of his hand and he reached up to unbutton her blouse.

When they were naked, they held each other tightly. Lanier kneeled to kiss her breasts. His eyes moistened at the feel of her nipples between his lips. Her breasts were medium size, very slightly pendulous, one noticeably larger than the other, the skin between them freckled a darker brown. Their size and shape did not matter. Lanier felt a sudden clean flow of passion, taking away all conflicting emotions. She led him to the bedroom and lay beside him as they kissed, nested shallowly together. He took hold of her hips and angled them and slipped deep inside, the muscles of his stomach and buttocks tight, compulsive. Then they rolled over, Patricia on top, and she slid against him, eyes closed but relaxed, as if she were making a gentle wish. She raised herself up and Lanier watched their connected motion without his usual isolation, knowing instead a completion and wholeness that made no sense. There had been not a hint of this between them—simply of duty, working together. He had had that with others.

405

And now he was in bed with Hoffman's little Chicana genius. He had been dismayed on first seeing her, he realized only now; his respect for Hoffman's judgment had hidden that initial reaction to Patricia's apparent fragility. He was inside that fragility, taking pleasure from her, all in the name of duty and that was a laugh.

Part of his dismay had been attraction.

Patricia moved of her own volition to the expected climax. With Paul, she had found herself to be a natural at lovemaking. She could feel the state subsiding, storing itself away rather than dissipating. Her thoughts became pellucid. Here was a focus.

She came and, after a short respite, continued moving. Lanier's hips arched once, then he fell back, and then again, higher, and he groaned against her lowered shoulder, and then her cheek, and opened his mouth in a stifled, quiet, hoarse scream. With the thrusting and release he felt everything loosen, years of tension he hadn't even consciously known about.

They lay together, silent, for long, damp minutes, listening to the grinding breakers beyond the glass doors.

"Thank you," Patricia said.

"Jesus," Lanier said, and he smiled at her. "Better?"

She nodded and burrowed her nose into his shoulder. "That was very dangerous," she said. "I apologize."

Lanier turned her face toward him and clutched her head between his shoulder and his cheek. "We're both odd birds," he said. "You know that?"

"Mm." She nestled into his shoulder, eyes shut tight. "You shouldn't sleep here tonight. I'll be okay. You should sleep with Karen tonight."

He examined her face carefully. "All right," he said.

She opened her eyes—wide and square—and stared up at him. Now she seemed less a cat than some strange inversion of the neomorphs they had seen the past few days. They were human within, with strange exteriors.

But there was something inside Patricia Luisa Vasquez—

something that had perhaps been there all along—which was not precisely human.

Only gods or extraterrestrials.

"You're looking at me funny," she said.

"Sorry. Just thinking how upside down everything is."

"No regrets?" she asked, stretching, eyes reduced to slits.

"No regrets."

As he left her room, he felt his skin prickle. Looking down at his arms, he realized that of all the things he had seen in the past few days, none had given him gooseflesh. . . .

Until now.

Chapter Fifty-nine

While day had not yet come to the resort, Olmy led the five of them to a waiting bus. Carrolson called them puppy-buses, because of their large white tires. The air was still and cool, and the stars gleamed clearly and steadily in the powdery blue-blackness.

Patricia was quiet, showing no sign of what had happened between her and Lanier the night before. Nor did Farley betray any awareness; Lanier had returned to their room to find her asleep. Sleep had come with much more difficulty for him; not since his adolescence had he put himself in such a situation.

Ram Kikura ran across a stretch of blue-green grass and boarded the bus a few minutes later.

"The President is unable to join us," she said.

"How disappointing," Carrolson said, not sounding terribly sincere. "Troubles?"

"I don't know. Ser Toller, the President and the Presiding Minister's partial are meeting now. You go on ahead; I'll stay here and follow the situation."

The bus's Frant driver looked back at Olmy, who nodded. They rolled smoothly across the lawn to a road paved with fine gravel, then to a whitetop highway that circled the resort and aimed toward the dawn, now deep red on the inland horizon. Patricia smelled something sweet, quite unlike the rich sharp smell of the Timbl ocean; a breeze was blowing over fields of low-lying thick yellow stalks growing outside the resort boundaries. In the fields, Frant farmers in red, many-pocketed aprons, accompanied by small automatic tractors, were already at work.

"They're harvesting biological personality elements," Olmy explained. "Tailored plantimals replicate complex biological structures, right down to preassigned memories. A cottage industry, you might call it—very advantageous."

"For humans or Frants?" Lanier asked.

"The plantimals can be adapted for most organics," Olmy said. "Installation of genetic codes is not difficult for carbon-based forms."

Lanier had meant whether the industry was more advantageous to humans or Frants, but decided not to restate his question. The bus took the white road through the fields and crossed the densely populated coastal plain. For dozens of kilometers in both directions along the coast, and for at least ten kilometers inland, the plain was covered with Frant villages.

As many as ten villages occupied tracts of land barely three kilometers square. Each village consisted of several nested circles of low-roofed rectangular houses. At the center was a stupa-like structure, often as much as fifty meters tall, draped with many-colored banners. As the sun brightened, the inland-facing banners on the stupas changed color, waving slowly in the gentle breezes like despondent rainbows.

"How advanced are the Frants, compared with your people?" Carrolson asked.

"More basic, but not primitive," Olmy said. "Their grasp of technology and science—I assume that's what you're referring to—is extensive. Do not be misled by styles of philosophies, or even by gentleness. Frants are resourceful. We rely on them a great deal."

Beyond the fields and villages, the road spiraled around a

low mountain crested with sky-pointing prisms of translucent gray rock. At the top of the mountain, resting on a plateau formed by the prisms, a squat white-and-copper-banded dome rose some sixty meters higher, ballooning at its base into a broad pavilion. The bus drove under the outlying skirt of the pavilion and stopped.

Olmy led them toward the well-kept but obviously ancient bronze, black iron and white enamel works beneath the hollow dome. Standing beside a five-meter-wide horseshoe-shaped mount was a muscular, apparently middle-aged man, naked from the waist up, a tool kit hanging from his broad belt. His skin had a deep brown color, with a faint rainbow sheen. Three Frants stood at other points around the equipment, talking among themselves in low tones as they worked with polishing cloths. Above them all towered a huge cage of crisscrossing black iron bars, like a misplaced Victorian bridge.

"It's a telescope," Heineman said. "It's beautiful!"

"It is indeed a telescope," the brown man said, smiling. "The last the Frants built before our gate opened."

"This is Ser Rennslaer Yates, secondary gate opener," Olmy explained, introducing them around. "He will accompany us to one point three ex nine."

Yates unhitched his tool kit. "This meeting has been long expected. Ser Olmy has kindly kept me informed about all of you. The Frants indulge me by letting me tinker with their historical treasures." He pointed with one hand to the telescope and the dome and pavilion, then donned a blue cloth shirt and closed it by pressing along a seam. "There's not much need for gate openers now. The primary can do most of the work very well without us." He approached Patricia. "Olmy's told me a fair amount about you. You've made some impressive discoveries."

Patricia smiled but said nothing. Her eyes, however, were bright and square: cat with a secret. Lanier felt a surge of—pride? something else?—as he realized how much she had improved since last night.

"I'd love to tinker with that," Heineman said wistfully.

"Perhaps someday you will—or one like it. Frants are not much for preserving their past, I'm afraid." He patted the telescope mount. "I will not be back here for some time," he said sadly. To Heineman and Carrolson, he confided, "I'd ask them to keep up the work, but they'll be reassigned—wander off and homogenize, as Frants do—and it will start decaying all over again. In its day, you know, this instrument and fourteen others like it were kept busy from dusk to dawn, searching for the comet sweeps." He waved his hand, bidding them to follow him beyond the rim of the pavilion and across a narrow, flat field.

At the lip of the steep precipice, they looked across the flatlands and the sea beyond. "The Frants were already moving into the space age when we arrived. They had built thousands of missiles with nuclear warheads—fantastic, ingenious and very jumbled technologies; jerry-rigged could you call them? It had been over nine centuries since the last major impacts, and they were waiting.

"If this instrument or any of the others had sighted comets, then trajectories would have been computed by thousands of Frants linking minds. Years it might have taken them, but otherwise they had only primitive computers. The villages would have been moved, placed in safer areas. Every village on the planet in motion! They were saved from that. Still, this"—raising his hand to the dome—"was a noble instrument." He shook his head. "Ser Olmy! Lead on. I am done here." He hugged each of the Frants and touched their hands in the homogenizing gesture, though for a human it was purely a formality.

They were about to board the truck when one of the Frants, standing in the sunlight at the edge of the pavilion, whistled and pointed toward the coast. Sweeping inland, three tiny white points were approaching the telescope. Olmy frowned.

"Mr. Lanier, please take your people back to the telescope. Ser Yates, could you stay close to them?" Yates agreed and followed them back to the center of the pavilion.

"What's happening?"

"I don't know," Olmy said. "We weren't scheduled to be met by gate police."

The three white points grew rapidly to full-sized, blunt-arrowhead craft. The craft circled the telescope and settled on the flat field to the north. The nose hatch of one craft opened, and out stepped Oligand Toller, four gate district representatives and a Frant marked with the green sash of diplomatic authority. Toller walked quickly toward Olmy, eyes directly on his.

"There are difficulties in the Axis City," he said. "I'm instructed to cut off your visit and return all of you to the Axis City immediately."

"Please explain," Olmy requested. "What are the difficulties?"

"Korzenowski factioners and orthodox Naderites have taken illegal authority and cut communications between the precincts. The President has adjourned the Jart conference and left Timbl and is now on his way back to deal with it. We must leave now."

"Wouldn't it be best to keep everyone here?" Olmy asked. "Until the situation becomes more clear."

"It is very clear. The secessionists are trying to force the issue." Toller resorted now to tight-beam picts. The color of his message was an agitated red-edged purple: "Our guests are key figures in this dispute. You know that, Ser Olmy."

Olmy did not pict. "I understand, Ser Toller. But you miss my point. Ser Yates is now ranking human on Timbl, if the President has left."

Toller sized the situation up quickly. "You refuse to release them? I am operating *under authority* of the President."

"I don't refuse to release all of them," Olmy said. "Only two will remain with us. You may take the others."

Lanier began to protest, but Olmy shot him a glance that demanded silence.

Toller backed a step away. "I could order the gate authority to arrest all of you."

"No bluffing, please, Ser Advocate," Yates warned. "Even

an inactive gate opener is obeyed by gate authority. Who is the other you wish to stay with us?" he asked Olmy.

"Mr. Lanier," Olmy said.

"Are you with the secessionists?" Toller asked him, clearly angry now. Olmy did not answer.

"We will keep Patricia Luisa Vasquez and Garry Lanier," he said. "You may take the others."

"We refuse to be separated," Lanier said, stepping forward despite Heineman's hand on his arm.

"You have no choice," Olmy said. "We're past the point of euphemisms and diplomatic games, Mr. Lanier. I choose you in order that you may assist us with Miss Vasquez. The others will be safe."

"We guarantee the safety of all," Toller said. "Except those who go with you, Ser Olmy."

"Ser Ram Kikura is their advocate. She will accompany these three, wherever you take them—and watch out for them," Olmy instructed.

Mechanical workers emerged from the craft and rolled or floated to surround Farley, Carrolson and Heineman. "Garry," Farley said, her voice strained.

"They will not be harmed," Olmy reiterated. "This is not that kind of struggle."

"The Thistledown is being cleared at this moment," Toller said, hoping to arouse more defiance. "Corprep Rosen Gardner is in charge of a campaign to evacuate the asteroid."

Olmy nodded as if that were obvious.

"What will you do with Vasquez and Lanier?" Toller asked.

"Please take the others now," Olmy said. "They are your responsibility."

"This is intolerable. When word gets down the Way, gates will be closed, lanes cleared—"

"That's what the Geshels planned anyway, isn't it? To expedite clearing the Way of Jarts. That's the decision the conference was about to reach, at the suggestion of the President, or am I wrong?"

412

Toller glanced nervously at the secondary gate opener. "You are cooperating with this . . . secessionist?"

Yates merely smiled, removed his torque from the tool-kit, and picted a symbol of Earth wrapped in a circular string of DNA.

Shaking his head, the advocate gestured to the workers, who guided Farley, Carrolson and Heineman toward the waiting craft. Carrolson was livid with anger. "Are we just going to go along with this?" she cried.

"I don't think we have any choice," Heineman said, his expression long and solemn. "There goes Patricia's birthday party. Watch your step, Garry."

Farley looked over her shoulder at Lanier, tears flowing down her cheeks. "Garry?" she called back.

"You sons of bitches," Lanier said to Olmy and Toller. "Patricia was right. We're nothing but pawns."

"Don't underestimate yourselves," Toller said. He returned to the craft with the gate district representatives in his train. The diplomatic Frant stayed behind. The craft took flight again, heading toward the gate reception area.

"My apologies for your distress," Olmy said. "Now. We must proceed to one point three ex nine immediately. Things are happening much sooner than expected."

Wu Gi Me and Chang i Hsing carried boxes of equipment and papers out of the tent with the help of Berenson's troops, loading them into the back of a truck. A cool breeze descended from the southern cap, stirring the tent fabric. Except for their heavy breathing and footsteps, and occasional guttural exclamations from Berenson, the evacuation was conducted in silence.

Six metal double-barred crosses hovered three meters above the road, their red spots seeming to watch every move the soliers and scientists made. Far above, at the center of the plasma tube, something long and black was aligned on the singularity, no more than fifty meters from the opening of the bore hole. Examining it through binoculars, Wu estimated it

413

was 150 meters in length. It had arrived less than ten minutes earlier, prompting Berenson to order the evacuation.

When the truck was full and the tent empty, the soldiers crawled on top and the Chinese took the remaining two seats in the front. Berenson grabbed a handgrip along the roofline and stepped up on the side ladder. The truck jerked forward and swung around to roll up the ramp.

With the chamber deserted, the crosses bunched into a cubic formation, then flew off to circumnavigate the chamber floor.

From the vantage of the flawship, twenty-five kilometers above, an assigned ghost of Corprep Rosen Gardner watched the proceedings, relaying everything by direct beam down the Way to the Axis City.

In the Axis City itself, communications between the three rotating cylinders and Central City had been severed. Axis Nader was completely blocked off from the transport systems. And major sections of City Memory—usually active around the clock—were now isolated and quiet. The tide had turned; the radical Geshels had tripped themselves up in their own haste to take advantage of Olmy's news and the five guests.

The incarnate Corprep Rosen Gardner had moved to the Nexus Chambers a few hours before, risking the uncertain location in Central City to be at the center of all Axis City activity. He had created four partials to handle the details of the revolt.

None of his factioners or supporters called it a revolt; for them, it was a necessary maneuver to protect their rights against action by radical Geshels. Whatever it was called, it was hideously complicated.

Word from the Thistledown was incomplete, but that was the least of Gardner's worries now.

His partials were in the three Axis cylinders and in the offices of the Way Commerce Committee at nine ex six. His militant factioners held all strategic transport sites within the Axis City, and along the Way nearby. Through City Memory and deep within the Axis City's infrastructure, orthodox

414

Naderites and Korzenowski factioners—his people—were consolidating the gains made in the past few hours. Sympathetic personalities in City Memory, including his father, oversaw the interdicted communications nets.

Everything was proceeding as planned. Yet Corprep Gardner was more unhappy than he had ever been in his two centuries of life. He cared little for the accusations of the Presiding Minister or the President. He had opposed them often enough in the past, and felt the sting of their power, to relish watching them squirm.

What made him miserable was the knowledge that the action violated all *he* had stood for in the Nexus, and all he had espoused before his election as Corprep by the New Orthodox Naderite precincts of Axis Nader. He felt peculiarly vulnerable, as if one of his own partials might chastise him for a breach of honor and faith.

Already, his factioners were preparing to move the city south along the flaw, toward the Thistledown. They would have to remove barriers as they went; that would take time.

In the center of the empty Nexus Chambers, surrounded by the armillary information rings, he awaited the return of the President and the senators and corpreps now convened on the Jart question. When they attempted to reenter the Axis City, and were denied, what Gardner called the action wouldn't matter.

Then the revolt would have truly begun.

A partial of the President appeared to one side of him and awaited his attention. Gardner took his time. Finally, satisfied that all was going well—and that the partitioning of City Memory had been particularly successful—Gardner allowed the partial to pict.

"Do you have the support necessary?" the partial asked. "My original is on his way. Director Hulane Ram Seija has already filed court proceedings. Needless to say, you haven't followed the usual Nexus procedures."

"No. Emergencies and opportunities." His last statement picted a wide range of emotionally charged symbols: the com-

415

plex Naderite sign for home, consisting of Earth surrounded by a circle of DNA; this symbol engulfed in fire, replaced by a singed animal skull; and the requisite meaning qualifiers. Then, more straightfoward, "Ser Ram Seija can try his case after secession. In absentia. Besides, we are working now to have him tried for violation of Nexus procedure."

"I've heard nothing of this," the partial said, incredulous.

"You've been busy, Ser President." He regretted the tone of his response; the President had been working hard on the Jart problem, and he did not wish to imply any dereliction of duty; it was enough for his people to have taken advantage of the President's absence. "It was a minor infraction, but I am within my rights. As long as there is a court question, all of Ser Ram Seija's duties are suspended. Senator Prescient Oyu is his replacement in command—she has left a partial here to carry on her duties."

The partial of van Hamphuis then picted that he had protested the insurrection and tried to muster the votes necessary to override Corprep Gardner. Gardner already knew this; by legal maneuvering, and with the advice of Senator Prescient Oyu's partial, he had declared the vote invalid— lacking a quorum of incarnate senators and corpreps, and called by a partial instead of an incarnate.

The fight was far from over. The incarnate Tees van Hamphuis would be in the vicinity of the Axis City in just a few hours.

Chapter Sixty

At the limit of the plasma tube in the first through fourth chambers, arrow-shaped craft patrolled back and forth. Other, larger craft flew at will above the valley floors, and the double-barred crosses were everywhere.

In the fourth chamber zero compound, Hoffman realized

that any attempt at defense would be useless. The technology and the force they were up against was insurmountable.

"There's no doubt they're from the corridor?" she asked Berenson in the middle of the compound as they stood by a truck prepared to evacuate them.

"No doubt," Berenson said, accent thick with nerves.

"Then we can hope for the best."

"And what would that be?" Polk asked. Her hair was wildly astray; for impeccable Janice Polk, that was a definite sign of frayed nerves.

"That they're human. Our descendants."

Rather than risk wholesale slaughter, she instructed Gerhardt to tell his soldiers not to fire unless directly assaulted. She could not, of course, instruct the Russians—they would have to figure out the situation on their own.

Wallace and Polk helped with the communications. They spoke with several Russians on the radio, but the Russians refused to provide any information on their situation—though, in all fairness, neither of the women were able to get in touch with an officer. Rimskaya stepped forward and offered to take a message to the Russian leaders, on foot if necessary. That was gallant, but Hoffman refused. By the time the Russians received the message, the situation would probably have changed.

Three crosses in a triangle formation flew over the compound. One broke away at the southern cap and returned to hover directly over the center, and over Hoffman. Bright flashes of light appeared between Berenson and Hoffman. Hoffman jerked and stumbled against Rimskaya; Berenson stood his ground with eyes wide and nostrils flared.

Then the cross spoke, its voice that of a woman.

"You are not in danger. Under no circumstances will you be harmed. You will also not be allowed to harm each other. All occupied chambers are under Axis City jurisdiction."

"So what do we do? Kowtow?" Beryl Wallace asked.

Gerhardt approached them slowly, one eye cocked toward the hovering cross. "Jesus, that's scary," he said to Hoffman

417

in a whisper. "My people don't know whether to piss down their legs or bow in submission."

"Sorry I can't reassure them," Hoffman said.

"What in hell is 'Axis City?' " Berenson asked.

"I could hazard a guess," Hoffman said. "Where everybody lives down the corridor—on the axis."

Rimskaya nodded too eagerly. "Talk to it, then," he suggested.

Hoffman looked up and squinted. "We intend no harm. Please identify yourself."

"Are you the leader of this group?"

"Yes," Hoffman said. She pointed to Gerhardt. "He's a leader, too."

"Are you the leaders of all groups in the chambers?"

"No," Hoffman said. She didn't volunteer any more information, deciding a witness's approach to questioning would be best.

Two of the larger blunt-arrowhead craft flew by slowly and took up positions at the north and south ends of the compound, hovering about twenty-five meters above the surface.

"Do you guarantee the safety of a negotiator?" the voice from the cross asked.

Hoffman glanced at Gerhardt. "Make sure," she said. Then, more loudly in the direction of the cross, "Yes. Give us some time." Gerhardt used his radio to contact the units in all chambers.

"Are you prepared now?" the voice asked.

"Yes," Hoffman said, at a nod from Gerhardt.

The craft at the southern point dropped gracefully to the ground ten or eleven meters from the center of the compound, lowering a single pylon as it touched down. A hatch in the nose dilated.

A man in a black suit stepped from the hatch and quickly examined the compound, then focused on Hoffman. He had walnut-colored hair cut in three stripes, with shorter fuzz between; he lacked nostrils and his ears were large and round.

"My name is Santiago," he said as he approached. He held

418

out his hand to Gerhardt, who was closest; Gerhardt took it and shook it once, then backed away. The man approached Hoffman and offered his hand again. Hoffman grasped it lightly; the man squeezed no harder than she did. "I apologize for your distress, whatever the necessity. I am instructed to tell you that all of your people are now honored guests of the Axis City," he said. "I'm afraid you can't stay in the Thistledown much longer, however."

"We don't have anyplace else to go," Hoffman said, feeling overpowered, more helpless than she had felt even when leaving Earth on the shuttle.

"You are in my care," Santiago said. "We must gather everybody together—your researchers, soldiers, your people in the bore holes—the Russians. And we must do it soon."

Mirsky disembarked from the craft and blinked at the bright tubelight. The interior of the craft had been quiet and dark, in sharp contrast to the bright glow of the seventh chamber. For the first time, he stared down the length of the corridor and felt as undeniable truth what he had hitherto only heard described. There had been so little time; the library had taken up whatever effort he had spared from being a leader. . . .

Five other Russians disembarked behind him. All had been deserters in the woods near the 180 line in the fourth chamber. They, too, blinked and covered their eyes. They, too, stared in awe down the corridor, the implications of that vast distance becoming more and more clear.

A kilometer to the west, hundreds of people gathered near the zero tunnel. They were mostly NATO personnel, Mirsky saw, also being evacuated. The Potato was being cleared, for whatever reason hardly mattered right now.

The Russian he had met in the woods touched Mirsky's arm and pointed east. Hundreds of Russian soldiers squatted in a square, flanked on all sides by at least a dozen crosses and three people he didn't recognize, dressed much like the woman who had taken him captive.

More blunt-arrowhead craft descended and landed near the

419

chamber's southern cap, disgorging more people. Mirsky wondered idly if they were all going to be killed. Did it still matter? Having died once? He decided it did.

He still wished for the stars. Now the possibility of attaining that wish was remote, yet the wish itself informed him he was essentially Pavel Mirsky. He still had a connection with the five-year-old boy who had stared up at the stars over winter-bound Kiev. In fact, that memory was pure, not reconstructed but original; Vielgorsky had not blasted that most basic experience from his head.

He wondered idly if Vielgorsky and the other political officers were in the crowds of captives. What could they do to him now? Nothing.

Only a Russian, Mirsky thought, could draw a free breath in such a situation as this.

Senator Prescient Oyu joined them at the resort and informed Yates and Olmy that the Frants were planning to close the gate, standard procedure in any temporary emergency involving the Way.

Olmy acted quickly. Before the gate could be closed, Yates requested that a small defense flawship be prepared to ferry the secondary gate opener and his guests. The request was denied, but Yates tested his authority on the Frant side of the gate by appropriating one of the two Axis craft left on the reception field. The human defense forces there—mostly Naderite homorphs—decided to abide by the letter of the law, and not Toller's parting instructions, and gave the secondary gate opener what he asked for, as well a two guards and a mechanical defense worker.

Taking the craft through the gate and up to the axis, they found three flawships that had been disengaged from the singularity to allow Toller's craft passage. One was unoc-cupied; it had been parked just minutes before and abandoned by its Naderite crew in a near-axis inspection area, tethered to the flaw by traction fields. Again, following the letter of the law, the crew had retired their small flawship for an inspection after a hundred thousand hours of active duty.

Yates's authority easily overrode the flawship's ambiguous instructions.

They boarded and restrung the flawship on the singularity. The flaw passage through the center of the ship simply extended to the outer bulkheads, reshaping the craft's nose-in-profile from an O to a U, and then closed around the flaw. They accelerated toward 1.3 ex 9.

"You have a lot of support, don't you?" Lanier asked Olmy as they watched the Way blur into black and gold.

"More than I would have gambled on," Olmy said.

"Radical Geshels have walked on the edge for decades," Senator Oyu said. "They have not been bad leaders, but they haven't prepared adequately for the fulfillment of their plans. And they have exacted a kind of revenge on the orthodox Naderites by benign neglect. Now you see some of the results."

"Are you all orthodox Naderites?" Patricia asked.

"No," Olmy said. "I've long since given up that heritage, and Sers Yates and Oyu were raised Geshel."

"Then why are you doing this?"

"Because there is a way for both sides to achieve their goals—if reasonable people intervene," Senator Oyu said.

The small flawship was designed for speed and rapid acceleration. They averaged some 4,900 kilometers a second, and reached the first defense station at 5 ex 8 within 28 hours.

The stations were located at three points along the Way from 5 ex 8 to 1.3 ex 9. Each was a solid fifty-meter-thick black layer hugging the corridor's floor for a hundred kilometers, the surface dimpled with weapons emplacements and field generators.

At all three stations, the crews requested their mission and authority. Yates identified himself, and since the station personnel had no orders to prevent craft from moving down the Way, they were allowed to pass. A hundred thousand kilometers beyond each station, mechanical flaw defense vehicles cleared the Way for them, then resumed their posts on the singularity, vigilant for Jart flawships or flaw-riding weapons.

Within fifty hours, Olmy decelerated their little craft and approached the atmosphere barrier at 1.3 ex 9, passing through the axial hole at little more than a crawl—a few dozen meters per second. What lay on the other side of the barrier was unexpected—and enchanting.

For as far as the eye could see, the Way resembled the fourth chamber in the Thistledown. If anything, it was even greener and more luxuriant. Clouds drifted at leisure beyond the plasma tube, over a landscape of forested hills partaking of a palette of greens and grassy golds. Rivers cut bright paths through the hills, reflecting the tubelight at every point to take on an aspect of shimmering silver.

Patricia floated in the nose of the flawship, arms crossed. Prescient Oyu explained that this segment of the Way was being adapted for eventual human settlement. The project had been started by those who wished to relieve the tensions arising from overcrowding in the Axis City. Even City Memory's enormous capacity was being filled and would soon need extensions.

The Way had other, smaller segments adapted for human living, but on the whole it had been reserved for commerce. The segment at 1.3 ex 9 was to have been devoted to homorphs and their special needs—in short, it had been chiefly intended for orthodox Naderites.

A year before, the settling of this segment had been delayed by a Jart incursion beyond 2 ex 9. Now the delay was indefinitely extended; the Jarts and their allies had grown in strength, and it seemed they might break through to 1.3 ex 9. Still, the humans did not pull back. They did not settle the segment, but they conducted other activities—including opening a gate at 1.301 ex 9.

The verdant areas of the segment extended for only a few thousand kilometers. The flawship passed over a terminal building covering the gate through which the segment's soil and atmosphere had been brought into the Way; they were accelerating again, over a stretch of sandy, barren territory much like the region just beyond the seventh chamber, and then through another atmosphere barrier.

There was no commerce in the next segment. No other gates had been opened; except for three more defense outposts, the Way was a featureless, darkly bronze tube along the entire million-kilometer stretch. Patricia contemplated the geometry of this undisturbed section of corridor. The geometry stacks would be of a different configuration without gates to bunch them, but they would exist—in fact, this segment might be ideal for her search. . . .

"Would you like to test your ideas here?" Olmy asked her quietly. She turned, startled, and nodded.

"Ser Yates and I have been discussing your theories," Olmy said. "We feel you should present them to Ser Ry Oyu. . . ."

Patricia's eyes narrowed suspiciously. "Would this have anything to do with Korzenowski?" she asked, deciding now was as good a time as any to probe Olmy's secrets.

Olmy lifted a finger to his lips conspiratorially. "If you wish to test your ideas . . . perhaps. But no more talk until our audience."

At 1.301 ex 9, they passed through another barrier. Beyond, a segment barely sixty kilometers long lay velvety green under a thick and hazy atmosphere. Four small terminal buildings— little more than a hundred meters on each side—were spaced around the as-yet-unopened circuit at the middle of the segment.

A disk a third as wide as the one that had transported them to the Timbl terminal ascended from a white landing field near the zero terminal, climbing toward the flawship.

Patricia's jaw hurt. She realized she was clamping her teeth and forced herself to relax. What was Olmy up to—and what would he and the gate openers possibly want with her? What could she exchange in return for the opportunity?

They descended to the surface in the smaller disk. This disk

423

was clearly more utilitarian in design; its bottom half was opaque, and its only illumination was the steady glow of traction fields.

A pie-shaped segment of the disk slid aside, and traction field chutes lowered them gently to the landing area. Olmy disembarked last. Prescient Oyu led them toward the terminal.

"We can walk," she said. "I think it would be best to meet with Ser Ry Oyu immediately."

They crossed the white pavement and then stepped on thick, fine-bladed grass. Oaks and maples were spaced evenly around the park-like grounds; beyond the trees, the yellow terminal pyramid possessed only four steps, each twisted in relation to the one below.

To one side of the terminal, a series of four traction pipes, each about three meters in diameter, wound for several kilometers around the terminal grounds just above head level. Within the pipes, suffused by a faint violet glow, shapes not even remotely human tracted over the landscape.

"Our clients and allies," Olmy said. He pointed to one individual, an eight-legged cylinder with a mane of fuzzy antler-like appendages surrounding its bifurcated, round "head." "Talsit," he said. "Tertiary form. They're a very old race—their history goes back at least two billion terrestrial years. You'll meet another Talsit soon—one serves as assistant to the primary gate opener."

The terminal was little more than a shell, about 100 meters high and 150 wide at the base. Within the terminal, a series of graceful gun-metal-blue scaffolds curved above the smooth-lipped pit about 50 meters in diameter.

Hanging from the center of the scaffold in an intersecting radiance of traction fields was an object tiny in comparison, no broader than three hands. To Patricia, it resembled an old-fashioned Japanese pillow, with its neck-receiving curve. The base was forked, however, like the handlebars on a bike. She stopped by the edge of the scaffold to inspect it, knowing almost by instinct what it was, and how important it could be to her.

To Lanier, it looked like a divining rod with a radar dish attached.

"What is that?" Patricia asked, her voice small.

"That is what a gate opener uses to dilate the Way manifold," Olmy said.

She seemed to shudder. "What's it called?" she asked.

"A clavicle. Only three exist. Ry Oyu has charge of this one."

"Where's yours?" Patricia asked Rennslaer Yates.

"Inactive," Yates said. "Each is tuned to a gate opener. When the gate opener is not performing his official function, the clavicle is deactivated."

She reluctantly looked away from the suspended clavicle and followed the others to the western end of the terminal building. There, under an incomplete cupola roughly sketched from racing black and gold lines, a tall, thin man with close-cut Titian-red hair stood next to a data pillar. Patricia looked first at the man, then at the cupola.

"Friends," Prescient Oyu said, "this is my father, Ser Ry Oyu." She introduced Olmy and Lanier. The primary gate opener nodded to each in turn.

"And this is Patricia Luisa Vasquez," Yates said, hand on her shoulder.

"I've learned the old language just to speak with this woman," Ry Oyu said. "And the old cultures and ways. Yet she gives me such a peculiar look!"

Patricia straightened and cleared a slight frown from her face.

"You were expecting something more impressive, weren't you?" Ry Oyu said. "Not the Wizard of Oz, I hope." He extended his hand to her, eyes narrowed in amusement. "I am deeply honored."

Patricia shook his hand, her thin black eyebrows drawn together.

Ry Oyu patted her hand paternally and glanced uneasily at Olmy. "Now this branch of the conspiracy is gathered. My researchers are at the first-quarter location now; they'll join us

425

in a few hours. They have no idea what's happened here. I'm not sure how I'll explain it to them—a person in my position, engaged in petty intrigues. Miss Vasquez—"

"I prefer Patricia," she said, voice still small, subdued.

"Patricia, do you have any idea what we've brought you here to discuss?"

"Some idea," Patricia said.

"Yes? Tell us."

"It involves my work on the corridor—the Way. And it somehow involves Konrad Korzenowski."

"Very good. How did she discover these things, Olmy?"

"I arranged for a rogue to visit her."

Patricia stared at him in shock, eyes square, touched with anger.

"I see. And?"

"The rogue revealed certain facts to her."

"Something of a risk, don't you think?"

"A very minor one," Olmy said. "She has the Mystery, after all."

"Does she, now." Ry Oyu approached Patricia. "Do you know what he's talking about—the Mystery?"

Patricia shook her head. "No."

"Do you know how important this might be to us? No, of course not. Too many questions . . . Patricia—"

"Olmy knows where a complete record of Korzenowski is," Patricia said abruptly. It was a wild guess—but she hated appearing completely ignorant.

"Actually, I doubt that," Ser Oyu said. "There are no complete records—not since the assassination."

Olmy tied together what she had already heard bits and pieces of: the story of Konrad Korzenowski. Called the Engineer, he had designed the inertial damping systems for the Thistledown, and had overseen the in-flight maintenance of the Beckmann drive. Working from inertial damping theory, he had then designed the sixth chamber machinery that created the Way.

That project had taken thirty years, and had been accomplished by forging an alliance between the largely Geshel governing bodies of the Thistledown, and the orthodox Naderites inhabiting Alexandria in the second chamber. Korzenowski himself—like Olmy—had been a Naderite by birth, and had given his word that Naderite wishes would be carried out. What the Naderites demanded was that the creation of the Way not alter the original mission, which was to find an Earth-like planet circling the distant star Epsilon Eridani. The Naderites believed their principal mission of settling distant worlds in the name of Earth was a sacred obligation, the only truly acceptable reason for venturing beyond the Solar System.

But Korzenowski had not reckoned with a number of problems. First, he had not known that the linking of the way with the Thistledown's seventh chamber would, in effect, whip-snap the asteroid starship out of its native universe, and into another. And he had not figured on the incredibly bad luck of having the experimental gates, opened by remote manipulation before the connection, allow Jarts into the Way and give them centuries to exploit their position.

Korzenowski had retired his corpus into Thistledown's City Memory soon after the first Jart wars, in the wake of the ensuing scandal. Even there, he had been harassed. Finally, radical Geshels, judging him to be a Naderite traitor, had arranged for the purging of his personality records—in effect, assassinating him.

"Then he *is* dead?" Patricia asked, confused.

"No," Olmy said. "In City Memory, he was supervising the construction of the Axis City. To do that, he placed partials of himself in different locations, to carry on his work more rapidly. The most extensive partials were retrieved by his fellow engineers and entrusted to a woman, who placed them in secret storage. This woman died in an insurrection in Alexandria, a century after Korzenowski's assassination. She was an orthodox Naderite, and at that time her sect did not allow implants. Her death was final.

"A century after that, the final Naderites were driven from

427

Alexandria, and for a time some were kept in Thistledown City. I was born there. And while I was experimenting with the abandoned private memory banks of our apartment building, I discovered the hidden partials of Korzenowski. I was very young then. I only had a few years to become acquainted with the engineer. But in that time . . ."

Olmy glanced at Ser Oyu. He had kept this secret for centuries and was reluctant to reveal it even now that the time was right. Ser Oyu nodded encouragement.

"In that time, I learned that the Engineer had sought to repay his people for the injury he had done to them, however inadvertently. After the Jart wars, the Geshel-ruled Hexamon decided it was unnecessary to proceed to Epsilon Eridani; the Thistledown's course was uncertain, and, to be truthful, they simply thought there was more potential for settlement and exploration in the Way. They were right, but that did not satisfy the orthodox Naderites. They had lost not only their mission in life, but their Earth, and their home universe. So before retiring his corpus, Korzenowski secretly reprogrammed the Thistledown guidance systems. The ship sought out and located the home Solar System, and began a return journey."

"I don't see how I can help," Patricia said.

"Korzenowski's partials, when assembled, almost equal the original," Ser Oyu said. "We lack only the final impressed shape, the Mystery, to have him back with us. In this way, we hope to repay him for what he gave us. We hope to let him see his success."

Patricia glanced at Olmy to Oyu, and then to Yates.

"And what will you give us?" she asked.

"Your colleagues will have their choice of returning to Earth or proceeding down the Way with the Geshels. You, on the other hand, will be given the means to play out your dream."

"My dream?"

Ry Oyu walked to a smooth black cabinet under the center of the shimmering cupola. He opened the cabinet and brought

428

out a small pearl-white box. Returning, he held the box to Patricia and instructed her to open it.

She lifted the lid. Within, lying in a hollow of green velvet, was a miniature version of the clavicle that depended from the scaffold. Yates looked upon it with her and sighed.

"We're offering you an exchange, a trade in which you lose nothing," Ry Oyu said. "You let us copy your Mystery, to complete the Engineer's personality record, and we will let you search for your home."

"You're saying that my soul, and Korzenowski's, are identical?" Patricia asked.

" 'Soul' is an imprecise term," the gate opener said. " 'Mystery' at least has the advantage of a more precise application. When everything in a personality—memory, thought patterns, skills—has been abstracted out, the sum of their parts is still not the whole. There is a super-pattern which colors the entire psyche, and which can be lost when even the great majority of fragments are reassembled. This is called the 'Mystery.' We have never been able to synthesize it. It is ineffable, and it can only be transferred by an imposition of all the patterns of one person on the assembled personality fragments of another. What is already present in the other is rejected; what is not present, the Mystery, is retained. That is the gift you could give to us—to Korenowski."

She took hold of Lanier's hand, suddenly afraid. This was not in the same league with the things that had gone before; it seemed abruptly mystical and unconvincing. For a time, she had thought that nothing could remain unknown to these descendants, and yet here it was, primary and basic; elaborated upon, manipulated, but not solved.

"You could take it from me by force," she said. "Why try to convince me?"

"Force is not useful in these circumstances," Ry Oyu said. "Either you give voluntarily or you do not give at all."

"Why do you want him back? Hasn't he served his purpose?"

"It's a matter of honor." Olmy smiled. "If the Knights of

the Round Table could have brought King Arthur back, don't
you think they would have? The Engineer must see that his
plan has come to fruition."

"But not as he expected."

"No," Olmy admitted.

Patricia looked down at her clasped hands. "Do I lose
anything?"

"No," the gate opener said patiently.

"And in exchange, I get to use this. . . ." She pointed to
the miniature clavicle. "Why is it so small?"

"It has been deactivated," Yates said.

"It's yours?"

He nodded.

"Yates will transfer its power to you, and you will learn
how to use it during the ceremony," Ry Oyu said. "You will
stand by my side."

"Is Korzenowski here—I mean, his fragments?"

"He is within me," Olmy said, pointing to his head.

Patricia looked at Lanier, her expression that of a little girl
uncertain whether she was being told wonderful lies, or
incredible truths. She shifted her gaze to Olmy. "He's in your
implant?"

Olmy nodded. "I carry additional implants in my body,
sufficient to contain him."

"Something big is going on in your city, isn't it?" Patricia
asked.

"Very big. Your companions back on the Thistledown
should know more about it by now."

"That's why the President couldn't stay with us?"

"Yes."

"We have to rest," Lanier interrupted. "We haven't slept or
eaten for hours—"

"You're going to push the Axis City into orbit around the
Earth? Destroy Thistledown?"

"Not precisely," Ry Oyu said. "But enough for now. Mr.
Lanier is right. After you've rested, we'll resume. Talk shop, I
believe you call it."

430

Patricia narrowed her eyes and shook her head slowly. "I don't know what you people would want to talk with me about. I have to be a complete amateur, a primitive, compared with you. . . ."

"If we haven't convinced you of your value, and your influence, then we are not being sufficiently clear," Olmy said. "You are the source of Korzenowski's work on the Way. You laid the theoretical foundations. That is why we believe you can share the Mystery with him. He was your greatest student.

"You were the teacher, Patricia."

Mirsky hunted through the crowd of Russians for Pogodin, Annenkovsky or Garabedian, keeping an eye on the crosses passing overhead. The soldiers that had once been under his command eyed him sullenly, moving out of his path with fated indifference. He lifted up on his toes, trying to scan the sea of heads, and spotted Pletnev's red face and fuzzy short-cut crown of hair. Maneuvering in that direction, he came up behind the former heavy-lifter commander and laid a hand on his shoulder. Pletnev turned quickly and brushed the hand away, then cocked his head to one side on seeing Mirsky.

"Where are the others?" Mirsky asked.

"Who? The other assassins? You left us with a hellish mess, Comrade General." Pletnev's voice was thick, his words mushy, frightened and angry at once.

"Pogodin, Garabedian. Annenkovsky," Mirsky prompted.

"I haven't seen them since this . . . whatever it is," Pletnev said. "Now leave me alone."

"You were with them," Mirsky persisted. "What happened?"

"What do you mean, what happened?"

"To Vielgorsky, and the other political officers."

Pletnev surveyed the sky suspiciously, looking for crosses. "They're *dead*, Comrade General. I wasn't there, but Garabedian told me. They were shot." He turned away from Mirsky,

431

murmuring, "I hope to God these hounds of heaven don't know."

More crosses flew overhead, causing heads to turn like a sea of wheat in a wind. Mirsky walked away, hands in pockets, bumping shoulders and ploughing his way through the men, face creased in concentration.

This must have been what it was like for the Stoners when the last holdouts were evacuated, Hoffman thought. Shuttle after shuttle of blunt-nosed craft flying back and forth to the bore hole and the huge tuberider Berenson said was waiting there, loading in groups of twenty from each chamber. She was glad Wallace and Polk were in her group; she had grown to rely on them. Ann was not; she was apparently still in the first chamber, or aboard already.

The woman in black, left behind by Santiago, tended her group of four hundred with all the mastery of a shepherd over a flock. Her dogs were the chromium crosses, which gently and insistently brooked no dissent, at least not dissent in terms of wandering away. Hoffman wondered vaguely if mood-altering devices were being used on them; she felt calm, not at all apprehensive, and clearheaded, even rested. Better in fact than she had felt in weeks.

About half in her group were Russians. By a kind of mutual consent, the Russians divided from the Americans, though the craft had brought them in mixed. Mirsky, as far as she saw, was not among them; nor were the officers who had taken command in his place.

Hoffman's time came. The woman asked them to step forward, pointing to each in turn, until twenty had been separated from the larger group. The blunt-arrowhead craft had landed as they were being chosen.

She took a deep breath when her turn came. In a way, this was a relief. All responsibility was gone now. This was a schism with all that had happened before. She found it surprisingly easy to let go.

Sheep-like, she boarded the craft with the others.

432

Chapter Sixty-one

Patricia and Lanier were given their privacy in a small cubicle at the south end of the terminal, to sleep and have time for Patricia to think. A pictor provided some semblance of familiar surroundings, using the same basic decor as Patricia's quarters in the Axis City, but Lanier was scarcely comforted; he was angry and confused.

"You don't have any idea what they're talking about," he told her as they sat on opposite ends of the "couch." "For all we know, they're out to steal your soul. . . . And I don't care what they say, it does sound suspiciously like that, doesn't it?"

Patricia stared steadily at the illusart window opposite, with its view of pine trees and bright blue sky beyond. "I suppose they could do that if they wanted," she said.

"Damned right they could. We don't know anything about them—they've manipulated our view of them ever since we arrived."

"They've tried to educate us. We know a lot more then we did then. What Olmy and Ram Kikura have been saying makes sense."

Lanier shook his head vigorously. He was having none of that; anger was a slow, smoking coal inside, and he could not damp it. "They aren't really giving you a choice—"

"Yes, they are," Patricia insisted. "They won't take anything from me I won't volunteer."

"Bullshit," Lanier exploded. He stood and felt wildly for the boundaries of the cubicle, which he knew was no more than three meters on a side. He could not feel them. The illusion was complete, even to the distance between them as he walked across the room. "Everything's a sham here. For all we know, nothing we've seen is real since we arrived. That would make sense. Why show us more than they have to?"

"They're not . . ." She tried to find the right word. "Not *bad* people."

"You accept that crap about your being the teacher, the precursor?"

"Why not?" Patricia turned to him and held out her hand. He walked back to the couch and took it. "I've seen some of the papers I will write. . . ." She scrunched her eyes shut and shook her head, putting her other hand to her cheek. "I probably will never write them . . . but someone else who is me will, or has written them. And they really do point to all this. It's what's been in my head, unformed, for years now. I've known for almost as long that I was the only one, in our time, our world, thinking seriously about such things. So, ego aside, I don't disbelieve that." She smiled up at him. "Judith Hoffman thought I was the only one. You accepted that."

"You love being a cultural hero? Is that it?" *Coming down on her too hard,* he thought. *Ease up. And why are you angry?*

"No," she said softly. "I don't care, actually. There's not much I do care about now."

Lanier let go of her hand and backed around the table, rubbing his chin, glancing at her repeatedly from the corners of his eyes. "You just want to go home."

She nodded.

"You can't go home again."

"I can."

"How?"

"You know the basics, Garry."

"I want specifics. How can you find your home?"

"If they teach me how to use a clavicle, I'll return to the blank section of the corridor we passed through, and I'll search through a geometry stack. For them, geometry stacks have been garbage areas—useless, or worse then useless. But that's where I'll find a way home."

"Not very detailed plans, Patricia."

"They'll teach me," she said, regarding him with her large black eyes, not square at all now, not feline, but round and calm.

434

"And what will they take?"

"Nothing!" She leaned her head back on the couch. "They'll copy, not take."

"How can you trust them?"

She didn't answer.

"You really didn't need time to think, did you?"

"No," she admitted.

"Christ."

She stood and hugged him firmly, touching her cheek to his shoulder. "I don't know what we are to each other, but I have to thank you."

He cradled her head with one hand and stared away at the juncture of wall and ceiling, blinking, lips drawn down at the corners. "I don't know either."

"I was beginning to think I wasn't human."

"You . . ." He didn't finish.

"What I've been thinking . . . in some ways, that makes me more like them than like you. Do you understand that?"

"No."

"I suppose it also makes my Mystery appropriate for Korzenowski. He thought similar thoughts, and he had similar goals. He wanted to take his people home."

Lanier shook his head, rejecting everything.

"They're not going to hurt me. They're going to teach me. I have to say yes."

"They're blackmailing you."

She raised her head suddenly, frowning. "They aren't," she said abstractedly. "No more than I'm blackmailing them. Garry, I just thought of something . . . and why didn't I think of it before? Why are they opening another gate?"

"I don't know," Lanier said quickly. Her question seemed completely irrelevant.

"I'll ask them."

He laughed. "You're serious, aren't you?"

"That's why we were brought here, to witness the ceremony. . . . Well, that's obviously not the main reason, but it was part of the package."

435

He thought for a moment, still holding her. Despite everything, despite his doubts and fears and suspicions, he had to admit . . .

That was something he would like to see.

"I think we should sleep," Patricia said.

It was not incidental that they made love, but Lanier realized the act was not necessary to Patricia. She was in sight of her goal; everything else, like the decor and the very bed they lay on, was window dressing.

That made him feel insignificant. And it made him wonder what Patricia had become since her arrival on the Stone.

"Am I human?" she asked as they lay together.

"Probably," he said, trying to keep his voice steady, and not completely succeeding.

By the time van Hamphuis's flawship arrived at the position formerly occupied by the Axis City, all gates up and down the Way had been closed and the lanes between them cleared. The situation was unprecedented in the history of the Way.

The Axis City had moved on. Under Corprep Rosen Gardner's direction, the city's flaw power stations had been seized from the last holdouts. Those who had been killed had had their implants carefully retrieved—some 183 citizens so far. The toll disturbed Gardner, but their deaths were not permanent. With the flaw shaft under his control, he had accelerated the Axis City, moving south toward the Thistledown. The journey had taken sixteen hours; van Hamphuis's flawship had followed, but there was little the President could do.

In the Thistledown's sixth chamber, four members of Gardner's Korzenowski faction had committed the ultimate crime—they had tampered with the Way machinery. The tampering was minor, but the penalty for even minor offenses was discorporation and complete wiping of all personality records. At this point, Gardner knew, there was no turning back.

The flaw did not need to extend beyond the actual northern

436

boundary of the seventh chamber; its present extension, near the chamber's bore hole, had been purely for convenience during the final stages of the Thistledown's evacuation and the construction of the Axis City. The machinery was now adjusted to reduce the flaw's length by twenty kilometers.

Four teams of three citizens apiece then exited to the exterior of the asteroid, riding elevator shafts undiscovered by the recently arrived visitors. These shafts opened directly onto buried Beckmann drive units.

Using these drives, the rotation of the asteroid was slowed, and then reduced to zero. The result at first was fairly minor in all chambers but the fourth, where wave action in the broad expanses of water forced huge globules into the air. There wasn't time to damp the effects. Gardner was working on a tight schedule.

Radical Geshels, and the moderates who had never actually committed themselves, were given the opportunity to join Gardner's factioners. For many, there was no choice— Gardner's plans had little room for radical neomorphs. Populations were shuffled between the various precincts as quickly as possible, and City Memory was rearranged and sectioned, all in preparation for the next step of Gardner's plan.

The Axis City was partially unstrung from the flaw, the section containing Axis Nader and Central City first. It was Gardner's plan to reverse the city, leaving these precincts for the Geshels who wished to travel down the Way at near light-speed and force out the Jarts. What he needed to complete his plans were the two rotating cylinders of Axes Thoreau and Euclid.

The re-tuning of the gravity gradient between the Thistle-down and the Way was extraordinarily delicate. The engineers within the sixth chamber had their hands full, especially when the large mass of Central City and Axis Nader was shunted to one side within the seventh chamber, allowing the remaining precincts to be unstrung.

The entire procedure took five hours. By the time it was

done, Axis Nader and Central City had reversed position on the flaw with Axes Thoreau and Euclid. The two pairs of precincts and their related structures were separated by a kilometer, and the pair reserved for the Geshels—Central City and Axis Nader—moved slowly north along the flaw.

The visitors had been informed of their choice. Of the roughly two thousand captives, only four decided not to cast their lot with the group planning a return to Earth.

Among them were Joseph Rimskaya and Beryl Wallace. The other two were Russians: Corporal Rodzhensky and Lieutenant General Pavel Mirsky.

The asteroid was then set into rotation again. Within all the chambers, some damage was unavoidable, but in the fourth chamber, the results were catastrophic. The water globules slowly broke over the basins and land, billions of gallons snapping trees, scouring the forests and forming new rivers as the centrifugal force returned.

The plasma tubes within all chambers were suddenly extinguished. The atmosphere barrier fields remained in force, but the chambers were plunged into abyssal night for the first time in twelve centuries.

And in the seventh chamber, at the boundary of the Way and the end of the chamber itself, mechanical workers began setting powerful charges to blast the northern end from the asteroid and cauterize the Way.

There was little the President or his followers could do. Gardner's organization was masterful, and the dedication of his followers complete. Once again, human history proved that the worst mistake possible in politics was underestimating one's opponents.

Van Hamphuis had no choice but to accept Gardner's offer of a settlement and take control of the precincts alloted to the radical Geshels.

Within Central City's Wald, weightless, assigned to a neomorph Geshel guardian, Pavel Mirsky began to regret his decision. He seemed lost in a Boschian nightmare, and he asked himself if the urge for exploration and new things was worth the strangeness and anxiety.

There were always some disadvantages to completely abandoning one's past and culture. . . .

And Mirsky had committed himself to what amounted to the grandest defection of all time.

Chapter Sixty-two

Olmy stood alone by the scaffold, staring at the clavicle. He wished the Engineer could interact with his thoughts, comment on his actions either positively or otherwise, but Korzenowski was stored inactively.

Vasquez and Lanier were still in their cubicle. For Olmy, the notion of sleeping for eight hours at a time was at once peculiar and attractive. To have a long, blank period in one's life, every day; to have that time free of thinking and immersed in a kind of other-world nothingness . . . Talsit cleansing was much more effective, but he was amused to find a primitive part of himself still longing for simple sleep.

He had never given deep consideration to the differences between humans of his time and theirs, except insofar as he had to plan for their needs. Even with all the accoutrements and additions and manipulations of his time, the similarities far outweighed the differences.

Yates crossed the smooth green carpet of lawn to the scaffold. His face was grim.

"Our time is limited," he picted to Olmy. "The defense station at one point nine ex nine says it's detecting excessive flaw radiation. The Jarts could be preparing to open a new, very large gate."

"Gate to a star's heart?" Olmy asked.

"That's the supposition. Station personnel are preparing to pull back."

The idea had been discussed in upper-level defense circles for decades. It was simple, if drastic: the Way at many points touched on stellar bodies. Since the Way was essentially a hollow, evacuated tube, opening a circuit of massive gates into the heart of a star would suck up the high-pressure, super-heated plasma and distribute it throughout the Way. Barriers— though constructed of modified Way space-time—would transmit the extreme heat and finally break down, becoming level with the walls. The Way itself would remain intact, but everything else for billions of kilometers would simply dissolve to component particles in the fury.

"How fast would the plasma front travel?" Olmy asked.

"It would only be slowed by turbulence effects. Its final velocity could be about six thousand kilometers per second."

"Then we'd have about thirty-two hours to evacuate."

"If they can't open a gate remotely . . ."

The thought of the Jarts' being able to manipulate Way gates from a distance had sobered defense planners for years. The Jarts had never demonstrated such a capability within the human-controlled sector, but data from Way disturbances had led many gate researchers—including Ry Oyu's team—to believe they were doing so beyond 2 ex 9.

"I've passed word on to Senator Oyu," Yates continued. "Her father is with his researchers now. She'll tell him when he's available."

Olmy saw Patricia and Lanier emerge from the cubicle in the living quarters on the north side of the terminal shell.

"Will Ser Vasquez agree, do you think?" Yates asked. "You've spent much more time with our guests than I."

Olmy picted a symbol of uncertainty, carrying implications of resigned humor: an incomplete neomorph choosing between two high-fashion body designs.

"I wish I had your calm," Yates said. "I could use a Talsit session right now."

Patricia spotted Olmy and Yates and waved at them, then touched Lanier's shoulder. Both crossed the grass toward the scaffold.

"I have to see Ser Oyu," she told Olmy. Lanier seemed haggard, his eyes darting back and forth.

"He's in conference with his researchers. Senator Oyu will relay any message," Yates told her.

"Well, I suppose I don't have to tell him in particular. Olmy . . ."

Lanier focused on Olmy, his expression unhappy and resentful.

"I've decided. I'll make the bargain."

Olmy smiled. "When would be convenient?" he asked.

"Our time is limited," Yates said.

Patricia shrugged. "I suppose now is fine. Any time."

"I'll hold you personally responsible," Lanier said to Olmy, emphatically jabbing his finger at him.

"I take the responsibility," Olmy said solemnly. "She will be protected."

Yates went to inform Senator Oyu that they were about to begin. Olmy led them to the unfinished cupola where they had first met Ry Oyu, and picted instructions to a monitor floating nearby. "It will summon a medical worker. I'll make a few modifications in the worker and transfer the partials. You will then offer your Mystery and the patterns will be conformed. It's quite simple."

"If it works, it's a goddamned miracle," Lanier said under his breath, "and you say it's simple."

" 'Lazarus come forth,' from your perspective, correct?" Olmy asked, hoping to amuse him.

"Don't patronize us," Lanier said. The man's anger was obviously building. Olmy thought he could understand why. Now that Patricia had made her decision, Lanier was cut out of the process. He was simply an appendage. Patricia had obviously ignored his misgivings.

The medical worker—an upright, elongated egg-shaped device about a meter tall, delineated with purple to show where manipulators and other instruments would emerge— approached them, floating a few centimeters above the grass.

Olmy picted modifying instructions and the worker extended a small cup-shape at the end of a thick metallic gray cable. He placed the cup below his ear and closed his eyes. Patricia watched, eyes wide, crossing and uncrossing the fingers of both hands. Her calmness seemed artificial now. Lanier's stomach knotted.

441

Prescient Oyu and her father joined them just as Olmy removed the cup. They said nothing, standing a few meters away to watch.

The medical worker moved closer to Patricia. A traction field spread out into a kind of cot before it, and Olmy asked her to lie down. She complied. The worker then spread a fan of black cables around her head like a hairnet.

The net adjusted itself, squeezing her hair. Patricia reached up to feel it. "I should never go out in public with this thing on," she joked.

Lanier knelt beside the cot and took her hand. "Just a couple of Hottentots," he said. "Blowing in the wind."

Patricia made a face, then rolled her head to look at Olmy. "I'm ready," she said.

"There's no pain, no sensation whatsoever," Olmy said.

"Well, whatever, I'm ready." She pressed Lanier's hand and released it. He stepped back.

The net tightened, and she winced at the pressure, not painful but strong nevertheless. Lanier winced in sympathy but did not move. Prescient Oyu walked to his side and placed a hand on his shoulder.

"She carries a part of our dream," the senator said. "Do not worry." Lanier squinted at her.

Patricia seemed to be concentrating, her eyes barely closed. Lanier felt a sick kind of fascination. There was no sound, nothing overt whatsoever, simply the transfer of whatever they were borrowing from her, copying.

She opened her eyes and turned her head toward him.

The net withdrew.

"I'm okay," she said, sitting up on the field. "I don't feel any different."

"The combination will take a few hours to mature," Olmy said. "Then Korzenowski should be with us again."

"Will he have a body?" Lanier asked. Patricia stood by him.

"He'll occupy the worker until one can be made," Olmy said. "He can project an image of himself, however. That would be one sign of his complete reconstruction."

442

Patricia took Lanier's hand in hers again and squeezed it firmly. "Thank you," she said.

"Thanks for what, for Christ's sake?"

"For being brave," she said.

Lanier stared at her in complete amazement.

Patricia, Lanier and Olmy followed the medical worker to the quarters where they had spent the night. Olmy judged it would be best if Korzenowski's first perceptions were in reasonably familiar surroundings—a normal room, sparsely decorated and without too many people—or nonhumans. Ry Oyu and Yates agreed. "Besides," the gate opener said, "you've been waiting for this moment for five centuries. It's your moment much more than ours."

In the quarters, they waited for fifteen minutes before Olmy prompted the worker to display an image showing the progress of the personality it contained. Patricia raised her hand to her mouth as the image manifested before them.

The image was grossly distorted, one-half of the body large and bulbous, the other small almost to vanishing. Its apparent solidity was imperfect, with some parts opaque and others transparent. Its color was predominantly blue. The elongated, side-slipping head seemed to watch them, turning from face to face.

"Don't be disturbed," Olmy warned them. "The awareness of body shape is the last thing to mature."

Across a period of minutes, almost imperceptibly, the distortions corrected themselves. The overall blue color became more natural, and the patches of translucency filled in.

When the adjustments were completed, Korzenowski's image was fully and accurately formed, Olmy noted with satisfaction. It matched the appearance the Engineer had once chosen for the official portrait miniatures: a slender, dark-haired man of medium height, with a sharp, long nose and inquisitive, humored black eyes, his skin colored light coffee.

Olmy still searched for deviations. The Mystery imposed upon the partials, however close to Korzenowski's original,

443

was not exact. However, it was sufficient to return Korzenowski to full awareness, and that awareness would be patterned by the virtually complete memories of the partials to reproduce closely the personality that had been erased—assassinated— before Olmy was born.

"Welcome," Olmy said aloud.

The image regarded him steadily, then attempted to speak. Its lips moved, but produced no sound. The image wavered abruptly, and when it was solid again, said, "I know you. I feel much better—very different. Have I been reconstructed?"

"As best we can manage," Olmy said.

"I remember so little—like bad dreams. You were a child . . . when we first met."

Olmy felt the rise of another emotion that Ram Kikura might have regarded as atavistic. "A boy, five years old," he said. He clearly remembered first seeing the Engineer's partials in the apartment memory, remembered his child-self frightened and fascinated at meeting someone famous—and dead.

"How long have I been incomplete, dead, whatever I was?"

"Five centuries," Olmy said.

The Engineer's expletive would have been extremely crude in his day; for Olmy, now, it was archaic and quaint. "Why was I brought back? Surely everyone was better off without me."

"Oh, no," Olmy said sincerely. "We are honored to bring you back."

"I must be completely out of date."

"We can correct that in a few hours."

"I don't feel . . . finished. Why is that?"

"You have to mature. Your reconstruction is still finding its pathways. You don't have your own body. You're occupying a medical worker."

Again the expletive, even stronger. "I *am* behind the times. Only a mental midget could have fit into the most advanced worker. . . ." The image tilted its head forward, regarding Olmy from beneath its brows, eyes questioning. "I was damaged, wasn't I?"

"Yes," Olmy said.

"What's missing?"

"The Mystery. We had to work from partials only."

"Whose Mystery replaced it?"

Olmy pointed to Patricia.

"Thank you," Korzenowski said after a moment of thoughtful silence.

"You're welcome," Patricia said lamely.

"You look familiar . . . I've seen you before."

"This is Patricia Luisa Vasquez," Olmy said.

Korzenowski's expression was at first incredulous. The image extended its hand to Patricia. Patricia gribbed the hand, no longer surprised by the solidity and warmth of projections.

"*The* Patricia Luisa Vasquez?"

"One and only," Patricia replied.

Korzenowski's image leaned its head back, grimacing. "I have an awful lot to catch up on." He released her hand, apologizing under his breath. He took Lanier's outstretched hand and shook it more briefly, his grip firm but not insistent.

Lanier was more than a little awed to meet the man who had designed the corridor. "I have a small . . . I don't know what it is, statue, hologram, whatever, of you. Back in my desk. You've been a puzzle to me for years. . . ." he realized he was babbling. "We're from Earth," he concluded abruptly.

Korzenowski's face was unreadable. "Where are we?" he asked.

"In the Way, at one point three ex nine," Olmy replied.

"Where is the Thistledown?"

"In orbit around the Earth and Moon."

"What year?"

"2005," Patricia said.

"That's Journey year?" Korzenowski asked hopefully.

"*Anno Domini*," Olmy said.

The Engineer suddenly looked very tired. "How long before you can educate me?"

445

"We can start now, even before your personality is mature. Is that what you wish?"

"I think we'd better, don't you?" Turning to Patricia again, he said, "You're very young. How much work have you done . . . how many of your papers?"

"None of my most important ones," she replied.

"This is not something I anticipated. . . . It is not an obvious result of our work. I mean to say, how could I have missed it? And you *must* tell me how you got here . . . and why you?"

Even before Olmy could arrange for the update of information, Patricia and the Engineer were deeper in discussion.

Within four hours, the researchers, representing seven of the species that utilized the corridor, had gathered around the scaffold. Each of these species had demonstrated its usefulness to the human patrons, though by no means their subservience; they were full partners in the venture of the Way, and they came in a wide variety of forms—though not necessarily much wider a variety than the neomorphs of the Axis City, Lanier thought.

There were three Frants, cloaked in the shiny foil jackets that seemed to be their usual clothing away from Timbl. A being shaped like two upside-down U's connected with a thick, gnarled rope of flesh—lacking visible eyes, its skin as smooth and featureless as black glass—stood unmoving on its four elephantine feet a few meters from the Frant, surrounded by a red line of quarantine. It apparently did not find the atmosphere uncomfortable, however.

A Talsit researcher stood on its eight limbs beside Yates on the north side of the scaffold, surrounded by a traction bubble containing its particular mix of atmosphere—very little oxygen, with a much higher percentage of carbon dioxide, at temperatures low enough to make condensation form on the field's flexible boundaries. Its mossy "antlers" were in constant motion. All the other nonhuman researchers were surrounded by similar fields, the most striking being a sinuous,

446

snake-bodied, four-headed being suspended in coils in a levitated sphere of deep green liquid, like a preserved specimen.

From the evidence, human-form beings were not common.

Before the gathering, Lanier and the Talsit had engaged in a strange conversation—strange in its clarity and uncanny *familiarity,* as if they had been no stranger to each other than new neighbors at a block party.

The Talsit had stood on the north side of the scaffolding, conversing with a Frant while a second Frant waited silently nearby. The Frants had homogenized several hours before; there was little need for the second Frant to contribute to the conversation, unless parallel thinking was required. Lanier and Patricia had eaten as much from a bountiful floating lunch table as they cared to. Patricia had then gone off with Olmy to resume her conversation with Korzenowski.

Lanier found himself speaking with the Talsit almost by default. The Talsit had approached Prescient Oyu to discuss her father's plans for the ceremony's aftermath. Their conversation had been picted at first, and then she had shifted to English, introducing the Talsit to Lanier. The Talsit spoke perfect English, though nothing moved anywhere on its body in any way to show sound production.

Lanier didn't even bother to be curious; he had had a surfeit of marvels, minor and major. It took his full attention just finding the right words to explain how they had come to be here. In conversation with a being not even remotely human in shape, and of unknown psychological character (if it could speak perfect English, surely it could also provide a screen for its real thought processes), he talked casually enough about the Death, about alternate universes and invasions in space. The Talsit, in turn, discussed its own kind. Lanier found himself nodding in understanding to a story that would have been incomprehensible to him only a few short months ago.

The beings called Talsit were offshoots of a unified biological-mechanical intelligence that had once occupied the fourteen planets of a very old solar system. At one point, the

447

intelligence had been entirely stored in memory banks, with no physically manifested individuals—not unlike the Axis City Memory. But gradually the intelligence had broken down into individuals—a condensation of consciousness within the system—and the individuals had created new forms for their physical manifestation. These had been the parent species of the Talsit. The parent species, this Talsit seemed to imply, still existed, but were introverted and isolationist; they had created the Talsit to act as mercantile representatives, consultants to younger civilizations. A circuit of gates happened to open onto one of their worlds, and they had begun trading, first with the Jarts who had opened the gates, and then with humans after the Jarts had been pushed back.

By implication, the Talsit and their ancestral forms were at least a hundred times older than humanity.

"Then why even bother communicating with us?" Lanier asked.

"Consider it a hobby of one's old age, or senility," the Talsit said, without a hint of condescension or dissembling. "My kind have services—particularly regarding the cleansing and reordering of information—which humans and others find invaluable. It pleases us to be useful, and in turn we acquire information of great value to us."

The call to the ceremony came a few minutes later, one of the Frants ringing a high-pitched, sweet sounding bell hung from a bar on the south side of the scaffold.

Lanier stood at parade rest, hands behind his back, next to Korzenowski's image and Prescient Oyu, while Patricia took a position of honor between Yates and Ry Oyu.

Ry Oyu's ceremonial clothes were simple, consisting of rough white cloth shirt and black pants. He wore black cloth slippers. Yates wore a forest-green robe, showing some signs of wear.

Ry Oyu stepped to the stairs that curved over the top of the rounded scaffold. He stood for a moment, head bowed, and then beckoned for Patricia to follow.

"You must learn this," Ry Oyu said to Patricia at the top of

448

the scaffold. "The clavicle can tell you where a gate is to be opened, but only in part; you must also sense the point, and tune it to that desired world. There is as much of what you would call intuition as calculation."

He bent down and gripped the handles of the clavicle, removing it from its holder at the center of the radiance of traction lines. Patricia stared down and became dizzy; the top of the scaffold was at least sixty meters from the pit bottom.

"And there is also ritual. It tunes the mind," the gate opener said. "It prepares. It may not be strictly necessary, but I've always found it useful. Now." He held out the clavicle and closed his eyes. "We're not looking for the usual game today. I've been seeking this junction for fifty years at least, and until now, it's always eluded me." He opened one eye and gave her a querying half-smile. "You've been wondering why we're still here, opening another gate that we must inevitably close when the Jarts come or the Axis City passes over. Haven't you been wondering?"

Patricia nodded.

"Because whatever our disloyalty to the present Geshel rulers, I remain faithful to the Hexamon. I will serve the Hexamon even if they believe I'm a traitor, as they must if they know the role I've played in the secession. So to redeem myself, I open this gate."

"I still don't understand," Patricia said, head cocked to one side, eyes on the clavicle.

Ry Oyu removed one hand and spread his fingers, swinging his arm to indicate a circle. "All gates have been tuned to open onto worlds, planets. The Way passes an infinity of possible junctions with other worlds, and we must choose from a large subset of that infinity when we tune at each optimum point. You've noticed, perhaps, that our gates are always spaced at distances no less than four hundred kilometers. That's because of the rhythm of the geometry stacks. Do you understand that rhythm?"

Patricia nodded. "Yes."

"We do not venture into the stacks themselves. They

449

commingle alternate universes and timelines in a way not useful to us. We work *between*." He axed the air with the edge of his hand. "We work within a range of ten meters, and within that range, there are perhaps a billion vantages. We tune as closely as we can to the location of an object with planetary mass; the clavicle tells us the mass by picting directly to our minds, giving us all the necessary information. Feel this." He took her hand and placed it on the opposite grip of the clavicle. Her mind was flooded with images, information. "Now look at me."

She stared at Ry Oyu, and into her head he picted a rapid, steady flow of techniques. "It would be much easier if you had an implant, but at least you have the *inclination*—and the motivation to learn. I cannot give you all the skill, but I can help you hone your intuition." He delivered another series of instructions. Hand still on the clavicle, she felt the flows of data merge.

"I can't help you find your way home," he said, tapping her hand to get her to remove it from the grip. "I won't be with you, and neither will Yates or Olmy. We all have business to attend to. But if your theory is correct—and I see no reason why it shouldn't be—then you can find the proper gate within the geometry stack. You have sufficient knowledge for the attempt. Now watch carefully. We do not open onto another world today. We open onto the Way itself."

Patricia frowned.

"You've seen the curve, Patricia; I'm sure you've calculated the curve of the Way."

"Yes," she said.

"Have you seen where it crosses itself?"

"No."

"It's a very subtle crossing, and the points are far-separated. At such distances, the Way's character may be very different.

"The Axis City will eventually reach those sectors in its travels, perhaps in millions of years, much sooner if the Geshels carry out their present plans. When we open the gate at this junction, we will know what the Way actually is, what

450

we have created and perhaps how extensive it is. We redeem ourselves to the Hexamon by pioneering. Now do you understand why we have stayed here?"

Patricia nodded.

Ry Oyu turned to the researchers and his colleagues at the base of the scaffold. "Is the Engineer ready to witness?"

"I am here."

"Can you experience everything clearly?"

"Yes. I think so."

The gate opener took a deep breath and glanced sidewise at Patricia. "Today, we are all privileged," he said to her.

The clavicle hummed as he stepped down onto the traction field. He beckoned for Patricia to accompany him. She stood on the lines beside him, and the field dimpled downward where they stood, forming a cup around them. They were within a few meters of the floor of the pit when they stopped their descent. Ry Oyu kneeled and replaced the clavicle in its holder. "I've narrowed the region down to a few centimeters," he said.

Lifting his head, to Patricia's surprise he began to chant.

"In the name of Star, furnace of our being, forge of our substance, greatest of all fires, Star give us light, give us even in darkness the gift of right creation."

He adjusted the clavicle and gripped it tightly with both hands, closing his eyes and lifting his face to the heights of the terminal shell.

"In Fate we lay our trust, in the Way of Life and Light, in ultimate destiny's pattern, which we cannot deny, whatever we choose, however freely we choose.

"In the name of Pneuma, breath of our minds, wind of our thoughts, born of flesh or carried in machine, guide our hands, enthuse us, that we may create in truth ourselves, that we may manifest what is within, without."

Lanier saw Korzenowski's image mouthing the words along with Ry Oyu. Had the Engineer written the ceremony the gate opener now used?

The clavicle's hum rose in pitch. Patricia clenched her hands

451

together in front of her, realizing that she was making a gesture of prayer. She could not persuade herself to untangle her fingers and put her hands to her sides.

"And in the name of the Eld, some of whom are with us this occasion, those born of flesh and those resurrected by the gifts of our past creativity; in the name of those who burned that we might find a truer path, who suffered the Death that we may live . . ."

Both Patricia and Lanier felt tears brim over and spill down their cheeks.

"I lift this clavicle to worlds without number, and bring a new light to the Way, opening this gate that all may prosper, those who guide and are guided, who create and are created, who light the Way and bask in the light so given."

He brought the clavicle out of its field receptacle and lifted it between his knees. The stream of picts issuing from the clavicle lit up his face with a fire-like intensity. The humming had passed out of range of hearing.

"Behold."

"I open a—*new world*. . . ."

The bronze surface of the Way beneath them seemed to degenerate into a crosshatching of black and green and red lines. Ry Oyu stood, keeping the clavicle level in his hands.

At the edge of the pit, standing as close as they could to the scaffold, the researchers, Yates, Prescient Oyu, Lanier and the image of Korzenowski stared down into the silent storm of the gate's beginning.

The traction cup lifted the gate opener and Patricia a few meters. Patricia became dizzy again, staring into the pregnant, whirling illusion of color and infinite possibility.

The illusion parted, an oily black circle forming at the center.

Ry Oyu handed the clavicle to Patricia. She took its grips firmly in her hands.

"Now feel the power of what is happening," he said in English. "Learn the sensation of a correct opening."

The clavicle was alive in her hands, part of her, connected

452

with her by its constant picting. Ry Oyu's instructions to her had been quite detailed and were now fixed in her head.

The power was exhilarating. She felt like laughing as the clavicle broadened the hole in the surface of the Way. Overhead, the incomplete cupola that had sheltered Ry Oyu's work area now moved into position on its own, seeking the center of the disturbance.

"This is a dangerous time," Ry Oyu said to her. "If it gets out of control, the cupola encloses us and smooths out the disturbance. If that happens, we are forever lost to the Way. We go wherever the aborted gate takes us, and we cannot come back. Do you feel that potential?"

She did. Her exhilaration changed into a sensation of having something indescribably nasty and unfriendly by the tail. She kept her eyes on the clavicle.

"That's it," Ry Oyu said. "Olmy could not have been more correct. You're more of our time than your own."

The cupola's sketchy, racing lines shrank into the familiar active bronze coloration they had seen at other gate sites. At the center of the pit, the vortex surrounding the black circle began to rise, and the traction field carried them higher still.

"Follow me," Yates told Lanier as the researchers moved outward. They regrouped about fifty meters from the scaffold, near the site of the gate opener's work area. The ground around the pit was buckling, breaking up and forming a tumulus over the rising slope of the gate.

The scaffold and traction lines remained level. Ry Oyu resumed his grip on the clavicle. "A hundred thousand possibilities here," he murmured. "Through the clavicle, I can feel them . . . experience them. I learn about a hundred thousand worlds now, but I only want one. I *listen* for it . . . I know its character . . . I know the particular tangent it occupies. The clavicle controls its own probing, keeping its position steady, but I direct. . . . And *find*."

His expression was exalted, triumphant. The oily black circle widened and became an intense cerulean blue. Around the circle, the bronze Way material again took on definition,

453

forming a smooth-lipped depression with the blueness at its center. The depression deepened; Patricia could not avoid characterizing the process as space-time healing, growing accustomed to the unnatural intrusion.

Around the circumference of the blueness, she received a camera-obscure, fish-eye-lens view of something long, bright and flowing, surrounded by massive dark objects.

"The gate is opened," Ry Oyu said, shoulders slumping. He slipped the clavicle into its receptacle and stretched out his arms. "Now we find out what lies on the other side."

"Do we enter?" Patricia asked.

"No," the gate opener said with a hint of amusement. "We send one of our mechanical friends. It makes its report, and we make our decision without immediately risking our lives."

The traction field cup brought them level with the steps at the top of the scaffold. Ry Oyu motioned for Patricia to precede him, and they joined the others near the work area.

A cubic monitor about half a meter on a side—large for such devices—floated up the new slope and passed through the bars of the scaffold. It slipped quietly into the depression and through the gate. Yates activated a pictor and tuned it to the monitor's signals, relayed by scaffold transponders.

To Lanier, Patricia's stature seemed to have increased. She appeared more self-assured, calm. Taking his hand and squeezing it between both of hers, she smiled at him and whispered, "I can do it. I felt it. I'll be able to follow through."

The monitor image had not yet come into focus. Yates translated picts carrying information about the conditions on the other side. "The monitor is in a high vacuum," he said, "with a very low radiation count. If we are indeed in another section of the Way, the flaw is particularly inactive and stable."

"There doesn't seem to be any flaw," Ry Oyu commented, squinting in concentration.

The visual image clarified.

"It's enormous," Senator Oyu said quietly.

At whatever point the gate had intersected the Way, the tube-shaped universe had expanded to a diameter of at least fifty thousand kilometers. "Geodesic drift," Patricia said.

"Well, that might account for it," Ry Oyu said. "But it may not be inherent."

Lanier didn't bother asking for an explanation; he doubted he could absorb it.

The Way was filled with cyclopean structures, dark crystalline masses thousands of kilometers long, some floating free, casting broad shadows against the opposite walls of the Way as they passed before an intense, meandering, snake-like plasma tube.

"Surface attraction is about one-tenth g," Yates said. "The parameters are substantially different, Ry. Do you suppose it's another Way, not our own?"

"Do we have reason to believe anyone else would have made a universe like this one?" the gate opener asked.

"No," Yates admitted.

"We imposed our own heritage on the shape of the Way when we made it cylindrical—I strongly doubt others would duplicate it. Not with the endless possibilities available."

"Still, there's a convenience to such a shape, a practicality if commerce is desired. . . ."

Ry Oyu agreed to that much with a curt nod. He seemed angry, surveying the results of his work. "It's very strange there," he said. "No detectable flaw, and the plasma tube is highly irregular. I'd say it's been tampered with."

"By Jarts?"

"No," the gate opener said. "Those structures are very un-Jart-like. I'm not sure I can conceive any practical uses for them—they're either distortions in the geometry, space-time extrusions and crystallizations, or . . ." He shook his head. "Or they're beyond our comprehension. And besides, I doubt very much if Jarts could have progressed so far. This junction—if it is a junction—has to be beyond one ex fifteen—over a hundred light years down the Way."

"There can't be any gates there, then," Patricia said.

Yates raised his eyebrows. "Why not?"

"Because that's beyond the end of our universe, in time. Gates would open onto . . ." She held up her hands. "Nothing. Null."

"Not necessarily," Ry Oyu said. "But you have an interesting point. The Way is adapted to fit conditions in its epoch of origin. Where it surpasses those conditions—extends beyond them—it may naturally reach other accommodations."

"Can the Axis City ever travel that far?" Prescient Oyu asked.

"I don't know. If the flaw ceases to exist, they would have to make adjustments . . . it would be difficult. And if there's no flaw beyond a certain point—"

"The Way is self-sustaining," Yates finished for him.

"It is indeed. It doesn't require sixth chamber machinery or any connection with the Thistledown."

"It looks empty," Lanier said, unsure he should enter into the discussion. "I don't see any traffic—there's no movement."

Yates instructed the monitor to survey the region. The images became greatly magnified, revealing the cyclopean crystals in more detail. The Way was filled with them—some soaring from one side to the other across tens of thousands of kilometers, the plasma tube curving around them.

All of the structures—even those floating free—were covered with cupola-like disks, each protecting the obvious blisters of open gates. The image magnified several more times. Shimmering strands of light passed in thick nets between the densely packed gates. There *was* traffic—commerce of some sort—but on an inconceivably vast scale, and of a different kind than they had ever witnessed.

More picts flashed beside the images. "Definitely no flaw," Yates affirmed. "The Way at this point is completely stable and self-consistent."

Patricia appeared half-asleep. She was in the state again, Lanier realized. She was struggling to understand what was happening—it was completely beyond him.

456

"It's causally connected," she said thickly.

"Pardon?" Lanier asked, glancing at the others and cupping her elbow in his hand. She opened her eyes wide and stared at him.

"If the Axis City travels at near light-speed down the Way, this is what will happen—even before the journey begins. The Way lies essentially outside time and has to accommodate any event within its length. This is what will happen—especially if the Thistledown end is sealed off."

"Yes? Please continue. . . ." Yates urged.

"She's right," Korzenowski said. "It's perfectly obvious. And you have somebody—not humans, not Jarts, not even of our universe—taking advantage of the adaptation."

Ry Oyu smiled broadly. "I'm afraid it isn't obvious to us. Please go on."

Patricia looked at the Engineer and felt a stir of recognition. *Herself* . . .Something about herself. Korzenowski nodded to her. "You're doing fine," he said.

"We're looking at the results, carried along superspace vectors, of what is about to happen in the Way," she said. "I was thinking about this before we left for Timbl, after the rogue came to my quarters. If the Axis City travels faster than one-third light-speed, it will twist the Way and create a space-time shock wave that will exceed light-speed, moving ahead of it. The shock wave will operate outside of time, arriving before its cause. The shock wave has already passed this point—perhaps centuries ago, perhaps even before the Way was opened. Something traveling at near light-speed on the singularity, the flaw, will strain it beyond its endurance. It will convert virtual particles into energy—radiate, 'evaporate.'" She took a deep breath and closed her eyes, seeing the mathematics being done even as she spoke. "The Way has been forced to expand to a stable configuration. The flaw has vanished."

Olmy said nothing, calmly listening to Korzenowski and Patricia. *He's proud*, Lanier thought.

"For several light-years, until the Way expands and the

city's shock wave dissipates, everything will be sterilized ahead of the city. Nothing will exist in these segments but the city. All features will be wiped out, all gates fused shut." She pointed to the structures. "Obviously, the Way has expanded here, and relativistic objects along its length won't bother it quite as much."

Lanier tried to puzzle out the flaw's vanishing even before the construction of the object that would force its "evaporation." He quickly lost himself in contradictions, but the contradictions didn't seem to bother Korzenowski or the gate openers.

"When we've prepared the documentation—you can do that, can't you, soon?—" he asked Patricia.

She agreed. "With Ser Korzenowski's help."

"—Then we will know most of what we need to know," Ry Oyu said. "We can present our report to the President. His faction can do with it what they please." He smiled. "What, apparently, they *must*."

Bright red picts appeared before the defense monitor, signaling an urgent message. Olmy went to receive them. When he returned, his expression was jubilant—paradoxically so, considering what he said next. "The Jarts have opened their gate. It's a remote, at about one point five ex nine. They've cut off the last defense station. There's a plug of plasma reaching top velocity—it's about seven hours from us. We have to leave now."

Prescient Oyu looked to her father. "The Geshels will refuse to let the Jarts push them out," she said.

"Then the President has no choice now, does he?" Ry Oyu said. "The Way writes his destiny, and so do the Jarts. He must take his precincts, and we must take ours, and follow our separate paths."

Chapter Sixty-three

Mirsky and the three other "defectors" had been given small spherical quarters in the Central City Wald. Three Geshel homorphs—two females and one of uncertain sex— had been assigned to host them and guide their short-term education and accustomization.

Mirsky sat within his sphere, tuned to various channels of picted information—some translated for them by pedagog partials of their hosts. He and Rodzhensky had accepted temporary implants to help speed tutoring and interpretation. They watched and listened and said little. Rodzhensky stayed close to him, while Rimskaya—the American with the feminine name—kept aloof. The others he paid little attention to. They were very small ciphers in a huge mystery.

The hosts came to them, incarnate to minimize alarm, and taught brief, high density classes while their guests absorbed as much as they could.

The sense of urgency was thick in the air; except for their hosts, the Geshels paid little attention to the defectors. The Wald was almost deserted, most of its occupants taking new work positions to ready the precincts for whatever might come.

The reports from the farthest-flung defense stations had reached the now-divided Axis City. The Jarts had opened a remote gate and allowed the deep interior plasma of a star to enter the Way.

It would take about seventy hours for the destruction to reach the end of the Way, but the occupants of the Geshel precincts of the Axis City had to decide their course of action quickly. If they wished to remain in the Way, and not give it over to the Jarts, they had to have their precincts up to at least one-third light-speed before encountering the plasma front.

459

With the entry of the star's material into the Way, the plasma temperature would drop considerably below the level required for fusing, but would still remain in the neighborhood of nine hundred thousand degrees. The passage of the Geshel precincts would change that, however.

When they actually hit the front, their space-time shock wave would smash the superhot plasma into a thin film. The film, lining the Way after their passage, heated to temperatures far beyond those necessary for fusion, would then fill the Way with an even more powerful plasma. In effect, the precincts would convert the plasma and the Way into a tube-shaped nova.

Mirsky, trying to keep track of the public discussions, thought their plans were deliriously, deliciously insane. Whether he died or not seemed minor; he was in the middle of a grand scheme, far more ostentatious than anything he could ever have imagined.

The Geshel politicians, given their freedom by the secessionists, made frantic plans. There had to be sufficient shielding front and rear to prevent the precincts' being flooded with hard radiation; that would place a heavy strain on the four main flaw generators left to them, which would be burdened enough with having to contact the flaw at such high velocities. Could it be done?

Yes, the physicists decided. But just barely.

There would also have to be shielding along the flaw passage. The flaw itself would be emitting very high levels of lethal radiation. Could *all* the required shielding be maintained?

Yes. But with even stronger reservations.

Despite the doubts, there was a surprising consensus among the precinct's occupants. They did not wish to return to Earth; they looked to the future, not the past. And having fought Jarts for centuries, they were not about to give up the Way to them now.

Rimskaya, drifting through the woods outside his sphere, avoided hearing all the details. He prayed devoutly, not caring who saw him or what their reaction was. His principal worry was, could God hear prayers spoken outside of normal space-time? Would there come a moment when they were completely cut off from God?

His assigned host, a female homorph, kept her distance at his request, realizing there was little she could do to assure him.

For her, his questions fell into an extinct classification of knowledge, as meaningless as how many angels could dance on the head of a pin.

Waiting for the news of the final plans to reach them, Rodzhensky and Mirsky floated a few meters from each other in the greenery. A macrame pattern of light-snakes brightened a deep three-dimensional glade beyond their quarters, casting leaf shadows over them.

Mirsky studied the young corporal carefully, noting the shine of his skin, the loose excitement around his lips, the way his eyes started from his face. *The future is a drug for him,* Mirsky thought. Was it that way for himself, as well?

"I understand so little," Rodzhensky confided, pulling himself along a branch closer to Mirsky's position in a crook. "But I feel I *will* understand—and they are so helpful! We are strange to them—don't you feel that? But they welcome us!"

"We're novelties," Mirsky said. He did not want to exhibit his own misgivings to the corporal. His own heart beat faster each time he thought of what they faced.

The female homorph assigned to the morose American tracted toward them.

"Your friend worries me," she said. "We're considering returning him to your people. . . . He won't admit it, but I think he's made the wrong decision."

"Give him time," Mirsky said. "We've all left a lot behind. We'll be very homesick. I'll talk to him."

"I will, too," Rodzhensky said enthusiastically.

"No," Mirsky said, holding up his hand. "Just me. We talked when I negotiated with the Americans, and we volunteered together."

Rodzhensky, abashed, agreed with a sharp nod.

Mirsky knocked on the pearl-colored translucent outer surface of the sphere. Within, Rimskaya answered, "Yes? What?" in English.

"Pavel Mirsky."

"No more talking, please."

"We don't have much time. Either you go back now, or you face up to our decision."

"Leave me alone."

"May I come in?"

The sphere's door dilated and Mirsky pulled himself inside. "They'll be leaving soon," he said. "There won't be any choice after they get started—you'll be here forever."

Rimskaya looked terrible—pale, his red hair sticking out in all directions, his face scruffy with a four-day's growth of beard. "I'm staying," he said. "I've made up my mind."

"That's what I told your hostess."

"You're speaking for me?"

"No."

"What does it matter to you? You're back from the dead. You don't give a damn about your position—your own people tried to kill you. Me, I've left . . . responsibilities, loyalties."

"Why?" Mirsky asked.

"Shit, I don't know."

"Maybe I do."

Rimskaya regarded him doubtfully.

"You want to see the ultimate," Mirsky said.

Rimskaya simply stared, neither confirming nor denying.

"You, me, Rodzhensky, maybe even the woman—we're misfits. We aren't happy with just living one life. We reach out." He held up a grasping hand. "I always wanted to see the stars."

"You wanted to see stars, so you went into space to fight a war!" Rimskaya said. "We don't know what we'll see. More of this godforesaken corridor." He wrapped his face in his hands. "All my life, I've been a hard-liner. Everyone thought

462

I was a passionless old . . . asshole. Math and sociology and university. My life, held within four walls. When I was sent to the Stone—God, what an experience! And then this opportunity . . ."

"We know it will be interesting, far beyond what we could find on Earth."

"The others are going back to *save* Earth," Rimskaya said, fists curled tight against his sides.

"That makes us irresponsible? Perhaps. But no more so than all the people in this half of the city."

Rimskaya shrugged. "Look, I've made my decision, and I'm sticking with it. Don't worry about me. I'll be fine."

"That's all I wanted to hear," Mirsky said.

"Are you wearing the implant they gave you?" Rimskaya asked.

Mirsky pulled his right ear forward and turned his head to show he was.

"I still have mine," Rimskaya said. He opened one fist to reveal the peanut-sized device.

"You'll need it," Mirsky said. He lingered a moment longer, and the American slowly raised the implant to his head and positioned it behind his ear.

Chapter Sixty-four

"We leave each other now," Ry Oyu told his daughter and Yates. He held out his hand, and the Senator grasped it between hers. Olmy, Patricia, Lanier and Korzenowski waited for them beside the disk.

"What's he planning?" Patricia asked.

"He's going through the gate," Olmy said. "The Talsit will accompany him; one of the Frants, as well. All the rest are coming with us."

"He can't survive," Lanier said. "They can't possibly take enough food, oxygen—there isn't time to prepare—"

"He's not going incarnate," Olmy explained. "None of them are. They'll transfer personality to a long-term gate worker. They can research as much as they wish—open other gates, wait for the Axis City if it reaches that distance. They have millions of years of energy."

Prescient Oyu shook her head slowly, watching her father's face. "You've done well with me," she said. "It won't be easy, not being able to speak with you . . . ever."

"Come with the Geshel precincts," Ry Oyu said. "We might meet again, far down the Way. Who knows what their plans will be, if they succeed? And besides, somebody can always reopen this gate, find us again. . . ."

"No one will ever find this gate again," she countered. "Only you could find it and open it."

"She's right," Yates said. "It was your skill."

Ry Oyu nodded in Patricia's direction. "Korzenoski, or the Earth woman. They could . . . but then, Korzenowski's returning to Earth, and she goes hunting for something even more elusive. Well, at any rate, nothing is final."

"This is," Prescient Oyu said. "I'm going back to Earth. It's what we've been working for." She let go of his hand.

The gate opener picted a symbol to her: Earth, blue and green and brown, clouds vivid and alive, and surrounding it, a loop of DNA; and around that, the simplified equation that Korzenowski had taken from one of the elder Vasquez's papers.

The Talsit in its cold bubble and a Frant in a white coat of permanent parting—unpacked just moments before—stood behind Ry Oyu. Prescient Oyu reached across and kissed him, then turned to join the rest at the disk.

The gate opener and his companions moved toward the workshop and the tumulus around the new gate.

"He fulfills his pledge to the Hexamon," Prescient Oyu said as the disk closed around them. "He'll guide the Axis City if it comes his way." She reached out to Patricia, whose eyes were again moist and touched the Earth woman's cheek. Removing a tear, Prescient Oyu placed it on her own cheek.

464

Olmy instructed the disk to take them out of the terminal, and up to the waiting flawships.

Both of the flawships, the gate opener's staff vessel and the defense craft they had arrived in, had removed themselves from the flaw and hung tethered by traction fields, a precaution in case evacuating defense ships came from the north. Olmy chose quickly; they needed speed, and the smaller defense craft was the faster.

They had to meet the accelerating precincts before they had reached one-third light-speed. There were two options then: the precincts could briefly pull in their generators and flaw grips, and allow the defense flawship to move through the passage; or the defense ship would have to disengage, hug the wall, and weather the pressure wave of particles and atoms pushed before the city.

But before they encountered the precincts, he had to fulfill his promise to Patricia.

In the barren sectors where she was likely to find the geometry stacks she needed, she would be sent with a clavicle to the surface of the Way. She would have very little time to accomplish her work; the plasma front would be right behind them.

Yates took Patricia to an isolated section of the ship and gave her final instructions on the use of the clavicle. "Remember," he told her when he was finished, "you have the instinct, and the desire, but not much skill. You have the knowledge, but not the experience. You must not be rash, you must be deliberate and careful." He took her by the shoulders and faced her directly. "Do you know your chances of success?"

She nodded. "Not very good."

"And you'll still take the risk?"

She nodded again, without hesitation. Yates let her go and produced the small box from his pocket. "When I press the clavicle into your hands and transfer its services to you, it will grow to its active size. It will work for you only; if you die, it

465

will crumble to dust. So long as you live, it will serve you—though what use it will be if you succeed, I don't know. It will open new gates only from within the Way, not from without. It will recognize the existence of prior gates, even should they be closed. . . ."

Yates removed the clavicle, now little more than twelve centimeters long, and pressed it into her left hand. "Take both grips," he instructed. She held both between the thumb and forefinger of each hand. The clavicle picted a steady stream of red symbols at Yates.

"It doesn't recognize you now," he said. "It's asking for instructions from its last master. I will reactivate it." He instructed the clavicle in picted code.

The device slowly enlarged in Patricia's hands, until it was the same size as the clavicle used by Ry Oyu.

"Now I pass its control to you." More instructions in code, and Patricia felt a sudden warmth between herself and the device.

Korzenowski watched from a few meters back. Lanier floated behind him, near the flaw passage.

"I can talk with it now," Patricia said in wonder. "I can tell it things directly. . . ."

"And it can communicate with you. It is active, and you are its master," Yates said. There was a touch of sadness in his voice.

Korzenowski came forward. "I have some thoughts on your search—suggestions for technique," he said.

"I'd love to hear them," Patricia said.

At a steady acceleration of twenty g's, the flawship moved south along the Way.

The plasma front reached the sixty-kilometer sector reserved for the last gate opening, slamming against the barriers, the extreme heat upsetting their subtle geometry. Down came the first barrier, and the little oasis was incinerated; the circuit of wells was fused shut, and the surface of the Way became smooth and undisturbed.

466

Final messages from gates along the human-controlled length of the Way told of evacuations. Millions of humans decided to remain on the worlds beyond their assigned gates, rather than choose between the separated sections of the Axis City. The last remnants of Way commerce were shut down, and the gates were sealed, preparing both for the passage of the Geshel precincts and the arrival of the plasma front.

Despite the nearness of the plasma front, Olmy began decelerating. The flawship had two blunt-arrowhead flyers; Prescient Oyu was outfitting one for Patricia's journey.

Patricia went to Lanier and hugged him strongly.

"I appreciate all you've done for me," she said.

Lanier wanted to convince her not to make the attempt, but he didn't try. "You've come to mean a great deal to me," he said.

"Not just a green kid you have to look after?" she asked, smiling.

"Much more than that. I . . . ." He looked away from her, face working through a variety of discomforts, and then shook his head. "You're something, Patricia." He laughed sharply then, through tears. "I'm not sure what, but you're really something."

"Would you like to go with her?" Olmy asked, tracting aft. In each hand, he held a small black sperical monitor.

"What?" Lanier asked.

"She'll need help. I'm going."

Prescient Oyu saw Lanier's confusion and explained. "You'll create a partial. The monitor will project the partial. It won't be able to report back to you, of course, since we must move on as soon as we release Patricia."

"The partials will die?" Lanier asked.

"They will be destroyed along with the monitors," Olmy said. "But we won't."

Lanier felt an eerie wind through his head. "Yes," he said. "I'd like that very much."

Ramon, reading Tiempos de Los Angeles, *Rita fixing a meal for the homecoming. Coming home. Paul, waiting. What will I tell Paul? "You wouldn't believe . . ." Or, "I've been unfaithful, Paul, but—" Or just smile at him, and start over again . . .*

Olmy and Lanier—rather, their partials—sat beside Patricia in the flyer. She carried the clavicle in her lap. The screen before her showed the barren, smooth surface of the Way. She held the clavicle grips tightly, feeling the quality of the superspace at each point "beneath" the surface, transmitted through the clavicle.

What she was looking for was far more difficult to find than a particular grain of sand on a beach. She was searching for a universe without the Death, and without herself, also—where the Stone had arrived, but not caused war, and where her alternate had somehow died.

Not finding that (and she was far from sure she could be that precise—though such a place would exist, and would be distinct from all the others), she would settle for a universe where there would be two of her. She would settle for anything that would take her home. She glanced at Lanier's image. He smiled at her, encouraging and uncertain at once.

And suddenly, without any reason, without any certainty of her success, she felt wonderful. Patricia Luisa Vasquez existed in a bubble of joy, independent of all that had gone before, not caring what would come after. She had never experienced anything like it. It had neither confidence nor euphoria in its character; it simply was an appreciation of all she had experienced, and would experience, a fulfillment of the compulsion she had had since childhood not to be *normal*. Not to live a normal existence, but to subject herself to the most extraordinary experiences she could possibly have. The world being what it was, she had long since decided she would have to create those extraordinary conditions in her head. And then, the world turned upon itself. The universes had twisted in some incomprehensible fashion and delivered to her an experience drawn *from* the visions in her head, made even more wonderfully strange and outré by history, by the actions of tens of billions of people, and who could tell how many nonhumans?

Her moment was not solipsistic; she did not feel in the least isolated or unique. But she realized how extraordinary her life was. She had already fulfilled her wildest and most deeply held dreams.

Anything else is gravy, she thought. *Even going home.*

The flyer landed smoothly on the surface of the Way. In her hands, the clavicle emitted a pleasant, busy hum, telling her that they would have to be several kilometers south. She informed Olmy's partial, and he lifted the flyer up for another short hop.

Overhead, the flawship accelerated south again.

She closed her eyes, letting the clavicle's sensations stream through her. She seemed to see a kind of digest of every cluster of alternate universes, tasting them, being part of them; but she could not grasp them. She could not do anything more with the sensations than guide the clavicle. No detailed knowledge about the other realms was conveyed; only the fact of their existence, and whether or not they fell within the range she was seeking.

The partials would not need a protective field, but she would. Olmy prepared a traction bubble and environment for her. Lanier stayed beside her. *How much of him is here?* she wondered. *What is it like when a partial is destroyed?*

Then she turned her full attention to the clavicle. The nose hatch opened and Patricia stepped out onto the surface of the Way, surrounded by the flexible, faintly glowing traction bubble. Lanier and Olmy followed, walking beside her without aid in the high vacuum.

"You have about half an hour," Olmy said, his voice conveyed from the monitor to her torque. "After that, the radiation from the plasma front will be dangerously intense. Will that be time enough?"

"I think so; I hope so." Patricia checked her bag and found everything in place: multi-meter, processor, slates and blocks.

She held the clavicle before her, searching. For ten minutes, she walked back and forth, north and south, the clavicle conveying the enormous stretches of alternate worlds she

469

crossed with each step. She discarded impressions from nearly all of them, trying not to jam her senses.

Within another ten minutes, she had located a line several centimeters long that seemed to harbor the point she was searching for. She kneeled, the traction bubble comfortably flexible beneath her. The clavicle guided itself within this tiny space, her hands merely completing the causal connection.

In five more minutes, she had the search down to fractions of a millimeter. The information from each separate universe was much more complex now; she was indeed close to an alternate Earth, and the time period was approximately correct—within a few years.

"Hurry," Olmy said. "The plasma front is near."

It was very difficult. Her theories proved to be not quite as precise as she had hoped. Within even the smallest segments of the geometry stack, worlds of substantial degrees of difference interwove. She could see now why Korzenowski and his followers had initially regarded the regions of geometry stacking as useless.

The clavicle stopped. She could not tell if she was tuning the region finely enough, but she could spend days searching and not be any closer. She closed her eyes and gave it one final tweak

"I'm ready," she said.

"Then do it," Lanier said. She looked back at the partial and smiled her gratitude.

"Thank you—for everything."

Lanier nodded. "You're most welcome. It's been fascinating."

"Yes . . . hasn't it?"

She began the gate dilation. To the north, the corridor was filling with a reddish glow. As the seconds passed, the glow progressed higher through the spectrum—orange, an awesome greenish blue—

The clavicle's whistle was painfully intense. She saw a circle of whirling possibilities at her feet, and then she saw the circle—little more than a meter wide—clarify, presenting a distorted picture of blue skies, something bright tan, large shapes and water—

She did not have the precise location. She would be on land—she could sense that much—but had no idea where on Earth that land would be. Wherever, the traction field would protect her.

Lanier's partial bent through her traction field to give her a parting kiss. His lips felt pliant, warm.

"Go!" Olmy commanded.

She stepped through the gate. It was like sliding down a hill. Everything twisted and spilled around her. She released the clavicle and then grabbed it again with one hand. There was the sound of water, something huge and sharp and white not far away, blinding sun—

Lanier and Olmy faced the oncoming radiation.

It's not like dying, Lanier thought. *There's another, complete me escaping even now. But he will never experience these things. I'll never "report" to him.*

They were surrounded by an intense brightness that went beyond light or heat. Olmy grimaced and grinned at once, relishing the sensation. He had sent partials to die before and had never known what their sensations were like. Now, he would experience it directly—

And the original Olmy would *still* never know.

"The monitors will last a fraction of a second in the plasma front itself," he explained to Lanier. "We'll spend the briefest moment inside a star. . . ."

Lanier, without pain, without much fear, faced directly north and looked into the heart of the furnace rushing down on them at six thousand kilometers per second.

There was not even time to savor the sensation.

On the flawship, perilously close to the ravening plasma, Lanier closed his eyes and told himself, again and again, that he had carried out his responsibilities and accompanied his charge to the very last.

* * *

471

Still clutching the clavicle, bag strapped to her shoulder, Patricia fell from an altitude of five or six meters into water.

She was not even wet. She lay in the bottom of the floating traction bubble, stunned. The water—a river or canal—carried her several dozen meters from the gate. She looked to one side to see where she was.

That was just as well. An intense, blue-white plume flowed from the gate and blasted the water behind into steam, covering everything with a thick white cloud. Fortunately for her, and for everything within a few hundred meters, the gate was fused permanently shut within millionths of a second.

She lay back in the bubble, partly blinded, with one hand over her eyes, and drifted for several more minutes until she grounded against a sand bar. Her sight had recovered well enough by then.

Standing, she surveyed the territory, heart pounding.

She was on the shore of a broad straight canal, the sluggish water a deep muddy brown. The bank was lined with tall green reeds. The sky was an intense, pale blue, cloudless—and the sun was very bright.

With some qualms, she shut off the traction bubble and took a deep breath. The air was sweet, clean and warm.

She was heavier than she had been since leaving Timbl. This time, she had no floater belt to buoy her up. The gravity was uncomfortable.

But this was undeniably Earth, and she was not in a nuclear wasteland. In fact, the scenery was hauntingly familiar. She had seen it all before . . . in the Bible classes Rita had insisted she take as a child.

Shading her eyes, Patricia looked to the west.

Across the canal and on a plateau were brilliant plaster-white pyramids, kilometers away but sharp in the clear desert air. She felt a moment of excitement.

It was Egypt. She could travel from Egypt—that would be a minor problem. She could get home from here.

She turned around. On a rickety-looking scaffold emerging from the reeds stood a small, slender brown girl, no more than

472

ten or eleven, naked except for a white cloth tied around her hips. Her hair was done up in many long, close-knotted braids, each tipped with a blue stone. The girl regarded Patricia with slack-jawed wonder mixed with fear.

"Hello!" Patricia called, trudging up the sandy bank. "Do you speak English? Can you tell me where I am?"

The girl turned deftly on the scaffold and fled. For a horrible moment, Patricia wondered if she had slipped several millennia in time . . . if in fact she was in *ancient* Egypt.

Then she heard a distant rumble and looked up. Her relief was so great she almost whooped. There was an airplane, probably a jet, flying high above the desert.

Walking along the edge of the canal, clutching her clavicle and considering whether or not to reactivate the traction bubble—the sun was becoming uncomfortably hot—Patricia found a road and followed it. Beyond a grove of date palms, she came upon a little, square town made of whitewashed brick, the houses as blocky as benches and about as uniform. Very few people were about; it was just past high noon, and no doubt they were all resting until the day cooled.

Something bothered her. She hadn't thought about it before, but now that she remembered . . .

Putting the clavicle down on the stone roadbed, shading her eyes with both hands, she looked west again. From this vantage, she could see that the pyramids were surrounded by thick groves of trees, she couldn't tell what kind. That didn't seem right. Weren't the Egyptian pyramids in desert?

And how many *large* pyramids had there been on Earth? Three?

She counted eight smooth-surfaced white pyramids in a row, filing off to the horizon.

"Wrong-o," she said softly to herself.

Chapter Sixty-five

Lanier floated in the flawship's prow, alone and content to stay that way for a long time. Kilometer after thousands of incommensurable kilometers flowed by, black and gold and indistinct.

What it had all come down to was that he owed more to Earth than he did to Patricia. And he could not help her complete her journey—see her through safely—because it was not *his* journey to make.

Did she survive? Reach her destination?

Even if she did, in this half-dream, half-nightmare Way of stacked universes, she was as far from him—and as inaccessible—as if she had died.

Olmy tracted behind him, clearing his throat.

"I'm fine," Lanier said testily.

"That was never at question," Olmy said. "I thought you might wish to know our situation. We're well ahead of the plasma front. The radiation is tolerable—though I'd suggest a thorough physical Talsit session when we arrive."

"What about the precincts?"

"We've communicated with them. As we suspected, they are accelerating toward us now. They've agreed to lift their grips and let us pass through them."

"Can we do that?"

"With some luck, yes," Olmy said. "They'll be at thirty-one percent light-speed."

"I suppose that will be something to see," Lanier said.

"I doubt we'll 'see' much of anything," Olmy said.

"Figure of speech."

"Yes. There's food available if you wish it. Ser Yates is equipped to eat and would enjoy your company."

"How long until we meet the precincts?"

"Twenty-seven minutes," Olmy said.

Lanier swallowed hard and rotated. "Sure," he said. "I could eat."

He ate very little, however, glancing nervously about the cabin—at the nonhumans, secluded in their traction bubbles, dormant or disturbingly active (the snake with four heads was doing a quick, jerky ballet in its greenish fluid); at Prescient Oyu, who frankly returned his look; at Yates as he ate, the most human-seeming of them all, the most natural in his habits, and yet an opener of gates.

Olmy was quiet and still. Not far from him, the worker that held Korzenowski's reconstructed personality—and part of Patricia as well—floated wrapped in traction lines, its image shut off as it continued the long process of final maturation.

Lanier put aside the rest of his uneaten meal and said he would rather wait at the bow. Olmy agreed.

They crowded forward, Lanier beside Olmy and Yates, with the odd U-shaped beast on the opposite side of the flaw passage, still surrounded by its quarantine field. The two Frants relaxed behind them all, curled up with only necks and heads extended.

Ahead, the black and gold became a warmer orange and brown. The flaw pulsed faintly pink, disturbed by their accleration.

"Just a few seconds," Olmy said.

The Way appeared to balloon outward in all directions. Lanier felt his hands tingle and his eyes grow warm. The flaw vibrated and glowed to a searing blue. The transparent bow grew darker and darker to compensate. The flaw passage through the middle of the ship vibrated and groaned.

Just a few seconds of life—less—

Lanier felt as if he were exploding. He yelled in pain and surprise and flung out his arms and legs.

Then it was over. He drifted against a net of traction lines, blinking. The Way was black and gold again. The flaw glowed faintly pink.

"There's no damage," Olmy said.

"Correction," Yates said, holding a hand over his eye. Lanier had struck him with an elbow. He apologized.

"Nothing to be upset over," Yates said. "All the more excuse for some Talsit. Quite exciting, actually."

Behind them, accelerating at four hundred g's, the linked Axis Nader and Central City met the plasma front with their building shock wave of space-time, beginning the process of converting the Way into an elongated nova.

The radiation level outside the flawship increased sharply.

The charges around the perimeter of the seventh chamber were set. Engineers had gone throughout the Thistledown, making final structural checks and testing the sixth chamber machinery. When the asteroid was blown from the beginning of the Way, the sixth chamber machinery would face an enormous strain—the end of its duties as stabilizer of the Way, and a sudden and violent increase in its policing of destructive forces inside the chambers.

The precincts of Axes Thoreau and Euclid had been moved north a hundred thousand kilometers from the seventh chamber. Within the twin cylinders, the confusion was enormous. Most of the Axis citizens—the Naderites, orthodox and otherwise, and a surprising number of homorph Geshels—had been reassigned to new quarters; few were completely familiar with their new precincts. There was a sense of holiday, of triumph, and also a heavy air of anxiety.

By the hundreds, the Earth people filled the processing halls, tended by Geshel doctors and watched over by advocates.

A male *homorph*—Hoffman noted the word and added it to her rapidly growing vocabulary—took skin samples from his group of twenty Earth people. She was seventh in line. For each he had a smile and a few well-chosen words of encouragement. He was handsome, but not to her taste—a little too finely honed, his characteristics not noticeably different from those of a dozen other homorphs. Or perhaps her senses weren't sophisticated; she was used to the broad varieties of physiognomy from her time, when unavoidable

476

defects—misshapen noses, corpulence, dental misalignments—produced a medieval carnival of features.

When the samples had been stored, he produced a face-shaped cup from his floating toolbox. "This performs a number of medical analyses," he told them. "These tests are also voluntary—but your cooperation will be most helpful."

They all cooperated, peering into the cup and watching a series of complex patterns for several seconds.

Throughout the proceedings, she felt a sense not of coming misery or servitude, but of camaraderie. So many of the attendants proudly flew projected flags over their left shoulders. Flags of India, Australia, China, the United States, Japan, the USSR, and other nations. All were willing—eager, even—to speak to their charges in native tongues.

When the medical exams were completed, they were led off to a series of elevators opening on one side of the hall. Ann Blakely, Lanier's secretary and now Hoffman's, crossed over from another group. With her was Doreen Cunningham, former head of security in the science compound.

"Everybody's so tense," Cunningham whispered to Hoffman.

"Not me," Hoffman said. "I feel like I'm on some kind of holiday. The big folks are taking over now. Oh, Lord." She had just peered into their elevator. It didn't have any floor. Even with explanations and a demonstration from the attendants, it took some coaxing to get them to move forward.

They hung on to each other as a group of sixty ascended. Cunningham kept her eyes closed. Most of the Russians were resigned to the worst, she told Hoffman; their gloomy pessimism kept them pretty much to themselves.

"Somebody told me a few of our people have defected," Hoffman said, keeping her eyes resolutely on the back of the person in front of her. The elevator walls were too uniform to show motion, and there was no sensation, unpleasant or otherwise, but she still wasn't enjoying the trip.

"Four—two Russians and two Americans; that's what I've heard," Ann said.

"Anybody know who?"

"Rimskaya," Cunningham said. "And Beryl Wallace."

"Beryl . . ." She raised her eyebrows and shook her head. "I wouldn't expect that from her . . . or Rimskaya." Did she feel they had betrayed her? That was ridiculous. "What about the Russians?"

"One of them is Mirsky," Ann said. "I didn't recognize the second name."

Mirsky didn't surprise her at all. She could read strangers clearly but not the people in her own command. So much for the instincts of a master administrator.

Their quarters were spread through the precincts. More homorphs met them as the groups were further divided and escorted to apartments on different levels.

"You'll be sharing quarters in parties of three," their escort told them. "Space is at a premium now."

"Roomies?" Cunningham asked Hoffman and Blakely.

"Roomies," Hoffman said. Blakely nodded.

Their group of twelve dwindled rapidly as attendants shunted them into vacant quarters. They were the last three, escorted by a single female homorph, who picted a Russian flag over her shoulder. Their apartment was at the very end of a long, gently curved cylindrical hallway. Green numbers beneath the door glowed brightly as they approached.

The rooms were small and very blank. The homorph remained to give them basic instructions on use of the data services. She then wished them well and departed.

"Such a hurry," Blakely said, shaking her head.

"Since we're out of the action," Hoffman said, "or along for the ride, whatever, we might as well settle in."

Within minutes, they were eagerly discussing the possibilities of decor with an assigned ghost from the library. They had several hours before the Breakout, as it was being called; Hoffman used that time to contact others in the precinct who had been assigned quarters.

Blakely and Cunningham decided on an interim decor which gave some color and shape—and considerably more

478

apparent living space—to the apartment. Hoffman joined them to examine the facilities, and to sample the food provided by an automatic kitchen tucked in one corner.

Citizens and Earth people alike, the assigned ghost informed them, would be able to witness the breakout, almost in its entirety. Monitors placed throughout the Thistledown would transmit detailed views of the events and their results; everyone had a ringside seat, if they desired one.

No longer hungry, or very interested in playing with the quarters, the three women sat before a continuous documentary of what was happening in the asteroid and the precincts.

The images were almost too real. After a few minutes, Cunningham turned away from the display and began giggling uncontrollably. "This is ridiculous," she said, clutching her cheeks and rolling back on the apparent Oriental-pattern carpet. "It's terrifying." Blakely caught the bug next.

"We're hysterical," she said, and that sent them both into fresh paroxysms. "We don't have any idea what's going on."

"Oh, I do," Hoffman said solemnly, feeling left out.

"What?" Cunningham asked, trying to be serious.

Hoffman rolled one hand into a near-cylinder. She peered through it at them. "Blow one end off—the end no one ever tried to drill through. The north pole."

"Jesus," Cunningham said, her giggles gone as quickly as they had started. "What would have happened it we had tried to drill through it? Where would the drillers have ended up?"

"Blow the north pole off," Hoffman resumed, ignoring the unanswerable question, "and knock the Stone off the corridor. And after that—"

"What?" Ann asked, owlish now and also very serious.

"This half of the city leaves the corridor. We become a space station."

"And the Stone?" Cunningham asked.

"Another moon."

"And we go back to Earth?" Blakely asked.

Hoffman nodded.

"Damn," Blakely said. "It's a . . . I don't know what it

479

is. A fairy tale. Maybe it's the day of resurrection. What did they call it? Rapture. Dead people flying up through the freeways. People leaving their cars right through the roofs." Embarrassed, Blakely turned back to the projected display. "That doesn't make any sense, does it? No freeways, no cars. Only angels coming from the sky."

Hoffman made a deep, shuddering sigh. "You're right," she said. "It's a fairy tale." Then, abruptly, she broke into laughter, and couldn't stop until her lungs ached and her face was wet with tears.

An hour before the scheduled breakout, Corprep Rosen Gardner picted a personal message to Hoffman requesting that he be allowed to visit. A few minutes later, he arrived at the apartment door in person—"incarnate," Hoffman reminded herself. She invited him in. By that time, they had all regained some semblance of control.

Gardner's political work on behalf of the divided Hexamon and the Naderites was no longer necessary, he explained; he had volunteered to act as Corprep in the New Nexus for the Earth people, and chose Hoffman as the most logical person to speak with. He offered to keep her informed by linking her with his private memory and information service.

Her vacation was over, she thought, not without some regrets. She was on call again.

"I also bring news," he said, standing before her with his hands behind his back. She was beginning to get a sense of the orthodox Naderites—dedicated, almost chivalric, not unlike some of the political conservatives she had dealt with on Earth. "We have word of Patricia Luisa Vasquez, and the four who were sent to find her."

"Yes?"

"Three of the four have returned to our precincts. They are Lawrence Heineman, Karen Farley and Lenore Carrolson. They were kept as captives for a time, I am ashamed to say, by the Geshels in Axis Nader and Central City. They were

480

released just before the Geshel precincts began acceleration. They will join your people shortly."

"And the others?"

"Patricia Luisa Vasquez was given an opportunity to find her way home," Ser Gardner continued. "What that means, precisely, I am not sure; the details are sketchy. She and Garry Lanier were detained and sent with the gate opener and his party to one point three ex nine; many in that party, including Lanier, are now on their way back, and have passed through the accelerating precincts safely. They will not return to our sector in time to join with us, however."

She had no idea what a "gate opener" was and didn't feel it was appropriate to ask. She could look it up later. "Are they going to leave the corridor?"

"I do not know," Gardner said. "Their leader, Ser Olmy, has been informed of the timetable. He believes they can escape the sealing of the Way. They have been delayed by stopping at several reopened gates to drop off nonhuman clients."

Hoffman absorbed the news quietly, slapping her left hand lightly against her thigh. She had assumed the four searchers and Vasquez had died or been irretrievably lost in the shuffle. For the time being, she had managed to forget about them. Now she once again had something to worry about, with little knowledge of the perils involved, or their chances for success.

"Our zero hour will be in forty-three minutes," Corprep Gardner said. "By the way, I thought I would inform you that numbers of Hexamon citizens have been solicited by a small group of your people. There is a 'wild party' going on in the quarters of Axis Thoreau. Some of your female personnel are bartering sexual favors, for what commodities I don't know. I have placed that party off limits to my people."

Hoffman looked at him, startled, not sure how to respond. "That's wise," she finally managed. "I don't know who would corrupt whom the most."

* * *

481

In the stone:

From end to end of the seven chambers: darkness and quiet. In the first chamber, clouds had built up since the re-rotation; rain threatened in the darkness.

In the bore holes, the absolute silence of vacuum, and no activity but the occasional flight of a tiny monitor.

In the second chamber, a faint whistle of wind as the atmosphere regained its equilibrium. More windows had broken out, and some buildings—including a mega—had collapsed despite the efforts of the engineers.

In the third chamber, much the same, though no buildings had collapsed. The scattered glows of still-active illusart windows in Thistledown City resembled a swarm of fireflies.

In the fourth chamber, the washed-out forests and unleashed waters had finally made their peace with each other. The compounds formerly occupied by Eastern and Western bloc personnel had been washed away, their debris carried down to the lakes or jammed up against trees near the shorelines.

Those who had died to invade or defend the Stone—the Potato—the Thistledown—still lay in their graves, unseeing, their patterns flown, personalities vanished, Mysteries made even more mysterious.

The fifth chamber: as dark and hollow as a vast cavern in the Earth, with only the eternal sound of waterfalls and rivers.

The sixth chamber, vigilant, the only chamber besides the seventh still illuminated by a plasma tube, although that was uncertain and unreliable.

The plasma tube flickered and was extinguished. No matter. All the preparations had been made, and now only monitors patrolled the Thistledown's vastness.

The seventh chamber. A wind blew gently down from the cap, rustling the copses of scrub forest; it lazed through the abandoned tent with a faint whistle, flapping the canvas. A section of the tent sagged where a pole had drifted loose during the de-rotation. Surprisingly little else had been disturbed.

The detonators waited patiently beside their charges.

The joined precincts of Axes Thoreau and Euclid were too

482

far down the Way to be visible from this point without the aid of a high-powered telescope. The Way seemed empty, infinite, eternal and serene: the greatest thing ever created by human beings.

Outside the Thistledown, black space and stars and Moon and poor battered, burned, winter-besieged Earth, where few if any were even thinking of the asteroid or the possibility of rescue. How could there be rescue from such total misery and death? History had passed them by.

The asteroid's overhauled Beckmann drive engines prepared for their part in the drama, stockpiling reaction mass to be slung out and dematerialized in the combined beams. They would reduce the kick of the separation, and the combined kick and counter-thrust would maneuver the Thistledown into a circular orbit around the Earth, at an altitude of some ten thousand kilometers.

The precincts of Axes Thoreau and Euclid began their acceleration, in an apparent suicide run to smash themselves against the seventh chamber cap. Within, twenty-nine million human beings—corporeal and otherwise—did the various things humans do while waiting to see if they will live or die.

Behind the precincts, half a million kilometers down the Way, a tiny defense flawship was decelerating drastically, the flaw ahead of it brightening to violet and blue. It had to slow to Earth orbital velocity by the time it followed the linked precincts out the end of the Way—if it managed that feat at all.

The charges buried in the walls of the seventh chamber synchronized.

The grips of Axes Thoreau and Euclid were withdrawn, and the huge cylinders coasted south toward the seventh chamber cap at just a little over forty thousand kilometers per hour, or eleven kilometers per second.

The detonators reached their appointed microsecond.

Within the seventh chamber, there was a noise beyond human description. Billions of tons of rock and metal rushed in toward the axis from the seven charge points, and immense fissures shot outward to the vacuum of space.

Around the northern pole of the asteroid, dust and debris spread out in a wide circular fan, followed by a white glow more brilliant than the sun. The glow faded to red and purple. A seventy-kilometer-wide monk's cap of rock was propelled away from the asteroid. The asteroid withdrew much more slowly from its severed end, and for the briefest moment, between them, there was a hole in space, filled with the light of the plasma tube, showing an infinite perspective—

Out of which flew the linked precincts of Axes Euclid and Thoreau, barely missing the asteroid itself, shunting aside debris with conical traction fields. Through the fading glow and spinning chunks of rock and metal, the precincts passed out of range of the Thistledown's Beckmann drives. The drives then fired to maneuver the Thistledown into orbit.

The Way was now an independent entity. The hole in space began to heal, wrapped in a thousand varieties of darkness— violet and sea green, carmine and indigo—venting winds mightier than a thousand hurricanes into the vacuum.

Closing.

Sealing itself off forever from this universe.

Olmy sat back and closed his eyes. Yates was more animated, rubbing his hands together. Senator Oyu appeared as cool as ever, but Lanier noticed her eye movements were frequent and jerky.

If Prescient Oyu was even slightly nervous, and Olmy resigned, then Lanier figured he had every right to be terrified.

"Are we going to make it?" he asked.

"Just barely," Olmy said, eyes still shut.

Lanier faced the bow.

The brightness of the seven coordinated blasts had reduced the bow to opacity. Now it cleared and gave them a view of the Way's beginning. Within a glowing circle of molten asteroidal debris and frozen streaks of rushing water vapor was a circle of blackness.

The circle was shrinking, being taken over by an iridescent nullity that hurt the eyes: the new terminus of the Way.

And then, within the diminishing black circle, Lanier saw a dull white crescent. He blinked.

The Moon.

The flawship twirled in the outrushing atmosphere. The iridescent nullity had almost completed its task; it seemed to take them forever to approach the rapidly shrinking blackness and crescent Moon.

Chunks of soil rose from the walls and shimmied up the fresh, nacreous boundary. The boundary eclipsed the Moon.

"Oh, God," Lanier said. He clasped his hands and closed his eyes.

Epilog: Four Beginnings

One/ 6 P.D.

And all the king's horses, and all the king's men . . .

The phrase occurred to Heineman often as he piloted a blunt-arrowhead flyer from point to devastated point around the globe. What the Death itself had not incinerated or poisoned, the Long Winter had ravaged; it had seemed for a time that even the ingenuity, technology and power of the New Hexamon itself could not make the situation right.

Yet, as Lenore—his wife of four years—reminded him during his worst, most discouraged moments, "They managed to climb back up even without our help—our presence *has* to make things move faster."

But even hope and the prospects of a brighter future could not take the edge off, or reduce the bitter gall of what he saw in the course of a single day's surveying.

India, Africa, Australia and New Zealand and much of South America had emerged from the Death with minor damage. North America, Russia and Europe had been practically sterilized. China had lost a quarter of its population in the nuclear exchange; another two-thirds had died of starvation during the Long Winter, which was subsiding only now, with help from the orbiting precinct. Southeast Asia had crumbled into anarchy and revolution and genocide; the destruction there was almost as complete.

Ashes, barren plains, snow-covered valleys and hills soon to become glaciers; scudding gray, snow-thick clouds casting black shadows over fallow earth; continents given over to bacteria and cockroaches and ants, and among these new ecologies, a few scattered animals who had once called themselves human beings, who had once lived in comfortable houses and known the basics of electrical wiring and taken newspapers and subscribed to provincial points of view about reality . . .

Who had once had time for the luxury of thought.

It was heartbreaking. Heineman came to think of his kind—the engineers and scientists and technicians of the Earth—as the very tools of Satan himself. His latent Christianity returned with a vengeance. He knew he severely tried Lenore's patience, but from his meandering visions of apocalypse and angels and resurrection he could at least take some solace, find meaning, and search for destiny and God's plan. If he had once been an agent of Satan, now—without switching occupations—he was an agent of the angels, of those who would transform Earth into paradise. . . .

Lenore tried, again and again, to point out that engineers were as much responsible for saving the Earth as for destroying it. Without the orbital platforms and the whole paraphernalia of space-based defense, the Earth would have been wiped utterly clean of life; the NATO and Soviet platforms managed to destroy some forty percent of all missiles.

Not enough, not enough . . .

And how many children, how many animals, how many innocent and—

But, Lenore would counter, no one born with a mouth and a need is innocent. . . .

She was often right, of course.

The masters he served now were not perfect, hardly angelic. They were intelligent, powerful, reasonable; their leaders lacked the ignorant erratic blindness of Earth's leaders. But they still differed with each other, sometimes strongly.

So Heineman, with his wife, flew the skies of Earth and charted the damage, and hoped for a day when grasses would grow and flowers bloom, when snows would recede and the air would be clear of radioactivity. He worked hard for that day.

And he was faithful to his new masters, for he was born again in more ways than one. On his first day back on Earth, he had suffered a fatal heart attack.

487

Larry Heineman was on his second body. Lenore assured him it was better than his first.

He had his doubts, but it certainly *felt* better.

New Zealand dusk, with another spectacular sunset in the offing. Overhead, the large beacon of the Thistledown rose clear and unobscured, and not far away, the speeding point of the orbiting precincts crossed the sky in the opposite direction.

Garry Lanier emerged from the Talsit tent and saw Karen Lanier speaking with a group of farmers at the camp fence. The farmers had brought their children to the camp two weeks before for Talsit cleansing; they, at least, would not give birth to monsters, or suffer the long-term effects of radiation poisoning. But for the adults, there was still much suspicion and distrust; the early rumors of alien invasions and hordes of sky-traveling devils had seemed peculiarly convincing in the aftermath of the world's end. Karen's obvious pregnancy—six months along—did much to reassure them they were dealing with real human beings.

Lanier still had not told their story to any Earth-bound survivors. Who could absorb such an incredible and complicated tale when one's thoughts were on simple survival and the health of one's children, or sheep, or townspeople?

He stood with his hands in his overalls pockets and watched Karen talking quietly with the shepherds. They had lived and worked together since returning to Earth and had married two years ago. Their life was busy, and they were good for each other, but . . .

He was not yet content, not yet free of the manifold neuroses he had picked up in the past decade. At least he could feel the edges of his mental wounds puckering and healing, scarring up, perhaps even smoothing away.

Lanier only took physical Talsit sessions to cleanse his body; they were required at least every six months to prevent ill effects from the atmospheric radiation. He did not indulge in mental Talsit, whatever Olmy's urging; he was, after all, a rugged individualist, and he would rather accomplish those things on his own.

In a few months, he and Karen, if they could be spared from their labor here, would join Hoffman and Olmy and perhaps even Larry and Lenore. They would reload their temporary implants with new training, new data, and work with Earth's corprep, Rosen Gardner, and Earth's senator, Prescient Oyu, to coordinate the massive task of cleansing the atmosphere and reorganizing the survivors.

Paradoxically, the Naderites would soon have to deal with the infant cries of their own creed, which was rapidly gaining power in areas not yet touched by the reconstruction.

Lanier did not often think of the Way now, or of what had happened years past. His mind was too occupied with more immediate concerns.

But every now and then he would shut his eyes for a moment and open them again. He would turn to Karen and meet her sunny smile and run his hands through her yellow hair.

No sense worrying about those who were farther away than the souls of the dead.

Two/ Journey Year 1181

Olmy stood in the Axis Euclid public observation chamber, hands folded behind his back, waiting for Korzenowski. Together they would try to convince Earth's chief advocate, Ram Kikura, that the legal rights of the survivors on Earth could not supersede the New Hexamon's duty to eventually force them to undergo Talsit purging. He gathered his arguments in his head:

If they were not purged mentally as well as physically, the condition of their thinking would be such that strife and discord would tear the Earth apart again, in centuries if not sooner. They had to be mentally healthy to face the future the New Hexamon was already structuring for them; there was no

489

room for the kind of archaic, sick thinking that had led to the Death in the first place.

Olmy was not sure he could convince Ram Kikura, however. She had been rereading the *Federalist Papers* and consulting ancient constitutional law cases.

Korzenowski arrived, late as usual, and together they spent a few minutes watching the passage of continents, seas and clouds below. The horizon was still orange and gray with dust and ash in the stratosphere; where clouds parted, much of the land was covered with snow.

"Is your woman going to give us a hard time today?" the Engineer asked.

"No doubt," Olmy said.

Korzenowski smiled. "I have a confession. Another young woman has been giving me difficulties lately. Oh, I realize we should all be concentrating on the reconstruction . . . but I think you'll understand why my mind wanders."

Olmy nodded.

"She probably did not succeed," Korzenowski said.

"At going home?"

"It's very unlikely. I've been thinking about Way theory. Part of me keeps pursuing those problems. We understood the geometry stacks so little. When Patricia expressed her theories, they seemed right at the time . . . and they very nearly were. But not right enough to take her home."

"So where is she now?"

"That I cannot say." Korzenowski held one hand to the side of his head. "This persistence, though . . . this pressure to keep working on the problems . . . I can't say I object. The theory is fascinating. Thinking about it is one of the most enjoyable things I can do. And perhaps some day we can try again."

"From Earth?" Olmy asked.

"We still have the sixth chamber," Korzenowski said. "It wouldn't be nearly as difficult as it was before. And we could do it better."

Olmy didn't reply for some moments. "It may be inevitable," he conceded, "but let's not mention it to the Nexus right away."

"Of course," Korzenowski said. "After all this time, we—I am very patient." The Engineer's intense, sharp gaze, like that of a cat waiting to pounce, made the hair on Olmy's neck tingle.

He hadn't experienced such an atavistic response in years.

"Let's go fight the good fight with your advocate," Korzenowski suggested. They turned away from the view of Earth and took an elevator to the Nexus antechambers, where Suli Ram Kikura waited.

Three/ Pavel Mirsky: Personal Record

If I am not too far off—or the distorting effects of our journey are not too difficult to calculate—then today is my thirty-second birthday.

I have settled in to life in the Central City, taking part in the rituals and exchanges of the Geshel life. I update my personality copies each week and make the acquaintance of dozens of citizens every day, many anxious to converse with me; and I work.

I study history. Those who assign work here believe that my perceptions and abilities make me a unique lens through which to view and interpret the past. Rodzhensky helps. He has adapted far more completely than I, and even plans, in his next incarnation, to take on a custom neomorph body.

I often meet with Joseph Rimskaya, but he is still morose and not very stimulating. I believe he is homesick and perhaps should not have defected. He plans to undergo Talsit therapy soon, though he has said that before. Beryl Wallace, the other American, we seldom see. She has been assigned to an observation party; a unique and sought-after job, in which I believe she must be serving more as a mascot than anything else, but I could be wrong. The implants can perform wonders.

I was never an intellectual. Philosophy bored me; questions of ultimate meaning and reality seemed pointless. I did not have the capacity for far stretches of the imagination. With the implants, all that has changed. I have taken a dozen more steps on the road to being a different person.

We have voyaged a considerable distance since achieving near light-speed. I do not believe anyone expected what is happening now. The Way is so complicated; even those who created it could not predict all of its possibilities.

We now journey down a ghost Way, its local nature altered by the violence of our near light-speed passage. It has no diameter or boundaries as such; objects with mass simply cannot exist beyond a distance of more than twenty thousand kilometers from the course on which we ride. (The flaw, or singularity, vanished three months ago. Simply evaporated in a pulse of newly created particles, some of them unknown even to the Geshels.)

We have traveled beyond the domain of the super-set of external universes which encompassed all our various world-lines. Even were we to stop now and open gates to the "outside," whatever that may be, we would encounter realms without matter, perhaps without form or order; it is highly doubtful we would find anything familiar.

There are an infinite number of alternatives to the Way, each originating in an alternative world-line, yet reaching beyond that world-line. Until now, Way researchers have not known quite how the alternate Ways were stacked or arranged, or indeed whether they could even be considered real. Since the Way intersects a large group of alternate world-lines— perhaps all—could there be more than one Way?

But by traveling close to the light-speed within the Way, we have answered these questions and found new ones to ask. We have distorted Way geometry in more than the requisite four dimensions; we have also contracted the fifth dimension, drawing the alternate Ways together. The Way boundaries have become transparent in a wide variety of frequencies, and we can perceive the shape of other Ways. We can select which Way we wish to inspect, using devices similar to the gate-opening clavicles. It is in observing these alternate Ways that Beryl Wallace is now occupied.

We can even see (and in some instances, communicate with) beings in other Ways.

So there are an infinite number of world-lines, and because of this one human artifact, an infinite number of connections between them. Our researchers devise schemes to allow us to cross over to other Ways, other super-sets of world-lines, but even with implants I have difficulty understanding what they are discussing.

This much I do know. There are Ways where the beings of thousands of completely different universes hold commerce, exchanging in some cases only information, in other cases actually exchanging different types of space-time. *Is it possible to conceive of the potential that would exist between two universes of differing qualities? Would that potential be called* energy?

Rimskaya, morose as he is, has continued working, and has even made some significant contributions to the researches. He believes he has found a definition of information: the potential that exists between all time-like dimensions (time itself, and the fifth dimension separating world-lines, for instance) and space-like dimensions. Wherever space and time interact, there is information, and where information can be ordered into knowledge, and knowledge can be applied, there is intelligence.

Lest anyone reading this journal of a primitive man should think we spend our time mired in abstractions, let me also say that I am discovering the richness *available to those who are willing to alter their major characteristics. The variety of emotions available to a reconfigured human mind, thinking thoughts impossible to its ancestors . . .*

The emotion of -*-, describable only as something between sexual love and the joy of intellection—making love to a *thought? Or &&, the true reverse of pain, not "pleasure" but a "warning" of healing, growth and change. Or (ˆ+ˆ), the most complex emotion yet discovered, felt by those who consciously endure the change between mind configurations, and experience the broad spectrum of possibilities inherent in thinking and being.*

I have barely begun to taste the varieties of human love. Personalities are not necessarily isolated here; I can belong to a wide spectrum of personality aggregates, and yet still retain my individuality. . . . I lose nothing and gain a thousand new tastes of human affection.

What use is it to try to measure the distances we have traveled? What use is the personality of the old Pavel Mirsky to comprehend them? Soon, I firmly resolve, I will gather up my courage and join with the extended personalities in City Memory.

And yet with all this to occupy me, I still mourn. I still weep for the lost part of myself, still feel sad for a land I cannot return to, a land doubly inaccessible now. But the weeping is buried deeply, where even Talsit sessions have difficulty reaching . . . perhaps lodged in the one area it is illegal to modify, known as Mystery. How ironic, that in this way I still feel like a Russian, and that so long as any part of me exists, it will be Russian!

Because I share the same Mystery with the old Pavel Mirsky, I feel continuity. I feel . . .

An urge for the stars, yes, but more than that.

When I was a child in Kiev (or so a few dim portions of my memory inform me) I once asked my stepfather how long people would live when the Worker's Paradise was achieved. He was a computer technician, very imaginative, and he said, "Perhaps as long as they wish. Perhaps a billion years."

"How long is a billion years?" I asked him.

"It is a very long time," he said. "An age, an eternity, time enough for all life to rise and all life to end. Some people call it an eon."

In geological terms, I learned later, an aeon *is indeed a* billion years. But the Greeks who coined the word were not so specific. They used it as a pointer to eternity, the lifetime of a universe, far more than a billion years. It was also the personification of a god's cycle of time.

I have survived the Worker's Paradise. I have survived the end of my universe, and may survive countless others.

Dear stepfather, it looks as if I will outlive the gods themselves. . . .

A true eon.

So much to learn, and so much change to look forward to. Each day I breathe deeply, count my choices and realize how lucky we are. (If only I can convince Rimskaya! Sad man.)

I am free.

Four/ Aigyptos, Year of Alexandros 2323

Young queen Kleopatra the 21st had just spent a long and drowsy four hours listening to the complicated testimony of five ostracized congressmen from the Oxyrrhynkhos Nome's Boulē. Their complaints, her most trusted counselor decided, were without merit, so she dismissed them with a stern smile and warned them not to take their complaints outside Aigyptos, to any other polity, or they would be exiled from the Alexandrian Oikoumenē and forced to wander east or west in the lands of the barbarians, or even worse, in Latium.

Three times a week, Kleopatra received such complaints, selected from thousands of cases by her counselors, well aware they were mostly for show and had been predecided. She was not entirely happy with the limitations of royal power imposed by the Oikoumenical Boulē in the time of her fathers, but it was that or exile, and an exiled eighteen-year-old queen had few places to go outside the Oikoumenē. How things had changed in the past five hundred years!

Kleopatra looked forward to her next visitor, however. She had heard many stories about the head priestess and sophē of

495

the Hypateion in Rhodos; the woman was legendary not only for the tale of how she had come to the Oikoumenē, but for her accomplishments in the last half-century. Yet queen and priestess had never met.

The sophē Patrikia had flown in from Rhodos two days before, landing at the Rakhotis airport just west of Alexandria and then taking up privileged residence in the Mouseion until an audience could be arranged. In those two days, the sophē had been taken on the virtually mandatory tours of the pyramidons of Alexandros and the Diadokhoi to observe (how tiresome, Kleopatra thought) the gold-wrapped mummies of the founders of the Alexandrian Oikoumenē, and then through the surrounding pyramids and tombs of the Later Successors. It was said that the sophē had borne the tours well, and some of her observations had been recorded for broadcast to the eighty-five nomes of the Oikoumenē.

Heralds arrived to announce that the sophē had come to the Lokhias Promontory and would shortly be at the royal residence. The counselors cleared the court and Kleopatra was surrounded by her flies, as she called them—her chamberlains and makeup maids, wiping sweat from her brow, powdering her cheeks and nose, arranging her robes around the golden throne. Across the courtyard, standing half in shadow and half in sun, was the phalanx of royal security. When they divided into two lines, one on each side of the portal, Kleopatra would assume her Attitude and welcome the sophē.

The lines formed and the heralds went through their wearisome rituals.

The date was Sōthis 4, old-style, Arkhimēdēs 27, new-style.

Kleopatra sat patiently on her throne, made of cedar from the troublesome hierarchy of Ioudeia, sometimes called Nea Phoenikia, sipping sparkling water from Gallia out of a cup manufactured in Metascythia. Thus in every single day she tried to utilize goods from the nomes, polities and friendly nations all around, knowing that they would feel honored and that their peoples would feel proud for serving the oldest of the old empires, the Alexandrian Oikoumenē. It would be well for the sophē to see Kleopatra fulfilling her duties, for in truth the young queen had little else to do; the Boulē and the Council of Elected Speakers now made the truly important decisions, in the Athenian manner.

The great bronze doors of Theotokopolos swung wide and the procession began. Kleopatra ignored the rapidly-swelling crowd of courtiers and chamberlains and petty politicians. Her eyes went immediately to the sophē Patrikia, entering the chamber supported on the arms of her two sons, themselves middle-aged.

The priestess wore a gown of black Chin-Ch'ing silk, simple and elegant, with a star above one breast and a moon above the other. Her hair was long, still luxuriantly thick and dark; her face appeared youthful despite her seventy-four years, her eyes black and square and penetrating. Kleopatra met those eyes with difficulty; they seemed dangerous, too provocative.

"Welcome," she said, deliberately eschewing all the ceremony. "Come sit. I am told we have things to discuss."

"Oh, yes, we do, my beautiful queen," the sophē said, stepping away from the arms of her sons and approaching the throne, one hand lifting the long hem of her gown. She was very spry, actually; no doubt she retained her sons in the temple for their own good, and not hers; the Oikoumenē was not the easiest place to find employment these days.

Patrikia sat on the pillow-covered chair, a body length below the queen's throne, and lifted her face to Kleopatra, eyes bright with excitement.

"I am also told you have brought some of your wonderful instruments, to show them to me, and reveal their purposes," Kleopatra said.

"If I may . . . ?"

"By all means."

Patrikia gestured and two Hypateion students carried up a wide, shallow wooden case. Kleopatra recognized the wood: pigeon's-eye maple from Nea Karkhedon across the broad

497

Atlantic. She wondered how their revolution was coming along; little news leaked out from the blockaded coastal territories.

The priestess ordered the case to be set down on a wide round table of beaten brass chased with silver. "Perhaps your Imperial Hypsēlotēs knows my story . . . ?"

Kleopatra nodded and smiled. "That you dropped from the sky, chased by a furious star, and that you were not born on this Gaia."

"And that I brought with me . . . ?" Patrikia prompted, for all the world like one of Kleopatra's tutors. The queen didn't mind; she enjoyed tutoring and learning. Indeed, she had spent most of her life in classrooms, learning the qualities and extent of her realm, and the languages, as well.

"You brought marvelous instruments, for which there are no exact equivalents in our world. Yes, yes, these stories are well known."

"Then I now tell you things known only to myself," Patrikia said. She glanced around the court and then returned her extraordinary gaze to the young queen. Kleopatra understood and nodded.

"This will be a private audience. We will adjourn and meet in my chambers."

The court was quickly cleared, and Kleopatra unceremoniously dropped her heavy robes and gathered a light cloak of byssos around her shoulders. With only two guards and the sophē's sons accompanying them, they strolled to the queen's chambers. Trays of quail and crystal goblets of wines from Cos awaited them, and the sophē ate with the queen, a very rare privilege.

When they were done, the sons ate, and Kleopatra and Patrikia made themselves comfortable on pillows in a corner. Chamberlains drew curtains around them for privacy.

Then and only then did Patrikia open the lid of the wooden case. There, in thick Tyrian purple felt—the felt from Pridden and the dye from Ioudeia—rested a silver-and-glass, palm-

498

sized flat object, a second slightly smaller object and something saddle-shaped with protruding handles.

These objects were almost as famous as the Cache of General Ptolemaios Sōtēr, especially among scholars and philosophers. Few had ever seen them, not even her mother and fathers.

Kleopatra regarded them with unabashed curiosity. "Tell me, please," she said.

"With this," and Patrikia pointed to the smaller flat object, "I can measure the qualities of space and time. Years ago, when I took refuge in the Hypateion, after the death of my husband, the tekhnai there made me new batteries, and these devices function again."

"I must commend them," Kleopatra said. Patrikia smiled and waved her hand as if at trivial matters.

"The philosophy and tekhnos of your world is not so advanced as mine in some respects, though very nearly. But you have wonderful mathematicians, wonderful astronomers. My work has progressed."

"Yes?"

"And . . ." Patrikia lifted the object with handles from the case. "This instrument tells me when others are trying to open passages to our world, this Gaia. It senses their workings, and it tells me."

"Does it have any other purpose?" Kleopatra asked, aware she was already out of her depth.

"No. Not now, not here."

To her astonishment, the queen realized that the old priestess had tears in her eyes. "I have never given up my dream," Patrikia said. "And I have never given up my hope. But I am growing old, my Imperial Hypsēlotēs, and my senses are not so keen. . . ." She lifted herself up in her seat and resettled, with a deep sigh. "Still, I am certain now. I have been given the proper signs by this device."

"Signs of what?"

"I do not know why, or where, my queen, but a passageway has been opened on our world. This device *feels* its presence, and so do I. Somewhere on Gaia, my queen. Before I die, I wish to find this passage, and see if perhaps there is some slight chance I might fulfill my dream. . . ."

"A passage? What do you mean?"

"A gate to the place from which I came. They have reopened my gate, perhaps. Or—someone has created an entirely new road to the stars."

Kleopatra was suddenly troubled. The instincts of a hundred and twenty generations of the Makedonian Dynastic Succession were not idle in her blood. "Are those in your world people of peace and goodwill?" she asked.

The priestess's eyes became momentarily distant and cloudy. "I do not know. Probably they are. But I ask the queen to locate this passage, this gate, with all the means at her disposal . . ."

Kleopatra frowned and bent forward to see the priestess's face from a better perspective. Then she took one of the sophē's withered hands in hers.

"Would our lands benefit from this passage, this gate?"

"Almost certainly," Patrikia said. "I am a very minor example of the wonders that could lie beyond such an opening."

Kleopatra frowned and pondered this for a moment. The Oikoumenē was beset with many problems, some of them, her counselors assured her, insurmountable, the problems of an elderly civilization on the wane. She did not believe this—not entirely—but the thought frightened her. Even in an age of airplanes and radio, there had to be other things, other marvels, which would rescue them from their plight.

"This is a shortcut to distant territories, places where we might extend our trade, and learn new things?"

Patrikia smiled. "Your understanding is quick, my queen."

"Then we will search. I will decree that all our allied states and empires will search as well."

"It may be hidden, very small," the priestess warned. "Perhaps only a test gate, as wide across as a man's arm is long."

"Our searchers will be thorough," Kleopatra said. "With your guidance, they will find this gate."

Patrikia squinted at her with almost insolent suspicion. "I have long been regarded as a crazy old woman, despite these marvels," she said, resting her hand on the case. "Do you believe me?"

"Yes, upon my heritage as a Queen of Alexandros's Egypt and the Makedonian Dynasty," Kleopatra said. She *wanted* to believe the priestess. Life in the court had been very dull the past few years. And the queen did indeed exercise some powers, chiefly in matters involving the political spirit and aims of the state. She could fit this quest into those territories nicely.

"Thank you," Patrikia said. "My husband never truly believed me. He was a fine man, a farmer of fish. . . . But he worried about me and said I should live this life only, and not dream of others. . . ."

"I *hate* limitations," Kleopatra said vehemently. "What will you do if we find this passage?"

Patrikia's eyes widened.

"I will go home," she said. "Finally, however futile it may be, I will go home."

"Not before you have finished your work for us, I presume."

"No. That will be my first priority."

"Good. So be it, then."

Kleopatra called in her counselors, warned them sternly this was an Imperial decree not subject to dissension, and issued a command that the search begin.

"Thank you, my Imperial Hypsēlotēs," the priestess said as they strolled back to the court. Kleopatra watched Patrikia leave through the Theotokopolos door, on her way back to the Hypateion until such time as the search would begin. Then the queen closed her eyes and tried to imagine . . .

The old woman's home. Where would such a woman have come from? A place of gleaming towers and mighty fortresses, where people might be more like gods or devils than the men

501

and women she knew. Only such a place could have produced this small, intense sophē.

"How strange," Kleopatra murmured, resuming her throne. The heavy robes were wrapped around her shoulders again. She felt a shuddering thrill. "How wonderful . . ."

"Unless you know *where* you are, you don't know *who* you are."

—Wendell Barry

Acknowledgements:

A book as complicated as this one cannot be written alone, and thank God for those willing, even eager, to help. My deepest appreciation to (in no particular order) Rick Sternbach; Ralph Cooper; John S. Lewis; Louis A. D'Amario; David Brin; Anthony and Tina Chong; Craig Kaston; LCDR Patrick Garrett, USN; LCDR Dale F. Bear, USN RET.; the Citizen's Advisory Council on National Space Policy; and of course Astrid.

Errors and misconceptions no doubt remain, and are my own.